There was an awkward silence.

From time immemorial, goblin surgeons and apothecaries had been remunerated in the old-fashioned way: a flat fee of fivepence if they cured the patient, or the carcass if they didn't. "Where's the incentive in that?" the Chairgoblin said angrily. "Threepence an hour, regardless of whether they get better or not? I mean, why bother?"

Mordak counted to five under his breath. "All your patients die," he pointed out. "And then you eat them. Admit it, that's not an ideal system."

The Chairgoblin was shocked. "That's social responsibility, that is," he said. "By weeding out the sick and infirm, we're making an invaluable contribution to the future of the species."

"Threepence an hour," Mordak said firmly, "and no more amputations for ingrowing toenails. You want drumsticks, you buy them in the market like everybody else. Next."

AN ORC ON THE WILD SIDE

TOM HOLT

orbit

www.orbitbooks.net

Orbit
Hachette Book Group
1290 Avenue of the Americas
New York, NY 10104
orbitbooks.net

Simultaneously published in Great Britain and in the U.S. by Orbit in 2019
First Edition: September 2019

Orbit is an imprint of Hachette Book Group.
The Orbit name and logo are trademarks of Little, Brown Book Group Limited.

The publisher is not responsible for websites (or their content) that are not owned by the publisher.

The Hachette Speakers Bureau provides a wide range of authors for speaking events. To find out more, go to www.hachettespeakersbureau.com or call (866) 376-6591.

Library of Congress Control Number: 2019931475

ISBNs: 978-0-316-27085-4 (trade paperback), 978-0-316-27084-7 (ebook)

Printed in the United States of America

LSC-C

10 9 8 7 6 5 4 3 2 1

For John Tyler, with many thanks

BOOK ONE

The Orcward Squad

In a hole in the ground there lived an advertising account executive. Not a nasty, cramped, smelly hole with no indoor plumbing, electricity or mains water; nor yet a ghastly primitive hole without air conditioning, broadband access, wi-fi or cable. It was a tastefully modernised halfling-hole, which the advertising account executive had bought for an absolute song and spent a fortune doing up; and that meant comfort.

When he and Pauline bought the place, of course, it had been a rather different story. After one look at it, they'd very nearly given up and gone back to Fulham. For a start, the front door was *round*—no, honestly; well, that had to go, naturally, which meant ripping out the doorframe, which was structural, wouldn't you know, so the whole frontage had to come out and be propped up with RSJs, and as soon as they did that they discovered the joists were completely shot, woodworm or termites or something, God only knows what was holding the place up, force of habit presumably, so they had to scrape off all the turf and go in from the top, because of subsidence or whatever, and you can imagine how much *that* cost, and then redo all the timberwork, really, it'd have been so much easier to start from scratch but you don't know that, do you, when you start bashing holes in walls; and once you got inside everything was panelled in this godawful gloomy dark wood, so all that had to come out and then the whole lot had to be plastered, and the floors, don't talk to me about the floors, just horrible great stone slabs, freezing cold underfoot and every time you walked across a room it sounded like Frankenstein, so that was no good; a hundred and six tons of concrete it took before we could get a floor level enough to lay a decent bit of carpet. And the plumbing, don't get me started on the plumbing. For one thing you just can't get a plumber, they're all dwarves and they live about a thousand miles away under some stupid mountain, it's three months each way just to get there, and of course the moment they start work they discover they haven't got some stupid tool or other and they've got to go back for it. And if you think it's hard getting a plumber, you just try finding anyone who's prepared to do a bit of cleaning and dusting. Which is hardly surprising, you should see the way the Short-arses, sorry, mustn't call them that, the locals keep their houses, it's disgusting, really, and they all smoke like chimneys. And the nearest supermarket's the Lidl in bloody Hobbiton, twelve miles away, I know it doesn't sound a lot but you try it rattling about on what they laughingly call roads in a stupid pony-trap, and they all drive like maniacs, and when you get there it's practically a dead cert they'll be out of Tunisian olives or parmesan. Thank God for the Internet, that's what Pauline and I say, if we couldn't order in stuff from home we'd starve.

Do we regret it? Oh no. No, once we'd got past all the teething problems, you can't beat it. I mean, I can work from home via the Net, and now we've built the pool and found a company back in England that's prepared to ship out Beefeater gin, Pauline's happy as a clam, and it's so quiet and peaceful and unspoilt. And the locals, once they've got to know you, they couldn't be more friendly.

Or take the Barringtons, Terry and Molly. He was something high powered in phosphates and she ran a thriving online boutique, but then they got sick of it and thought, wouldn't it be nice to get away from the pressures of the big city and rediscover the simple life. She could carry on with her business but sell locally sourced artisan craftworks, while he'd always fancied having a crack at writing that novel ... And then they heard about the Hidden Realms from the Hendersons, who'd just sold their poky little flat in Ealing and bought what was effectively a castle, with a sodding great deer park and a lake and its own windmill, and still had enough left to pave over the rose garden for extra parking.

Getting to the Realms was a bit weird but incredibly quick and easy, and almost as soon as they arrived they saw the place of their dreams and knew they just had to have it—

Terry Barrington craned his neck until he could feel something go click, but still he couldn't see the top of the tower. He took three steps back, but it didn't help. The black stone seemed to swallow up the light—it wasn't so much a colour as an absence, a rip in the fabric of reality— and when Molly Barrington touched the wall it was so cold it tore skin off her fingertips, as though it was covered in superglue.

"Who did you say used to live here?" Terry asked.

The guide smiled. "Well," he said, "according to local folklore, a great wizard once dwelt in Caras Snorgond."

"A wizard," Molly squeaked, "that's wonderful. I can almost feel the aura. Can you feel it, Terry?"

"When was the last time this lot was rendered?" her husband asked.

"Recently," the guide said smoothly. "They used a local process, very reputable contractors, and it comes with a twenty-five-thousand-year guarantee." He didn't add that the re-rendering had been necessary to cover up the scuff marks left by the war engines of the Kings of Men during the Great Siege, when for six weeks a thousand trebuchets had pounded the tower day and night. Because of the spells of Gorman the Blue, they had succeeded in causing only minor cosmetic damage, but an offcomer might be sceptical about that and demand a full structural survey, which would confirm the futility of the assault but which might well turn up other issues which a purchaser might find off-putting. A quick dab over with coal tar and a freezing spell, however, covered a multitude of sins.

Terry took a further step back and felt something snap under his heel. He stooped down and picked it up. "What's this? Looks like a bit of dowel."

"Arrow shaft," the guide said. "Stuff like that's always turning up. This site is particularly rich in historical arte-facts and antiquities."

"Is that a fact."

"Absolutely. The locals can't dig their vegetable patches without coming across a dozen arrowheads or a bit of rusty armour."

You can make good money selling historical artefacts on eBay. Terry casually dropped the fragment in his pocket and took a few steps towards the tower. Something was missing. It took him a moment to figure out what it was.

"Where's the door?" he asked.

"Ah." The guide beamed at him. "I was going to tell you about that. One of the special features that makes this property so unique is the amazing security system."

"Great. Where's the door?"

"There isn't one," the guide said. "That is, unless you know the secret incantation." He made a very peculiar noise, like someone gargling with gravel, and four glowing red lines appeared on the face of the black stone and slowly joined to form a rectangle. There was an audible click, and the rectangle swung open. "You can forget your triple-bolt deadlocks and your infra-red motion detectors and your CCTV," the agent went on. "Without the magic words, no force on earth can get in here. It's also handy," he added, "for anyone who has trouble remembering where they put their keys."

"Mphm," Terry said, trying hard not to sound impressed. "So how about windows?"

"Ah. Just step inside and see for yourself."

They followed him, through the almost invisible entrance and up a long flight of winding steps. It was pitch dark and bitter cold. Terry was just about to say something when the guide did some more of that weird muttering, and suddenly—

"The walls, you see," said the guide, "are transparent."

Molly squealed with delight, and Terry had to admit he was impressed. It was a 365-degree picture window, looking out over green pastures and vast tousled forests towards the gaunt grey outline of the distant mountains—

"With," the guide added, "built-in magnification."

—which were suddenly right up close, in your face, as if you'd just teleported a hundred miles and were hovering in mid-air just short of the cliff face. Then lift your head just a little and suddenly you're looking *over* the mountain-tops, down through the clouds (which part and dissipate instantly) at purple moorlands, golden wheat fields, and then a rocky coastline and the sky-blue sea . . .

"That's amazing," Terry said. "It's like Google Earth without a mouse."

"Quite," the guide said. "Or, if you prefer, you can mute them so they're just slightly translucent." The view vanished abruptly, and they were in a bare circular room with walls of faintly glowing mother-of-pearl, and a polished pink marble floor.

"That'll have to go," Molly said firmly. "I'm not spending the rest of my life on my hands and knees keeping *that* clean."

The guide smirked. "No need," he said. "Self-cleaning. Just say the appropriate spell."

Terry looked at him suspiciously. "You keep saying that," he said. "Spells and rubbish. Are you trying to tell us this place is powered by *magic*?"

"Good heavens no," the guide said, and in the pocket of his jacket his fingers were tightly crossed. "It's just really sophisticated voice-activated, solar-powered technology, so advanced and discreet it *looks* like magic. But perfectly normal, I promise you. I mean, *magic*. Would I ask you to believe in anything like that?"

"Mmm," Terry said. "Where's the toilet?"

"There are garderobes," the guide corrected him gently, "on every floor, naturally." He mumbled something, and a door appeared in the wall. The *outside* wall, Terry was about to point out, but then the door swung open to reveal a large bathroom, with pale green marble walls and what looked suspiciously like a solid gold bath and lavatory bowl. Terry reached in and fingered the toilet paper. It was amazingly soft, as though woven from cloud.

There comes a point when there are no more tyres left

to kick. "How much did you say they want for this place?" Terry heard himself say.

The guide quoted a sum of money that would just about buy a lock-up garage in Chiswick, provided you weren't fussy about roofs and stuff. "There's got to be a catch," Terry said. "What about rates and ground rents and local taxes?"

"Ah," said the guide. "They come to about five thousand silver marks a year."

"That's a bit—"

"*They* pay *you*," the guide added quickly. "As Lord of the Tower of Snorgond and Prince of Falthithuil. The titles come with the property."

Terry's mouth moved up and down for a bit, but no sound came out. Molly said, "Does that mean we'll be lords and ladies? That's so exciting."

"Something like that," the guide said. "Of course, there's a few purely nominal obligations that go with it; basically, just letting the locals use part of the grounds for fetes and flower shows, that sort of thing. No big deal. Of course you don't have to accept the title, but—"

Five thousand silver marks a year; what exactly was a mark, and how much did it weigh? Gift horses' teeth, Terry thought. "Oh, I think we ought to enter into the spirit of things, don't you, Moll? I mean, what's the point of coming to a place like this if you aren't going to make yourself part of the community? That's what the big society is all about."

"That's the spirit," the guide said cheerfully. "Now, if you'd like to follow me up onto the roof, I think you're going to like the view. You can see right out over the Entwoods as far as the Great River."

"Whee!" Molly said, gazing up at the eagles circling overhead. "What's an Entwood?"

Maybe the guide hadn't heard her. "Over there," he said, "you can see the White City, with its celebrated shopping facilities, entertainment complex and folkloresque Old Town. There's a carrier's cart three times a week, but I expect you'll keep your own carriage. Now, if you look closely you can just make out the remains of the curtain wall, which marks the boundary of the property. It's about five square miles, give or take."

Just before they came to the Realms they'd had drinks with the Lushingtons, who'd made them both feel sick, banging on about their wonderful converted *mithril* mine in the foothills of the Taram Asalat, which they'd snapped up for a trivial sum and had such plans for. Already, in his mind's eye, Terry was showing the Lushingtons this view, before adjourning to the patio for a glass of wine from his own vineyard, which would be somewhere about *there*—"What do you think, Moll?" Terry said. "Will it do?"

Before she could answer, they heard a scream. It started low and rose to a piercing shrill crescendo, blending all the hate and all the sorrow in the world into one heart-stopping, anguished leitmotiv. Then it died away as abruptly as it had begun.

"Ooh," Molly said. "That's a bittern. They're dead rare, they are."

The guide had gone white as a sheet and stepped back into the shadow of the ramparts. The sound had apparently awoken some old memory; once bittern, twice shy, or something of the sort.

"Well?" Terry said.

"I love it, Terry. We are going to buy it, aren't we?"

Only last year the Cordwainers had paid nearly as much for a beach hut at Lyme Regis. "Not at that price," Terry said, with what he hoped was genuine sincerity.

"Knock off ten per cent and maybe we'd be interested."

"Done," the guide said.

Terry blinked twice. "When I said ten, what I actually meant was twelve."

"Of course you did," the guide said, contorting his neck so he could peer up at the sky without coming out of the shadows. "Twelve per cent it is. Now, by some extraordinary chance I happen to have a draft contract in my pocket, all we need to do is fill in the blanks and we're away." A shadow had fallen across the sun; a slick, fast-moving shadow that flew against the wind. "Just sign the last page, where the pencil cross is, and initial the first paragraph. You can use my back to rest on if you like."

Before he succeeded the Nameless One as Dark Lord and Prince of Evil, King Mordak had acquired a justly deserved reputation as the greatest proponent of liberal social reform in the history of Goblinkind. True, he was the greatest goblin reformer in the same way that the Sun is the hottest star in the solar system, or seven is the biggest whole number between six and eight; but his agenda had been ambitious, and he'd given it everything he'd got. Under the banner of New Evil, he'd come a long way in a short time, although he was painfully aware that there was still an even longer way to go before he could declare victory in any credible sense.

Getting the Dark Lordship had, naturally, put a bit of a crimp in things. There had to be a period of consolidation. The honeymoon hadn't lasted long. He'd barely seated himself on the Iron Throne (his feet didn't quite touch the floor; he had the engineers looking into that) when the infighting started in earnest; wraiths against trolls, Dark Elves siding with the revisionist faction of the Undead against the Erlking and the cobolds, the Queen of the Fey shamelessly pulling every string in sight to get herself appointed to the vacant chair on the Finance Committee. Sorting all that out had taken a long time and rather too much of his reserves of mental and spiritual energy; and while his attention was elsewhere the goblin Old Guard had been quietly gnawing away at everything he'd managed to get done in the last ten years of patient, agonisingly slow effort.

Take, for example, his flagship universal healthcare programme—

"No," he said. "And that's final."

The Chairgoblin of the Apothecaries' Guild scowled at him. "It's traditional."

"I know. That's why it's got to stop. From now on, you get paid in money, or not at all."

There was an awkward silence. From time immemorial, goblin surgeons and apothecaries had been remunerated in the old-fashioned way: a flat fee of fivepence if they cured the patient, or the carcass if they didn't. "Where's the incentive in that?" the Chairgoblin said angrily. "Threepence an hour, regardless of whether they get better or not? I mean, why bother?"

Mordak counted to five under his breath. "All your patients die," he pointed out. "And then you eat them. Admit it, that's not an ideal system."

The Chairgoblin was shocked. "That's social responsibility, that is," he said. "By weeding out the sick and infirm, we're making an invaluable contribution to the future of the species."

"Threepence an hour," Mordak said firmly, "and no more amputations for ingrowing toenails. You want drumsticks, you buy them in the market like everybody else. Next."

Next was the Defence Committee. Mordak glanced at the agenda and sighed. "All right," he said, "would somebody care to explain to me why we're at war with the dwarves *again*?"

A thickset goblin in troll-scale armour shuffled his feet. "They started it."

"Of course they did. What did they do this time?"

The goblin stuck out his chest. "They failed to comply with an ultimatum to evacuate Grid Section 34992/XP/239 by the date specified."

"Fine." Mordak unrolled a map and peered at it. It was a sad but undeniable fact that the Dark Eyesight wasn't getting any better as time went by. The humans, so he'd heard, had these bits of ground glass you stuck in your eye, and it helped you see better. Sounded promising. Goblins had something similar, of course, but designed to achieve the opposite effect. "Hold on," he said. "Did you say 239?"

"Sir."

"According to this map, that's the guest wing of King Drain's palace."

The goblin shrugged. "It's directly above one of our main supply tunnels," he said. "If they were to neglect it and it all caved in, our ability to transport vital materiel from the depot to the front-line tunnels would be seriously compromised."

"Just a second." Mordak fiddled about with a ruler and a pair of dividers. "By directly above, you mean separated by a thousand feet of solid rock."

"Solid *at the moment*, sir," the goblin said. "All it'd take would be a bit of water erosion and some tectonic shift and we'd be staring disaster in the face. Much better to act now, sir, from a position of relative strength."

Mordak closed his eyes for a moment. "Oh, come on,"

he said. "We only just managed to patch things up after the last war. They wiped the floor with us."

"I did say relative strength, sir. Who knows, in five thousand years' time they could be ten times stronger than us, instead of just three, like they are now. That's why we should strike *now*, sir, while we've got the chance."

"Scribe."

A bored-looking Elf sprawling in a chair to his left took a pencil from behind her ear. "What?"

"Write a nice polite letter to King Drain reassuring him that we have no hostile intentions and that we hope he wasn't unduly alarmed by our April Fools message."

"It's September."

"Backdate it."

The Elf shrugged and went back to her newspaper. That was one area, at least, in which he could reasonably claim to have succeeded; there were now Elves living (for longer than ten minutes) and working in Goblinland, performing such essential administrative functions as reading, writing and adding up, and making a valuable contribution to goblin society. True, they were if anything even more insufferable than they'd been before the great rapprochement—there's nothing like living and working with a species, they delighted in saying, for confirming all your deeply entrenched prejudices—but at least they were here, tolerated and uneaten, and someone was doing the paperwork and telling him where he was supposed to be and when.

"All right," Mordak said to the Defence goblins, "you lot clear off, and try not to start any more wars without at least telling me. Next."

Ah yes, the civil engineering programme. New roads, bridges, infrastructure of all kinds, just what was needed to create jobs and boost sustainable economic growth—

"What do you mean, you've stopped work?"

The chief engineer shrugged. "Can't get the materials."

"For a *road*? Oh, come on."

"It's not just any road, is it?" the engineer retorted. "It's a road from the State ordnance factory to the principal supply depot at G'nash G'vork."

"I know that. It's so we can move cartloads of iron ore on the flat, instead of having to go up three levels and then back down again."

"Ah," said the engineer. "But if you look at the map, see, there's this half-mile section here that goes straight past the royal palace, right?"

"Well, yes. I don't mind. Roads have got to be built. I'm not one of those not-in-my-backyard whiners who—"

"Yes, Your Majesty, but with all due respect you're missing the bloody point. If it goes past the palace, you might walk on it."

Mordak's head was starting to hurt. "There is that chance, yes. So?"

"So," said the chief engineer, "everybody knows, the King of the Goblins tramples on the bleached bones of his mortal enemies, it's traditional. You can't just go walking about on *tarmac*. You got your royal dignity to think of."

"Yes, but—"

"So," the engineer ground on, "if we're going to build this stupid road, it's got to be bones, and the thing of it is, there just aren't enough of 'em to go round. You aren't executing enough mortal enemies, all due respect. So, either you start chopping off a few more heads, or we're going to have to reroute to bypass the palace area altogether, which'll mean digging seven miles through solid rock and coming out *here*"—he stabbed at the map with a splintered foretalon—"which is three levels down, so you'd need a bloody great big embankment *here*, and if you're going to have to do all that, I ask you, where's the bloody point?"

Mordak looked down at his hand. He'd just bitten clean through one of his own claws. Never mind. "You know what," he said, "you're quite right."

"I am?"

"Yes. And I'm a fool not to have thought of it before. Silly me. What we need, obviously, is a whole lot more executions."

The engineer grinned. "Now you're talking. There's the Highways Committee, for a start. Chop the lot of 'em and who'd ever notice?"

"Quite," Mordak said. "But that's still only, what, thirty yards' worth of bones. Whereas your department—just offhand, round numbers, how many goblins have you got working for you in Construction? Yourself included."

"Um."

"Got to be at least seven thousand. That's, let me see, best part of half a mile. Which would cover the stretch of road that goes past the palace just nicely."

"Yes, but—"

Mordak smiled. "I know," he said. "You're going to point out that you and your colleagues aren't my mortal enemies, and therefore not suitable for deployment as roadmaking material. Isn't that right?"

The engineer seemed to be having difficulty speaking, but he could still nod his head.

"That's what I thought," Mordak said. "Because in order for someone to be my mortal enemy, he'd have to do something to get me seriously annoyed, like making difficulties, or deliberately holding up one of my pet projects, or not doing as he's damn well told. Agreed?"

"Anything you say, boss."

"Which you would never dream of doing, it goes without saying. So, that's fine. Oh, and by the way, did I ever tell you how I feel about concrete?"

"Boss."

"I *hate* concrete. One of these days I'm going to have all the concrete in Goblinland rounded up, stood against a wall and shot. And then I'm going to dance on its shattered rubble. Get the picture?"

"Absolutely."

"Good man. Down with concrete. Death to aggregates. Two, four, six, eight, they're the stuff we really hate. Now get on with it. Next."

Next was the president of the Equality Commission. And, he had to admit, just for once, here was someone in charge of something who'd actually made an effort. Just, perhaps, a trifle misguided.

"It says here," Mordak said, "you've had nine hundred and forty goblins arrested and their feet cut off. Is that right?"

"Nine hundred and forty-*six*."

"I stand corrected. Out of interest, why?"

"They weren't equal."

You know that feeling of having just walked into a plate glass door? "Excuse me?"

"It says in the Universal Declaration of Goblin Rights," the president said patiently, "henceforth, all goblins are to be equal. Well, they weren't."

"Um?"

"Too tall. So, we shortened them a bit. The mean average height of an adult goblin is forty-nine-point-seven inches, so—"

"Ah." Mordak nodded. "So presumably the reason why you locked up eight thousand goblins in a dungeon with no food for a month—"

The president nodded. "Too heavy. The mean average weight—"

"Yes, all right." Mordak drummed his fingers on the arm of his chair. "And the ones you had squashed between two huge slabs of stone were too wide, I think I get the picture. May I ask, what definition of *equal* are you using as your point of reference?"

The president frowned. "You told me, look it up. So I did. It means being the same in quantity, size or amount. So I looked up size, and it said—"

"Mphm." Mordak took a strangely shaped metal object from the baggy sleeve of his black robe, polished it on his cuff and balanced it carefully on the arm of the throne. "Come on, S'nrrg, it's me you're talking to. I know you. You're doing this to be awkward, aren't you?"

"What, me? Perish the—"

"You and all the rest of them. You don't like the reform package, you've never really got behind the core values of New Evil, and you're trying to make me look like an idiot. Well?"

The president looked at the metal thing, then at Mordak, then back at the thing. "All right, so me and some of the lads don't hold with all this new stuff. But we're loyal goblins. Dead loyal. We're just doing like you said. Honest."

"S'nrrg, I wouldn't trust you if we were sitting under a clock and you told me the time. The question I always ask myself before I appoint someone to high public office is, is this man more scared than bolshie? I think I may have misjudged you, old friend." He smiled. "I admire you for that. You've got to take your hat off to someone who's prepared to die horribly for what he believes is right."

"Honest, boss, I never—"

"Of course," Mordak went on, picking up the metal

thing and turning it slowly in his hand, as if trying to find the sweet spot, "if I could convince myself that you were capable of true, sincere cowardice, not just a bit frightened but genuinely terrified out of your—"

He paused and glanced down. A dark, treacly pool had appeared around the president's feet, and Mordak could smell the sharp fumes of dissolving marble. He nodded and put the metal thing back in his sleeve. "In that case," he said, "I might feel justified in giving you a second chance. Well? What do you reckon?"

"Oh, I think so, boss," the president whimpered. "I mean, why not? Just for the hell of it."

"Quite." Mordak gave him a warm smile. "In that case, I suggest we start by amending article one of the Declaration so that it says something like equal rights and opportunities for all goblins, regardless of age, size, rank, gender or religious preference. How would that be?"

"Um, boss."

"What?"

"Sorry, boss, but you can't do that."

Mordak sighed. "You're being brave again, S'nnrg." He pulled the object a little way out of his sleeve, just far enough so that the torchlight could play on its burnished steel. "In fact, not just brave but downright bloody heroic. Now, what did you just say?"

"You can't do it, boss." The president screwed his eyes closed and braced himself. "Sorry."

"I see. Why not?"

"You can't promise equality regardless of gender, boss. We haven't got any females."

"Ah." Mordak sat back in his throne, frowning. He'd been quoting, of course, or rather paraphrasing, from the Elvish Declaration of Superiority. But goblins practised parthenogenetic reproduction, fishing their newly spawned offspring out of bubbling vats of beige goo with very long tongs and confining them in fortified rearing pens until their acne cleared up. Hence, no female goblins. It was a good system. It worked. "All right, then, regardless of age, size, rank and religious whatsit. No worries. Go away and see to it, there's a good lad. And send someone out here with a mop and some potash."

The president tottered unsteadily away. Mordak sighed, took the egg whisk from his sleeve, turned the crank a few times and listened to the whirr of the blades. It was an artefact of human origin, he knew that, but unlike anything he'd seen before. The scouts had told him it came from one of the new human settlements far away on the south bank of the Great River, near the dreadful Tower of Snorfang. Apparently you used it for making meringues, though what it could do that a bundle of the desiccated neck sinews of your mortal enemy tied together with a bit of wire couldn't, he was at a loss to guess. He put it carefully back in its cardboard box and stowed it under the throne.

No women. Yes, it was a damn good system. It had served the goblin race well for millennia. It worked.

Hmm.

Ever since he'd started the New Evil project, basing his reforms on measures successfully adopted by other species and other cultures, he'd gradually come to the conclusion that goblins weren't like most life forms. He wasn't quite sure he could put his claw on what made them so different. Sure, there were the obvious, superficial things—the cannibalism, the mindless aggression, the loathing for sunlight, the three-inch fangs—but he knew it went deeper than that. Loyal goblin though he was, he couldn't help thinking that his species was incomplete somehow, that Goblinkind was missing out on something it needed if it was ever to take its proper place among the mature liberal societies of the sunlit world. For a long time he'd worked on the assumption that it was intelligence; and it wasn't a bad hypothesis at that, because goblins could be incredibly stupid at times, to the point where it made his head hurt wondering how they'd managed to survive so long. But his studies of dwarves, humans and Elves—especially Elves—had made him realise that crass stupidity wasn't an exclusively goblin attribute. Yes, goblins could be pig-headed at times (and dog-headed, and goat-headed, and there was that colony out on the Freep River whose inhabitants had made him swear never to eat cheese late at night again) but generally speaking they had a modicum of basic common sense, and definitely knew which side their shin bones were larded on. So: if it wasn't brains, what was it? Could it possibly be—? No, that was just plain silly. What possible difference could it make if you were hauled out of a goo vat rather than squeezed out of the guts of a fellow goblin? If anything, surely, it was a sign of superiority, because the other way of doing it, he was a bit hazy about the details but it sounded down-right *yuck*. How could something so primitive and, well, let's not mince words, barbaric possibly constitute an advantage?

Quite. He shivered, and drank a skull of water to settle his stomach. Just then, the door behind the throne opened and his secretary came in, holding a big folder of papers.

"Oh," she said, "you're still here."

You can get used to Elves, eventually, if you try hard enough. "Tinituviel," he said. "Tell me everything you know about non-parthenogenetic reproduction."

She raised one gossamer-thin eyebrow. "Certainly not."

"Fine. Tell me everything you know about females."

"Are you feeling all right?"

"Broadly speaking, do you think they're a good thing?"

Elves, by the same token, can get used to goblins. It just takes longer, and why would they want to? "You've been thinking again, haven't you?"

He stuck his tongue out at her. "Of course I have. I'm an intellectual. Thinking is what I do."

"Of course it is."

"Thank you."

She smiled at him. "It's just a pity you're so bad at it. Still, that doesn't alter the fact that you try." She sat down beside him and pushed a dozen or so sheets of parchment at him. "Sign."

"All right. What am I signing?"

"Bits of paper."

"Fair enough." He took the pen and scrawled *Mordak R* where she'd marked the place in pencil. In the process, he lacerated the palm of his hand with his talons, but that couldn't be helped. "Females," he said. "You were about to fill me in."

"Why do you want to know about females?"

"I was thinking," Mordak replied. "Maybe it's time we had some."

"What, dancing girls? Or lightly grilled on a bed of steamed spinach?"

Mordak sighed. "As valued members of goblins society, taking their rightful place in the hierarchy of rights, duties and obligations."

"Oh, you mean *cleaners*. I can get some sent in if you want. Dwarves or humans?"

"Goblin females."

"Don't be stupid," she said almost kindly. "There aren't any. You know that."

"Maybe there should be."

He waited for her to reply. He counted to twenty under his breath. Then he took off the brooch that fastened the Black Cloak, yanked off the pin and dropped it on the floor. There was a faint tinkle.

"Thought so," he said.

"What?"

"I heard a pin drop. I take it," he went on, as she stared at him, "that the idea comes as a bit of a surprise."

"You broke your brooch."

"A present from King Drain. I didn't like it much anyway. *Well?*"

"I don't know," she said. "It's certainly—"

"Refreshing? Imaginative? Radical?"

"Weird," she said. "Weird as a butter churn full of ferrets. Why?" she demanded. "What would be the point?"

"You're asking me what's the point of females?"

"Goblin females."

"Ah, I get you. You're saying, why innovate when the goblin race is perfect as it is."

"No, actually that's not—hello," she said, catching sight of something. "What's that?"

"What?"

"In the box under your chair."

"Oh, that." He reached forward, pulled it out and handed it to her. She opened it and frowned. "It's an egg whisk," he said.

"I can see that." She turned the handle and the blades whirred. "Not bad. What do you want it for?"

"It's human."

"No, it's an egg whisk. If it was human, it'd have arms and legs."

"Of human origin. Apparently it came from one of those new human settlements out by the old wizard's tower."

"You turn the little crank and the blades spin round and round."

"You noticed that, too?"

"That's quite a neat idea," Tinituviel said, with grudging admiration. "Takes much less strength and effort than the conventional type. And quicker, too."

"It's a very fine egg whisk," Mordak conceded. "So what?"

"Humans made this?"

"So?"

"It's better—" She stopped abruptly. "Almost as good as the Elvish pattern. Better than anything the dwarves make." She looked at him. "How did you say you got hold of it?"

"One of the scouts brought it back. He found it. On a trash-heap. Look, what about my goblin women idea? I want your honest opinion. What do you think?"

"I think," she said, frowning, "that people who can make something as ingenious and advanced as this, and then throw it away even though it's still working just fine, are not your ordinary run-of-the-mill humans." She looked at him. "What do we know about these colonists?"

"Don't look at me. You're the one who gets all the reports."

"We know nothing about these colonists," she amended. "Which won't do at all. I'll send out more scouts."

"You do that. Listen, what about goblin females? Do you think it's a good idea or not?"

"Straight away. I don't like this. We need to find out about these humans. Just look at the work that's gone into this," she went on, turning the whisk over and staring hard at the flywheel. "That's a casting, not forged. And look at how evenly the gear teeth are cut. I bet if you measured it with a pair of dwarvish callipers, you'd find it was made to really fine tolerances, like maybe thousandths of an inch. Which is why it runs so smoothly."

"Fascinating. So you think I should go ahead, then."

"And it's *plated*. Not with silver, it's something much harder than silver. A bit like *mithril*, I guess, but it isn't that. Something harder and shinier than *mithril*, then. The dwarves are going to be livid when they find out about this."

"Or would it be better to forget the whole idea and carry on as we are?"

"And what this stuff on the handgrip is I have absolutely no idea. It's not horn, it's not bone, it's not ivory, it's definitely not any kind of wood—"

Mordak reached out, grabbed the egg whisk and took it away from her. "Hey," she snapped. "I was looking at that."

"For crying out loud," he said, "get over it, will you? It's a kitchen appliance, that's all."

She made a half-hearted grab for the whisk, then glared at him. "You don't get it, do you?"

"Get what?"

"Look at it. Go on, look. Well?"

"It's an egg whisk."

"Fine." The basilisk stare. Elves do it so well. "Now, I want you to ask yourself. What sort of people go to all that time and trouble and expense on a gadget for fluffing up egg whites?

"I don't know, do I? Idiots?"

She shook her head. "Look at it another way," she said. "If they can come up with something like this just so as to produce a better omelette, what else do you think they're capable of making?"

*

Drain son of Dror son of Drifel, King under the Mountain and hereditary Convener of the Dwarvenhold, cautiously opened one eye, then closed it again. The only light in the room was the faint amber glow of a single baked clay oil lamp, resting on a low table in the far corner. It was far too much for a dwarf with a bad migraine. He groaned; then his head swam, his stomach lurched and the molten lava started to pump through his hiatus hernia into his windpipe. Must've been something I ate, he told himself.

In which case, it could only have been either the slack half-handful of dry roasted peanuts or the cocktail olive, which were the only things he'd eaten the night before, when he'd presided over the Grand Lodge Gala of the Ironworkers' Guild. Doctor's orders, naturally. That damned Elvish quack had told him he needed to lose weight; and, to be fair, maybe he had a point. It's never a good sign when you're taller lying down than standing up, and the only part of his ceremonial armour that now fitted him was the scabbard. Well; you don't pay good money in ridiculous quantities to a needle-eared sawbones and not take his advice, so Drain had gone on a diet. Dry bread, lettuce, celery and skimmed-milk yoghurt. Washed down with all the beer he could get down him without falling over, of course, but that was drinking, not eating, and the Elvenquack had specifically said; you're digging your grave with your teeth. Teeth, please note, not gullet. Drinks, therefore, were clearly not included in the regimen.

Maybe it was lack of food that was making his head hurt so much; that and overexposure to searingly bright lamp-light. It also appeared to be affecting his memory. They'd been celebrating something last night, he was pretty sure about that, but what was it?

Signature. He'd signed something. That narrowed it down to five possibilities: treaty, contract, death warrant, banker's draft or autograph. He could probably rule out three and five, and signing number four wasn't something you'd celebrate. Contract or treaty? One or the other.

He left his bedchamber and wandered down the corridor to the Royal Forge. Dunking his head in the water bucket stopped the throbbing in his temples but wasn't much help in getting him to remember. He staggered another three doors down and kicked open the kitchen door.

"Coffee," he shouted.

The trouble was, you couldn't get the staff. Any dwarf with two hands and at least one leg worked in the forges or the stone yard or down the pit; cooking, therefore, was traditionally the remit of the infirm, the half-witted and the hopelessly unemployable, and tended to consist of porridge. If you wanted anything else, you had to hire foreigners, which generally meant humans, because you'd have to be dying of starvation to eat that Elvish muck, and the associations between goblins and eating that lurked in the dwarvish subconscious were enough to put anybody off his dinner. And humans—well. With an alternative like that, you quickly came to appreciate the finer points of porridge.

Unless—

It came flooding back; the reason for the celebration. A contract; a contract of employment.

He looked round to make sure nobody was about, then backed up and looked at his reflection in a burnished copper pan. His hair was a mess and his beard looked like it should have blackberries growing in it. He wiped his fingers on a nearby pat of butter and did a bit of emergency slicking. Just in time.

"Your Majesty."

She called him that. He wasn't the pompous sort, always standing on ceremony, and dwarves have always prided themselves on their sturdy egalitarianism; but after all, if you've got a title, it's quite nice if people use it now and again, as a change from *bumface* or *hey, you.* "Ah," he said. "Yes. Hello. I was just wondering—"

"Coffee?"

"Yes, please."

"Coming right up."

Another thing. Ms. White knew how to make coffee. She ground the acorns herself, knew just the right amount of lamp black and iron filings to give it that subtle boost, and always added just enough treacle. Until yesterday, she'd been head cook in the kitchens of Barn Ironteeth, deep under the passes of the Taupe Mountains. Yesterday, though, she'd put her name to a five-year contract to work exclusively for the House of Driri, starting immediately. It would almost certainly mean war. The first time he'd been over to a feast at Barn's, the old fool had spent ten minutes describing in loving detail exactly what he'd do to anybody trying to poach his amazing new cook—but what the hell. Dwarves like war, Barn's lot were rubbish at fighting, and with a bit of finesse and the help of a few Elvish intermediaries there was a better than even chance of selling the Taupe Mountains crowd a few thousand of those substandard mail shirts the humans had sent back the autumn before last. All that and decent coffee, too. No wonder he'd been celebrating.

"You look a bit under the weather, Your Majesty."

Strictly speaking, dwarves are always under the weather, not to mention everything else, but he didn't correct her on it. "Bit of a headache. Hay fever, probably."

"Hangover?"

"Mm."

"Just a moment." Ms. White went away, opened a few cupboards, mixed a few things and handed him a tin cup that fizzed disturbingly. "Try that."

"What is it?"

"Good for you."

Ah well. King Drain hadn't had an official food taster ever since the last incumbent had shouted, "I'm not eating *that*" when presented with a plate of human-style lasagne, and stormed off back to the iron-ore mines. He knocked it back in one, and a strange thing happened. Several strange things. His head stopped pounding. The lava flow slowed, then stopped. The coating of potter's clay that had turned the inside of his mouth into a tandoor vanished, leaving a faint residual taste of apples. "Thank you," he said.

"You're welcome. Breakfast?"

Two minutes earlier, if someone had told King Drain that he'd ever want to eat again, he'd have pulled their beard out by the roots. "That's not a bad—hang on." He pulled a face. "Better not. This diet I'm on—"

She smiled at him. "Oh yes," she said. "I was meaning to talk to you about that."

A tiny ray of sunshine broke through the gloom that had descended when he'd said the D word. Passing through the lens of Hope, it grew so bright that you could've read a book by the glow from his ears. "Go on."

"Well," she said, "obviously I'm not a doctor, and I'm sure this Elf knows his business and is properly qualified and everything, but I took a look at what he reckons you're allowed to eat, and it did seem to me it was a teeny bit harsh."

The way to a dwarf's heart is not through his stomach. If you're a goblin, the best bet is an upward thrust to the armpit, whereas humans and other Tall Bastards are recommended to try stabbing down at the small gap between the spine and shoulder blade. That said, I quite like her, Drain thought, even if she is a human.

"I mean," she went on, "all this salad stuff. And yoghurt. You do know about yoghurt, don't you?"

"What about it?"

"It's crawling with bacteria. That's Elvish for germs. Nasty little bugs," she translated, "which you can't see but which eat you alive from inside. Personally, I wouldn't touch that stuff if you paid me."

"But Dr. Glorien—"

"Yes, well. Where did you hear about him, by the way?"

"From King Gnorin of the Olive Drab Hills. Recommended him very highly."

"Mphm. And King Gnorin is a close friend of yours?"

Point. It wasn't all that long ago that the Olive Drabbers had made a concerted effort to muscle in on the corrugated *mithril* trade, which had been a monopoly of the House of Driri for three hundred years. "Not close, no."

"Just as well. Friends like that should ideally be as far away as possible. Sorry," she added quickly, "I'm speaking out of turn. But when I see people torturing themselves unnecessarily, it makes me so mad—"

"Unnecessarily?"

"You're not *fat*. Well-built, maybe, but not fat."

King Drain gazed at her for a moment. A human could never be beautiful—skinny, tall, clean-shaven—but there's such a thing as a beautiful soul; and as far as he was concerned, her soul was centrefold material. "My mother," he said, "used to say I had big bones."

"There you are, then."

Mostly in his head, was what she'd actually said, but

no need to elaborate unnecessarily. "So all the lettuce and stuff—"

She frowned thoughtfully. "If I had a suspicious mind," she said, "I'd be wondering if it wasn't all part of a plot to sap your strength and diminish your standing in the world arena. If you ask me," she went on, "what you could really do with is feeding up."

"You think so?"

"Definitely. A man in your position, after all, at any moment you might be called on to defend the Mountain against Mordak and his evil hordes. You can't be expected to do that on a few scraps of dandelion leaf and a chive."

It was in his mind to say that, actually, King Mordak wasn't all that bad once you got to know him, and these days the goblins were probably the least of his problems. Something told him, however, that Ms. White wouldn't approve of sentiments like that. Maybe it was the look of loathing that had contorted her face when she mentioned Mordak's name. You learn to pick up on subtle little things like that when you're a king. "Quite right," he said accordingly. "Um, you've come across King Mordak then, have you?"

"Him?" She scowled. "No, and I wouldn't want to. Would you believe, his lot actually had the nerve to offer me a job, when I was still with King Barn? Head cook and royal housekeeper. I told them what they could do."

"Really."

"Oh yes. Well, for a start, head cook—you know how literal-minded goblins are. And cleaning up after those horrible creatures, I'd rather not think about it."

"So you came here."

"Yes. Maybe I'm old-fashioned, but I like to work for people who have standards, you know?"

A bit of a non sequitur, that. True, he had standards, loads of them, mostly topped with goblin skulls or the

Iron Fist of Driri. Just one more thing to dust and iron, he'd have thought, but maybe she enjoyed that sort of thing. You could never tell with humans. Gentle seismic activity in his stomach reminded him that he was drifting away from an important issue she'd flagged up earlier. "Breakfast," he said.

"Yes," she replied crisply. "How about sausages, three fried eggs, a dozen rashers of streaky bacon, hash browns, mushrooms and two slices of fried bread?"

Tautology; but he didn't mind that. "And coffee."

"Of course coffee. You like it extra strong with treacle, don't you?"

There were six other dwarf-lords in the Realms, but the King under the Mountain was reckoned to be equal in wealth and power to the rest of them put together. All of which wealth and power, Drain vowed silently, he would unhesitatingly spend, down to the last man and the last grain of gold dust, to keep any of those six thieving bastards from doing to him what he'd done to that pinhead Barn. "Ms. White."

"Yes?"

"I don't think I quite caught your first name."

"Um."

"Excuse me?"

She flushed slightly. "It's Snow."

"Snow White?"

"Yup."

"That's an unusual—"

She looked at him. "It's short," she said, "for 'S-no-business-of-yours-what-my-first-name-is. Now if you'll excuse me, I have sausages to fry."

His mouth had fallen open, and it took him time and effort to get it closed again. He'd offended her, he could see that, but how? Still, that's humans for you. He remembered King Gnuin telling him once about a human he'd met at some function. "Lovely weather we're having," Gnuin had said, knowing that humans are interested in all that climate stuff, "absolutely glorious sunshine again, that's three days in a row, most unusual for the time of year"; and the human had burst into tears and rushed off sobbing. Turned out he was an ice merchant, and all his stock was held up in a bonded warehouse somewhere, quietly melting. Moral: to avoid embarrassment, never say anything at all to a human if you can possibly avoid it.

Barry and Patricia Lushington were just beginning to settle in to their new home, after a shaky start. The word shaky is used in its literal sense. Two days after the furniture arrived, the walls started to wobble and they found the master bedroom lying in heaps on the games room floor.

"You've got to expect a bit of subsidence in these converted mineworkings," the agent had told them, when they Skyped him to complain. "The place is ten thousand years old, after all. It's there in the surveyors' report, if you care to look."

The trouble was, Barry and Pat had fallen in love with the place when they were first shown round it, and had therefore read the report with a certain degree of optimistic scepticism. They've got to say that, Barry had said more than once, to cover themselves. After all, Pat had replied, it's been there ten thousand years, it's not going to fall down now, is it?

Indeed. For nine thousand of those years, of course, it had been empty, ever since the previous occupants moved out in something of a hurry. Aggravation from the neighbours, the agent had explained; but that was all a long time ago, you shouldn't have any trouble on that score.

So they had the tunnels shored up and the pit props replaced; and it was great fun, because round every corner there was a new Great Hall or guard house or throne room waiting to be discovered, and, once the electric light was working and Pat had got some carpet down in the Chasm of Mazar-Glûm, it wasn't long before the place started to feel homey and lived-in. It was exciting to think that their water came from their own artesian well, and they relished the thought of the savings they would make on their energy bills, thanks to the geothermal generator—

("How does it work, exactly?" Barry asked the engineer, a rather standoffish man with strangely pointed ears.

"Simple," the engineer replied. "Down in the basement it gets very hot. The heat boils water in a big kettle thing. The water gives off steam. The steam turns a big wheel round and round, very fast."

Barry pointed out that he had a degree in engineering from Imperial College London.

"The big wheel turns a thing called a turbine," the engineer went on, "which gives off electricity, and the electricity runs along the inside of copper wires and makes all your machines go. Pretty basic stuff, in fact."

"Yes, quite. But what are you using for a heat source in the first place?"

The engineer looked past him and changed the subject.)

They were mildly disconcerted when they found a load of perfectly preserved skeletons in chainmail armour in what they'd already decided was going to be the guest bathroom. But the armour was hardly rusty at all, and Barry pointed out that it'd look great hanging on the walls of the breakfast room. They contacted the agent about the bones. He asked them if they had a dog.

The heated indoor pool was a breeze; there was one already. The water was a sort of greenish colour, and bubbled, and there was a big sort of palm tree thing grow-ing on an island in the middle. Pat said she could've sworn she saw its fronds wave, but Barry pointed out that they were several hundred feet down and there was no draft, so she must've been imagining it. They also found a little wooden boat drawn up at the water's edge. Just think, Pat had said, we can go boating on the lake without having to leave the house. Barry didn't reply. He was sure he'd caught a glimpse of a pair of very pale green eyes, watching him from the shadows. But if Pat could imagine waving fronds, he could imagine green eyes. He put it out of his mind, went back upstairs and had a drink.

The only thing about the new place Barry and Pat Lushington found really annoying was the plumbing. It worked all right, but there were these awful noises—loud clanking and thumping deep down in the basement, like somebody beating a huge drum. They called out the plumber and told him what the problem was; he went bright green, made some excuse about being late for another job and left. Pat's theory was that he was afraid of the dark, but Barry said no, he's a dwarf, that's impossible. Spiders, probably. Or confined spaces.

He sent in his bill for the call-out charge, though. It was addressed to "the executors of Mr. and Mrs. B. Lushington". Weird mistake to make, Barry thought, but what can you expect from a species that don't even use Excel?

Ms. White wasn't her real name. Neither were any of the others she'd worked under and answered to over the last few years—Neige La Blanche was her favourite, it had class, though it was obviously too much for the bank and the electricity company, who insisted on writing to Nigel

La Blanche, which wasn't the same thing at all. Every single one of the various permutations was, of course, just the same thing translated into a different language. Obvious, really, but fortuitously the police and revenue authorities in several jurisdictions hadn't figured it out yet. So that was all right.

Who, or what, is Ms. White? Well, for one thing, she really is a seriously good cook. It used to be nothing more than a hobby; a useful one, since quite a few of her gentlemen also enjoyed a proper home-cooked meal at the end of a hard day at the bank or on the set or wherever, but really only something she did to unwind and remind herself that she was a human being and not an exquisite artefact (with ever such a lot of moving parts). The thought that one day she might achieve the Big Score, the one that'd set her up for life, through her work in the kitchen rather than the bedroom had never occurred to her until that momentous day when she—

But let's not go there yet. Two weeks ago she'd found a book. It was huge and heavy, bound in what she feared was probably trollskin, and written in runes and sadly faded, foxed, pierced with arrow holes and permeated with dark brown stains, and she'd come across it lying in an inch of dust on the tomb of King Groin under the Mountain in a ghastly sort of box room on one of the upper levels. She'd homed in on it because it was a book, and she liked reading, and it was the first and only book she'd come across in this dump. And it was fabulous. Just what she needed.

Take six orc livers. She frowned. Not likely, she muttered under her breath, but calves' liver would do just as well, and she could get some next time she went to the Lidls in Hobbiton. *Fourteen ounces of oatmeal, two roc's eggs*—she looked again, to make sure it wasn't a misprint. But orcs don't lay eggs, they have that disgusting beige goo. What was a roc? No idea, though some faint, far-distant memory suggested *big*. All right, make that two dozen ordinary eggs, what else?

The Red Household Management Book of Khored-Zûn was a treasure, no doubt about it. When she'd first started housekeeping for the Heirs of Snorin, naturally she'd stuck to what she knew, which meant human cuisine, in all its many-splendoured permutations. In retrospect, that had been a bad idea and she'd been lucky to survive it. Quite by chance, early on she'd hit on the one area where the Venn diagrams of human and dwarf cuisine kiss, if not actually intersect, namely breakfast. Give them a lorry driver's fry-up three times a day, she'd discovered, and they're happy.

She could also readily understand why King Groin had chosen to be buried with The Book, rather than the usual ironmongery and bling that dwarvish custom dictated. As far as she was aware, there was nothing like it in dwarvish culture, about which she'd learned ever such a lot since she came through the—And that was odd, because the dwarves really did enjoy their food, and it was only silly pride and dwarfismo that made them stuff themselves with porridge instead of nice things. Cooking is cissy, they'd tell you to your face, we're above such things (figuratively speaking), food's just fuel to keep you going at the coalface or on the battlefield. Like hell it was. Knock them up something tasty and watch the almost sublime look of joy spread across their craggy little faces. But try and get them to admit it? No chance. A dwarf café typically had two choices of *plat du jour*: salted porridge or salted porridge with extra salt. No wonder the poor dears were so bad-tempered.

Beat the eggs together with the icing sugar. She frowned. She could use an iron spoon—no wooden spoons under the Mountain; wood came from forests and forests are crawling with Elves, so we avoid them and anything derived from them. A typical dwarf spoon weighed three pounds and doubled as a ladle for pouring molten bronze. On the other hand, say what you like about the dwarves, when it came to metalwork anything they couldn't make wasn't worth having. The problem was convincing them to make it for you. *Make me an egg whisk* would be an invitation to give her a blank stare and a less than courteous refusal. If she wanted an egg whisk made, she'd have to draw it out, precisely to scale, with the gearing ratios of the flywheel clearly marked and the appropriate alloys for the various components written at the bottom, with the right SDE numbers. Then you'd just say *make me one of these* and they'd do it, no questions asked. Trouble was, she was hopeless at drawing and couldn't do long division, let alone gearing ratios. So, an iron spoon it'd have to be. Damn.

It was a book that had got her into this in the first place, let's not forget that. Her favourite book of all time, though whether she could ever bring herself to read it again she wasn't sure, not now that she'd seen what she'd seen and found out that large parts of it were, well, sort of true. To be precise, it had been a poem in her favourite book. To be exactly precise, one line from that poem—

Seven for the dwarf-lords in their halls of stone.

So it stood to reason there were seven dwarf-lords. Seven dwarves. Now that rang a bell.

Seven presumably very rich dwarf-lords, since her favourite book of all time was for ever banging on about gold and treasures stored deep in the roots of mountains; and when she'd first read that, when she was twelve, she hadn't taken much notice, because dwarves were rich the same way heroes are brave and Elves are wise and goblins are nasty, what the philologists call a fixed epithet. But time passed and she pursued her chosen career, and met a lot of very rich men who she never really liked much, if truth be told, and who had certain characteristics in common with dwarves but not good ones. And then some-one—someone's poor, long-suffering wife—had called her a cheap little gold-digger, and she'd suddenly thought about the dwarves and laughed. And not long after that she'd stumbled on It, and since then, everything—

Add the grated auroch's cheese, fry lightly until golden brown. The sort of men she'd always associated with require women for three things, and she was good at two of them, and of those two she knew which she preferred. But it would be nice if she could get her hands on a spatula that she could actually lift.

Marinade the bat goujons in a mixture of oil and balsamic vinegar. Hmm. You could get bat easily enough—walk down any Level Three gallery without a hat on and at least one of the little horrors would obligingly tangle itself in your hair—but for some reason she felt the recipe would probably taste nicer if she substituted guinea fowl, which she'd got from the Lidls in Hobbiton. Balsamic vinegar was no problem; the dwarves didn't actually have any, but dwarvish homemade bindweed wine was indistinguish-able in taste and had the extra merit of killing all known bacteria stone dead. Oil—well, it was a dwarvish book, and when they said oil, they weren't referring to anything that involved olives, sunflower seeds or oilseed rape. She sighed and set off for the winch sheds. Plenty of oil there, in big steel cans.

The dwarves didn't stare at her any more, for which she was quietly grateful. She was used to being stared at, came with the territory in her previous line of work, but not shud-dered at. It had taken her a while to get her head around the idea that to these people she was perfectly hideous (tall, slim, soft skin, beardless) and although on one level it was rather refreshing not to be ogled at, peered down or peeked up at, there were self-image issued involved which at some point she was going to have to deal with. Crepe hair and spirit gum, maybe.

Instead of staring, these days they tended to look just past her, or off to one side, or (if they happened to be standing on something at the time) over her head. Even the king, bless him, and he was completely besotted, ever since she'd persuaded him he could lose weight by eating fried onion rings in batter. They might avoid looking at her but they took extreme care not to bump into her in the corridors; also mildly insulting, if you stopped to think about it. The sensible thing, therefore, was not to think about it at all.

To get from the kitchens to the shed which housed the mechanism for winding the winch that hauled the ore up from the face, you had to go along a quarter-mile of gallery, down two flights, along another quarter-mile and up four flights, across the swaying rope bridge that crossed one of the many bottomless chasms so beloved by dwarvish interior designers and through the Hall of Factory-Reconditioned Columns (waste not, want not); third on the right leads you down nine flights to the winch house.

She'd been walking for quite some time, not recognising anything she saw around her, when it occurred to her that she might just possibly have taken the second on the right (which led to Armoury #674) or the third on the left, which led to the dungeons. She pressed on another hundred yards or so. The passageway got narrower and lower, and then she came to a door.

It wasn't in front of her. It was set into the wall, and it had a little grille at the top. She peered through and saw someone lying on a heap of grubby looking straw, reading a book by the guttering light of a tallow candle.

Doing *what*?

She banged on the door with her balled fist. The figure on the bed looked up; male but no beard. A fellow human.

"Excuse me."

The man peered at her, then marked his place with a wisp of straw. "My God," he said.

"Excuse me," she repeated, "but what's that you're reading?"

He was staring at her; not the way the dwarves used to, before they gave up. A bit like old times, in fact. "Are you real?" he said.

For his part, he probably didn't get stared at much. He was young, about her age, maybe a year younger; short, square, heading rapidly towards podgy, with the first tidemark of a receding hairline. "The book," she said.

"What? Oh, right. You wouldn't like it."

"I'll be the judge of that."

"Whatever." He wriggled round so his back was to her and went on reading.

She counted to five under her breath, then yelled, "Hey!"

"Pack that in," he said without moving, "or you'll wake the guards."

"What's the damn book?"

He looked at her over his shoulder and grinned. "Pay me twopence and I'll tell you."

"Get lost."

"That would be hard. It's a small cell, and perfectly square."

"What's the *book*?"

He got up, walked to the cell door and held up the spine so she could read it. *Luvien and Tinoriel on Environmental Law.*

"Oh," she said.

"You can owe me the twopence," he said.

"I'll give you sixpence for it."

That stopped him. "You're interested in Elvish law?"

"No, but it's a book and I'm desperate. Is it any good?"

"Weak on plot but the characters are fully realised. Two shillings."

More than she earned in a month. "What's it about?"

He looked at the book, then back at her. "It's about seven hundred pages, give or take. You give, I take. Two bob."

"Couldn't I just borrow it?"

"Of course. A shilling and ninepence."

She frowned at him through the bars. "You're a lawyer," she said.

"Lucky guess. My name's John. John the Lawyer."

"What are you doing that side of the bars?"

"Ah." He shrugged. "Slight error of judgement on my part."

"Really."

"Mphm. I issued proceedings against King Drain for nuisance, damage to property and release of a noxious substance under the Rule in *Rylands v Fletcher*."

"Um."

"And made the mistake of trying to save threepence by serving the summons personally. That was a week ago. But they were quite nice about it. Let me keep the book."

She hesitated. She wasn't sure she liked him very much, but he was a fellow human, incarcerated in the dungeons of the dwarf-king. "I'll talk to King Drain," she said. "I'm sure he'll let you go if I ask him nicely."

"Don't do that."

She blinked. "Say what?"

"Don't *do* that." He calmed down a bit. "Look, all the time I'm in here, I can bill the client at my standard hourly rate for languishing in jail. Fivepence an hour, plus two farthings a day for candles. It's a really sweet thought, but I'm way behind on my target for the month and I could do with the billable hours."

She counted to ten under her breath, then smiled. "Yes," she said, "you're a lawyer."

He nodded. "A human lawyer," he said, "in a region where the profession is traditionally dominated by Elves. I'm hoping I can spin this gig out for a month, so long as some idiot doesn't come along and spring me."

She widened her smile. "Here's the deal," she said. "Sixpence for the book and I won't go to King Drain and beg him on bended knee to release my long-lost cousin John."

"Ouch."

"I'll take that as a compliment."

He peered at her. "Are you sure you want to read about Flangábrithil's doctrine of privity of contract?"

"Yes."

He nodded. "Actually, it's rather interesting. Suppose a party X contracts with a party Y to deliver a specified quantity of goods to a certain point on or before a speci- fied date—"

"I don't want to *hear* about it," she said. "That'd be boring. I want to *read* about it."

"Ninepence."

"Don't worry about a thing. I'll have you out of there before you know what hit you."

Definitely a grudging respect in his eyes as he backed away a step. "Tell you what," he said. "You can have the rotten book. Something tells me you're as sharp as my senior partner's ears. That," he added, "is meant to sound like a compliment but is in fact ambiguous."

"Take your word for it." She took her purse from her

sleeve and scrabbled for coins. "You wouldn't happen to have change for a florin, would you?"

"I said, take the book. Free of charge. Gift."

"But then you'll be stuck in that horrible cell with nothing to read."

"I can amuse myself with mental arithmetic. Five times twenty-four times seven—"

"Eight hundred and forty," she said quickly. "That's seventy shillings. Three pounds ten." Her eyes widened. "You've made three pounds ten shillings just lying on a heap of straw."

"Languishing," he corrected her. "You're good with numbers, then."

"Am I?" She shrugged. "I suppose I am."

"What do you do around here?"

"I'm the cook."

He whistled. "The one everybody's been talking about back in Elvenhome."

A slight shiver ran down her spine. "Really. What have they been saying?"

"You make a wicked apple charlotte."

Which was true. "And?"

He shrugged. "And what's a competent domestic servant doing working for these semi-literate barbarians when she could be making nearly twice as much waiting tables at the Marshmallorn Tree?"

"That's what they're saying, is it?"

"Yes."

"Typical.

She paused and looked at him again. One thing she'd gathered from the self-made multimillionaires of her past acquaintance was that you can be quite smart and still look remarkably like a badly stuffed sheep. "What do you think?"

"You're not from round here, are you?"

"What makes you say that?"

"A human working for dwarves."

"Right. Almost as weird as a human working for Elves."

"A human female working for dwarves."

"Cooking, cleaning and tidying up. Woman's work."

He gave her an odd look; rather as if he'd found a counterfeit coin in his small change, all wrong because it was pure silver rather the regulation silver plate. "So where are you from?"

"A faraway place of which we know little. You wouldn't have heard of it."

"Try me."

"It's just a village. Well, more like a hamlet, really. A few neglected cottages clustered round a narrow strip of green, where pigs and chickens wander aimlessly."

"Called?"

"London."

He shook his head. "You're right, it doesn't ring a bell. Faraway, you said?"

"You couldn't begin to imagine."

"And you left there to come here."

She nodded. "To better myself. Seeking my fortune in the big city."

"Mphm. Well, don't let me keep you." He hesitated, then tried to poke the book through the bars of the door. It was too wide and wouldn't go through. "Well," he said. "Fancy that."

He didn't actually grin, but she knew he'd known all along it wouldn't go through. "No problem," she said. "Open it about halfway through and try again. There," she added, tugging it from his reluctant fingers. "Piece of cake."

Definitely respect in those pale blue, slightly piggy eyes. "Nice of you to stop by. Enjoy the book."

"I will. That's what's so desperately sad."

She left him lying on his back with his hands folded behind his head, the default attitude of long-term prisoners everywhere. On the way to the winch house, she read the whole of the chapter about conflicts of jurisdiction. Interesting.

The oil was black and sticky and poured out of the jar at the pace of rush-hour traffic. It took her two hours with a fistful of wire wool to clean up the frying pan.

"You know what," Mordak said. "I'm not sure you should've put in quite so much cayenne pepper."

The beige goo bubbled and heaved, giving off clouds of foul steam that stank of ammonia and boiled cabbage. The Goblinmaker General gave him the sort of look that laymen who offer advice to experts so richly deserve, and said, "Mphm".

"Is it meant to do that?"

"Yes."

They stood and watched for a long time while nothing ostensibly happened. On the surface, that is. Down there somewhere, seething away in the depths between the unspeakable thousand-year-old sediment and the fissured biscuit-hard crust of topscum, the miracle of parthenogenetic reproduction was in full swing. But with a difference—

The original recipe, as handed down by the Old Ones and reverently transcribed on the back of an empty packet of candied teeth by Gror the First when the Realms were young, was perhaps the most closely guarded secret of the goblin race. Sure, everybody knew the main ingredients, because they saw them arriving in huge carts: slugs by the bushel, snails in towering clay jars, bale after bale of sun-dried puppy dogs' tails from the vast, sprawling puppy dog ranches of the Ogain Mord. But the special blend of herbs and spices that acted as a catalyst and served to galvanise the goo into frantic, squirming life was known only to the king, the Goblinmaker and, for some reason, the Postmaster General. It was rumoured to include turpentine, mandragora, formic acid, rosewater, acetone and bicarbonate of soda, but mostly that was just ill-informed guesswork.

A bubble, ten feet wide and high, welled up out of the exact centre of the goo, quivered soapily for a moment in the pale red torchlight and burst, spraying the faces of the bystanders with a fine beige mist. Mordak wiped his eyes, instinctively licked his lips, pulled a ghastly face and spat.

"For crying out loud," he whimpered. "It's like *treacle*." The Goblinmaker ignored him.

To create a female goblin, however, it soon became clear that they were going to have to go right back to square one and start again; no preconceptions, no fiddling around trying to save a buck by using stuff they'd already got in stock. Out went the slugs and snails. In their place came hundredweight sacks of sugar beet, barrels and crates of oregano, cumin, turmeric, caraway, fenugreek, garlic and cayenne pepper, and dried jalapenos in special lead-lined boxes. As to the third core ingredient required by the formula painstakingly compiled by the senior technical officer of the Goblin Institute for the Advancement of Science, there was a sharp difference of opinion between the Chief Science Officer and the Goblinmaker. The latter insisted on dried tails; you can't make goblins without at least 40 per cent puppy dogs' tails, he swore passionately, it wouldn't be right, that's what makes us what we are. The Science Officer, though sympathising to a considerable extent with this view, pointed to the blackboards that covered his office walls, each one crammed to bursting with tiny chalked formulae. The equations can't lie, he pointed out. It's All Things Nice, or forget the whole project. To which the Goblinmaker replied that if there was anything nicer in this world that a properly matured sun-dried Labrador tail with the hair still on, he'd never been told about it. Being goblins, they should've decided the issue with a duel to the death, but Mordak made them toss a coin instead.

The Goblinmaker dipped the tip of his claw into the edge of the vat. It fizzed and dissolved. "It's time," he said.

He, it should be noted, had lost the toss. Accordingly, a massive crane lifted a colossal iron bucket high into the air above the vat; a chain tightened, the bucket tilted. The Goblinmaker grabbed Mordak by the scruff of his neck and dragged him back out of the way of the splash, as forty-seven tons of axes, spears, scimitars, daggers, poisoned arrows and assorted body parts of mortal enemies burst through the crust and plunged into the deep goo. There was an explosion of effervescence, the sort you get when you add sugar to a fizzy drink, and beige suds flooded the floor. All things nice, goblin-style.

"Don't blame me if it all ends in tears," the Goblinmaker said.

The fizzing was dying down, and something strange was happening. Mordak took a long step backwards and made the Sign of the Claw on his forehead. "That can't be right, surely," he said.

The Goblinmaker shrugged. "Don't ask me," he said. "I've never done this before."

The goo was changing colour, from beige to pink.

The Science Officer, who'd been watching the proceedings from behind a large oak vat, cleared his throat. "It's probably all that iron," he said, "reacting isothermically with the—"

"Oh be quiet," snapped the Goblinmaker. The goo had started to glow. "I told you we should've stuck with tails, but would you listen?"

Pink vapour, thick and cloyingly aromatic, rose from the meniscus of the goo. It, too, was faintly luminescent, like the unearthly light of the Dead Marshes at night, only pink. "I recognise that," mumbled the Science Officer, "it's *Nuits d'Amour* by Maison de Luthiel. Sorry," he added quickly, as Mordak turned and looked at him. "No idea how I come to know that."

The Goblinmaker took a long stride forward, as close to the vat as he dared get, and peered through the clouds of billowing vapour. "You know something," he said. "I think it's working."

Mordak stared at him. "But it's *pink*."

The Goblinmaker shrugged. "Perhaps it's supposed to be. We just don't know, that's the thing. Maybe pink is, I don't know, natural, in these circumstances."

"I wouldn't go any closer if I were you," muttered the Science Officer. "I don't like the look of it one bit."

A fat drop of sweat ran down Mordak's snout and landed on his projecting lower lip. "I say we pull the plug and start again with puppy dogs' tails," he said. "Nothing good ever came of pink, trust me."

"No," the Goblinmaker said. "It's working. He was right and I was wrong. This is—"

A long crack suddenly appeared in the side of the vat. Mordak lunged forward and grabbed for the Goblinmaker's sleeve, but too late. The vat gave way, and a pink tidal wave spurted through the fissure. The Goblinmaker tried to back away, slipped, lost his footing and went down. A fraction of a second later, he was completely engulfed. Mordak tried to go in after him, but the Science Officer grabbed his knees and wouldn't let go.

"Leave him," he shouted, "there's nothing we can do for him. We've got to get out of here, now!"

True; the flood level was rising, groping for their toes with outriders of fizzing pink foam. "It's expanding," Mordak yelled. "Is it meant to—?"

"Who gives a damn? Come *on*."

They scrambled up the steps, slammed the door behind them and shot all six bolts. Then they caught their breath and looked at each other. For a long time neither of them spoke. Then Mordak said, "This never happened, right?"

"What never happened?"

"Good man."

The Science Officer wasn't listening. He was staring at the door, from under which a creamy pink pool was rapidly spreading out into the passageway. "Oh, *nuts*," he said. "That isn't good."

Mordak thought quickly. "The best thing," he said, "would be to evacuate this entire level, then divert the main sewer and flood it good and proper. Anything else down here, do you know?"

The Science Officer scowled in thought. "State archives," he said, "Treasury Department offices. Armoury. Crown jewels. Oh, and most of the gold reserves."

The goo was eating away at the foot of the door. Mordak quickly snatched his feet out of the way. "Nothing we can't do without, then," he said. "Which way's the exit?"

The door shattered into splinters. A torrent of foaming pink goo swept them both off their feet and washed them away. Mordak grabbed the Science Officer by one cauliflower ear and stuck out his other arm, so that his claws scraped the wall as they were carried bodily by the current down the passageway. The Science Officer started squealing; definitely conduct unbecoming a goblin under any circumstances, but the only reason why Mordak wasn't doing exactly the same thing was that his mouth was full of the loathsome sweet pink goo. The flood was shooting them inexorably towards a ventilation duct, down which the pink stuff was gurgling away into the bowels of the earth; we can fit through that easily, Mordak calculated, but only after our heads are snapped off like carrots. Oh well.

And then his trailing claw lodged in something, which turned out to be an iron ring, fitted to a door in place of the more conventional lifter-type latch. Hooray for unconventionality.

"Your Majesty."

He could barely hear the Science Officer over the roar of the pink flood. "What?"

"I think you were right. Too much cayenne pepper."

In spite of everything, Mordak smiled. "Shut your face," he said, not unkindly, and hung on grimly, ring in one paw, ear in the other, waiting to see what happened next.

Secretary Tinituviel—in Elvish, her name meant the soft tinkling of silver bells, melodious but unceasing, somewhere in the back of one's head—was worried about the egg whisk.

She'd interviewed the scouts, who repeated what they'd said before. Out back of one of the new human dwellings on the south bank of the Mouthwash, just down the road from the dark Tower of Snorfang, they'd come across a shiny new trash can. Inside it, among other wonders too bizarre to contemplate, they'd found the Machine. They had no idea what it was but felt it was their duty to bring it back for the boss to see. They had no idea how to find out whether it was loaded or not, so they brought it home in a bucket of water, just in case.

Right, Tinituviel had said. What other wonders?

You don't want to know, the scouts had told her, they're too bizarre to—well, if you insist. There were bags, wrought of some shining white fabric that was smoother than silk, thinner than gossamer, of a weave so fine that you could neither see nor feel the weft; most remarkable of all, moisture (there were lots of wet, sticky things in the trash can) didn't seem to soak into it, but, rather, was repelled, as by the finest oilcloth. There were perfect cylinders of fine steel, like helmets but no bigger than a goblin's handspan, closed at one end, roughly cut open at the other. There were small trays made of—here the scouts fell to arguing among themselves, one claiming that it must be some sort of fungus, the other plumping for a kind of inedible bread; anyway, it was white and light as a feather, and if you bent it, it snapped like a dry twig; and wrapped round these trays were shreds of an unearthly transparent substance, soft and pliable, the colour of slug trail, like very thin sheets of dry water; yes, well, we told you it was too bizarre to contemplate but, no, you had to know best.

"And you found all this," Tinituviel asked, "in the *trash*?"

Yes, because in the same receptacle were apple cores and chicken bones and potato peel and a sort of gravelly breakfast cereal stuff that tasted tantalisingly of cat. Evidently all stuff they'd slung out, as being of neither use nor value; all that and this machine. The trash can hadn't even been padlocked, showing how trusting these humans were.

"Thank you," Tinituviel had said, then remembered she was an Elf. "Go away, I'm busy." The scouts bowed low and backed away, muttering something under their breath in an obscure goblin dialect she found it expedient to let people believe she didn't understand. Ever since then she'd sat silently multitasking, the egg whisk lying on the desk in front of her.

Who *were* these people?

Just humans, that was all. Crass, ignorant; marginally prettier than goblins, most of them, but looks aren't everything, and in all other departments there wasn't a lot between them. Except that goblins were often brave, intermittently loyal and solidly based around a handful of core values (nasty, but core) which as often as not they'd rather die than betray. Humans, as had often been observed, would sell their own grandmothers, although only other humans would be foolish enough to buy them, even with an extended warranty. Above all, though, humans were *dumb*. To them, the white heat of technology meant burning their fingers on a tinderbox. Human inventions? Human achievements in the field of technology? Name one. Right. Knew you couldn't.

And yet humans had built this *extraordinary* egg whisk. The other stuff the scouts had talked about was probably fantasy, the products of overheated goblin imagination— transparent clingy filmy stuff, for crying out loud, who could possibly believe in that? But the whisk was something she could see and touch, she had no choice but to believe in it. And if they could make that, just think of the weapons they'd be capable of producing. Or had already produced.

Um.

Advanced military hardware is (wait for it) a two-edged sword. You can get hold of it and use it on your enemies. Or your enemies can get hold of it and use it on you. You have two alternatives only, and inertia isn't one of them. Oh damn, she thought, I'm going to have to *do* something. And quickly, before someone else does it. And sneakily, of course. Goes without saying.

Well? The first thing she needed was solid, reliable information. No use, in that case, sending more goblin scouts, she needed observations from someone with a brain larger and marginally less dense than a walnut. A dwarf? Since Mordak's epoch-making Treaty of Bad-Tempered Tolerance with King Drain, there were a few dwarves on the payroll—moderately smart, no, make that cunning, and sending a dwarf to investigate the possibility of new and deadly forms of weapon was like asking a cat to babysit fledgling sparrows. It had to be an Elf; an Elf, furthermore, with energy, intelligence, resourcefulness and the determination to see the mission through.

"Oh damn," she said aloud.

Still, she'd defined the parameters herself, and there was only one candidate, who was currently wearing her underwear. She sighed and reached for a scrap of paper.

Mordak—
    Gone out. Back later. May be some time. Don't whatever you do attempt to file anything, make appointments or answer letters. Do NOT move anything that we may conceivably want to find ever again.
    T.

Experience had taught her that the best way of slipping quietly out of the palace was to go up to the fourteenth level, ride back down to the seventeenth level on the service elevator, cut across through the Museum of Cultural Artefacts and take the back stairs direct to the East Gate. As she paused for breath on the level twelve landing she heard some sort of commotion on the far side of the massive steel door. She hesitated. If there was a problem, she ought to stay and sort it out, before Mordak made a mess of it that she would have to clear up later. But that would take time, and that was a commodity which she suspected was in short supply if she wanted to get to the whisk-makers before anyone else. She shrugged and carried on up the stairs, and in due course emerged into the sunlight.

There was, of course, a sentry on duty outside the East Gate. He was covered from head to foot in black cloth, apart from his eyes, which were in there somewhere behind two two-inch-thick discs of smoked glass held together with wire. Goblins don't like sunlight much.

"You," she said. "Get me a horse."

The sentries all knew her, by sight and by the sting of her extensive vocabulary. "Sorry, miss. No horses. Not till Tuesday."

She rolled her eyes. "What?"

"No horses, sorry, ma'am. Wolves and flying lizards only, till Tuesday."

"What happened?"

"Well, your ladyship, some id—somebody thought it'd be a good idea to save money by amalgamating the royal messenger service and the household cavalry. Have 'em share the same stables, that sort of thing."

She knew that. She'd forged Mordak's signature on the order. "Well?"

"The household cavalry ride wolves, Your Grace. So, no horses. Not till Tuesday."

She sighed. "Fine. Get me a winged lizard. Now."

(After all, she said to herself, how hard can it be? The wraiths fly the horrid things, and they aren't even *there*. And the lizards were held to be sentient and telepathic, and anything that could read her thoughts could be brought to a keener appreciation of its own shortcomings and made to do as it was damned well told. And it was that or walk, and it looked like rain.)

The sentry looked at her. "Are you quite sure about that, your excellency? Only, they can be a bit—"

"*Now.*"

The sentry didn't smile, let alone grin, but there was something about the enthusiasm with which he trotted off to obey her orders that made her wonder if the investigation couldn't wait till Tuesday after all. But it was too late now, of course. An Elf doesn't back down or show nervousness in front of a goblin. And if a wraith could do it—She'd watched them, showing off; *look, no hands*—

"Here you go, miss." The goblin was back, leading her trusty steed on a very long rein. It looked like two earthworms grafted onto each end of a turtle, with vast leathery wings added as an afterthought, probably using non-standard parts. She looked at it. It looked at her and winked. The goblin pushed the reins into her hands, saluted and backed away, with the sort of utterly fixed expression on his face that could only mean that, if he relaxed just one muscle, he'd collapse into fits of uncontrollable laughter.

Then a voice spoke to her inside her head.

The relationship between a wraith's steed and its rider is one of the greatest and most complex mysteries in all the Realms. It begins at the moment the lizard hatches, and ends—who knows when? Death is only a staging point on that shared journey. It is more than mere symbiosis. It constitutes a joining of minds and souls at a level so profound that if you were to ask where does one end and the other begin, all you would achieve would be to show how little you knew and understood. It is a welding, a mingling, a blending that simplifies rather than complicates. It is beyond dependency and love. It can only be the rejoining of two parts of one whole that should never have been sundered in the first place.

Hello, gorgeous, said the voice.

She sighed. "Pack it in," she said aloud. The lizard sniggered, and nuzzled her thigh with its nose. *Do you want to ride me,* it said, not in her head but in the very recesses of her soul, worst luck. *I think I'd like that very much.*

She closed her eyes, counted to ten, picked up a fair-sized rock and bashed the lizard's head with it. *Ooh,* said the innermost fibre of her being, *you can do that again, any time you like.*

She whimpered. But what the hell. The walk would do her good. She tied the reins to the massive bronze knocker of the great gate, hitched up her socks and started to walk towards the distant eaves of the forest.

She hadn't gone more than a few yards when a horrible tearing noise, followed by a crash, made her stop and spin round. The lizard was trotting after her, dragging one of the Black Gates behind it on the end of its rein. *Wait for me,* said the quintessence of her existence.

"Go away."

Can't. We are joined. Nothing will ever part us. Talking of which, what are you doing after you get off work?

Elves don't swear or scream or have hysterics or burst into floods of tears. When confronted with the inevitable, they proceed with a cold, calm dignity, together with a steely resolve to take it out on the next member of an inferior species unfortunate enough to cross their path. "Fine," she said. "If I'm stuck with you, I suppose you'd better make yourself useful. Oh, come on," she added, as the lizard sank to its knees and wiggled its hindquarters, "you can do better than that. Here, twist your head round a bit more, so I can stand on it."

She was wearing her four-inch stiletto heels. Unfortunately, the lizard really liked that.

*

The flood of pink goo subsided to a steady flow, then a trickle. When he judged it was safe to do so, Mordak cautiously let go of the iron ring, then the Science Officer's ear. "Well, then," he said. "That's all right."

"Say what?"

"I think it's stopped now," Mordak said, slowly and clearly. "Crisis over."

Brave words. He had no idea what volume of the stuff had washed past him and gone down the ventilation duct, but he had an idea it was going to be sticky underfoot in Levels Thirteen to Twenty-seven for a day or so, and he didn't want to think about what would happen to productivity if the stuff had managed to find its way into the winch mechanism or the elevator shafts. The smell, likewise, was going to take quite a bit of getting used to. Still, as far as he could tell at this stage, there was no irreparable harm done; and they'd managed to prove beyond reasonable doubt that creating a female goblin was impossible. Which advanced the sum of goblin knowledge one tiny step further, and good science is never wasted.

"What the hell's that?"

The Science Officer was pointing up the corridor. Unfortunately his newly enlarged ear was blocking Mordak's view. He folded it down out of the way, and saw—

"Oh, darn," he muttered.

The first and most obvious thing was the sheer size. Twice the height of the tallest goblin he'd ever seen, taller even than a human or an Elf, and monstrously broad in the shoulders, chest and thighs. Gigantic muscles knotted under the coal-black skin, and the legs were straight and unbowed, the knees unknocked, so that it strode rather than scuttled. The only really goblin thing about it, in fact, was the tusks, and the little red piggy eyes.

"What are those things on its front?" Mordak whispered. "That can't be right, surely."

"Cayenne pepper," said the Science Officer. "you just can't be too careful with that stuff."

The monster advanced on them, stopped and looked down at them, blinking confusedly. Then, with a lunge so quick that Mordak never knew it was coming, it grabbed the Science Officer round the throat, lifted him off the ground, held him up, nose to snout, and bared its dreadful teeth. It growled, and its voice was as deep and menacing as an earthquake.

"I want my mummy," it said.

"You," the jailer said, "on your feet. Jump to it."

John the Lawyer woke up out of a dream in which he was suing the Creator of All Things for product liability and opened his eyes. "What?"

"Your lucky day," the jailer said. "You're going home."

An icicle pierced John's heart. "Now just a minute. Let's not be too hasty."

"Out."

And ten minutes later he was, bathed in harsh, unfamiliar sunshine and cursing fluently under his breath as the sentries lifted their crossed spears to let him pass. As he started off down the long road to the forest, he heard a ghastly shriek directly overhead and instinctively ducked as a huge flying creature shot through the sky, briefly blotting out the sun before dwindling, arrow-swift, into a dot on the far horizon. Maybe he imagined it, but he was sure he heard the echo of a woman's wailing voice carried back to him on the breeze; the ghost of a plea to, for pity's sake, slow down, the last dying susurration of bad language. He slicked back his hair, which had been ruffled by the slipstream, and trudged onwards.

If optimism and pessimism are defined in terms of glasses half empty and half full, John was a dry martini. He blended the harsh gin of realism with six parts of the rich, sweet vermouth of hope, and if he ever considered it, revelled in the contradiction. Thus he knew in his heart of hearts that even with the time he'd spent in King Drain's dungeons he hadn't clocked up enough billable hours this month to meet his target and avoid the sack. But the month still had one day to go, and who knew what that day might hold? Answer: twenty-four hours maximum, and the shortfall in his hours was twenty-seven. But the Realms are a strange place, teeming with dark and gorgeous wonders. There were caves under the mountains and dappled glades under the Marshmallorn trees where Time was reputed to stand still. If he happened across one of them and managed to find someone to sue while he was there, he'd be laughing.

Intriguing, to find a human at the dwarvish court. Humans and dwarves didn't mix much, outside of business dealings. The reason why was, of course, implicit in everyday speech. You look up to people you fear and respect (Elves, say) and down on those you despise and, well, belittle. The fact that a dwarvish five-year-old could arm-wrestle a six-foot human into blubbering submission or carry a sack of coal that humans would need a cart for was neither here nor there. Dwarves were short, therefore inferior and funny. One of John's daydreams was being instructed by the Heirs of Snorin in a class action against the whole of humanity, for defamation and aggravated looming.

He stopped in a small glade of willow beside a silvery brook, sat down on a big rock and took off his shoe. As he suspected, the sole had worn through. Time for a new pair, except maybe this wasn't a good time for major capital expenditure, if he was going to get fired from Thanduil & Gluvien. On the other hand, if he lost his job he'd need to find a new one, which meant interviews, for which it's essential to look smart, well dressed and prosperous. He put his hand in his pocket and came up with four silver pennies and a goblin *zlotyl*. Awkward.

And then he caught sight of something that made him think; whoa there, steady on. For on the bank of the quicksilver stream, in the middle of a patch of grass gilded by bars of sunlight lancing through the overhanging trees, he saw a pair of shiny black boots, practically new, just lying there.

Did he just do that? A wishing-grove, maybe, where all you have to do is ask and it shall be given to you. A million gold florins, he thought hopefully, and waited. Nothing happened. Ah well. The boots, however, looked to be just his size.

He hopped up, scampered over and grabbed the nearest boot. It was so heavy he could barely lift it. Then it kicked him in the chest.

He toppled backwards and sat down in the brook. He was soaking wet, but hadn't even noticed. All his attention was fixed on the boots, which were moving. They were, not to put too fine a point on it, scrambling to their feet.

"Do you mind?" said a voice.

It was high, faint, cracked and somehow far away, and in it John could hear unquenchable malice, endless sadness and distinct annoyance. "You're a wraith," he said.

A black cloak appeared from behind a thorn bush, swirled briefly in the air and settled to define a humanoid shape. Unseen hands lifted a hood and pulled it into place. "What of it?"

"What were you doing?"

"Sunbathing, if you must know."

"With your boots on?"

"My feet burn easily. Look," the voice added irritably, "I don't need to explain myself to you, thank you very much. And leave my stuff alone, all right?"

John shook his head. "Wraiths don't sunbathe."

"How would you know?"

A valid point, actually. "They just don't. They're creatures of shadow and darkness who abhor the sunlight. Everybody knows that."

"Bigot." A twig bent sideways, then relaxed. "First you help yourself to my stuff, then you insult me."

"Sorry," John said quickly. "Obviously I don't know very much about wraiths. No offence intended."

"Fine. Now, would you mind turning around, please?"

"What? Why?"

"Because," said the voice, "I'm about to put my bra and knickers on. So if you wouldn't mind."

John turned red as a beetroot and spun round so fast he nearly fell over. "You're a—"

"Yes. We do exist, you know."

"I thought it was just men."

"Yes, well, you would. All right, you can turn round again now."

John stayed where he was. "I really don't mean to be offensive," he said. "The truth is, you're the first wraith I've ever met."

"There's a surprise."

"Don't be like that," John said, and slowly turned round. The black cloak was closed again, but a brightly coloured silk scarf shot up like a firework from behind a fallen log and wound itself round an invisible neck. "It's all come as a bit of a shock, that's all. That's probably why

I keep putting my foot in it. My name's John, by the way.
John the Lawyer."

"Charmed, I'm sure. And now I really think I ought
to be going." The hood turned, first left, then right, then
left again. "All right," the voice said icily. "What have you
done with it?"

"What?"

"My horse. Where is it?"

"What horse?"

A sigh that seemed to come from deep inside his own
soul. "Yes, all right, I know. Let's all go and rag on the
wraith. Out of sight, she won't mind. All terribly amusing
and let me assure you I'm grinning all over my face, but
can I please have my horse back now? I'm late as it is."

"I haven't seen any horse," John protested. "Honest."

"Did you just say honest?"

"Yes."

"What did you say your name was?"

John sighed. "Now look who's doing the stereotypes. I
would never, ever, steal a horse. Never."

"You tried to take my boots."

"I thought they were empty."

"Sure. And you were going to walk a mile in them, just so
you could understand me better." The black cloak seemed
to slump a little. "You haven't seen my horse, then."

"No. Sorry."

"Bloody thing's probably wandered off somewhere.
Wouldn't be the first time."

"Would you like me to help you look for it?"

The hood swayed from side to side. "It'll be back in the
Black Stable by now, eating its head off. Which means I'll
have to walk. Sod it."

"Where are you headed?"

The tip of the hood dipped south-east.

"Me, too," John said. "Mind if I walk with you?"

"Suit yourself, as the tailor said to the mirror."

John blinked. "Did you just make a—?"

"Yes. We do that, too."

"Gosh."

It was mildly disconcerting, walking along beside an animated cloak, but John decided he didn't really mind. "So," he said, "how long have you been a wraith?"

"Why?"

He shrugged. "Just curious."

"I couldn't actually say," the voice replied. "Since about the middle of the First Age, I think. I don't know how long that is in years. I sort of lost count after twenty thousand."

"You're over twenty thousand years old?"

"At least."

You don't look it, John managed to stop himself saying, just in time. "I'm twenty-six," he said.

"There, now."

Actually, once you got used to it, the voice wasn't unpleasant at all. "So," he went on, "you work for King Mordak."

"He's the Dark Lord of the Wraiths these days, so, yes, I suppose I do. Though I'm not what you'd call exactly front line. More sort of support and administrative."

"Ah."

"Personnel management, that sort of thing. Inhuman resources."

"That must be an interesting job."

"Not really, no," said the voice, as a gust of wind lifted the skirt of the Black Cloak, revealing the tops of the empty boots. "So it's just as well there's so little of it to do. Mostly I just loaf around and amuse myself."

"Fair enough," John said. "I'm not sure it'd suit me, but each to their own."

"Fact is," the voice went on, "I seem to spend most of my time shopping. I know it sounds awful, but I really do like clothes."

"Well, you would. Sorry, was that an insensitive remark?"

The shoulders of the cloak rose and fell. "Don't see why. Of course, I've got to wear all this tatty old rubbish for work. But that's no reason why I shouldn't pamper myself a bit in my free time."

"Why not?" John said. "Live a little. So, what's King Mordak really like? I've never met him, but he sounds— well, different, for a Dark Lord."

"I've never met him either," said the voice. "He doesn't seem to hang around Admin much, for some odd reason. It's just conceivable, I suppose, that he might have more important things to do. Ouch," added the voice. "Stone in my boot," it explained.

"Lean on me, if you like."

"Better not. Frostbite."

"Ah."

So the Black Cloak sort of folded itself on the ground, and a boot separated itself, waggled about in the air, then went back the way it came. "I hate walking," said the voice. "There are some species who do it for fun, but that's just weird." Both boots were back on the ground, their toecaps visible under the Black Hem. "I hope that stupid horse does find its way back home. I'll be in ever so much trouble if it gets lost."

"Oh?"

"The thing is," the voice said diffidently, "I'm not really supposed to borrow horses from the Black Stable, and specially not for shopping. They're reserved for the executive grades and above. I'm just junior admin."

John nodded. "Because you're a female, presumably. Typical."

"No, because I'm younger than everyone else in the department, and promotion is strictly on an undead-men's-shoes basis. Think about it," she added, and John said, "Oh."

"Quite. There are times when I'm tempted to pack in the Service and get a job in, well, you know." The voice was silent for a moment. "The World."

"I see. Doing what?"

"Well—no, it'll sound silly."

"Try me."

"What I always wanted to do," said the voice, "ever since I was a little girl, was modelling."

"Ah."

Sigh. "I told you it was silly."

"Not a bit of it," John said briskly. "You can be whatever you want to be. It's just that some things take an extra little bit of determination and resolve."

"Oh, I've got *those*."

"Well, then, there you are." John thought hard for a moment. "Here's what you do. You get two dozen eggs and some flour and a quart of milk—"

"Yuck."

"Well, it works for fish," John said vaguely. "No, maybe you're right. We're coming at this from the wrong angle. I mean, what's the actual purpose of a model?"

"To show the clothes off, I guess."

"Exactly. You can do that, better than anybody. No distractions. All the emphasis will be on the garments, not the person inside them."

"I think the distraction is the whole point, actually. But it's sweet of you to suggest it."

"How about paint?"

"I'm allergic to linseed oil."

They crossed another brook and started the long uphill

climb to the eaves of the forest. "So," said the voice, "what about you? There aren't many human lawyers."

"Only because the Elves won't give us a break. There's no reason why a human shouldn't be just as devious and sly and money-grubbing if he gets the chance."

"Hm." The gradient didn't seem to bother the contents of the Black Cloak. John found himself having to trot to keep up, which wasn't easy. "Personally, I'd say an invisible model stood a better chance than a human lawyer."

"There you are, then. My point exactly."

"You're doing well, then. Soaring ahead in your chosen profession."

"Well, no," John confessed. "Actually, I'm that close to getting fired. But I'll bounce back, you'll see."

"When they throw you out, you'll bounce. Quite possibly. Depends on whether you land on a hard surface."

"I'll get another job. Or, better still—" Suddenly the thought welled up inside him, like violet-flavoured acid reflux. "I'll set up on my own. Start my own firm. Rent a little hut somewhere, second-hand desk, couple of chairs, that's all you need."

"And customers."

"Not a problem," he said cheerfully, though he had no idea where they might possibly come from. It didn't seem to matter. Of course there'd be clients, queues of them halfway down the street. All he had to do was want it, and it'd happen. "Tell all your friends. Special discount for members of the transparent community."

The voice laughed. "All right then, it's a deal. You can come and watch me on the catwalk, I'm come and listen to you in court."

"I'm serious."

"Of course you are."

Ahead of them loomed the tall, high pines that grew

on the fringes of the forest, the border of Elvenhome. Here the road forked; to the left, it plunged into the deep valley where grew the towering oak trees in whose upper branches the lawyers built their offices, while the right path skirted the edge of the forest and came out at the entrance to the Mall-Orn shopping centre. At the last possible point before the division they stopped, and for a long moment, neither of them spoke.

"Well," said the voice, "be seeing you."

"You t—" John stopped. An indescribable and unfamiliar melancholy swept over him, as though he'd just realised he was out of time for serving a request for further and better particulars. With the sorrow, however, came a sort of reckless daring. "Now listen to me," he said. "I meant it. If you want something badly enough, you'll find a way, I promise you."

"But not paint. Or batter."

"You'll think of something."

The voice laughed. "I can't kiss you," it said, "because if I do your lips will fall off and shatter like crockery. But you're very sweet."

He watched the Black Cloak until it merged with the shadows under the trees, which didn't take very long. Then he shook himself like a wet dog and turned left.

Updating the blog had become the purpose of Terry Barrington's life. It was the mast he clung to when the storm winds blew, the pillar that supported him as he struggled to bear the weight of his new world on his shoulders, the cross of obligation and duty to which he was nailed. Especially the latter; because this experience had to mean something, or why the hell carry on with it? And the meaning must be, to endure and communicate, to suffer so that something valuable should be created. People used to put caged birds in the sunlight to make them sing; overheated and wretched, they warbled their complaint, and the room was filled with sweet music. It had to be that. There was no other logical explanation.

So he sat in the room at the top of the tower, looking down on impenetrable fog for the seventh day in a row, and spread his fingers over the keyboard like a concert pianist. *Day 12*, he typed, and paused.

Something vast with leathery wings flapped past. Because the walls were transparent, it felt like the horrible thing was in the room with him. He had no idea what it was, but there seemed to be an awful lot of them around here; like pigeons in London. He shuddered. The thing receded and was folded into the mist. He stretched his fingers again and rested them lightly on the keys.

Day 12.
How can I begin to describe the unutterable beauty of the Realms in autumn? From my vantage point on the top of our ancient, historic watch-tower—

A fat droplet of water fell on the back of his hand. He looked down at it and sighed. Soon the tympani section would start up; the tinkle of raindrops on the bottoms of every saucepan and casserole they owned, tink tink tink. He'd been on to the agent about it five times in the last three days and all he'd got was a load of muttered promises about renewing the damp-proof incantations. It had been mildly amusing the first time, but he'd got sick of wizard's-tower jokes. What he wanted was a builder, with a long ladder and dustsheets and a toolbelt and a wireless belting out Radio 2. He wiped his hand on his trousers, deleted what he'd written and started again.

Day 12.
Season of mists and mellow fruitfulness was how Keats
described autumn, and how better to describe the
Realms at this uniquely lovely time of year? From where I
sit on the top floor of our historic ancient watch-

The screen went black. It did that. He'd asked the agent
about it, and apparently it was something to do with high
altitude electromagnetic discharges—the agent had called
it something else, more magic-and-wizardry humour,
but it was obvious what he meant—and they could try
installing a full-length copper strip down the side of the
building, but it would cost a lot of money and there was
no guarantee it'd work, so probably the best thing would
be to get used to it.

Terry Barrington had his faults; giving up easily
wasn't one of them. He closed the lid of his laptop,
covered it with a plastic carrier bag, opened his desk
drawer and took out a pad of paper and a pencil. If he
had to write it in longhand and type it out later, so be
it. Come the three corners of the world in arms, and we
will shock them.

Day 12.
    If I was ever tempted to regret my decision to buy this
ancient historic watch-tower in the heart of the Realms,
all I would have to do is look out over this amazing
panorama of rolling hills and lush green forests. Words
cannot begin to express the beauty of the late morning
sun breaking through the clouds as I write these words,
while sixteen storeys below, Pat is starting work on a
delicious lunch, using fresh organic ingredients sourced
from our local—

"Terry. Terry! There's someone at the door."

Remarkable how well sound carried in this place. "Can't you answer it?"

"Not bloody likely."

She had a point. Actually, everyone who'd turned up on their doorstep so far had been perfectly nice, which went to show the danger of going by appearances. Even so. "Coming," he said, and put his pad away in the desk. The first *ting* told him he wouldn't have got much work done anyway, so that was all right.

Forty-seven flights of stairs in this place. Well, it's a tower, what do you expect? The agent had promised to get back to him right away about finding someone to install a lift, so any day now—

He muttered the security code and the door did that weird thing it did, and he found himself facing a tall young woman with pointed ears. "Hello," he said. "What can I do for you?"

The Elf looked at him. "Probably very little," she said. "Are you the new owner?"

Terry sighed and moved sideways to let her in. Elves, he knew by now, were generally local government, of which there seemed to be rather a lot in an area that offered no public services whatsoever. "If it's about the barbecue, I asked our agent and he says he's never heard of any smoke abatement order in this area, and even if there is one—"

"The what?"

Terry explained what a barbecue was. The Elf sat down and looked at him. "You cook outside over an open fire. I see."

"Only in summer. Look, I explained all this to the other Elf, and she said we had to apply to the district planning office for a hazardous processes permit, and I've done that, so I don't see what the problem is." He paused. He was forgetting his manners. "Sorry. Can I get you a drink?"

She didn't appear to have heard him. Her attention was fixed on Pat's computer, on the table in the middle of the room. "What's that?"

"What? Oh, that. That's just Pat's old desktop. I'm always on at her to upgrade to a notebook, but she likes it, bless her."

"A notebook." The Elf got up, walked to the computer and gently tapped the screen with a shapely fingernail. "Glass."

"Yes. That's the VDU. The screen," he explained.

"A glass screen."

That was the thing with Elves, he'd noticed. They were so assured and full of it that you found yourself assuming they were, well, like normal people, us; and then they said something and you realised how different they were, how many things they didn't have and didn't know about. "They usually are," he said. "It can be a bit of a nuisance sometimes."

"What's it for?"

"Oh, Pat mostly uses it for going online." The blank stare again. "Shopping—for stuff we can't get locally—and keeping in touch with the family and friends back home, that sort of thing."

The Elf's eyes widened for a moment. "And you believe your wife would be better off with a notebook."

"Well, they're smaller."

"So?"

He shrugged. "Better for when you're on the move, that sort of thing."

He'd clearly said something she didn't like the sound of, but he couldn't think what it could be. "Do you eat meringues?"

"What? Yes, occasionally. I can't say they're a favourite."

"How about your wife and family? Your friends—" She paused, and her nostrils flared. "Back home. Do they eat meringues?"

"Occasionally. They're all right. For a change. Now and then."

"Do you eat them every day? Once a week? Once a month?"

"I don't know, I don't keep a food diary or anything. Why? What's wrong with bloody meringues? And what's that got to do with our barbecue permit?"

"What is that?"

She was pointing at his golf bag. "Oh, that's just my clubs."

The Elf stood up quickly, with a vaguely intimidating grace. She drew out a three iron and peered at it, then ran her thumb along the edge of the blade. "Very fine steel," she said quietly.

He relaxed a little. "Actually," he said, "that's a chrome-molybdenum alloy. Lighter without compromising on strength. Forged, not cast. The cavity back makes for a lower centre of gravity, so it's easier to feel the sweet spot. Titanium shaft, of course. Again, you've got the strength of steel, but it's lighter and faster in the hand."

By this point most women's eyes would have glazed over, but the Elf seemed genuinely interested. So he explained a bit more, about blade angles and edge geometry and the trade-off between impact velocity and mass transfer, and she was hanging on his every word; and then, quite suddenly, she dropped the club back into the bag, pointed at the wall and said, "What's that?"

"Oh, just a dartboard."

He'd done it again. This time, he'd earned himself a

look of deep suspicion. "Here, look," he said, and took his darts out of the sideboard drawer.

"Arrows."

He laughed. "Sort of." He turned sideways, got his feet right, and threw. As luck would have it, straight into the bull. Couldn't do that again if he tried.

The Elf had gone white. "I think I may have come to the wrong house," she said. "Is this number seven, Old Smials Drive?"

Well, that explained everything. "No, this is the Old Tower." He grinned. "I know, pretty unimaginative name. I'd have quite liked Xanadu, but Pat can never remember if it's spelt with an X or a Z."

"Xanadu." She made it into two words, for some reason. "I apologise," she said gravely. "I hope I haven't disturbed you, or given offence in any way."

"No, not at all."

"We do not seek conflict. All we wish for is to live at peace with our neighbours."

"Jolly good," Terry said. "Well, don't let me keep you."

In order to open the door to let her out, of course, he had to do the security code. The agent had told him, don't say it out loud where anybody can hear—well, just common sense, really—and so he'd got quite good at muttering it under his breath; but the Elf—well, with ears like that, it was only to be expected that her hearing was pretty good.

"What did you just say?" she rasped at him.

"Sorry? Oh, that's just to open the door."

One seriously freaked-out Elf. She backed out, still staring at him, and nearly fell down the steps. The hell with it. Maybe word would get about, and they wouldn't be getting quite so much hassle from the town hall. If so, wonderful.

He trudged back up the stairs to his study, just in time to duck and cower instinctively as another of those ghastly flying lizards flapped by. In theory, the walls turned opaque whenever you wanted them to, but it didn't work reliably. What we need, Terry decided, is proper net curtains.

BOOK TWO

Many Claws Make Light Orc

"**T**hey grow up so quickly," the Science Officer said wistfully.

Mordak adjusted the box so it was stable, climbed onto it and peered through the grille at the top of the cell door. "She's grown," he said in a horrified voice. "I wouldn't have thought it was possible."

"Seven feet four inches," the Science officer said proudly. "That's an extra nine inches since yesterday. Four hundred and sixteen pounds three ounces." He smiled. "She ate her first guard this morning."

The she-goblin didn't seem to know she was being watched, which was probably just as well. "What's she doing?" Mordak whispered.

The Science Officer joined him on the box. "Ah, that. We're not quite sure."

From where Mordak was standing, it looked like she was anointing her claws with blood, using a little tapered brush. Fair enough. But apparently she'd figured it out all by herself, untaught.

"She puts stuff on her face as well," the Science Officer said, "round the jaws and the jowls and under the eyes."

"Is that right?"

"To make them look bigger, we're guessing. Impress the enemy with your superior eyesight. Pretty advanced stuff. We never thought of that."

"She's not stupid, then."

"Far from it. Frighteningly smart, in some ways. See that thing she's wearing? That was a blanket this time yesterday."

"Quick work."

"She's raised the hemline twice since then."

Mordak frowned. Something that size, and with brains, too. He had an uncomfortable feeling that he might just be looking at the future of the goblin race. As that race's leader, with its best interests at heart, he could see it might well be no bad thing. Even so. Nobody, no matter how altruistic, rejoices at the thought of being out-evolved.

"I suppose we'd better let her out at some point," he said.

The monster raised its arm to tuck its hair behind its ear. The forearm was thicker than Mordak's thigh. "No rush," the Science Officer said.

"What's she doing now?"

She'd got hold of a scrap of metal from somewhere—a bit of the unfortunate guard's armour, probably—and was rubbing it industriously against the sandstone blocks of the cell wall. Every now and again she would stop and peer at it, then back to work again. "I think she's polishing it," the Science Officer said.

"What for?"

"I don't know. Maybe to make a mirror."

Mordak was impressed. With a mirror, you could keep watch on the cell door (the only point of entry for a potential enemy) even when you were lying down or facing the other way. Intuitive tactical thinking, something his soldiers conspicuously lacked. Size, muscle and brains; just think what could be achieved with an army of these creatures. King Drain wouldn't stand a chance; nor would the Elves, let alone the humans. The thought should have elated him. He paused for a moment, wondering why it hadn't.

"Has anyone tried talking to her yet?"

"No. Why?"

Why indeed? His predecessor on the Iron Throne wouldn't have bothered, that was for sure. In his view, the only vocabulary a servant of the Dark Cause needed was *yes, boss* and *charge!* Mordak, of course, saw thing differently. He'd spent a lifetime watching the armies of Evil getting beaten into a cocked hat by vastly inferior forces, snatching defeat out of the jaws of victory at the last possible moment; *this is all wrong*, he'd said to himself, and from that epiphany New Evil had been born. Learn from your enemies, adapt their winning ways, figure out the reasons for their success and see if you can't use a few of them yourself. While staying 100 per cent committed to the values of the Dark Cause, needless to say. Oh yes. Absolutely.

All well and good, so long as things stayed as they were, with the enemy still superior in intelligence and technology. But what if that no longer applied? What if he was looking at the ultimate game changer, a new weapon that would give Evil a sporting chance not just to live to fight another day but actually *prevail*? Of course, they'd said the same thing when Azog III issued his armies with scythe-wheeled chariots five centuries ago, and all that Goblinkind had gained from that was a series of giant hops forward in leg armour and artificial limb technology. If there was a way of wasting a shining new opportunity, trust the goblins to find it. But—he took another peek through the window—something like *that*; there was no way of knowing where it would lead to.

Maybe even victory?

"Oh, look," said the Science Officer. "She's brushing her teeth with a bit of stick."

Mordak looked. "It'll take her for ever to get them sharp that way."

"Yes, but she hasn't got a proper grindstone. I call that initiative."

"That's not stick, it's shin."

"Whatever."

Because, Mordak reflected, what's the defining experience of Evil, taken as a whole, throughout three Ages of recorded history? It loses, that's what. It gets hammered. It gets the stuffing bashed out of it, every single time. A Dark Lord rises, for a while everything goes swimmingly, vast swathes of territory fall under the Shadow; and then a handful of pointy-ears or a bunch of uppity humans or even a solitary furry-toed, knee-high hooligan stops us dead in our tracks and it's straight back to square one, do not pass Go, do not collect two hundred *zlotyl*. A wise man, observing this trend, decides not to fight it. He rolls with it instead. He doesn't get his hopes up. He climbs slowly up the ladder and puts a nice soft cushion under the tail of the snake. He compromises. He's a realist.

And after a while he gets to thinking; maybe Evil always loses because that's how it's meant to be, because Evil shouldn't win, because Evil is *bad*. And, following that silvery snail trail of logic to where it seems to want to go, maybe the job of the leader of Evil is to make sure it keeps happening that way. He can do it by overreaching himself, or turning on his allies, by unbelievable stupidity (a firm favourite, that one), or he can do it on purpose, deliberately, controlled failure, designed to reduce the

impact of defeat and keep collateral damage to an acceptable minimum.

That, years ago, had been Mordak's road-to-D'mashkûz
moment. To achieve victory, first you have to define what
you mean by it. New Evil; if you can lose as advantageously
as possible, you've won.

There was this little voice in the back of his head. It
had a sort of whiny, bleaty tone and it sounded distinctly
worried. *Perish the thought*, it was saying, *we've been through
all this, we decided; Evil isn't meant to win, see above, Victory,
definition of. And if you think this, or anything, is going to
make the slightest bit of difference, you're just another dumb-
ass Evil Overlord with dark matter for brains. That thing in
there is basically just a Ring of Power 1:2. It'll take you so far
and then dump you in the brown and sticky, and the Elves will
sing snide songs about your downfall until all the Realms are
sundered. You want that? Really?*

Maybe. But the little voice, Mordak couldn't help but
feel, doth protest too much. After all, he didn't have to
make his mind up right away. Let the project run a bit
longer, see what we come up with, and then decide.

"Well?" said the Science Officer.

Mordak looked at him. "Well what?"

"What do you think? Do we carry on and let her get
absolutely *huge*, or—?" He did the familiar finger-across-
throat gesture. "Up to you."

Mordak took a moment, but he didn't have to think
too hard. You don't have to when you already know the
answer. "I think she's kind of cute," he said.

"You do?"

"Oh yes. A terrible cutie is born. Get on with it, and
don't let her eat too many guards. It'll stunt her growth."

*

It had all started, as so many things tended to do, at a party on Bogdan's yacht. The regular crowd were all there: oligarchs and their trophy wives, oil sheikhs, an Indian steel magnate or two, a few movie faces and a selection of the finest politicians money could buy. And Ms. Neige La Blanche, of course, pretty in canary yellow and bored out of her exquisitely contoured skull.

And a little roly-poly bald man in a Hawaiian shirt, open sandals and socks, who said his name was George; he was quite obviously nobody, compared to the sleek and the mighty all around him, but people were talking to him and laughing at his jokes, and Ms. La Blanche found the incongruity intriguing. So she asked the maître d', an old friend and ally.

"Him?" He shrugged. "English."

"Nobody's perfect. Why do they all like him so much?"

"He's rich."

"English rich?"

The maître d' shook his head. "Genuinely rich," he said. "Look, if money was weight, he could sit at one end of the boat and everybody else could be at the other, and his end would sink like a stone."

"Rich as in?"

The maître d' frowned. "Property," he said. "Sort of."

So, when the opportunity presented itself, she went and sat next to George the Englishman and smiled at him, and he smiled back and offered her a plate of horrid sticky cakes.

"No thanks," she said sweetly. "I only have to look at a cake and suddenly nothing fits any more."

"That's a pity," he said. "Because these cakes are for looking at, not for eating."

She assumed that was supposed to be a joke and did the silvery laugh. But George said, "No, seriously. You don't eat them, you look at them. Or, more precisely, through them." He grinned and held out his hand. "I'm George," he said. "And this is what I do for a living."

"You're a baker."

"No. But these are what you might call my stock in trade."

Going nowhere. "That's a nice shirt," she said. "Where did you get it?"

"Here." George picked up a doughnut, his finger and thumb meeting through the hole in the middle. "It's safer if you hold it like that," he said. "Just a second, I'll wrap it for you." He took a paper napkin, wrapped the doughnut and put it on her knee. "You think I'm stark raving bonkers, don't you?"

"Yes," she said, "but in the nicest possible way."

He nodded. "The last person I gave one of these doughnuts to paid me fifty thousand quid for it," he said. "But I like you, you've got nice eyes, so this one's on me. Oh, and you'll need one of these." From his top pocket he took a folded piece of paper. "Tells you how it works," he explained. "Excuse me, I'm going for a pee."

Some time later, when she was alone in the cabin, she opened her bag and there inside it was the napkin-wrapped doughnut, which she thought she'd thrown over the side of the boat, but clearly she hadn't. Also the folded bit of paper the mad rich man had given her. She unfolded it and started to read.

Half an hour later some fool came and disturbed her, and she had to go and be nice to people, and it was three in the morning before she had a chance to get some peace and quiet and read it through yet again. It was, of course, entirely crazy and impossible; in exactly the same way as flying in the air was before the Wright brothers came along.

So she found George, who was sitting on deck drying his socks in the sun. "You read it, then?"

"I don't believe it."

"Suit yourself."

She sat down next to him, picked up one sock and held it over the side. "Explain it to me," she said. "Or the sock gets it."

"Let's not be hasty," George said. "Actually, it's really quite simple."

And then he told her about the late Professor Pieter van Goyen, of Leiden, who'd spent his life exploring the endlessly fascinating and lethally frustrating field of multiverse theory. Van Goyen started from the premise that there are an infinite number of parallel universes and alternative realities, of which our neck of the spatio-temporal woods is only one, and a pretty drab one at that. But what if someone invented an interface, a device that let you cross over to the alternative version of your choice, at will, just by wanting to go there and doing some simple, painless, inexpensive act? If only, thought Professor van Goyen; and then, why not?

And then he disappeared without trace, shortly before his favourite student Theo Bernstein accidentally blew up the Very Very Large Hadron Collider and found himself out of a job; and Bernstein took over where van Goyen had left off, and it's a long story, and let other pens dwell, et cetera. But how would it be (George said) if there really was such an interface, and you could use it to travel to parallel universes where things are very different, easy as falling off the proverbial log?

"Well," Ms. La Blanche said, after a long pause for thought, "I imagine you could make a great deal of money."

George beamed at her. "Done that," he said. "Care to speculate how?"

"Something to do with property?"

"Sort of," George said. "Well, you know how there's a killing to be made buying up derelict old farmhouses in the back end of France and Spain and God knows where else, and flogging them to jaded urban Brits with half-baked dreams of authentic colour-supplement Arcadian living? Fine, only that market's a bit passé and prices are going up; what's needed is somewhere completely unspoilt and undiscovered and derelict and dirt-poor, where (allowing for exchange rate fluctuations) the entire GDP wouldn't buy you a Big Mac and fries in London, and a man with vision and the courage to aspire could make out like a bandit."

"And is there such a place?" asked Ms. La Blanche.

"Sure there is," George said, and told her about the Hidden Realms.

She listened carefully, and then asked, "And how did you say you go about getting there?"

"I didn't. But it's really very easy. You just need a doughnut."

"Doughnut?"

He nodded. "The sort with a hole in the middle. Or a bagel, or even a Cheerio. Any sort of circular, centrally perforated foodstuff. That's the genius of it. The equations are set up to focus the exochronomatic field through the hole, thereby punching a hole through the transmorphic barrier while simultaneously creating a massive Uncertainty effect, and bingo, you're there. Piece, no pun intended, of—"

"Does it have to be a special doughnut?"

"Any doughnut will do. I tell the punters it's got to be one of mine, but that's just bull. Theo Bernstein proved that, bless him, shortly before he disappeared. What they're actually paying for is attunement to the vast and eye-wateringly expensive Van Goyen Matrix Generator I've had built in a disused salt mine in Silesia. But a magic doughnut sounds better. It's called YouSpace, by the way. Catchy, don't you think?"

"No. But it really works?"

George pointed at his shoes, beside him on the deck of the yacht. "Dinnington's of St. James's," he said, "hand-made, cost me five grand. It works."

She knew a pair of Dinnington shoes when she saw one. "And people actually buy—"

George shrugged. "I know," he said. "Wouldn't suit me. Uproot yourself and swan off lock, stock and barrel to some faraway place of which you know little, you can't speak the language and the locals are a load of bloody savages who'd murder you for your earwax. But once you've made up your mind to it, Provence or the Hidden Realms, what difference does it make? Except your money goes ever so much further in the Realms. And the locals aren't so snotty, either."

"Talking of the locals," said Ms. La Blanche, "what are they like?"

So George told her; about the proud, supercilious Elves, the industrious and warlike dwarves, the feather-duster-footed halflings, the primitive but noble humans; the trolls, the wraiths, the Dark Elves and, of course, the goblins. "Bloody lunatics, the lot of them," he concluded, "but I don't give a stuff, I don't have to live there."

"These dwarves," said Ms. La Blanche. "Are they really rich?"

George laughed. "There's more to life than just money, pet."

"Wash your mouth out with soap and water. Well, are they?"

George looked round at his fellow guests on the deck of

the yacht and lowered his voice. "Tell you what," he said. "They could buy and sell this lot and still have change out of their beer money. And a nicer class of person, too. Marginally."

She looked where he'd just looked, and gave her opinion that that wouldn't be difficult. "Present company excepted," she added politely.

George was amused. "Thinking of trying your luck, then?"

"When I left school," Ms. La Blanche said, "the careers adviser told me, the modern world is crying out for intelligent, capable, dynamic women with solid core values and the will to succeed. I can see now that she was right. She just neglected to specify which world, that's all. Silly me, I thought she must've been talking about this one, but obviously not. Now I know."

Well, she'd gone away, she'd thought about it, and now here she was. Regrets? A few, but then again, too few to mention—except, had she known, she'd definitely have brought some books to read. The funny little lawyer's offering was quite hard going (and she'd read *On Chesil Beach*, so she was no quitter) but it was that or the recipe book, and she saw enough of that when she was working.

She was gently sautéing some liver when the door flew open (dwarvish hinges are half an inch thick and made of heat-treated carbon steel; there's a reason for that) and King Drain lumbered in, knocking over a pan of chopped leeks and spilling flour all over the kitchen table.

"You're human," he said.

She knew that tone of voice. Usually it said, "You're a woman", and ended up lumbering her with the task of choosing somebody's wife's birthday present. "I know. Why?"

"And you're not from round here."

Proceed with caution. "True. Why?"

"What do you make of this?"

He slammed something down on the table in front of her. She looked at it. "Rephrase the question. Ask me what I make *with* this."

"All right. What?"

"Soup," she replied. "Or sauces. Sometimes, if I'm feeling lazy, fruit salad. Where'd you get it?"

"You recognise it."

"Sure. We have them where I come from."

"How do you make soup with a small rotary shear?"

She smiled at him. "We open a tin. That's what it's for. It's a tin opener."

Most of King Drain's face was beard, but he had very bright pale brown eyes. Almost golden. "It's not made of tin, and what do you open with it?"

"Tin *can*. We preserve food by sealing it in little metal tubes. This is how you cut the tops off to get at what's inside."

"It's remarkable," Drain said. "I've been a metalsmith all my life, and my father before me, and his father before him. My great-grandfather, Grain son of Groin son of Grisli, built the Bronze Gates of Thingogram, which weigh five hundred tons each, but a child can push them open. But I've never seen work as fine as this."

She shrugged. "It's no big deal. Everybody's got one, back home."

"Everybody? Even poor people?"

"Mostly."

Drain thrust the tin opener under her nose. "But look at it. Look at how precisely the gear teeth are cut. I measured them with callipers, there isn't a thousandth of an inch difference between them. Are you trying to tell me you humans have craftsmen who can do work like this?"

"No idea. But it's all made by machines."

For a moment, she thought he must be having a stroke or a coronary. "A machine that can file?"

"I don't know, that's all rather specialised. All I know is, we have factories full of machines in a place called China, and they make all kinds of stuff. Everyday things. Cheap." She peered at him through the beard. He really didn't look well at all. "Where did you say you got this from?"

"The wizard's tower, Snorfang. It was lying around in the dirt. I thought it must be a product of dark wizardry."

She laughed. "Nothing to worry about on that score. It's just a cheap old tin opener."

"That's what I'm so worried about," Drain said feebly. "Wizards we can cope with. Machines that can file metal to exact tolerances, *cheaply*, will be the ruin of us all."

Ah. She really ought to have thought of that, before she blundered along and put her foot right in it. "A very long way away," she said soothingly. "Ever so far."

"Really. So how did it get here?"

Through a doughnut, presumably, she didn't say. "Besides," she went on, "it's no threat to you, is it? Nobody can cut you out of the can-opener business, because there isn't one, because there aren't any cans. So you've got nothing to worry about at all."

She was drivelling and she knew it. So, she suspected, did King Drain, who didn't look the least bit reassured. Nor should he be, of course. He might look like a clown with his stumpy bow legs and his ludicrous Afrikaaner-church-elder beard with a tiny point of nose sticking out of it like a carrot out of a snowman; but one thing her years in the profession had taught her was not to judge people by how they looked. She'd known a lot of men who looked even more grotesque than King Drain and who'd made ever such a lot of money in places where money was hard to come by, and a lot of beautiful women (including the one who lived in her mirror) who weren't nearly as angelic as they looked. And Drain wasn't to know, because she'd seen fit to withhold the key information from him, just how unlikely it was that the Chinese were poised to flood his domestic market with cheap manufactured goods.

Point: why hadn't she told him? Because he wouldn't believe her? Because the technology involved was so advanced it sounded like magic? Magic *worked* around here; to a limited extent and not particularly usefully, it was true, but it was genuine magic, not just science in fancy dress. How or why it worked she didn't know and preferred not to speculate; local variations in the laws of physics was her guess, and as an experienced traveller she knew that so long as you observe the local laws and don't argue the toss, you're generally all right, so if E chose to equal mc^3 rather than mc^2 in these parts, it was no skin off her nose provided she knew what to expect and looked where she was putting her feet. So, if not for fear of being thought crazy, why hadn't she said anything about doughnuts and YouSpace and how she'd got there and so forth? Partly, she suspected, because nobody had actually asked—well, you don't, do you? When was the last time you met a stranger who dresses a bit funny and has an accent you can't quite place and immediately demanded to know if they come from an alternative reality? You just assume they're a bit foreign and think no more of it. And partly—face it, she told herself, because the secret of the interface is your edge, your get-out-of-trouble-free card, your ace in the hole should things not go well, and there'd be no point giving that away without a very good reason, in which sector King Drain's peace of mind doesn't fall, unfortunately. Tough, but there we go. If he wasn't worried about that, it'd be something else.

And also—

A thought burst into flower in her mind, beautiful and terrible. But why not? She'd come here, after all, to make money, preferably without having to stare at too many ceilings. And this idea was an absolute peach.

"Maybe," she said, "you're looking at it the wrong way."

"Oh?" Drain turned the tin opener over and squinted at it from underneath. "Sorry, you'll have to explain. What am I supposed to be looking for?"

"This whole issue," she said, taking it gently away from him and putting it down on the kitchen table. "The cheap goods thing. I mean, why should it be a problem?"

"Are you kidding?" The point of his nose had gone bright red. "If these China people are going to start bringing their goods here to sell—"

"Ah." she smiled. "You're afraid because they can make things cheaper and better than your workers can, so they'll all be out of a job."

"Yes."

"What's so bad about that?"

There was an interval—about two seconds—when his mouth opened and closed but no words came out. Then he roared, "Are you—?"

"Back home," she said calmly, "we call it outsourcing. Why pay five silver pennies to have something made here by expensive, truculent workers who don't know when they're well off, when you can get the same thing run up by smiling, obedient, grateful primitives for a penny three-farthings? Then, suppose you normally sell one for ninepence. You can cut the price to eightpence, which means you sell more, and still make a much bigger profit. Now that's smart." she smiled. "That's the sort of thinking that's made my homeland the sort of place it is today."

He had that sort of bewildered look on his face; the sort that can't make its mind up whether the rosy glow in the sky is a bright new dawn or the end of the world. "But that's crazy," he said. "I'm King of the Dwarves, I'm responsible for them. I can't just throw the whole lot of them out of work, simply to make money."

"Of course not," she said soothingly. "That would be very naughty. So, you find them other things to do instead."

Drain blinked. "Such as?"

"Oh, there's loads of things. Information technology, financial services, entertainment, hospitality and tourism. All very worthwhile and fulfilling, and so much better than toiling away in a dirty old factory all day, or being stuck down a mine. We made the changeover years ago, and you wouldn't believe how happy and content everyone's been ever since. You'll be Drain the Great before you know it. Statues of you all over the place."

She watched him think. It was like observing speeded-up tectonic shift; huge masses of preconceived ideas colliding and forming mountains or sinking for ever beneath the oceans. "And these China people would sell us the stuff—?"

"No problem."

"How would they get it here?"

"Oh, I can see to all that," she said, as if undertaking to pick up a few groceries on her way to the office. "You wouldn't have to be involved at all."

A flicker of suspicion, which died away. "Really?"

"Sure. For a small percentage, naturally. But, yes, I can make all the necessary arrangements."

"I'll have to think about it."

Yes, she thought, but not too hard. "Of course. Take your time. I don't suppose there's any real risk of anybody else getting the same idea and beating you to it." She paused and smiled. "The Elves, say, or even the goblins. You think about it as long as you like."

There are worse things than goblins, so the proverb says, in the dark places of the Earth.

Goblins, naturally, resent that and regard it as a slur on their bad name. Mordak's predecessor took it so much to heart that he had posters put up on the walls of the lower galleries: *Your Worst Nightmare*, and *Nothing's As Bad*, with his portrait, in full regalia, drinking from the skull of his mortal enemy. That was fine, people said they brightened the place up; but then they started to disappear. Either they were removed completely or else torn down, ripped diagonally across by some sharp instrument, just conceivably an enormous claw. At the time it was put down to some of the lads larking about, and nobody thought very much about it.

That would have been around the time when the dwarves suspended mining operations in some of their lower galleries. Flooding, they said; subsidence, geological instability, and, besides, the seams down there are so thin they aren't worth the bother. All perfectly reasonable explanations, and no reason whatsoever not to take them at face value. As for worse things than goblins—too right, the dwarves say with a merry laugh, there's King Drain's socks for a start, you really wouldn't want to be trapped in a deep hole in the ground with those things; and then they change the subject.

And besides, even if there were any truth in the rumours, which there isn't, needless to say, who in his right mind would want to go that far down anyway? It's below the coal and the iron ore, you'd be chipping your way through solid rock and nothing worth having to show for it. Waste of time and energy. Why go down needlessly when there's still plenty of sideways left for everyone? No, only a complete and utter halfwit—

Pat Lushington pulled back the cloth, embroidered with strange sigils, that covered the Eye of Snorgoth, folded it neatly and gave the Eye a tap with her knuckle. No dice. The milk-white crystal globe was still cloudy, nothing but swirly white bits, just like the Christmas ornaments of her youth that you shook to make a snowstorm. "Bloody thing," she muttered under her breath.

You were supposed to be able to get video as well as sound on these contraptions, but she hadn't managed it yet. The agent, when taxed with its inefficiencies, tended to mutter *you're six hundred feet under a mountain, you can't expect perfect reception*, whereupon she'd read him the bit about it in the brochure, guaranteed to work flawlessly under any conditions. Call that flawless, she'd say, and he'd go all quiet.

"Hello?" she said.

She felt such a fool, saying hello to a glorified goldfish bowl. In theory, it was supposed to connect you instantaneously to anyone you wanted to talk to, anytime, anywhere. In practice, you had to chirrup at it pleadingly for half an hour, and then if you were lucky you'd get through to *somebody*, usually some crazy old man who cackled fiendishly and asked you to speak up, and then maybe he'd put you through or maybe the stupid thing would just glow bright green at you, in which case the best thing to do was put the cover back on, leave it for an hour and try again later. All in all, she wasn't pleased. It was easier and more reliable than broadband, but once you'd said that, you'd said it all.

Today, though, her luck was in. The ball went coal-black, and then filled with a single luminous red eye, its pupil like the filament of a light bulb. It stared straight at her, and she had the uneasy feeling it was trying to look down the front of her dress, even though it was on the table and she was standing up.

"Hello," she repeated.

Speak.

"I'm trying to get hold of a plumber," she said, "because we've got this terrible banging noise in the pipes some-where, but the little man who came out the last time was completely useless, and he hasn't been back since, so I need someone reliable who actually knows what he's doing, because if I have to spend another night in this place with that ghastly noise going on, I'm going to go loopy. Hello? Are you there?"

I am here.

She waited. Nothing. "Well?"

You seek a plumber.

"Yes."

What is a plumber?

She sighed. "Look, no offence, but is there someone else I can talk to, like the supervisor? Um, *puis-je parler avec votre superieur? Por favor?*"

The red eye blinked. *My superior.*

"If you don't mind."

I have no superior. I am not of the body. I am not of Time. I am alone.

The night shift, she might have known. Sorry, there's no one here, I'll leave a note for them to call you in the morning. She'd heard that before. "Look, I'm sorry, but you'll have to do. I need a *plumber*. Our hot-water system no work, make bangy-bang noises. Plumber man with bag of tools, he come fix. Savee?"

You seek a wizard.

"What? Oh, for crying out—yes, I seek a wizard. A wizard who can come and stop those bloody pipes making that bloody awful noise. You send one? Chop chop, wiggle wiggle?"

I was a wizard once. I will come.

She sighed. "*Thank* you, so bloody much. Arividerci. Bye."

She grabbed the cloth and slung it over the globe, and the red light instantly went out. She sat down, kicked off her shoes and poured herself a drink. Why did everything in this horrible place have to be so *difficult*?

Barry wandered in, looking vexed. "Have you seen my pliers?"

"Half an hour," she replied, not looking up. "Half an hour to get through to a call centre, and they may be sending a plumber but I wouldn't hold your breath."

"Mphm. Have you seen my pliers?"

"No. What pliers?" She poured herself another drink. "What are you up to, anyway?"

"Me? Nothing."

She narrowed her eyes. "You're not trying to fix it yourself, are you?"

He had the grace to look guilty. "I thought I'd take a quick look."

"You promised." She rolled her eyes. "After the last time, we agreed. No more DI bloody Y, if something's wrong, we call in a professional. Get it done properly."

He always got angry when he was in the wrong. "I'm just *looking* at it."

"With pliers."

"There's no point spending good money if it's something minor I can fix myself."

"No." She folded her arms at him.

"I'm perfectly capable of doing a simple little—"

She shook her head. "It's bad enough with the banging. Think about it, Baz, we're *underground*. If you break something and it floods, we could *drown*."

"Oh, don't be ridiculous. I'm not going to—"

"You said that the last time."

At this point, he was supposed to shout, flounce off and leave her in peace. Instead he went sort of cold and calm. "You said you can't get a plumber."

"They're sending one."

"Don't hold your breath, you said."

He was getting cunning in his old age. Also, he was listening to her when she spoke to him; a new departure for him, so presumably he'd figured out that if he listened he could occasionally pick up things that could be used in evidence against her. She'd have to watch that. "For the last time, Baz, you're not to go tinkering. Got that?"

"Fine." He did the big shrug. He had the shoulders for it, bless him. "Only, I don't want to hear any more about not being able to sleep because of the banging. Fair enough?"

"They said they'd send a plumber. Well, that's not what they actually said, but as good as."

"I do not tinker," he said coldly. "I do household maintenance."

She sighed. In theory, they could be trained to perform simple tasks, but you wouldn't want them let loose where you *live*. Meanwhile, the weather forecast was for heavy sulks blowing in from the north-east. Life, she decided, is too short. What the hell. She could swim. "Tell you what," she said. "We'll give them till Thursday, and if the plumber hasn't shown up by then, you can take a look at it. All right?"

"Today's Thursday."

He could well be right. It was so easy to lose track, stuck in this miserable hole in the ground. "Next Thursday."

"Suit yourself. Only, like I said, no more whining about the banging noise. All right?"

She could agree to that with a clear conscience, because she never whined. She expressed herself clearly and with feeling, which is different. "Whatever."

"Fine. I think I'll go up to the workshop for a bit."

She smiled vaguely at him, and he went away. Workshop; bless him. All that expensive carpentry stuff he never used. He'd probably have a drink and read the paper. And why not? The paper, of course, would be six weeks old, but he liked the ritual. It reminded him of—

She caught herself just in time. I will *not* feel nostalgic for home. Which isn't home anymore, because this is. Home, I mean *England*, is a noisy, smelly place where we used to live in a rabbit hutch surrounded by feral youths and litter, and everything was a rip-off, and it was only marginally easier to get a plumber, and when he did turn up he only spoke Lithuanian. And we're far better off here, I mean, we've got space, we've got *miles* of space, literally; vast echoing halls that make the temples of ancient Egypt look like a bungalow, which is what we always wanted. Isn't it?

She picked up her drink and walked through the long gallery to the pool. Something else they'd always wanted and knew they could never have back home, an indoor pool. She sat down and closed her eyes, listening to the faint drip-dripping noises. And not just a pool; a *huge* pool, so big it had an island in the middle, with that big fern thing. Only film stars and MPs could afford pools with islands in them, back home. No, they'd done the right thing, no question about that.

Funny; she couldn't feel a draught, but the fronds of the fern thing looked like they were stirring slightly. She frowned. Maybe the third drink hadn't been such a good idea. She really ought to keep an eye on that. But it was so easy, especially now she didn't have to drive anywhere; one little drink, and then another, and you don't even notice that you've poured a third one.

She decided she didn't like the fern thing. It was big and thick and ugly, and there were times when it had a distinctly creepy look about it, as though it was watching you. Right, she decided. As soon as we can get a reliable gardener, it's coming out, and we'll have a nice flowerbed there instead, bedding plants and maybe a couple of standard roses.

It was almost as though the fern thing had read her mind, because its fronds—if you could call them that; more like nasty big green tubes—definitely waved a bit, and if it had had fingers she knew what gesture it'd have been making. Same to you, too, fern thing. In fact—she looked down, and there was a stone, a bit of rock crumbled off something, God, this place really does need some work doing or one day it's going to fall down. She picked up the stone and threw it at the fern thing, but it fell short and went splash in the water. Screw you, fern, she muttered under her breath, and closed her eyes. Just resting them for a second. Sleepy.

She woke up out of a dream, in which a boy she hadn't seen for thirty years and whose name escaped her was tickling her ankles. She opened her eyes and blinked, then looked down at her feet. A frond from the damn fern was lying next to them, its revolting little pale green tendrils just touching her feet. She jumped up and stamped on it. How the hell had it got there? She looked and saw that it had come up out of the water. Yuck. It'd have to go. Otherwise it'd be like the Collingwoods and their Russian vine, which got in everywhere and did thousands of pounds' worth of damage to the foundations.

Wearily she clumped back up the stairs, pulled the cloth off the stupid crystal ball thing and waited for it to go black. Oh, come *on*, she thought, that's not right, it's taking longer and longer to get started, probably needs an upgrade or a reboot or whatever. "Hello," she said. "Hello?"

The red eye was back. What joy.

You again.

Her sentiments exactly. "Oh, hello," she said. "Look, I need a gardener. Man who pulls up weeds. Comprendez?"

"This is *serious*," Tinituviel said. "You need to *do* something."

Mordak nodded. "Yes, right," he mumbled. "Soon as I've got five minutes."

She had a wonderful knack of choosing her moments. He'd climbed all the way up to the top of the Dark Pinnacle in the hope of having five minutes' peace so he could really think things through, and suddenly there she was, nagging, telling him to *do* something. And the trouble was, when she was in this mood, she simply wouldn't take yes for an answer.

"You should have seen the stuff they've got there," she went on. "Amazing."

"Jolly good. I mean, well done."

"Which is bizarre," she went on, "because they're primitives, just like other humans, maybe worse. I mean, they cook outside over an open fire, so obviously concepts like chimneys are way too advanced for them, but in other respects they're quite terrifyingly advanced."

"Is that right?"

"Oh yes. You should see their weapons."

The W word snagged his attention. "Weapons?"

"Never seen anything like it."

"Spears? Swords? Axes?"

She was frowning. "He called them clubs," she said, "but they looked like a sort of precision poleaxe to me. Cross between a poleaxe and a halberd, but without the spike. Nasty piece of work. I would guess you need a lot of skill to use it, but the damage it could do—"

"*Without* the spike."

"But with a really carefully contoured slanting blade. He started to explain, but it was a bit technical. Impact velocities and mass transfers. They obviously take it very seriously."

Mordak looked at her. "You did say," he conceded, "if they can make a superior egg whisk, they might well have superior weapons."

"And I was right. But that's just for starters. Mordak, I'm worried."

The admission, and the use of his actual name, correctly pronounced, made him sit up straight. "What?"

She came a bit closer and lowered her voice a little. "I think they may have one of the lost Stones."

He whistled softly. "You're kidding."

She glowered at him. "It's not something to joke about," she said. "If I'm right, and they've got hold of one of the Stones of Snordor, there's no knowing—"

"Calm down," Mordak said. "Let's not jump to conclusions. What makes you think it's one of the Nine?"

She took a deep breath. "I had a good look at it."

"And?"

"Well," she said, "what do we actually know about the Nine?"

"Me? Practically nothing." His face went blank. "Look, we were told, the Nine came up in last year's exam, and the year before that, it won't be in this year's, you can bet. So I skipped that chapter and concentrated on the Black

Breath, which *did* come up, and I got ninety-seven per cent. *What?*"

She clicked her tongue so sharply it made his eyes water. "All right," she said, "since you've been honest and courageous enough to confess your ignorance, I'll fill you in. The Nine Lost Scrying Stones came across the sea in the White Ships from Scoobidoobidorëon, before the Fall. Made by the hand of Glondel himself—"

"Yes, I know all *that*," Mordak interrupted. "I'm not stupid."

"Made by the hand of Glondel himself—" (maybe she had wax in her ears) "—the Stones will show you what was, what is and what is yet to come, though they are perilous and seek to lead the foolish to their doom. Nine there were, but five have fallen into shadow, two the dragons consumed, one stands in the Hall of the Woodland King in Saras Mithron, and one—"

Mordak nodded. "I know," he said. "Upstairs. Doesn't bloody work."

She sighed. "That's because seven of the Nine are lost and out of Communion, and the eighth is hidden from you. There is nothing for your Stone to talk to. But if one of the five that were lost has been found—" She shrugged. "What concerns me more is what the humans use it for."

"I'm guessing you asked."

"Oh yes." She shivered. "The human said that the she-human talks to Home through it." She paused. "Through a screen of glass."

Mordak waited, then said, "That's significant, isn't it?"

Nod. "If you could've been bothered to read the chapter in your book even though it wasn't likely to come up in the exam, you'd have learned that after the Fall, between the Hidden Realms and Scoobidoobidorëon the Golden the Iaressë raised a screen of glass, invisible but impenetrable, so that seafarers might cast their eyes on the Golden Land but never ever reach there."

"That's just mean," Mordak said.

"The she-human," Tinituviel went on, "speaks to her family and friends in a faraway land through a screen of glass. If I were you, I'd put your helmet on at this point."

Obediently, Mordak reached for it. "Why?"

"So that when the penny eventually drops it won't knock your brains out through your ears. Faraway land? Screen of glass? Oh, come on."

Mordak put the helmet back under the throne. "Yes, I see what you're getting at. You think these idiots come from Scoobi-whatsisface. Maybe they do. What about it?"

She was counting under her breath. She did that, a lot. "Let me guess," she said. "The Prophecies were in the previous year's paper, too."

"Not even on the syllabus," Mordak replied. "Lot of Elvish nonsense. Well, aren't they?"

"I don't know why I bother with you."

"Money," Mordak replied succinctly. "So? There's a prophecy, then."

"Yes, there's a prophecy. When the Children of Fluor leave the Golden Land and pass through the Gate of Flour and Eggs, then shall the Realms be plunged in darkness and the Nameless One will arise."

"What Nameless One?"

"I don't know, do I, he's Nameless. Anyway, that's what it says, as you would know if you were even semi-literate, and that's why I'm worried. All right?"

Mordak took a moment to think about it. "But surely that's all fine and good, as far as we're concerned. All the Realms plunged in darkness? That's what we want, surely. I'm the Dark Lord, remember. We're the bad guys."

"Mphm. And when the Nameless One arises, you'll just

meekly hand him over the keys and retire to the seaside, presumably. And of course, he'll let you."

"Um."

"Quite. You see, I do have your best interests at heart, I have no idea why. So if you want your head to stay on your shoulders, rather than on a hook in the crockery cupboard, I suggest you start worrying. Hard."

Mordak scowled at her. "Oh come, now," he said. "It's just a prophecy."

"*Just* a—"

"Just another Elvish prophecy. Like Reluctant Hero for the Snordor Derby. That one cost me a hundred and sixty *zlotyl* that I'll never see again, so please don't give me all that infallible wisdom stuff—"

"That wasn't a prophecy," she said coldly, "it was a prediction. And I would venture to suggest that there's rather more at stake this time than a handful of coins. I mean, we could be looking at the ultimate victory of Evil."

"But like I said—"

"*Real* Evil. Not your peelie-wally alternative tree-hugging bleeding-heart New Evil, the genuine article. And I don't think either of us wants that."

Let her have the last word, he told himself, it might mean she'll go away. He was right about that; and after she'd gone, he was able to get back to his thinking.

Peelie-wally bleeding heart? The hell with that. Yes, he was right behind bleeding hearts, one hundred per cent, especially if they were still beating as he ripped them from the ribcages of his mortal enemies. Not, he had to admit, that he'd done an awful lot of that lately. It's always the way. You get bogged down in admin and paperwork, and quite soon you've lost sight of what it was you originally went into the profession for. But all this drivel about Nameless Ones was just Elvish scaremongering, surely.

Besides, there's no such thing as a foregone conclusion in the fight game, that much he knew from long experience. A phantom rival with no name was one thing, but it'd take a phantom rival with no name and a very large contingent of heavy infantry to get him seriously concerned. And besides, even if we lose we're used to that. It's what we do . . .

Which brought him back full circle; New Evil and the monstrous creature currently plaiting its hair into braids down in the dungeons. Damn, he thought. Why has everything always got to be so difficult?

It took him an hour to find what he was looking for, down in the Black Vault, where even the Wraith-lords are reluctant to go; an old battered trunk, with five massive padlocks, the keys to which he no longer had, it went without saying. Half an hour with an axe that would never be much use for anything again, and he had the trunk open. He lifted the lid, and couldn't help smiling.

He'd put the trunk in the Black Vault because he didn't want anyone to find it, not ever. The goblins would laugh at him, Tinituviel would say it was just a load of old junk and throw it away, but to him these were treasures way beyond gold and gemstones, magic weapons or rings of power.

"Hello," he said. "Long time no see."

Reverently, using only the tips of his claws, he lifted out a small, crumpled shape. The years hadn't been kind to Willy the Werewolf. Most of his stuffing was gone, and he was missing one of his button eyes, but that was all right. Sarah Spider wasn't much better off; if she was real, she'd be scuttling with a distinct limp, and she could definitely do with a decent meal or two. But they were still there, that was the point. He put them gently back on their bed of straw and carried on looking.

Ah. He took out a crumbling book and opened it at the flyleaf

Mordak

Form IVb

If this bûk shold dare to rome box its ears and send it hoam

There were other books—the Black Library was full of the things, shelf upon shelf of uniform editions, with the Dark Bookplate pasted inside every front cover, but none he trusted like this one. He sat down cross-legged on the floor, looked up *Prophecies, Elvish* in the index, and began to read.

"It's nothing personal," the senior partner said, gazing at him as though he'd just found him stuck to the sole of his shoe. "It's a simple question of arithmetic. You're seven billable hours short of your target for the month, which gives us a nice straightforward equation. T minus seven equals the sack. Sorry," he added, with a certain lack of sincerity. "Clear your desk and be out by noon."

John didn't have much to take away with him: a few books, a cheap whalebone slide rule, a framed cameo portrait of his mother. The doorman sold him an old wooden box to put them in, and some string to make a rudimentary carrying strap. He slung the box over his shoulder and climbed down the long ladder to ground level, a free man.

Bastards, he thought cheerfully. Ah well.

He left the forest, whistling a sprightly tune, and headed for the halfling village a few miles down the Old North Road. There he stopped at the carpenter's shop and asked the man there to make him a sign.

"A what?"

"Flat piece of wood," John explained, "about a foot by

eight inches, half-inch thick, oak or ash, something hard-wearing. And I want you to carve my name on it."

The carpenter frowned. "You mean, letters and stuff?"

"Is that a problem?"

The carpenter blinked. "I can do letters," he said. "No bother at all. Come back in an hour."

So John went to the Pink Oliphaunt for a coffee and a slice of simnel cake; and when he went back, the carpenter was just slapping on a coat of linseed oil. "Like it?" he asked proudly.

John looked at it.

JON THE LIAR
ATURNY AT LOR

John considered the literacy level of his target demo-graphic. "It'll do," he said. "How much do I owe you?"

"That'll be twopence."

Which was precisely half of his total capital, but what the hell. Every mighty tree was once a tiny pip, and some of the greatest lawsuits of all time have grown out of trivial incidents, like an idiot not reading the label or putting his foot in a pothole. At any rate, he had a sign. Now all he needed was somewhere to hang it up.

He asked around, but nobody knew of vacant premises to let. He asked at the inn, but they told him there was no room; all they could suggest was a lowly cattle shed out the back, which was a bit lacking in the structurally sound walls and weathertight roof department, but if he wanted it he could have it, twopence a month, two months payable in advance. That came to exactly fourpence, which by some strange coincidence was exactly how much money he had. An omen. "Deal," he said.

"Really?" The innkeeper quickly wiped the grin off his

face. "I mean, that's settled, splendid. See you in a couple of months, then."

Something is usually better than nothing at all. So, though his office was a stable and his desk was a manger and his filing cabinet was a stall, and the best he could do for a door was a couple of old feed sacks slung over a bit of rope—in spite of all that, he was back in the business, only this time without a bunch of pointy eared millstones round his neck. His own boss. Master of his fate and captain of his soul. Gosh.

To begin with, business was quiet. The chickens left in a huff and the pig moved out to the broken-down tool shed on the other side of the yard—choosy, presumably, about the company it kept—but the rats didn't seem to mind him at all, which was broad-minded of them. Then one night, as he was lying on his pile of vintage straw looking up through a hole in the roof at one especially bright star he couldn't remember having noticed before, he heard a strange flapping noise, followed by a stifled curse.

It only took him a moment to identify the sound as that made by a man trying to knock on a sack hung over a bit of string. "Come in," he called out. "It's open."

Light filled the shed, coming from a lantern in the hand of a tall figure in dark robes. "Are you the liar?" said a deep voice.

John pulled a face, which was fortunately masked by the shadows. "No," he said. "I'm a legal practitioner and notary public."

The stranger looked at him, and his eyes were a pale green gleam. "Not the liar."

"No."

"Well, you would say that, wouldn't you? Mind if I sit down?"

John shrugged. "Pull up a straw bale and be my guest. Now then, what can I do for you?"

"I need someone to tell lies for me. Convincingly. With style."

"Sorry," John said. "I can't do that. It's against my code of professional ethics."

The stranger studied him for a moment. "That was very good," he said. "If I didn't know any better, I'd have thought you meant it."

"I do. Really. If they catch me distorting evidence or perverting the course of justice, they'll take away my licence and that'll be that. It's just not worth it."

The stranger frowned. "Really?"

"Really and truly."

"You're not a professional liar, then."

"No."

"But that's what you say you are, on your sign outside."

"I was lying."

"Ah. Oh well," the stranger said, and as he stood up to leave he made a soft clinking noise, as of coins jingling together in his pocket. "Sorry to have wasted your time."

"That said," John said smoothly, "what I can do, and in fact do exceptionally well, is present a body of purported facts, which I then invite the opposition to prove to be false, on the understanding that, should they fail to do so, my version of events is deemed to be true by default."

"That's not lying?"

"Of course not. It's a dialectic-based methodology for ascertaining the truth based on adversarial debate, founded on time-honoured rules of evidence and proced-ure and governed by hallowed conventions, such as the presumption of innocence and the burden of proof, the final outcome of which is universally regarded by society as tantamount or equivalent to the truth, even though it usually isn't. Quite different, obviously."

The man nodded slowly. "So what you're saying is, if you tell people a pack of—a load of stuff, and you can get them to believe you, or at least put it in such a way that they can't prove it's all garbage, then it *becomes* the truth." He whistled softly. "Neat trick."

"Indeed. Which is why I can say, hand on heart, that I don't tell lies. Honest as the day is long, me. Especially the day at midwinter at the North Pole. Trust me, I'm a lawyer."

"Mphm. Sounds like the sort of work people would be prepared to pay a lot of money for."

"It has been known, yes."

"You any good at it?"

"The best," John said simply.

"Really. In which case, what are you doing in a dump like this?"

John smiled. "Starting out on my own. Which means," he said, "you have a once-in-a-lifetime opportunity to engage my services before they become too shatteringly expensive. I mean, you could chance it and come back in a week, and who knows? You might be able to afford me, or you might not. Up to you, really. I mean, are you a born gambler?"

"All right," the stranger said. "How much do you charge?"

"For straightforward presentation of true facts? Shilling an hour."

"That's a lot of money."

John's smile spread, like oil on water. "If I charged less, how would you know I was any good?"

The stranger's face was more or less invisible in the shadows, but John was fairly sure, on the balance of probabilities, that he was smiling, too. "Agreed," he said. "I can see now, less than a shilling an hour wouldn't be enough. All right. Consider yourself hired."

A peal of bells rang out in John's heart; at least, he attributed the vague rumbling to joy rather than the interval since he'd last eaten. Accentuate the positive, it's the only way.

"Excellent," he said. "Now, what would you like me to do?"

One of the first things Ms. White had done, once she'd satisfied herself that King Drain liked her enough to do her small favours, was to ask for the loan of a safe.

Dwarves make the best safes anywhere, and the House of Driri Mk7A Warranted Dragonproof is the absolute top of the line. King Drain had fifteen of his best men deliver it to her room, and they ended up having to knock through two walls and a ceiling and lower it on ropes from the gallery above.

"Out of interest," Drain asked, "what've you got that's so valuable?"

She showed it to him: a small, flat thing about a third the size of a roofing slate, glass on top and some material he couldn't identify underneath. "It's a religious artefact," she explained. "Among my people it has deep cultural and spiritual significance."

"Get away."

"No, really. We believe that if someone steals your phone—that's what this is called, a phone—they can steal your entire identity."

Drain handed her the safe key without another word. Later he asked if she wanted a few additional padlocks, but she said no, it was just fine as it was.

The good thing was that the phone worked. With it, she could call Home. Presumably it, too, was attuned to George's doughnut thing. The bad thing was that she only had $1.17 credit left on it, and she'd left her credit card behind in her native reality.

Enough for one call, two if she kept it snappy. The question was; did the amazing opportunity that now confronted her justify blowing her one call?

She agonised over the problem for a long time before the obvious solution occurred to her. She cursed herself for being an idiot, unlocked the safe and made the call.

"I thought I told you," said the voice at the other end of the line, "never to call me on this number. Or any number, ever again."

"Don't be like that," she said sweetly. "Listen. This is business."

Sigh. "Look, I know the IT revolution has changed the way we all work and there are countless things we used to have to go to the office to do that we can now do at home over the phone. Your speciality isn't one of them. Besides, you've been replaced. Now go away."

"Funny man. Listen, how would you like to get rid of some of those cancelled orders you were always telling me about?"

A long silence—ten cents' worth, which in context was practically unbearable. "You're kidding me."

"I don't joke about money. Listen to me. I have a potential buyer."

"You do? What for?"

She smiled. "I have a customer who might just possibly want to buy all those combination bean slicers and mango de-stoners you got stuck with five years ago; you know, the ones you sob hysterically about in your sleep?"

The voice was barely a whisper. "How many of them?"

"How many have you got? No, wait, listen, there's more.

Have you still got that consignment of O-So-E-Z clock-work sock stretchers, the ones the Finns decided at the last minute they didn't want?"

"Oh yes."

"Great, I can place them, I'm sure of it. How about the two hundred thousand pink powder compacts with the picture of George W. Bush on the back?"

Pause. "This is a wind-up, right? Nobody in the whole wide world could possibly—"

"I have a customer for them, ready and waiting." She hesitated. This bit might be awkward. "Oh, and he'll be paying in gold."

"Say again? This is an awful line. It sounded like you just said—"

"Gold," she repeated. "Chemical symbol AU, atomic number 79, density nineteen point three grams per cubic centimetre. Sort of a yellowy colour. Your wife has a rather nice brooch made of it," she added pleasantly, "which I chose for her, for your twentieth anniversary. This stuff my customer's talking about is around 99.999 fine, give or take a smidge."

"He wants to pay in *gold*?"

"Yes. Is that a problem?"

"Um, no. No, definitely not. Look, are you sure about this?"

"Pretty sure."

"Who is this lunatic?"

"Ah," she said, "that would be telling. Of course, if you're not interested, that's fine. You can go on paying warehouse charges for a load of stuff you'll never get rid of, and in due course no doubt your heirs will eventually find a big enough hole in the ground to dump it all in, and that'll be that problem solved. Entirely up to you. I just thought I'd mention it."

"How much?"

She stated a figure, in pounds avoirdupois. He whistled. "Are you *sure*?"

"Look, I haven't got much money left on this phone. Which reminds me; put a hundred bucks' worth of credit on for me, there's a sweetheart. No," she added quickly, "don't argue, just do it, within the next ten minutes, or the whole thing's off. This is a deal-breaker. I mean it."

"Sure," he said mildly. "So what now?"

Relief flooded through her like the first sweet rains of spring. "Soon as you've put the money on my phone, I'll call you back with the details, all right? Oh, and in the meantime, you might give some thought to whether you've got any more hopelessly unsaleable junk littering the place up that you might consider parting with at twenty-five per cent above cost. Ciao, honeybunch."

She cut the call. *You have $0.46 credit remaining.* Well, she'd always been a gambler. It remained to be seen whether this one would pay off.

Six anxious minutes later, her phone went *ting!* and congratulated her on a successful top-up in the sum of one hundred dollars. For a moment or so her heart was like a singing bird; then she put the phone away in the safe, locked it and went to find King Drain.

"Where the hell have you been?" he said, and she noticed a bowl of porridge on the table in front of him, a golden spoon standing in it, upright. "I want a bacon sandwich and I want it now."

She beamed at him. "You think you want a bacon sandwich," she said, "but you're wrong. What you really want is a vast consignment of incredibly valuable imported artefacts at a ridiculously low price. Which is the most amazing coincidence, because I just happen to have one."

He really did have genuinely nice eyes, even when they were practically popping out on stalks. "You what?"

"Genuine authentic artefacts," she said, "from China. You remember China? We were talking about it only the other—"

"Like the Opener of Tins?"

"Better than the Opener of Tins," she said seductively. "Much, much better. I can honestly and sincerely swear that these are items you can't buy in any store. Even back home, where I come from, they're incredibly rare and hard to come by."

The mills of King Drain's mind ground slow but exceeding small. "How much?"

"My, aren't you the sharp one? Does it matter? These things are unique. There's never been anything like them anywhere in the Realms. Once you've got them, your main worry will be how to keep the dragons from swooping in and stealing such a bewildering accumulation of treasure."

"How much?"

She stated a figure in dwarvish pounds, which are just a tad heavier than human ones. The figure was exactly double what she'd just told her friend. King Drain frowned. "A vast consignment, you said."

"Yup."

"How vast, exactly?"

She told him. He did mental arithmetic, a discipline at which dwarves traditionally excel. "Deal," he said. And then, a moment later, "What did I just buy?"

She patted the back of his hand. To do him credit, he barely winced. "Wealth beyond the dreams of avarice and a bright new future for the dwarvish race," she told him. "And at a price you can afford."

"Really?"

"Really and truly. Just trust your aunt Snow White. Who," she added, "will now go and fix you a bacon sandwich."

Drain gazed at her, his eyes filled with longing. "Mustard?"

"Loads of mustard." She smiled at him. "Now be honest," she said. "Does it get any better than this?"

"Just listen to this," Terry Barrington roared. "We acknowledge receipt of your application for a permit to burn charcoal in a designated conservation area, blah blah blah. However, we cannot process your application since it was not accompanied by four duplicate copies duly countersigned and witnessed by a registered notary. We have therefore cancelled your application, should you wish to proceed further you should file Form 38837/C, notice of intention to reapply where a previous application has failed, together with all requisite copies and supplementary documentation, also duly notarised, for crying out loud, what does it all *mean*?" He threw the roll of parchment onto the table and folded his arms. "Well," he said, "I've about had it with those clowns. If you really want a barbecue, you damn well sort it out."

Molly Barrington looked up from the flowers she was arranging. "All right, dear," she said. "Leave it to me. I'll deal with it when I've got five minutes."

Terry laughed. "You reckon? They're *impossible*. How anything ever gets done around here I can't begin to imagine. And to think, we came here to get away from all that kind of thing."

"I'll just pop down to the council offices and have a quiet word with them," Molly said. "I'm sure it can all be straightened out, calmly and reasonably."

Terry scowled at her. "You're saying I'm not calm and reasonable."

"I didn't say that, dear."

"I am beautifully calm," Terry shouted. "I am perfectly fucking reasonable."

"Yes, dear. Now, would you make me a cup of tea? My hands are a bit full."

Another thing. It took for ever to boil a kettle in this dump. Theoretically, the whole tower was one great big solar panel and they ought to have enough power to keep the lights on right across Europe and barely notice. But, as with everything else in this ghastly place, the gap between theory and practice—

Almost out of tea, he noticed. She'd ordered a fresh supply from home, stuff was supposed to get here within forty-eight hours but that was a laugh, and he really didn't want to be cooped up with Molly in a confined space if they ran out of tea. Or, saints and ministers of grace preserve us, gin.

He made himself a coffee and stumped up the many, many flights of stairs to his study. At times like this, he told himself, waiting for the bloody laptop to wake up, it's only updating the blog that keeps me going; the thought of all of them back in the foggy, rain-sodden UK gawping at the gorgeous sunny pictures of the spectacular view from the ramparts and all that guff, wishing they were here, dying slowly and painfully of envy—

Day 17.
Another spectacular sunrise over the distant mountains.
Sometimes I wonder what I've done to deserve
the uniquely special privilege of being here, in this
amazing place.

No, that could do with rephrasing. Start again.

Day 17.
Woke up to another amazingly spectacular sunrise,
seen from the top of our ancient historic watch-tower
overlooking unspoilt virgin forest and a stunning
panoramic view of the nearby snow-capped mountains.
Downstairs, Molly is busy arranging some choice blooms
from our garden, which promises to be especially
spectacular over the coming months

No, sod, already said spectacular once. He changed
the first one to *breathtaking*, which was just as good. He
scrolled through the photos he'd taken that morning, but
they were all a bit blurry and indistinct—bloody perpetual
mist—and wouldn't do at all. OK, then, Plan B. He called
up another gallery of pictures, diligently culled from the
Net, and chose three—one of New Zealand, the other two
a remote corner of Albania—and posted those instead.

This afternoon we plan to stroll down to the nearby
village, where the produce stalls in the marketplace are
piled high with mouth-watering local fruit & veg

That made him laugh out loud. Packet soup and tinned
peaches, more like. In theory, the local yokels were supposed to come round door to door with a wheelbarrow. If
so. they were mighty discreet about it, and quite unnatur-
ally timid about knocking on the door. But you had to
have masses of stuff about food and drink in these blogs,
giving the impression that every day was one long five-star
cordon bleu blowout, and all for less than a kebab and a
Coke back home. Now somewhere he had some old photos
of him and Molly sitting outside a café in St. Paul de Vence,

blurry enough that they could be practically anywhere. A bit of Photoshopping to get rid of any actual lettering on the signs, they'd do perfectly for the blog. He smiled. Maybe it wasn't such a bad life, after all.

The nerve of it, though, bloody town hall bureaucrats telling him he needed a licence for a barbecue in his own backyard. He might just possibly understand if it was a question of aggravating the neighbours; but there weren't any, not as far as the eye could see, which from the top of the tower was a very long way indeed. So, who the hell gave a damn, apart from a bunch of pointy-eared, pointy-nosed paper shufflers with nothing better to do than tear up perfectly good application forms—

I wouldn't stand for it if I were you.

Absolutely. If there's one thing that really ticks me off, it's being pushed around by—

Who said that?

He looked round, but there was nobody else in the room.

He considered those of his electronic devices that were capable of simulated speech, then inspected them, one by one, eliminating them from his enquiries. That just left voices inside his head. Unless you're Joan of Arc or an American evangelist, not a good sign. He made a promise to himself to throttle back a little on the drinkies, and not get so worked up about things.

The mist was starting to clear, and the view through the to-all-intents-and-purposes-non-existent wall was, he had to admit, pretty damn spectacular; the Snentwood, the sinuous curve of the Mouthwash sparkling in the sunlight, the rags of mist softening the peaks of the distant Taupe Mountains. You could learn to put up with a lot for the sake of a view like that. He wondered how you went about learning to paint; and soon he'd slipped into a reverie in which he was celebrating the success of his first one-man show in Bond Street, interspliced with shots of himself with palette and easel; pan out over the landscape, then close in on the same image miraculously transfigured on the canvas. Definitely, he told himself, as his eyelids began to droop, definitely look into that, painting. Can't be difficult, after all, because look at some of the deadheads who make a living at it.

He slept; and as his eyes closed, inside his head another Eye opened, and looked around. It peered through the walls of Terry's skull as easily as he looked through the ad-lib-transparent walls of the tower. It was bemused by much of what it saw; not worried, because it didn't do stress, or fear, or doubt, but curious and not entirely sure it approved, though it was nothing if not, no pun intended, open-minded. This human, for example; judged by appearances, or even by the layer of accumulated garbage littering the surfaces of its mind, it was worthless, no use to itself or anyone else, a fat, old, redundant consumer of resources better applied elsewhere. Kill it, on grounds of tidiness and good taste if for no other reason, and move on.

But the Great Red Eye knew better than that. It had been open and looking about for a very long time; it was wise, patient and long-suffering (three Ages of the World spent enduring chronic conjunctivitis teaches many things, particularly if throughout most of that time One has no knuckles with which to rub), it knew better than to judge anything by superficialities or to discard anything that might be made useful. It knew that even the most unlikely, vain, effete, contemptible little creature might have hidden depths or special talents, all of them grist to the mill, all of them potentially nutritious, like the tiny edible core of an artichoke. It would be simply untrue to say that there could be more to Terry Barrington than met the Eye; but what there was of him was there for it to see, and merited a close inspection.

Filtering out the rubbish, therefore, the Eye looked for qualities, and found persistence, a sort of dogged determination that others, Mrs. Barrington very much included, might be misled into filing under obstinacy; intelligence, too, limited—not the right word; constrained and confined, like a light shone down a tube, and capable of being concentrated to great effect, like the same light through a lens. Imagination, always worth having, though neither necessarily nor exclusively useful to its owner; a latent but strong sense of self-worth, robust enough to override the evidence, flexible enough to find the gaps and the crevices in the facts; an offshoot of that, an invincible sense of entitlement; pure gold, in context.

Give the choice, the Eye would have preferred someone else; an Elvenking, a dwarf-lord, a wizard or one of the Kings of Men; well. It had had plenty of those over the years, and look at it now: a disembodied faculty, marginally extant, bed-and-breakfasting in the minds of lower animals. Perhaps it was time for a different approach. After millions of years trying to bash down the front door, it's only sensible to consider digging up from the sewers.

The Eye fell on the curious object lying on the table in front of the sleeping human. It was unfamiliar. At first the Eye had assumed it was a book, or a slate for writing on, because there were letters, and a picture of some place. Something about the picture caught the Eye; it took it a moment to realise that it didn't recognise the place depicted—but that was impossible; the Eye had seen every corner of the Realms, from the moment when they were first formed out of the fiery catarrh of Iluvendor, through all Three Ages, every tectonic fashion, every whim of geology and afforestation; the Eye had seen and knew it all, every square inch, but this image it did not recognise—in which case either it was fiction, a work of the imagination, or it was a view of somewhere *else* . . .

The Eye studied the image closely, distinguishing every pixel, every photon of every pixel, and pronounced it unfamiliar. No pencil or brush had made the picture. It had been produced by taking light and capturing it some-how, like a fly in amber; incredibly powerful magic, the Eye noted in passing, though it would have to come back to the implications of that later. No; the picture was *true*, not a figment of imagination. It was an accurate representation of a real place, somewhere. Somewhere else.

The Eye blinked.

There had been long passages of time when the Eye had been closed, not daring to show itself. During those dark ages, since it could not sleep it had turned inwards, giving all its infinite energy and power over to contempla-tion of the intangible, the infinite, the very fundamentals of existence and reality. Much it had calculated and proved; much more was extrapolation and mere specu-lation, more likely than not but still not susceptible of proof, and among this material was what the Eye had decided to call Multiverse Theory; the hypothesis that this is only one of an infinite number of alternate real-ities—parallel universes might be a better way of putting it—all occupying one indivisible point on the x, y, z and t axes, but stretching away as far as even the Eye could see in another, equally valid direction, whose existence it could apprehend but never *reach*. The rational part of its persona held that, since none of this could be proved, it could not be considered to be true or real in any meaning-ful sense. The more speculative part held that there were more things in heaven and earth than are dreamt of in any discipline of philosophy, and it would be foolish to leave any possibility out of account when planning long-term strategies. The two halves had argued long and hard over this during the long night, and had come to the conclusion that, since they were never going to see Eye to Eye on the point, it was best not to dwell on it.

But the picture was evidence; genuine hard data. Once, in a place and at a time unknown, light had licked and slithered round these mountains and these forests, before splatting against a screen or getting caught up in a cobweb and ending up here, in the despicable little human's remarkable book. Light can do many things, but it can't lie; no dog ever ate Light's homework. So, if the picture was real, the mountains and the trees were real, and if so, *where were they*?

Not round here, that was for sure. Nowhere in the Realms. In which case, it followed ineluctably that outside or above or below or beyond the Realms lay Somewhere Else. And the only possible way of accounting for that was, yes, you guessed it . . .

Multiverse theory.

The Eye couldn't grin, but it could shine. Told you so, it told itself, I told you but you wouldn't listen, well, that's one in the Eye for you. Yes, all right, the logical aspect of its persona agreed grumpily, but so what? Don't you *see*, demanded the speculative part, and the logical part asked if that was supposed to be funny.

Multiverse theory. There are other worlds, like this one but different, other Realms, filled with other mountains, other oceans, other cities, other millions and millions of people, none of whom have ever encountered the Eye or what it stands for, or been given the opportunity to listen to its message and doctrine. Millions and millions and *millions* of people who, to put it bluntly, didn't know any better.

Fresh meat and pastures new. Yum.

It took the Eye a long time—several milliseconds—to recover from the shock. Then it set about absorbing as much data as it possibly could. It downloaded the human's brain; large parts of it were apparently encrypted, but that shouldn't be a problem. It swarmed through the human's book, which it was able to do even though it lacked fingers to turn pages, hitherto an insuperable problem in the quest for knowledge—I like this book, the Eye decided, I wonder if there are more where this one came from—and found a tantalising portal that appeared to lead somewhere completely unimaginable, except that it was for the time being closed, or *offline*, to use the human's word for it; sorry for any inconvenience, please try again later. The Eye resolved to do just that, and moved on. In a neglected cupboard at the back of human's mind, it came across the sentiment *if thine Eye offend thee, pluck it out*. It did the metaphysical equivalent of cordoning off that area with yellow tape, but decided it wasn't a serious threat at the moment.

Exhaustion; it had done too much. It was horribly frustrating to be so weak, even here, in the greatest of its strongholds. But the Tower could only draw in and retain so much power, and the wretched humans and their strange devices tapped off an infuriatingly high percentage of that, so the Eye had had to come to terms with certain limitations, which it wisely accepted. It closed itself and withdrew from the human's mind, and he woke up.

Bloody bureaucrats, he thought.

He yawned and stretched, found he'd woken up with a headache. Aspirin; had they got any? Probably not. Molly had ordered some, but that was the trouble with having to get every damn thing mail order via the Net, you ran out of something and then God only knew when the replacement supply was going to get there.

This is a horrible place, he thought. We ought to go home.

Now where did that come from, all of a sudden? Never once, in spite of all the buggerations and tribulations, had he considered admitting defeat, giving it best, crawling back to Putney with his tail between his legs. Nor, he resolved, was he going to consider it now; not after he'd posted all that stuff on the blog about being so happy, and having spent so much money. The latter point especially; God only knew what they could expect to get for this place if they sold it again, even with all the improvements— which, he knew only too well, had barely scratched the surface. Not enough to buy anything decent back home, that was for sure. They'd end up in a grotty little rat hole somewhere, with no money. No; he'd made this apple-pie bed for himself and now he had to lie on it. No alternative. Sorry, but there it is.

He looked at the screen of his laptop and swore under his breath. Somehow, in spite of the fortune he'd spent on anti-virus software, it had contrived to pick up something nasty. He flipped through to see what the damage was, but it appeared to be limited to the screensaver. Gone was the view from the top of the Tower on a clear day (amend that slightly; *the* clear day, there'd only been one so far), and in its place a horrible glaring cartoon red eye. He couldn't decide whether it was a still or an animation; he couldn't see it moving, but he was sure it did, when he looked away for a split second. Someone's sense of humour. He did everything he could to get rid of it, but nothing seemed to work. Still; it looked horrible but it didn't seem to be doing any harm. He added *get rid of horrible thing* to his list of things to do, and dismissed it from his mind.

*

"I read the prophecies," Mordak said.

Tinituviel stopped dead, one hand wrist deep in a filing cabinet drawer. "Well done. Bet your finger's sore."

Mordak sat down on a footstool. The Iron Throne was all very well, but the front of the seat chafed the insides of his knees. "They're drivel," he said.

That got him a look, which he ignored. "You can't have read them properly. You did make sure the book was the right way up?"

"Half of them," Mordak said, "are later interpolations, which is obvious, because they're written in New Low Elvish, you can tell by the increased use of the pluperfect subjunctive and the decrease in reliance on enclitic demonstratives. Any fool could see *that*," he added.

Tinituviel pursed her lips. "Arguably," she said. "Though Uviel and Picalillilion, in their landmark paper in the *Elvish Journal of Superior Thought*—"

"And half of the remaining half are about stuff that had already happened when they were written, which to my mind isn't entirely honest. Still, what would I know? I'm only a goblin."

"Yes, you are. Talking of which, are you sure you looked up all the long words? You didn't just skip them?"

"Which leaves," Mordak said, "the other half of a half, which I'm guessing came from a different source. There, I'm prepared to concede, we might be onto something."

"Aha."

"Actually," Mordak said, and no doubt those needle ears picked up the slight change in his tone of voice; you didn't have to explain every damn thing, like you do when you're talking to goblins, which was nice. "Actually, I'm a bit concerned."

"A bit."

"A bit, yes. Which is pretty hot stuff, bearing in mind

that I'm a High Vat goblin, possibly the most dangerous life form you'll ever meet, and traditionally we don't even know the meaning of concern."

"Along with lots of other words."

"Traditionally," Mordak said. "But on this occasion I'm concerned bordering on mildly apprehensive." He paused. "If you feel you need to run away screaming and hide behind something, please do so now. No? Right, here we go. This Nameless One. Bit of a piece of work, isn't he?"

"Mphm."

Mordak refreshed his memory from the notes he'd jotted down on the back of a desiccated troll's ear. "It says in the Prophecies that he is the destroyer of worlds." He paused. "That's not good."

"Quite. It's evil. Presumably you don't have issues with that."

"Yes and no." Mordak scratched his chin with his foreclaw. "On the face of it, yes, destroying worlds is a perfectly legitimate Evil activity, and one which, as Dark Lord, I might feel obligated to go along with."

She was grinning. "I can feel a spurt of New Evil coming along," she said. "Do go on."

"Yes, all right, there's no need to get all letters-to-the-editor at me. I'm just saying. Destroying worlds; is it really in the best interests of evil, in the sense that we've come to understand the word, or is it in fact misguided and downright counterproductive? I feel we need to ask these questions."

"I bet you do."

"For example," Mordak went on, "let's start with a basic and widely accepted definition of evil; the greatest harm to the greatest number. You're all right with that, presumably."

"It'll do, I suppose."

"Fine. So, you've got this world, on which a large number of people are living, let's say for the sake of argument peacefully and in a state of moderate contentment. With me so far?"

"I think I can just about get my head around that, yes."

"And then someone comes along and destroys this world. Blows it up, hits it with a falling star, whatever. All the people die. Evil?"

"Definitively so, I'd have thought."

"Ah," Mordak said eagerly, "but is it? Let's go back to our definition. The greatest harm to the greatest number. A planet is destroyed, millions are snuffed out in the blink of an eye. Do you see where I'm headed?"

She frowned. "Frankly, no."

"In the blink of an eye," he repeated. "No lingering in pain and dread. Most of them won't even know what hit them. No suffering, no agony, it's practically *merciful*. Probably they're better off in the long run."

"You know, maybe you're reaching just a teeny bit there."

"I don't think so," Mordak said robustly. "*Phut* and you're gone, never even knew you were in trouble. Where's the evil content in that? Also, once that world's been snuffed out, it means that there'll be no more people. No more people, no more misery, unhappiness and grief. If we look at it in terms of productivity quotients, taking the malon as our standard unit, a world of six billion people produces, what, eighty billion malons of evil per annum for fifty thousand years, OK? That's twenty-four million billion malons. All right. Destroy that world in one fell swoop. Agreed, that's pretty bad, but twenty-four million billion malons' worth of bad? I don't think so. Ten million billion malons, tops. That's a net loss to the cause of the Great Darkness of fourteen million billion malons. Call that evil? Because I don't."

Shouldn't that be mal*a*?"

"The greatest harm," Mordak went on, "to the greatest *number*. Again, the figures just don't add up. Let's go back to our planet of six billion people. That's six billion at any one time. But they have kids, they die; over the course of, say, three Ages we're looking at ten thousand billion people. Trash the world at a point, say, halfway through the second Age, that's five thousand billion people who'll never have the opportunity to encounter or experience evil. Five thousand billion potential customers, thrown away. Hardly," he added, beaming, "the greatest possible number. So, as far as both halves of the definition are concerned, this joker isn't evil at all. He's a bloody *philanthropist*."

Tinituviel looked at him for a moment with what could almost have been admiration. "And you thought up all that by yourself? That's so sweet."

"Counter-productive," Mordak said firmly, "counter-revolutionary and downright heretical. This Nameless One isn't on our side at all. Therefore, he's the enemy."

"And therefore isn't entitled to your job, agreed." She tucked a stray wisp of hair behind her ear. "I really like this New Evil. It can be anything you want it to be. Which is good," she added, as Mordak glowered at her. "Flexible, adaptable, therefore instantly relevant to the needs of modern society. Or not having your head chopped off, as the case may be."

Mordak shrugged ruefully. "Well, there's that consideration, too. But I genuinely believe I happen to be the right orc for the job. I mean, look at the progress we've made. Giant leaps forward in free healthcare, housing, education, employment—"

She nodded. "Evil jobs for evil workers."

"There wasn't much of that sort of thing going on under

my distinguished predecessor," Mordak pointed out with a certain degree of feeling. "And by the sound of it, he and this Nameless twit are practically interchangeable. I mean, take that other bit in the Prophecies. He will plunge all the Realms into darkness impenetrable." He shook his head sadly. "Oh dear."

"Not keen?"

"I should say not. Look, I've just spent a hell of a lot of time, effort and money trying to improve our image, so that when people hear *goblin* and *Dark Lord* there isn't that instant knee-jerk reaction. Oh, them. The bad guys. The nasty party. I've bust a gut trying to make the dwarves and the humans and, heaven help me, your lot, realise that just because we have our ideological differences, that doesn't mean we can't work together constructively in those areas we can agree on, such as trade, communications, the environment, all that stuff. Then along comes some frothing-at-the-mouth born-again reactionary and turns all the lights out. Result: years of painstaking diplomacy down the toilet in a matter of seconds. That's what some people just don't seem to realise. Evil can no longer afford to regard itself as some sort of monolithic isolationist bloc, it's got to get out there and start a meaningful dialogue with the greater community of species and ideologies. Evil right or wrong just won't cut it any more. I do wish people could see that, it's so blindingly obvious."

"Quite," Tinituviel said, and if she was smirking she had the grace to turn her head away a little. "So that's decided. We don't like the Nameless One and we don't want him in our backyard. Fine. What are you going to do about it?"

"Ah." Mordak frowned. "There I think we have a problem. These Prophecies."

"Hm?"

"Well." He made a vague, resigned gesture. "They're *prophecies*, aren't they? Not warnings, not this is what'll happen if you don't pull your claw out and deal with it. More like, well, statements of fact, really. The Nameless One *will* arise, and so on and so forth."

Tinituviel smiled. "That's not how it works."

Mordak looked up hopefully. "Isn't it?"

"The art of prophecy, lesson one. Feel free to take notes, by the way, because this is proper Elf stuff, and you may find it hard to follow. Prophecy," she went on, "is, as you say, a statement of fact. The following things *will* happen—"

"See? That's what I—"

"*Provided*," she went on firmly, "a certain precisely defined set of circumstances arise. Note the word precisely. The prophecy can only come about if all the requirements are exactly fulfilled. If there's just one thing that isn't exactly right, then the whole deal's off. The prophecy goes into a sort of holding pattern and stays up there hovering until the great wheel of Destiny comes full circle and the circumstances are sort of attracted to it, like iron filings to a magnet. That," she added impressively, "is the wisdom of the Elves, handed down from generation to generation."

"To explain why so many of your prophecies don't actually work?"

"Precisely. Which means," she continued, "if the prophecy says the Great Dawn will come about when an iron frog sits on a blue lily pad in the dead centre of the Lost Lake of Dimmithduin, it's no earthly good if the frog's copper, or the lily pad's mauve, or if an iron frog sits on a blue lily pad eighteen inches to the right of the dead centre of the lake. The prophecy takes one look at it, says *does not compute*, and wanders off and amuses itself for another ten thousand years. Which means," she went on, "that if for some reason a person has a vested interest in a prophecy *not* coming true, it's usually no big deal to make sure it doesn't."

Mordak gazed at her with big, round eyes. "Straight up?"

"Elf's honour. All that stuff," she added, "is not widely known, for obvious reasons. There's a lot of money and kudos in the making-sure-bad-things-don't-happen sector, so it wouldn't do if people realised just how easy it is. But—"

"It can't be terribly difficult, or Elves couldn't do it," Mordak said happily. "Or humans, even. Probably explains why your lot keep winning, come to that. Something must," he added bitterly. "But anyway, what you're saying is, if we can snafu just one condition of the prophecy, this Nameless One can go take a running jump."

"Very good." She clapped her hands together twice. "Now then, I take it you've made a detailed analysis of the conditions set out in the Prophecy. You have, haven't you?"

"Yes, actually." Mordak pulled another shrivelled troll's ear from the top of his boot. "One, a great portal shall open. Two, she who should never have been born will rise up among the chosen people. Three, the Children of Fluor will leave the Golden Land, lit by another sun, and pass through the Gate of Flour and Eggs and occupy the high places and the low places and the Seat of Seeing, and they shall speak to those who are here and yet not here through the Stone of Snordor that rests in Shanad-Dûm. Four, those who dwell in the low places will forsake the old ways and be turned around and will answer the call." He paused. "Have you got any idea what that's all about?"

"Not a clue. Go on."

"And, finally, five, he who made all things will rattle the small stones together in the place of great tidiness and fall the wrong side of a dot, and the hour of some-word-nobody's-ever-managed-to-translate will be at hand. That's it," Mordak added, turning the dried ear over to make sure there was nothing on the other side. "That's all we have to go on. Well?"

"What's the word you can't translate?"

He pointed. She craned her neck and peered. "Looks like *R'xit*," she said.

"What does that mean?"

"No idea." She grinned at him. "Tell you what," she said. "If you can't banjax just one thing out of that lot, I'm a cave-troll."

He relaxed a little. "So you're not too worried, then?"

"Oh, I'm worried all right. I'm worried because the fate of the Realms depends on a goblin doing something right, no matter how easy or trivial. But I reassure myself with the thought that the goblin in question has a wise Elf to advise him, and by and large he's been trained to do as he's told."

"Four thousand eggs," said the grocer's wife, "one ton of flour, four hundredweight of butter, thirty gallons of milk, six hundredweight of lard." She looked up, then down. "What's all this, then?" she asked. "Throwing a party?"

The dwarf shrugged. "Don't ask me," he said. "I just run the errands."

"Not sure we've got four thousand eggs," the grocer's wife said. "Hang on, I'll ask him." She stuck her head round the side of the door to the storeroom. "Customer wants four thousand eggs. We got that many?" A muffled voice spoke. "Sorry," she told the dwarf. "I can do you nine dozen, and that's your lot." She peered at him. "What do you want with that many eggs, anyhow?"

The dwarf sighed. "Forget it," he said. "I'll try somewhere else."

It was turning out to be one of those days for Train son of Tram son of Tori. Here you, his supervisor had grunted at him, go and get some stuff from the store. He'd neglected to mention it wasn't mining supplies he was being sent for, or consumables for the foundry or the toolroom; *food*, of all things; groceries, women's concerns. But you didn't answer back to the foreman when he gave you a direct order, so off Train had trotted, memorising the list as he trudged up the slope and down into the valley to the Human town. No big deal, he wouldn't have thought. A bit of flour, some butter and lard and a few eggs. So why were the Tall Bastards making such a fuss about it?

"*How* many eggs?" demanded the boss at the Mercantile & General.

"Four thousand," Train said, for the tenth time that morning. "Is that a lot, then?"

Whereupon the boss of the mercantile terminated the conversation, on the grounds that he didn't appreciate Train's sense of humour. Odd thing to say, but what can you expect from Snowheads?

"Of course we can supply four thousand eggs," the Duke's steward told him. "Not a problem. And the very finest quality, it goes without saying, His Grace has the finest collection of laying poultry in the Realms."

"Good," Train said.

"Just not," the steward went on, "all at once. Two hundred a week, say, over twenty weeks, we could manage that easily. And you won't find a better egg locally, I can assure you of that."

"Four thousand eggs *now*," Train clarified. "And we don't give a stuff about quality."

The steward gave him a smile you could've sharpened axes on. "The door is right behind you," he said. "Thank you so much for dropping by."

The annoying part of it was, everything else wasn't a problem. A ton of flour? Sure, where do you want it delivered? Butter and lard? We've got stacks of it, see those barrels over there? It was just the stupid eggs. He scowled, and kicked a small stone down the dusty street. Not his fault. If there weren't any eggs, there weren't any eggs; nobody could hold him responsible for that. He could hear the foreman's voice already. You're useless, you are. Can't you do just one simple thing?

"Excuse me."

He looked up and saw a human; at least he assumed it was, because of the ridiculously excessive height, bloody show-offs, but he couldn't tell for sure. He was all wrapped up in a swirly dark cloak and his face was overshadowed by his hood. Stupid, Train said to himself. Bet he keeps bumping into things all the time.

"You talking to me?"

"Yes," the human said. "Look, please don't take this the wrong way, and if you aren't I really don't mean anything by it, but you look to me like a dwarf who could do with some eggs."

Train glared at him. The taller they are, the easier it is to reach their kneecaps. "You being funny?"

"I don't think so. Only, it just so happens I have a huge consignment of eggs I need to get rid of in a hurry, before they go off."

"Go off."

"Yes. They do that, in this weather."

"Have you tried penning them in?"

"I'm so sorry, I put that rather clumsily. Before they go bad. Spoil. In the heat."

Well, Train thought. It's possible he could have over-heard, when he was talking to the stupid grocer. He hadn't exactly kept his voice down, after all. "Huge consignment?"

"That's right, yes. About four thousand. Customer ordered them, then cancelled at the last moment. If I turn round and go home again, by the time I get there, they won't be any good for anything, barring a large political rally."

"Four thousand."

"Give or take one or two. Of course, I can do you a very good price.

"Chicken eggs? Not ants or herring roe or anything?"

"Chicken eggs. Look, do you want them or not? Only I'm in a bit of a hurry, for obvious reasons."

Dwarves are by inclination and upbringing cautious businessmen, solid plodders rather than quicksilver entrepreneurs. Sometimes, though, you just have to go for it. "Done," Train said. Then he remembered something he should've asked earlier. "How much?"

"Shilling a thousand?"

The foreman had apportioned twelve shillings for eggs. "Go on, then," Train said. "If you can't help a fellow creature out of a jam now and then, what sort of a world are we living in? Even a Tall Bastard," he added magnanimously.

"Jolly good," the stranger said. "Is that your cart over there?"

The stranger may have come across as a big vague and not-all-there, appearance-wise, but he was clearly enormously strong. It took him no time at all to load the egg boxes onto Train's cart; every single crate neatly stacked, and tied down with rope so they wouldn't shift about in transit. The coins didn't jingle when Train dropped them into the stranger's gloved hand, which was a bit odd.

"Thanks," the stranger said. "Pleasure doing business with you." Then he turned away, and he must've walked very fast and gone into a building or behind a tree or something, because when Train looked for him to point out that he'd only given him three shillings by mistake, not four, he was nowhere to be seen. Ah well, his loss.

The foreman was—well, not pleased exactly, because nothing pleased him apart from shouting and terminating contracts of employment, but he wasn't angry when Train got back to the Mountain and confirmed that, no, he hadn't forgotten anything. Needless to say, the foreman went over everything, trying to find fault; but the best he could do in that line was draw attention to the eggs. "Where'd you get them from?" he wanted to know.

"Some tall git. Why?"

The foreman was grinning. The seller must've had way too much time on his hands, he said, because he'd gone to all the trouble of drawing little numbers on every single egg, along with a tiny picture of a lion.

BOOK THREE

All Orc and No Prey

"**A**re you sure," Tinituviel said, "that this is a good idea?"

The goblin army, forty thousand strong, was camped out on the plain. Ten thousand black tents stood in ruler-straight rows like a field of nightmare cabbages, while from a thousand campfires thin plumes of smoke rose up into the eerily still air, and a thousand cauldrons gave off the thick, stifling aroma of goblin military cuisine; troll pie, dissident tikka masala and sweet and sour orc.

"It's got to be done," Mordak said firmly, as he nibbled listlessly at a spare rib. "Condition three, the Children of Fluor will leave the Golden Land and pass through the Gate of Flour and Eggs and occupy the high places and the low places and the Seat of Seeing, right? You reckon these new humans are the Children of Fluor. So, they've got to go."

"Hm. Picking a fight with people you know nothing about, armed with impressive high-technology weapons—"

"There's forty thousand of us and a handful of them," Mordak said grimly. "First we ask them nicely, piss off or we do you. Hopefully, that'll be that. Otherwise—" He shrugged. "It's OK," he said. "We're used to being slaughtered like sheep, we take it on the chin and move on. Today is a good day to die, and all that crap. It'll be fine."

Contempt and respect don't usually work and play nicely together, but they were strangely blended in the look she gave him. "This is just so goblin," she said. "Still, far be it from me to interfere with deeply rooted cultural mores."

"Fine. So what would you do?"

"Diplomacy," she said firmly. "Backed up by dumping a few dead goats in their water supply. But, no, if your heart is set on playing soldiers, you go right ahead."

"It's our way," Mordak said simply. "We believe that warriors who die gloriously in battle, sword in hand, striking a blow for Goblinkind against the common enemy are eventually, after twelve Cycles of the Wheel, reborn as termites."

"*Termites?* That's so—"

"You don't want to know what goblins who don't die in battle get reborn as. Suffice to say, the lads are up for it, motivated, ready for a crack at Johnny Human. Of course the overwhelming odds in our favour helps a bit."

Tinituviel wasn't listening. "Who's that?" she said.

Climbing slowly down the winding track that led down the side of the mountain were two tiny figures. As they drew closer, Mordak could make out a white flag. "Told you," he said, trying not to let the relief show. "They've come to surrender."

"Don't bank on it," Tinituviel said. "Could be they're going to give you one last chance to go home, before they charge."

They proved to be humans. One was a little man in a brown coat and a curious flat-topped cap. He looked to be very old, though he hobbled along surprisingly quickly. The other was hardly more than a boy, very tall and impossibly skinny. He was carrying the white flag and eating a large slice of pizza.

"Excuse me," the old man said, "sir, miss. Would you happen to know where I can find King Mordak?"

"That's me. Who are you?"

"Herald, sir. On behalf of the ladies and gents in the new estates, back up over the hill." He studied the goblin camp for a moment, then nodded approvingly. "Fine army you got there, sir, very fine indeed. Reminds me of when I was in the service, forty years in the Supply Corps, happy days. Oh, this is my nephew Art. Say hello to His Majesty, Art."

The boy nodded and carried on chewing.

"Herald," Mordak reminded him.

"'Scuse me, sir? Oh yes. Art and me, we're here on behalf of the, um, newly arrived community. Couldn't help noticing, sir, not meaning to be nosy. All these soldiers."

Mordak nodded grimly. "Tell your people," he said, "they've got twenty-four hours to go back where they came from. Otherwise—"

He paused, assuming clarification was unnecessary. But the old man just blinked at him. "Otherwise, sir?"

"We kill the lot of them. Sorry," Mordak added, "but there it is. Go or die. Their choice."

That seemed to make the old man very sad. He turned and whispered something to the boy, who nodded and ate a cheese sandwich. "With respect, sir," the old man said, "and Art and me, we can see absolutely where you're coming from, strong arguments on both sides, not in any way wanting to imply there's anything wrong with your position, nothing like that. But you can't do that, sir. Sorry."

The bristles on the back of Mordak's neck were chafing against the iron bands of his gorget. They did that sometimes, though usually only when he was nervous about something. "You know what," he said. "I rather think I can."

"Sorry, sir," the old man repeated. "But I don't think we can let you. Art and me, that is. More than our job's worth, if you see what I mean."

"You're going to stop us? You and the bottomless pit over there?"

The old man frowned and the boy glared at Mordak as he unwrapped a fruit scone. "Yes, sir," the old man said. "And please, don't say things like that where the boy can hear you, he's sensitive, gets upset easily. Brings on his allergy. So if you wouldn't mind—"

"Let's get this absolutely straight," Mordak said. "You two are going to stop us."

"Oh, I do hope not, sir. Greatest respect for you personally, sir, all these splendid reforms you've been doing lately, crying shame if all that was to come to an end before you'd had a chance to carry it through. May I just say, sir, we're both great fans of yours, Art and me, Art especially, aren't you, son? We really admire your guts and vision and yes-we-can attitude."

"But you're going to stop me. You and him."

"Yes, sir. If we got to."

Mordak looked at him, and then at the boy, who was nibbling the chocolate off a mini Swiss roll. "Don't go away," he said. "I'll be right back."

Tinituviel was sitting on a rock, picking the petals off a rare moorland orchid. "Well?"

Mordak lowered his voice. "Those two."

"What about them?"

"I don't know. They seem harmless enough."

"There you are, then."

"Yes, but I don't like it. If you were a small, vulnerable

settlement and you happened to notice a vast horde of goblins bearing down on you, are they what you'd choose to hold the line against the darkness?"

She frowned. "Probably not, no. But bear in mind, this is humans we're talking about."

"You're the one who keeps banging on about how well armed they are."

"I suspect they may be trying to lull you into a true sense of security."

"I don't know," Mordak repeated. "I have a really bad feeling."

"Then don't eat so many candied toenails."

He shrugged and tramped back up the hill. "Twenty-three and three-quarter hours now," he said. "I suggest you tell your people to start packing."

The old man sighed. "Maybe if you and the young lady could spare a few minutes," he said sadly. "There's something that maybe you ought to see."

Those damn bristles again. He could hear them scratching his armour. "What?"

"Much simpler to show you than try and explain. Come on, sir, it's only a few yards up the hill."

The old man did look very old indeed, but Mordak found he had to trot to keep up with him, which was no fun with such a steep gradient, while Tinituviel gave up trying and trudged slowly along the path he'd gouged through the heather.

"Yes, sir, forty years in the military, time of my life, until I decided it was time to try my luck on Civvy Street. So me and the boy, we set up our own private security agency, and, I have to say, we been going great guns ever since, no pun intended. Great guns."

"What's a—?"

Eventually they reached a small plateau, where Mordak

saw a row of steel plates sitting on wooden stands, like easels. The plates were about two feet square and half an inch thick. "Just for demonstration purposes, you understand," the old man called back over his shoulder. "Now then, Art, not so fast. Got to tell the gentleman and lady what they're looking at first."

The boy was sitting down on a low stool, eating a ham and cheese baguette. In front of him was a sort of tripod arrangement, on which sat a weird looking thing: a rectangular box fitted to the back of a thick-ribbed tube, with a sort of spout thing sticking out of the end. Hanging from a small opening in the side of the metal rectangle was a canvas belt, into which were stuck a lot of tiny brass bottles, each one with a long copper stopper or bung, pointy as an Elf's ear.

"Wouldn't stand there if I was you, sir, miss. Come over here by me, out of the way."

Mordak did as he was told. "What is that thing?"

"That, sir? That's a Vickers machine gun. Effective range two thousand yards, cyclic rate five hundred rounds a minute. You don't see 'em about much these days, but this one's quite a nice one, all matching numbers and still got most of the original paintwork. All right, Art, let 'er rip."

The boy stuck the baguette between his teeth like a pirate's cutlass, rested his hands on two spade-type grips and squeezed something. There was the most horrible noise, like someone banging very fast on an unsupported sheet of heavy tin with a sledgehammer. Empty tiny bottles flew out of one side of the rectangular box and formed a little pyramid. The racket went on for about fifteen seconds, which was a very long time, in context. Then it stopped. The boy let go of the handles, reclaimed his baguette and carried on eating.

When Mordak had recovered from the shock he glanced quickly round. Tinituviel was on her knees, her hands clamped over her ears; super-sensitive hearing isn't always an unmixed blessing. He stared at the old man, who was flicking dust off the ribbed tube with a bit of yellow duster. "What the hell was all that about?"

The old man smiled. "Come and have a look," he said.

The steel plates were a mess. If they'd been oak planks, you'd have diagnosed a century of intensive woodworm. Not so long ago, they'd been pristine.

It took Mordak a moment or so to get his voice working. "What happened?"

The old man's grin was faintly condescending. "Bit technical, sir. Just think of it as being hit by a hundred and fifty invisible arrows shot from a bow so big not even a troll could lift it. Doesn't really bear thinking about, sir, does it?"

Mordak had to strain to hear him. "That thing did all this?"

The old man nodded. "Now," he went on, "from here to where your army is, sir, I make that about one thousand seven hundred yards. Of course, you could order all your brave goblins to charge up this hill, entirely within your rights there, you being the king and all, and I wouldn't doubt for a second they'd do it, a fine, well-disciplined army like that, a real credit to you, sir, if I may say so. Only—" He paused, just for a moment. "Don't suppose many of 'em would actually get here, if you follow me, sir. About six or seven maybe, possibly a dozen. And that'd be a shame, sir, if you don't mind me saying so. A real shame."

Mordak licked his lips, which were strangely dry. "I don't suppose you'd consider—"

"Sorry, sir, not for sale. Normally I'd go a bit out of my

way to oblige a fine gentleman like yourself, especially with all the good things you've been doing lately, the peace process and all, but the thing of it is, sir, it's not actually mine to sell. On loan, properly speaking. Young Art'd have my hide just for considering it."

Mordak nodded slowly. "Who did you say you work for?"

"Actually, sir, I didn't. Not allowed to, see." He tapped the side of his nose with a gnarled finger. "Client confidentiality, sir. Very important in our line of business. If you haven't got the customer's trust, what I always say is, what have you got?"

"A large sum of money?"

A look of genuine compassion glowed from behind the old man's finger-thick spectacle lenses. "If only it was that simple, sir. But it isn't, so there you go. Now then, sir, if you wouldn't take exception to a word of well-meant advice from an old hand, one soldier to another, like, if I was you I'd get my men back where they belong, sir. Only it can be dead chilly in these mountains this time of year. Camping out, they could catch their death."

The boy was still sitting behind the terrible machine, eating digestive biscuits. Mordak hadn't noticed him move, but the spout of the machine had shifted slightly and was now directly in line with Mordak's head. "Eats a lot, doesn't he?"

"About the same for a normal boy his age, sir. Growing lad, got to keep his strength up." The old man frowned, just a little. "I really do think you ought to be heading back home now, sir. It's getting late."

"It's not, it's—"

"Later than you think, sir," the old man said gravely. "Take care, now."

Being careful to maintain eye contact, Mordak backed away until he felt something soft under his heel and heard a loud squeak. "Mind where you're going," Tinituviel said. "That's my toe."

"Sorry. We're going now."

"Did you see what that ghastly thing did to all those—?"

"Yes. Wave goodbye to the nice gentlemen."

"What are you—?"

"That's an order."

The old man waved back ever so nicely, and even the boy waggled his chunk of apple pie at them before swallowing it whole. "Who the hell were they?" she whispered in his ear as they edged backward slowly down the hillside.

"No idea," Mordak said.

"I told you, didn't I? I said, I wouldn't be the least surprised if they had really powerful, advanced weapons."

"Yes, you did."

"And I was right."

"Yes, you were."

She looked round. A stray beam of sunlight flashed off the cylindrical part of the horrible machine. She shivered. "You know what," she said. "I really wish I wasn't."

A small, squat door opened in the lower panel of the left-hand Great Gate of Snordor. A goblin guard peered out and scowled at the smiling human standing in front of him. "Was that you making that godawful racket?" he asked.

The human nodded. "I knocked. Sorry, was that wrong?"

"What do you want?"

"To give you a present."

The guard made an anatomically impractical suggestion designed to convey scepticism. "No," the human said, "straight up. This is your lucky day."

There was something so honest and open and trustworthy about the human's broad, fat face that the goblin checked himself in the act of slamming the door. "Don't give me that."

"Not that." The man's smile broadened, and from the sleeve of his coarse woollen robe he took a shiny gold tube. "This. For you. Because it's your lucky day."

"What are you on about?"

The man's beam was almost bright enough to fry an egg. "Congratulations," he said. "You have been chosen as our lucky winner in this week's Open-the-Gate competition."

"How's that work, then?"

"Simple. We knock on a door, and the first goblin to open it receives this splendid prize, to keep, absolutely free."

The goblin peered at the tube. "Is that real gold?"

"Twenty-four-carat."

"Stone me." He reached out his paw, hesitated, then lunged impulsively and snatched the tube from the human's hand. "All right, then, what is it?"

"It's called a writ," the human said. "What you do with it is, you take it to a person in authority, such as the guard commander or the field marshal of the goblin host, or better still King Mordak himself, and he opens it and sees what's inside, and then he gives you a fabulous reward."

"And I also get to keep the tube?"

"For the rest of your life, probably." The human took a couple of steps back. "Have a nice day, now. Bye."

Neatly done, John the Lawyer congratulated himself, as he hurried down the narrow track toward the eaves of the forest, and it's good to see you're learning from your mistakes. That said, goblins were an order of magnitude more gullible than dwarves. Even so.

He couldn't wait to tell the client. He was looking forward *so much* to seeing the look on his face, or any look, come to that, assuming the client actually had a face to have looks on. Guess what, he'd tell him, I've made legal history—

"Have you? How splendid."

Where he came from, John could never figure out, though he spent several sleepless nights trying. He was just there, so close that John had great difficulty stopping himself from cannoning into him. Still the same swirly black cloak and hood. Probably a uniform, or the customary habit of some religious order.

"Sorry," John said. "Was I thinking aloud?"

"You must've been," the client said. "Either that or I can read your mind, which isn't very likely, is it? So presumably you were talking to yourself. Which is perfectly all right. Most people do, actually, though not many of them admit it."

John took a deep breath. The air seemed unusually thin, probably because of the altitude. "I'm so glad I bumped into you," he said.

"But you didn't. You stopped yourself just in time. Rather cleverly, I thought."

"Happened to meet you quite by chance," John amended. "We're making progress. The game's afoot."

"Hopscotch?"

"Matters," John translated, "are going forward. I've just served a writ on the goblins."

"I saw," said the client, sitting down on a boulder. His back was very straight and he folded his hands neatly in his lap. "That was extremely brave of you."

"Oh, you just need to know how to handle them. Which reminds me. You did say expense was no object?"

Not a quiver. "Yes."

John closed his eyes and took a run at it. "Fine, because I owe the dwarves for a solid gold document tube, and I was wondering if it'd be possible to have a bit of money on, well, you know—" His voice had dwindled to a whisper. "Account?"

"Certainly. How much would you like?"

How deep is the ocean, how high is the sky? To keep his heart from exploding, John rephrased that to *how much do you need?* It was still an amazing phrase to have echoing around inside his head, and he looked forward to replaying it on an endless loop every morning and evening for the rest of his life. "Um, fifty florins?"

"Make that a hundred," the client said, and from some hidden pocket in his robe he produced a bulging leather sack the size of a prize cooking apple. Which was odd, because it weighed ever so much, so it should've dragged down the client's robe on one side, but it hadn't. "Don't bother about a receipt," the client added. "I trust you."

"What? Oh, right. Thank you." John's knees had gone all weak. He looked for a rock to sit on, but there wasn't one, so he subsided into a scruffy heap on the bare ground.

"You were saying," said the client. "About making legal history."

"Was I? Yes, of course I was. Sorry, I got side-tracked." Another deep breath. Was he really as high up as all that? "I served a writ on King Mordak and the goblins."

"You already told me that."

"A writ," John continued, "for vacant possession of Snangorodrim, the Caverns of the Aubergine Mountains, the Dark Fortress of Gruin and the Mines of Snoria. It gives him twenty-eight days to clear out, failing which we immediately institute legal proceedings against them for forfeiture of premises, damages and costs. So? What do you think?"

"It sounds like you've worked really hard and been both resourceful and imaginative," the client said. "Purely out of interest, though, what are you basing this claim on?

Those places have been goblin territory for thousands of years."

"Ah." John beamed happily. "My point exactly." He fumbled in his pocket for a scrap of parchment and a stub of charcoal. "You'll recall that in the beginning, the High Ones created the heavens and the earth, and sundered the Realms from the Surrounding Sea."

"I've heard it said, yes."

"Fine. And on the eighth day they assigned the heavens and the Blessed Land to the Not Quite So High Ones, the woods and groves of Luviendor to the Elves, the caverns of Groth to the dwarves, the plains and meadows of Nithruil to the Children of Men, and the Dark Places to the goblins. With me so far?"

"You've explained it all beautifully, if I may say so."

"Thank you. Now then. The Dark Places include, among other locations, Snangorodrim, the Caverns of the Aubergine Mountains, the Dark Realm of Gruin and the Mines of Snoria. We're not disputing that."

"Aren't we? Ah well. Jolly good."

John shook his head. "I spent two days in the archives of the Woodland King, and I managed to find the original charters." He grinned. "Wonderful people, the Elves, they never throw anything away. They just refuse point-blank to tell you where it is. Anyway, I went over the charters with a fine-tooth comb, and they made pretty interesting reading, I can tell you. For one thing—"

"Why a comb?"

"What?"

"I'd have thought a magnifying glass would have been more useful. Still, I'm not going to try and teach you your job, which you're clearly very good at indeed. Please go on."

"Very interesting reading," John went on, though his

head was starting to swim a bit. "Because, and this is the key point here; no doubt you'll recall that at the end of the First Age, Thungor was cast down and the Isle of Innocence sank for ever under the sea. Then, halfway through the Second Age, the Iaressë grew wroth at the wickedness of Men, cut off the Golden Realm behind a crystal barrier and split the Inner Realm with a great earthquake, which raised the Taupe Mountains, created the Great Chasm and buried the entrance to Gol Dinûr under millions of tons of rock. And then, about a quarter of the way into the Third Age, the Venar overthrew the Iaressë and imprisoned them on a rocky island which they raised from the seabed, which in turn led to a massive tidal wave that swept away the Silver Cities of the Coast and turned Pondor into what we now know as the Middle Sea. Agreed?"

The client shrugged. "Absolutely."

"In other words," John said gleefully, "since the date of the original charter, the Realms have on three occasions been subject to intense seismic activity leading to geological movement and accelerated tectonic shift. Which, in layman's terms, means that pretty much everything is now at least fifty miles to the left of where it used to be. I intend to argue that, in accordance with the fundamental tenets of the law of real property, what the goblins were granted in the charter was the *original locations*, not the places where stuff that happened to be at those locations has now ended up. So—" He was sketching furiously on his scrap of parchment. "If we move Snangorodrim, the Caverns of the Aubergine Mountains, the Dark Realm of Gruin and the Mines of Snoria fifty-odd miles sideways, you'll find they're now out on the inner perimeter of the Great Salt Desert, which nobody wants and which has no development value whatsoever, leaving four great big chunks of prime real estate just sat there, not belonging to anybody."

"But full of goblins."

"*Unlawfully* full of goblins," John corrected him, "because as soon as I realised all this, I shot over to the Land Registry and filed vacant land claims on all four locations in the name of JTL Holdings Inc.—that's us— and since more than twenty-four hours have passed and no counterclaim had been received, all that beautiful property now belongs to us."

"But is full of goblins."

"Well, yes. Hence the writ, telling them to clear on out of it or else."

The client nodded. "Or else what?"

"We have them thrown out. Send the bailiffs in, pre- sumably, I don't know, that's an enforcement issue. The point is, we now have legal title. That's what you wanted, isn't it?"

The client thought for a moment. "Yes," he said, "I sup- pose it is. Actual vacant possession would have been nice, but like you say, that's an enforcement issue, and we have other people for that. So, yes, legal title is a substantial step forward. You've done extremely well, I'm very pleased. You must allow me to pay you considerably more than we originally agreed. No, I insist."

"Oh." John waved his arms helplessly. "Go on, then."

"Splendid." From another pocket the client produced another fat bag of coins, this time the size of a sheep's head. It nearly pulled John's arms out of their sockets when he took hold of it. "Now then," the client went on, "I'd like you to do the same for the Elves, the dwarves and the Children of Men."

John looked at him. "Excuse me?"

"I want their land," the client said. "All of it. With them

gone if possible, but if you can't manage that, then just the legal title. Let's see, what's today, Thursday. Would next Monday be possible, do you think?"

"*All* of it?"

"Yes, please." The client stood up. "You really have done outstandingly well," he said. "I wouldn't hesitate to recommend you to any of my friends or acquaintances. Goodbye."

"But where will they go? All the Elves and dwarves and—"

Big floaty shrug. "That's hardly our problem, is it? Remember, expense no object. Ciao for now."

There is nothing like a dwarf, Ms. White told herself, nothing in the world. Where else but the Dwarvenhold could you place an order for a twenty-foot-diameter wrought-iron doughnut pan in the morning, and be heating fat in it the same afternoon? And what a pan. Not just a stunningly efficient, irreproachably ergonomic kitchen utensil but a thing of beauty, sinuously contoured and perfectly balanced, its rim chased with gold-inlaid runes, its ten-foot handle defiantly arched like a springing leopard. Not just an object, a mere thing; but to the dwarves, things are never mere. Dwarves paint no paintings, compose no operas or symphonies, write no sonnets or Great Dwarven Novels, but into everything they make they pour the very essence of their being, their hearts and souls. They don't go much on fancy, useless decoration—floral borders, embossed panels of vine leaves, birds and grazing deer; that sort of thing they dismiss as Elvish side salad. Instead, without sacrificing an iota of utility and function, they put beauty in every line and curve, every proportion and ratio, everything that, taken together, makes up a shape, a symmetry, a design.

It took fifteen strong dwarves to lift it, and twelve tons of charcoal to make a fire hot enough to melt the lard.

"What's its name?" she asked, as they hauled it into position.

"You what?"

"Oh, come on. Something as big and beautiful as that's got to have a name."

Pause. "All right, if you say so. We name this pan Kharez-Zhâraf."

Kharez-Zhâraf. The echo of the words rolled away like distant thunder, mysterious and grand. She smiled. "That's a wonderful name," she said. "What does it mean?"

"Large Pan."

"I think I'll call it Peter," she said.

So, into Peter went all the flour, the beaten-up eggs, the milk and the butter, and shortly afterwards a crane, hastily shipped in from the mine head, winched a huge, glistening brown O out of the roiling fat. A specially adapted winch raised it seven levels to the Great Inner Hall, where the masons had just finished shoring up a wall for it to stand against. There was an awkward moment when a rope broke and the enormous object tottered and threatened to fall, but quick thinking on the part of the gangmasters saved the day; a volunteer jumped down from the boom of the crane, drove a handspike into the pastry and made a chain fast to it, and then it was every hand to the ropes, to haul it back upright while the fixing brackets were screwed in. And when it was all done, King Drain took a step back, scratched the back of his neck and said, "What in God's name is that all in aid of?"

"Ah," Ms. White said.

"Ah what?"

"Just ah. For now."

"Suit yourself. So, how's that going to help you get all that stuff we were talking about?"

"Ah."

"You know what? You're starting to get on my nerves."

She blew him a kiss; he shuddered and stomped away, leaving her alone in the vast echoing chamber with the giant doughnut. Splendid. She looked round to make sure all the workmen had gone, then took her LoganBerry from the pocket of her apron, hit the appropriate key and waited. Three rings. Then, "Hello?"

"White here. All right, everything's ready this end. In your own time."

"What about the money?"

"When I've had a chance to look at the stuff."

"Oh, for crying out loud. All right. Stand back."

The line went dead. She hopped and skipped back a couple of paces, and just as well. The towering stack of crates that materialised out of nowhere would've been right on top of her if she hadn't moved.

She stared at it for a moment, then noticed an envelope sellotaped to a front-row crate.

You said that if I had any other stuff, to send it through. Same terms. Prompt payment will oblige. How did you say this thing works, exactly?

She hadn't said, naturally. That technology wasn't hers to license, and she had an idea that anyone who tried to double-cross smiling, harmless looking George would quickly find themselves in a depth and diversity of trouble beyond the capacity of the human brain to imagine. Ms. White's motto had always been a simple one: don't be *too* greedy. It had served her well over the years and she respected it.

She chose a crate at random and peered at the label, but it was in Chinese, which she could speak after a fashion but not read. So she looked round and found a crowbar left behind by the construction crew, hauled the crate down off the stack, and prised open the lid.

Five hundred sets of wine bottle stoppers in the shape of letters of the alphabet. Cool. The next crate held a thousand leather-look cradles for carrying a bottle of wine suspended from the crossbar of a bicycle. Perfect. Eighteen thousand combination beard combs/bottle openers. Pure gold. Five hundred mahogany iPhone covers, sourced from sustainable forests. Well, the last bit would be wasted on Drain and his lot, but never mind. Some fool would buy them. Some fool always does.

She lined up an assortment of the stuff on the lid of a crate and gazed at it for a while. The dwarves—bless them—had never seen anything like this. Designed by cynics for sale to morons, stamped out by machines and shipped by the ton; the total antithesis of everything the dwarves stood for, and therefore as irresistible as blue jeans and rock music in Soviet Russia. The original plan had been to flog this garbage to the simple-minded Sons of Men in the surrounding villages, but now that she saw it with her own eyes, she knew with total certainty that the principal consumers would be the domestic market. Ugly, useless, thrown together any old fashion and built-in obsolescence. How could any dwarf possibly resist?

She tiptoed out of the chamber, as though afraid she'd wake up the sleeping treasure, and went in search of the king. She knew exactly where to find him. Behind the Royal Bedchamber, connected to it by a narrow passage that even a dwarf had to stoop to get through, was a tiny little cell where Drain kept his tools. Not the ancient and glorious Tools of Office, which were on display in the Royal Treasury under round-the-clock armed guard, but the ones he actually used, on the rare occasions when he managed to sneak off for ten minutes to tinker with something.

He looked up as she squeezed through the doorway. "Now what?"

"I thought you might like to come and see."

Drain was making a watch. On the bench in front of him lay dozens of tiny brass cogs, wheels, ratchets, springs and pinions; he was filing the teeth of a gearwheel no bigger than a fingernail, by eye. Dwarvish watches are the best in the multiverse but there are very few of them. Precisely seven are made every two years, because by ancient custom only the dwarf-lords themselves are permitted to make them. Meanwhile, three levels down in a wooden crate, she had five hundred white plastic combination cufflink-tidy-digital-alarm-clocks.

"See what?"

Talking of seeing; the teeth of the gearwheel he was filing were minute—if she'd had a Vernier calliper handy and measured them, she'd have found they were forty thousandths of an inch long, and all precisely identical in length, thickness, rake and pitch—but he wasn't using spectacles or a magnifying glass or a jeweller's loupe, for the same reason she didn't walk with a Zimmer frame. No need.

"The stuff, of course. It's all here."

"What, already? All of it?"

She nodded. "Come on," she said. "It'll blow your socks off."

In her cell in the dungeons of the Black Castle, the one and only female goblin sat on the stone shelf that served as a bed and stared at the wall. She was bored.

Having no frame of reference, she assumed that this was normal and as it should be. She didn't like being bored, but you can't argue with normality and the way things are.

Can you? She didn't know, because nobody had bothered to tell her.

Nobody had bothered to tell her *anything*, which was also normal—presumably—and which implied that it was her job to find out anything she needed to know, assuming she needed to know anything, which was a fairly big assumption. She extended her left paw—such pretty, pretty claws—and counted off the things she did know; of which there were six, one per claw, which she assumed was no coincidence:

Every now and again, not at regular intervals because she'd counted, the door opened and a funny little creature came in with a wooden bowl of food. She always ate the food and sometimes she ate the creature, which she knew instinctively was an inferior variant of herself. Nobody seemed to mind, so she assumed that that was normal, too. The food tasted marginally nicer than the creatures, but there wasn't enough in it to make any odds That was the first thing.

At rather longer intervals, again irregular, two creatures of the food-bringing type came and stared at her through the grille in the door. They did so either because they liked looking at her (she could understand the concept of getting pleasure from looking at something, ever since she'd made herself a mirror) or because they were watching her to see how she was getting on; figuring out the things she had to figure out for herself, presumably, which in turn implied that at some stage they'd be satisfied with her progress, and then something else would happen, possibly involving going out through the door into the World. On balance, she hoped this would be the case, since the World might prove to be marginally less boring. That was the second thing.

She knew that she existed and was alive. She knew about all that because the food-bringing creatures she'd eaten were no longer alive and didn't exist any more.

Which raised an interesting point. They were, she'd intuited, related to her in some way, but they were very much smaller and weaker than she was, so there was no way of knowing whether the not-existing state of affairs would someday apply to her or not. Anyway, that was the third thing.

She knew that she was bigger, stronger, faster and smarter than the food-bringing creatures, because she ate them, rather than the other way around. However, dozens if not hundreds of similar creatures scuttled backwards and forwards up and down the corridor all day, as against being confined in this boring little cell. It was logical to assume that the better you were, the more privileges you got. Therefore it stood to reason that being bigger, stronger, faster and smarter didn't make you better; the exact opposite, in fact. That was the fourth thing, to which she appended a query; am I being kept in here because I'm *bad*, or simply because this is where I belong, in the great scheme of things? Would quite like to know the answer to that one.

She knew that she was different from the food-bringing creatures in respects other than size, strength, speed and intelligence, because there were bits of her that didn't seem to correspond with the equivalent bits of the food-bringing creatures she'd dissected. That raised the issue of whether these differences also (further or in the alternative) consti-tuted badness, resulting in confinement. Would *really* like to know the answer to that. Anyhow, so much for known thing number five.

The sixth thing she knew was that the Others were able to communicate with each other using a system mostly based on sounds, though supplemented with movements of the head, paws and body. She was gradually figuring this out, though her progress was frustratingly slow, because she heard so little that she could learn from. She knew *no, stop, help, oh shit that hurts* and *aargh,* and had a pretty good idea what they were designed to communicate, but that was about it so far. Query: was this communication skill one of the things she was supposed to be figuring out for herself, and was her eventual release from confinement and boredom conditional on it? All things being equal, it seemed likely that it was, but so far she'd resisted the temptation to make that an assumption, on grounds of lack of compelling evidence.

Boring. Boring, boring, *boring.*

She had another look in her mirror. It was her favourite thing. From it she'd learned that she was beautiful (although it was probably pushing it a bit to assume that the Others realised this) and that thought gave her great pleasure; and pleasure was nice, though in deplorably short supply, though presumably that was normal and in accordance with how things are, see above, ad nauseam. It seemed odd to keep something as beautiful as she was locked up all day, but she could sort of understand why you might do such a thing; it might get away, wander off somewhere a bit less boring, and then where would you be? That sort of tied in with the two Others who came and stared at her—which, for all she knew, was normal and how it should be, etcetera. Really, she wouldn't mind quite so much if only somebody would take five minutes just to explain to her what was going on.

Back to the mirror. And then something curious happened.

Instead of showing her herself, it was filled with a funny looking object; a bit like one of her eyes, except that it was red and shiny; and it was looking straight at her with obvious interest (thereby giving a degree of evidential support to the Beautiful hypothesis, see above).

"Hello," it said.

She knew that one. It meant, initiate communication. "Hello," she said back.

"Can you understand what I'm saying?"

She blinked. "Yes," she said. "Hey, that's amazing."

"Glad you think so. I think it's pretty amazing, too. Would you like to do more saying-and-listening?"

"Ooh, yes please." She paused. "I'm *talking*."

"And very effectively, too, if I may say so. You're very good at it."

"Am I? Wow."

"You sound surprised."

"I am. It's my first time."

"Really? I'd never have guessed. You must be pretty smart, in that case."

She hesitated. "I think I probably am," she said, "because the little not-all-that-nice-tasting people-a-bit-like-me aren't clever enough to get away when I want to eat them. Am I smart?"

"I think so."

"Ordinary normal smart or smarter than normal?"

"Smarter than normal, I would say. I wouldn't have thought any of *them* would be able to talk so well if it was their first time. Do you?"

"Gosh, no. But that's just guessing. I don't know enough about them to be sure, you see."

"Well," said the Eye, "I know quite a lot about goblins—that's what they're called, by the way—and it's my opinion that you're considerably smarter than they are. And bigger, and stronger. And prettier, too, if you don't mind me saying so."

Any doubts she might have had about the Eye were thereby put to rest; because the Eye knew she was pretty, so it had to be smart and well informed. So that was all right. She could trust it implicitly. "Yes," she said. "Much prettier."

"Which is odd," said the Eye.

That troubled her. "Odd?"

"Yes," said the Eye. "Because here's you, a specially clever, big, strong and beautiful individual, and they've got you locked up in a tiny little space with nobody to talk to and nothing to do. To be honest with you, I find that hard to credit."

"Really? I thought that maybe it was normal and how things are."

The Eye took a moment to consider that. "No," it said, "I would say that's not normal and not how things are, or should be." It paused, then went on; "Can you account for it?"

She nodded. "I think it could be one of two things," she said. "It's either because I'm pretty and they like to look at me, so they keep me here so I don't get away."

"Plausible." the Eye conceded. "Or?"

"Or I'm bad, and I don't deserve to be let out."

The Eye glowed even brighter than usual. "I wouldn't want to speak out of turn," it said, "but I think I can set your mind at rest on that score. I don't think you're bad. In fact, I'm sure you're not."

"Really?" She bit her lip. "I thought maybe it was because I eat the Others who bring food."

"Oh, I don't think so. After all, if you weren't meant to eat them, they wouldn't keep sending them. Well, would they?"

"No, I guess not. I never thought of that."

"I think," the Eye said, "that there's another possible explanation."

"Oh. What's that?"

"This is just a suggestion," said the Eye. "I'm not saying it's true or anything."

"Yes, I understand. What is it?"

"Well," said the Eye, "maybe they keep you stuck in here because they're afraid of you." Pause. "Do you know what afraid is?"

"I think so. The food-bringy people I eat are afraid. Is that what you mean?"

"Same sort of thing, yes. I think the Others are afraid of you, because you're bigger and stronger and faster and smarter and *much* prettier than they are. So that's why they keep you locked up."

She frowned. "I don't follow. Why would they do that? If I'm all those better-thans, it must mean I'm good. If I'm good, they should like me more, not less."

"Ah." The Eye seemed to twinkle at her. "That's people for you."

"Is it?"

"Sadly, yes," said the Eye. "People are afraid that if someone comes along who's bigger and stronger and smarter and prettier, then other people will like the big-strong-smart-pretty more than them. That kind of being afraid is called *jealousy*."

"Jellersey," she repeated. "Ah, right. That would explain quite a lot. But it's silly," she objected. "For one thing, it's not fair on the big-strong-smart-pretties."

"Lots of things are unfair," said the Eye. "Sorry about that."

She frowned and was silent for a moment. "Oh," she said. "So the World isn't—?"

"Perfect? Unfortunately not. And that," the Eye added, "explains a lot of other things, I think you'll find. But don't be too upset about it. *I'm* not jealous of you."

"No, you aren't," she said. "I like you."

"Good. I like you, too."

"I'm glad about that." She paused again, then said, "Why are you just an eye?"

"Ha! It's a long story."

"I don't mind. I like listening to you."

"Fine. All right, then, here goes. A long time ago, I was just like you."

"Were you? Oh, I'm so glad."

"Really?"

She nodded quickly four times. "It means we can really be—" She waited, and the word came to her. "Friends."

"I'd like that. Anyway, I was like you once. I was bigger, stronger and smarter than everybody else in the whole World."

"And prettier?"

"Naturally. Though I have to say, I don't think I was ever quite as pretty as you."

"I bet you were. Almost as pretty."

"I was extremely pretty," the Eye said firmly, "but nowhere near as pretty as you are. Even so," it went on, "people were jealous of me. Very jealous."

"That's a shame."

"Very jealous indeed," said the Eye. "And you know what they did to me, because they were so jealous?"

"No," she said, in a low voice. "What?"

"They locked me up in a small, cramped cell," the Eye said. "Rather like this one, now I come to think of it. Maybe a bit smaller. It's a long time ago, so I can't quite remember."

"What, just because they were jealous?"

"Yes. Makes you think, doesn't it? Anyway, that's not all they did. When I managed to get out of the cell a couple of times—which I don't think was unreasonable, do you?"

"No, of course not."

"Well," said the Eye, "they didn't like it, because they took my body away. Really."

She could feel drops of water oozing out of her eyes. Was

that something to do with what she'd just heard? Rather a coincidence if it wasn't. She wiped them away with the back of her paw. "That's awful," she said. "What, your whole body?"

"That's right," said the Eye. "All that's left of me now is, well, what you can see. I don't like to complain, but it's a bit of a nuisance."

"I think it's—" She remembered; the perfect word. "Unfair. I think that's *so* unfair."

"Me too."

"And all just because they were jealous?"

"Oh, they made excuses," the Eye said. "They claimed I was disruptive, and a bad influence, and I was setting a bad example, and I wasn't a team player."

"That's just silly."

"I thought so. But no, they insisted. Said I had *antisocial tendencies*, of all things. Told me I had to shape up and fly straight. There is no Eye in 'team', they kept saying."

"But you didn't take any notice, I bet."

"I didn't," said the Eye, "and look where it got me. Remarkably similar," it added, "to where you are now."

She thought about that for a bit. "I don't think I'd be a team player, either."

"I don't suppose you would. You're bigger and stronger and smarter and prettier than everybody else, so why should you be?"

"And they took your body away, just for that?"

"That's what they told me."

"Gosh." A horrible thought struck her. "Do you think they'd do that to *me*?"

A long silence. Then: "It's possible, yes. Or they may just kill you."

She frowned. "Can I be killed?"

"I think so," the Eye said gravely. "I know I can't,

because they tried. But I think they could kill you, if they wanted to."

She shivered. "That's horrible," she said. "I don't think they should be allowed to do that."

"It's called *authority*," the Eye said. "Basically, it means, there's more of us and we have all the weapons, so we can do what we like to you. Personally, I don't hold with it."

"Nor me. I think it's awful."

The Eye gazed thoughtfully at her for a while. "How would it be," it said, "if I made it so you could get out of there?"

She stared at it. "Could you?"

"It's possible," the Eye said slowly. "I can't promise anything, mind, but I can certainly try. Would you like that?"

"Very much indeed."

"Well, then."

She hesitated. It seemed a lot to ask. But she had to try. "If I get out of here," she said, "can I come and be with you? I'd really like that. A lot."

"I'd like that, too," the Eye said gravely. "A *big* lot. Watch out," it added in a loud whisper, "someone's coming. Look, it'd be best if you don't let them know you can talk now, all right? You'll be able to understand them, but don't talk back. Promise?"

"I promise."

"That's great. Well, be seeing you. A little visual humour," it added with a wink, and vanished.

"Oh, come *on*," Tinituviel said, yet again. Mordak winced. *Oh, come on* seemed to land on exactly the same little cluster of nerve endings every single time; amazing accuracy, of which any championship-grade goblin archer would be justly proud. "It's so glaringly, blindingly obvious that even a particularly stupid rock ought to be able to see it. Or, provided it's explained slowly, you."

But Mordak shook his aching head. "It's ambiguous," he repeated.

"Ambiguous my ear tips. *She who should never have been born will rise up among the chosen people.* And what have you got down in the cellars right now? The one and only ever *female* goblin. I know you have severe issues with two plus two, but surely you get it."

Mordak selected a dry roasted ear from the small dish on the table in front of him; not too hard, not too wrinkled and furry. The green ones were his favourite. "You're jumping to conclusions," he said with his mouth full. "Really, I'm surprised at you, a smart lady like you. Conclusions," he added loudly, before she could get started, "that aren't warranted by the available data."

About the only way to get her to be quiet for a moment, he'd learned the hard way, was to bombard her with syllables. It always took her a split second to get over the shock of finding that he knew words that long.

"For example," he went on, "the prophecy says, *the chosen people*. A prophecy, mark you, concocted by *Elves*. Surely, if an Elvish prophecy wanted you to think goblins, it'd say something like evil little bastards. Chosen people's got to mean your lot, surely." He looked at her and narrowed his eyes. "She who should never have been born," he said. "An Elf. Hm."

She knew he was kidding. "Prophecies are like that," she said, "you know that perfectly well. They're supposed to be totally misleading while telling nothing but the truth."

"Mphm. Out of interest, why is that?"

"I don't know, do I?"

"Because they're exclusively composed by Elves? No, there has to be some other reason. Anyway, you've got to admit, when you see *chosen people*, you don't immediately think of goblins. Well, do you?"

Her fists were clenched into little hard knots. "Of course you don't. That's the *point*. Look, will you stop trying to score points off me and look at it constructively?"

That one went home, just below the sore spot caused by all the oh-come-ons. Yes, he admitted, I'm arguing with her because I *can*, which is no good reason. And also because—

"I don't want to execute Bolgette," he admitted. "It seems so unfair, somehow."

"*Bolgette?*" For a moment he thought she was about to explode. "You've given it a *name?*"

He shrugged. "Bolg after my revered predecessor, because we used a bit of his adrenal gland to get her bump-started, so to speak, and ette because that shows she's a she. I think it's a nice name."

"I'm starting to get seriously worried about you."

"All right, then, the experimental prototype female goblin. Killing her just for the sake of a maliciously obscure prophecy strikes me as excessive."

She looked at him. "It's the Evil thing to do," she said.

"Yes," he snapped, "the Old Evil thing to do, exactly what dear old Bolg would've done. Nasty, violent and *stupid*." He made himself calm down. One does not yell at Elves, because if one does they've won. "You should go down and take a look at her some time. She's *magnificent*. Oh, don't do all that," he added, as Tinituviel raised an eyebrow and smirked. "It's true. She's three times as tall and at least five times as strong, reactions like lightning, and the way she's learned stuff without any prompting at all, she must have so much brain it's a wonder it doesn't dribble out of her ears. With a hundred thousand more like her, I could build an army worthy of Snordor. I could *win*."

He'd shocked her; and he hadn't meant to say it, not out loud. One of the implicit terms of their unwritten contract was that she worked for him on the strict assumption that Evil could never win. He had a nasty feeling he'd just signed Bolgette's death warrant.

"All right," he said, "maybe you're right, maybe that's what the prophecy means by she-who-should-never. And when it says chosen people, I guess that means from our perspective. Though," he added, "chosen is still going it a bit strong. The people I got lumbered with would be closer to the mark, if you ask me."

She was giving him that serious look, the one that usually came before, *you've simply got to do this paperwork now.* "I think you've got a choice," she said.

He hadn't been expecting that. "Me?"

"Yes," she said, "you. Think about it. Evil always loses, you said it yourself. But, just before it loses, it reaches a point where anyone would think it's inevitably going to win. And then, from the quarter where you'd least expect it, the smelly stuff hits the fan or the ring hits the molten lava, and suddenly it's all over bar the interminable singing. I think we're building up to just such an event."

Pointy ears and snarky manner or not, you had to hand it to her. Smart. He could see it now, but only because she'd got there first. "Let me save you the bother," he said. "The she-goblin makes me think—with good reason— that I can win. Under that impression, I spare her and ignore the prophecy. Therefore a key term of the prophecy is fulfilled, and ten minutes after that, the Nameless One is drinking his morning coffee out of the back of my head." He paused. "That was what you were about to say, wasn't it?"

"Pretty much." She looked at him, as if he was the small print in a contract. "Not bad."

He sighed. "Fine," he said. "You win. No army worthy of Snordor for me. But killing her still seems a bit—"

"Harsh?"

"Oh, come on," he quoted, though he couldn't do it nearly as well. "You're the Daughter of Light around here, for crying out loud. We don't have to scrag the poor thing, we can just keep her locked up until all this aggravation's over and done with." She looked at him. "Can't we?"

She shook her head. "She's a goblin," she said. "Goblins don't count. Well, they don't," she added quickly, before he could say anything. "It's like feeling sorry for a biscuit. The whole purpose of a biscuit is to be eaten. The whole purpose of a goblin—"

He sighed. She was right, of course. *It* wasn't, but she was. "Fine," he said. "Off with her head, then. Go on."

She nodded, then hesitated. "You don't mean me personally?"

He'd learned the unblinking stare from her, along with a lot of other things.

"You don't mean me personally."

"Well, let's see," he said. "From what I've gathered, she's likely to make mincemeat of any detachment of less than a dozen goblins, and more than a dozen wouldn't fit in her cell, they'd have to form an orderly queue outside the door. I could probably do it, but, as you keep telling me, I owe it to my people to stay out of fights if I can help it. You, on the other hand, are an Elven warrior princess, it says so on your CV." He drew a sheet of parchment from a drawer and laid it on the table, the palm of his paw covering the writing. "Fifth-level archery, seventh-level longsword, distinction in unarmed combat and gracefully fighting dirty. Which reminds me," he went on, "one of these days you really ought to get around to putting copies of your diplomas on the file. Obviously I believe you have all these qualifications, but you're always saying the road to hell is paved with missing duplicate copies."

She'd gone a funny colour. "You know, on reflection, perhaps it'd be simpler all round if we just put something in her food."

Mordak grinned at her. "She eats *goblins*. Poison just won't cut it. No pun intended. Sorry, but I think this is a case where the old cold steel is called for. And since you're eminently qualified—"

"I'd have to check my diary. I do have rather a lot of work piled up right now."

Enough fun for one day. "Or," Mordak said, "I suppose we could call in a wraith."

"Yes, that's a really good idea." The words came tumbling out in a sort of heap. "How silly of me, I should've thought of it earlier."

"It's all right," Mordak said nicely, "it's hard to think straight when you're paralysed with fear. So they tell me," he added, slipping the sheet of paper back into the drawer after she'd had a chance to see it was blank. "All right, see to it, would you? Thank you so much," he added, as the door slammed behind her.

"Are you the plumber?" Pat Lushington asked.

The newcomer frowned. "I don't think so. Please may I use your telephone?"

The thing about him was that he looked normal. That should have made him stick out like a sore thumb, in a neighbourhood where everyone who called at the front door was either an Elf, a dwarf, one of the half-witted local humans or a delivery man (and she knew both of them by sight; a very old man in a flat hat, and a beanpole teenager who never stopped eating). The newcomer was dressed in concrete-coloured slacks, a light blue short-sleeved shirt and white trainers, all perfectly clean and tidy; mid-thirties, good-looking in a gormless sort of a way; if he was on TV, he'd probably be playing a vet. Normal; therefore, in context, all wrong.

Also, he knew about phones. "You're not from round here," she said.

"I don't think so. But I really do need to make a call."

Euphemism for toilet facilities? He had that air of desperation about him. But he was a man, and the foothills of the mountains in which stood the Great Gate of what Pat had resolved henceforth to call Mariposa were full of shady crevices, and a few hundred yards further down was the forest, offering an outstanding choice of trees. In which case, she could only assume he wanted to use the telephone. Odd.

"Well," she said, "we haven't got a landline because they can't connect one up through the whatsit, though that's not what they told us when we came here. A landline, high-speed broadband and cable TV, they said. Now it's, oh, well, we're hoping to have all that in place within the next two years, going forward. Honestly, it's been like that with everything. If we'd known what we were letting ourselves in for, we'd have stayed where we were. And you try and get a plumber. Forget it."

"OK," the newcomer said, with a twisted smile. "I should be able to manage. I seem to have forgotten everything else."

There was something about him that made her feel uneasy. "Are you feeling all right?" she said.

"Yes and no. Look, I hate to be a pest, but do you have a phone of any sort? It's quite important."

She sighed. After all, the indications were that he was a fellow citizen of the Civilised World, with a faint accent that was either Scottish or New Zealand, and a shirt made of polyester cotton rather than thirty thousand interlocking steel rings. On that basis he was probably One of Us, and deserved her help. "I suppose you could use my mobile," she said. "But you'll have to climb up the Gimbrill Stair and stand on the Ramparts of Mazhad-Bazhan. It's the only place you can get a signal."

The Gimbrill—sorry, the *historic* Gimbrill Stair, although what had actually happened there to earn it that sobriquet nobody had ever seen fit to tell her, and she was quite sure she'd rather not know anyway—consists of a hundred and nine spiral stone steps, and brings you out, panting and admiring the pretty twinkling lights just behind your eyelids, on the pinnacle of a windswept crag. She'd been tempted to say, through that doorway, turn left, you can't miss it and let him find his own way, but the thought of a perfect stranger wandering about the place wasn't one she was comfortable with. He proved to be in pretty good shape, at any rate; he was hardly puffed at all after the abominable climb.

He knew how to use a mobile phone; but all to no avail. "No answer," he said sadly and handed it back to her. "Just voicemail."

"Aren't you going to leave a message, after all that?"

He gave her a tragic look. "I wouldn't know what to say."

Pat Lushington's heart wasn't marble. "Come and have a cup of tea," she said. "You look ever so sorry for yourself."

His reaction to the decor in the morning room (she refused to think of it as the Treasury of Zharad-Püm, no matter how historic it might be) was interesting. He seemed not to notice. Now the locals all reacted with horrified fascination, while One of Us would be vividly reminded of Home. But the newcomer might as well have been sitting in a field for all the interest he took.

The tea, though, seemed to go down very well. "Thank you," he said. "Can I have some more?"

"Help yourself," she said, and he got up and operated the teapot as to the manner born. "I have to say, the local water's pretty good, it makes a lovely cup of tea. It must be extra soft, or is it extra hard, I can never remember."

The newcomer thought for a moment. "I'd imagine it'd be pretty hard," he said, "since it drains through all that limestone. I think I take sugar. Is there any?"

She pointed out the sugar bowl. "You think you take sugar."

He nodded. "It feels like I do. But I don't actually know." He added a heaped spoonful, stirred and sipped. "Now I do. Yes. One sugar in tea. Well, that's something."

From a few stray shards of data she'd picked up along the way, she was beginning to piece together a working hypothesis. "You've got whatsit," she said. "Am-thingy."

"Amnesia?"

"That's the one. You've lost your memory."

He beamed at her. "I rather think so, yes."

"You poor thing. When did that happen?"

Gentle smile. "Trick question?"

"What? Oh, I see. Well, did you have a fall or something? Bang your head, that sort of thing."

He frowned again. "Not that I'm aware of," he said, "and I haven't got any unexplained bumps and bruises, no blurred or double vision, drowsiness or nausea. Of course, if it's transient global amnesia or dissociative fugue, you don't need a bash on the bonce to get those. Basically, though, yes. The first thing I can remember is waking up on the mountainside about a mile and a half north of here, and apart from a load of useless information about science, history and the arts, the only thing in my head is a phone number, which I just tried calling, but no reply."

He smiled. "And there you have it. You now know as much about me as I do."

Pat looked at him closely for a while. "Actually," she said, "rather more."

"Really?"

"Yes. For a start, I can tell you for sure you visited a branch of Marks & Spencer within the last three months and bought a pair of trousers."

He blinked. "Marks & Spencer," he said. "A large British-based chain store specialising in clothing."

She nodded. "And you sound like you could be English. Or Scottish. Or from New Zealand, or possibly South Africa. Maybe Canada. I don't think you're American," she added reassuringly.

He considered that. "So possibly I've spent a lot of time in more than one of those places. Which would give me a sort of fifty-seven-varieties accent."

"See? Aren't we doing well?"

"It's a start," he conceded. "Where is this, by the way?"

"Ah."

"Ã," he repeated. "That's what it's called."

She shook her head. "It's a long story."

"I'm not in any particular hurry if you're not."

"Well." She poured herself some more tea. "It all started when my husband and I—my husband's Barry and I'm Pat, Pat Lushington."

"Pleased to meet you."

"Anyway," she went on, "we were at this party, office bash, Barry's work, and some people we knew a bit were telling us all about this amazing new scheme, like moving to France or the Algarve, only your money goes much, much further, and it doesn't rely on the cheap air fares because transportation is basically free. Well, we were desperate to get out of London, and Barry's always wanted to retire early and write his blessed novel, and the kids are settled, so we thought, well, why not? And here we are."

"That's wonderful. Only you haven't said where here is."

She gave him a slightly cold look. "I was coming to that. Apparently it's all to do with something called multiverse theory."

The newcomer sat up straight in his chair. "You mean the one that says that a generic prediction of chaotic inflation is an infinite ergodic universe, which, being infinite, must contain Hubble volumes realising all initial conditions."

"Um."

"From which it follows that there's an infinite multiverse containing an infinity of Hubble volumes which may or may not operate under the same physical laws as each other, depending on whether you agree with Tegmark or Wheeler and Smolin, though also see Everett and Feynman. That multiverse theory?"

A moment or so passed before she replied. "Probably," she said. "I really wouldn't know, I'd have to ask Barry. But anyway, *this* multiverse theory means you can zap across from our universe to a different one where property prices are ridiculously low, and still get a phone signal and the UK newspapers. Well, a couple of days late, but it's not like there's anything much in them these days anyhow."

The newcomer nodded. "A van Goyen portal," he said. Then he added, "Isn't that all still highly theoretical?"

She shrugged. "Search me. Anyhow, here we are, and it's really quite nice once you get used to it, the locals aren't too bad and anyway they keep themselves to themselves, and we order in pretty much everything via the Net, and if you place your order before 11 a.m. local time you've got a fairly good chance of getting it within forty-eight hours, except for fresh milk, which is a pain, so we use the long-life milk, which is OK in tea and coffee, because you wouldn't want to touch the local stuff, trust me, Barry had a tiny splosh of it in his Jamaican Blue Mountain and that was the last I saw of him for the next three days. And, of course, you can't get a plumber no matter what you do. Not even a Pole."

He nodded, waited a moment, then said, "You still haven't told me where we are."

"What? Oh, right. I think it's called the Realms. I don't suppose it means anything, Like, there was a new estate down the road from us in Tottenham and they called it The Elms but there wasn't a tree for miles, I think the local youths dug them all up and sold them on eBay. But we don't have any trouble like that round here, thank goodness."

The newcomer was thinking something through. "You say your husband drank some local milk and you didn't see him for three days. Did it turn him invisible?"

She laughed. "He was stuck on the toilet, poor old soul. But the water's all right. Not like the Bristows in that ghastly place in Portugal."

"I see," the newcomer said. "So you don't actually know where you are."

She found that mildly annoying. "Well, no, not in a point-at-a-map-and-say-you-are-here sense, I suppose not. But it doesn't actually matter, does it? Home is where the heart is, my gran used to say."

The newcomer nodded slowly. "I think, if it's all right with you, I'd like to try phoning again."

By now she reckoned she could trust him not to loot the place or start pawing the contents of her underwear drawer. She handed him the phone. "You know the way."

He wasn't gone long. "Still no answer," he said sadly.

"Did you leave a message?"

He shook his head. "You said something about a van Goyen portal."

"No, I didn't."

"Sorry." He smiled. "You said there was a whatsit. The way you got here. I'm guessing, since I don't think I come from this place, I must've got here the same way as you. Maybe if I go back through the whatsit, I can find out a bit more."

That seemed like a sensible idea. "You could try that," she agreed.

"I think I will, then. Where do I find it?"

"Ah."

His mouth twitched just a little bit. "Ah?"

"I don't actually know where it is."

"Fine."

"It sort of comes and goes," she explained. "Probably because of multiverse thingy. But it's all right, because the little men from the management company deal with all that, as well as doing the deliveries. If you ask them, I'm sure they'll point you in the right direction."

"Excellent. Where do I find them?"

Pat frowned. "I couldn't rightly say," she admitted. "They come here, we don't go to them. But we see them most days, when they bring stuff we've ordered from home. There's an old man who looks like Albert Steptoe and a skinny kid who eats all the time."

Something in that description made the newcomer blink. "Right," he said.

"You look like something just rang a bell."

"Very fleeting mental image," the newcomer said. "Came and went in a flash. Which would suggest I've met these people at some point."

"So you must've come through the whatsit, like you just said."

"Probably something like that." There was a faraway look on his face, and she got the feeling he was preoccupied with something else. "So when are these men likely to come here next?"

"I don't know," she admitted. "I'm expecting a Waitrose delivery, but that usually comes on a Thursday, and I know Barry's sent away for some DVDs and a new golf umbrella from Amazon, but if I know him he'll have chosen the Super Saver delivery to save a few pennies, and that always takes ever such a long time." A terrible thought struck her as she spoke. The newcomer was, after all, One of Us, helpless and alone in a strange land. The sacred laws of hospitality would, therefore, seem to apply. Fine, she was all in favour of sacred laws, provided they didn't park themselves in her home for three to six days, needing to be fed, housed and entertained. But if the stranger were to look at her with those soft brown eyes and say, I don't suppose I could possibly wait here till they show up next, I promise I won't be a nuisance, what excuse could she possibly make?

An ounce of pre-emption is worth a pound of cure. "Here's a thought," she said. "Terry and Molly Barrington live just down the road from us, and they're always sending off for stuff. You could try popping across to their place. Then, if they aren't expecting anything, you can come back and wait here. How would that be?"

"It sounds like a very good idea. How far away is their house?"

"Actually, it's a sort of tower. You can see it from our front door."

Which was perfectly true, on a clear day. And it couldn't be much more than thirty miles, forty-five at the outside, and he'd have the flash of the sunlight on the tower battlements to guide him every step of the way, so not much risk of getting lost. And the Barringtons liked having people to stay, they'd said so often enough. "I'll make you some sandwiches," she said, as much to her conscience as to the newcomer. "We've got some cold chicken from the weekend."

After he'd gone, she sat by the pool for a bit, reading her book. Several times she could have sworn the damn plant tried to tickle her ankles with its horrid fronds, but, whenever she looked at it, it was perfectly still.

Ask anyone who knows them what single word springs to mind when you say *wraiths*, and chances are they'll say *aaargh*, whereupon you'll say apart from that, and they'll frown and reply, well actually it's two words, does that count? The two words in question are *work ethic*.

The Slaves of the Curse are the willing horses of Evil, the grafters, the first to arrive and the last to leave. If Evil had bank holidays, wraiths would spend them at the office, or pounding the trail in all weathers, uncomplaining, conscientious, always putting the job and the outfit first. Some say they do it for the uniform. Others, more cynical, say they have no choice, because of the dark spell that binds and possesses them, and there's an element of truth in that. The power of the rings they wear has long since eaten away the last vestiges of individuality, transforming them into little more than extensions of the Dark Mind. A hand, the cynics say, could no more disobey the brain than a wraith point out that actually it's owed six weeks' paid holiday from last year, and if He wants it done so badly, why doesn't he do it Himself?

Nearly all wraiths. There are a few who aren't quite so remorselessly enthralled; and it was one of these who happened to be on duty at the station house when the Black One himself came stomping in through the door.

Because of the sense-of-duty thing, nobody in the Hierarchy expects wraiths to make themselves deliberately inconspicuous when they're on call; and an unscrupulous officer could use that to her advantage. When the adamantine door flew open and the Black Voice yelled, "Shop!", the officer in question was huddled by the fire trying to keep warm, mostly because her mantle and hood were hanging on a hook behind the door.

I'm going to be in so much trouble, she thought. But possibly not, if she kept perfectly still and quiet as a little mouse. Requiring no breath, she had no need to hold it.

The Dark Lord was looking round the room. Then he stopped. He was looking straight at her.

"Lieutenant," he said. "You're out of uniform."

Oh, snot, she thought. So it's true about the Black Eye.

"Let me guess," the Terrible One went on. "It's honking it down outside, so you've hung your kit up to dry, which accounts for why you're sitting in front of the stove with nothing on. Which is fair enough. Yes?"

She tried to agree, but all that came out was a little squeaking noise.

"Thought so," said the Voice of the Abyss. "Here." He threw her a blanket. "I have to say, this is not the sort of conduct I expect from one of the Enthralled. Skiving off, were you?"

Here it comes. "Yes, sir."

The Dark Face grinned. "Good on you," he said. "If there's one thing makes me want to throw up, it's sucking up to the boss. A shortcoming," he added, "to which your lot are distressingly prone. You won't catch a goblin brown-nosing, I can tell you that." He sat down on the table and let his legs swing. "You the duty spook?"

"Yes, sir."

He nodded. "Got a job for you. Right up your alley, I should think."

"Yes, *sir*!"

Mordak pulled a face. "Oh, don't you start. Try and look a little bit disgruntled and pissed off, if only for my sake. Now, then. In the deepest, darkest cell in the lowest level of the dungeons, there's a goblin." He drew a claw across his throat. "Capisce?"

"Sir."

"Jolly good. Make a good job of it, and there's a good chance promotion—"

He must've caught the look of dismay that flicked across her face before she could stop it.

"—will pass you by for some considerable time," he continued smoothly. "Failure, on the other hand, will see you bumped up to captain so fast your feet won't touch. Do I make myself clear?"

"Sir."

"Oh, *don't* do that," he said, a split second too late. She froze the salute as best she could, and he nodded his appreciation. "And you can tell your fellow see-throughs that the next one of them who clicks his heels at me had better be clog-dancing. All right, carry on."

She didn't manage to catch her breath until he'd been gone for best part of a minute. The Dark Lord! Himself! Of all the station houses and guard posts in all the dark strongholds in all the Realms, why did he have to walk into hers? Not quite what she'd expected, though; maybe that was this New Evil everyone was so snotty about. If so, she decided, she was all for it.

Now, then. Execute a goblin; shouldn't be any problem with that.

She caught herself shivering, even though she'd put

on her mantle and hood. Shouldn't be any problem, she repeated firmly to herself, we did it often enough in class, and it can't be much different with a real one. Except that the ones we did in class weren't, well, alive. Shouldn't make any difference, though, should it?

Should it? No, of course not. Rule one: the wraith who's tired of killing is tired of life. She knew that all too well, having once had to copy it out a thousand times for running in the corridors. It had been lodged in her mind for so long that she'd never given it a moment's thought. Even now, if she closed her eyes, she could see good old Miss, or, rather, her cardigan, sensible shoes and walnut-sized fake pearls, leading Year Four in the chant: *What do we do? What are we for? Killing the foes of dear old Snordor!* She could remember the pride and the nervousness as she walked out in front of the whole school on Speech Day to recite the Fifty-Two Vulnerable Points; did it well, too, got them all right and never a stutter. Well, now. Finally the time had come to put all that into practice. Good.

Um.

Pull yourself together, girl, and get on with it. She went to her locker and got out her dagger, a genuine Snorgul-blade, deeply engraved with Black Runes; they spelt out her name and class number and the year she'd won Best Improver in Grade Three Stealth & Menaces. I expect you'll get lots of use out of it, the Headmistress had told her, with a big wink; and they'd shaken hands, all very grown up, and she'd backed away blushing furiously as all her classmates clapped and cheered. She slipped the scabbard into the loops on her belt and straightened her hood in front of the mirror. For the old school, she thought. You can't let them down. Not Miss Most Likely To Succeed of FA 2376.

Ten minutes later she was standing outside a cell door,

accompanied by a petrified looking goblin captain. "That's her," the captain said. "In there."

"What did you just say?"

"I said, that's—"

"*Her?*"

"See? You heard me the first time."

"Don't be stupid. It can't be a *her*. There are no goblin females."

The captain snickered. "Well, in about a minute and a half there won't be. She's the only one. Prototype," he explained. "Didn't work out, see. So, clear up the mess and move on."

That sort of nipped at her, like a small, aggressive dog. "What went wrong? Did she turn out sickly and weak?"

"Look for yourself."

She threw back her hood, then peered through the window in the cell door. Then she turned back to the captain. "What's wrong with that?" she said.

The captain shrugged. "They don't bother explaining stuff like that to the likes of me. But my theory is, they're scared."

"Scared."

"Too right. I mean, if they made a whole bunch more like her, where would the rest of us be? Out of a job, is where. Next thing you know, they'd be taking over."

Wraiths do not debate policy with goblins, so she couldn't very well say any of the things that came rocketing into her mind at that point; just as well, because another thing wraiths simply don't do is criticise the decisions of the Dark Hierarchy. Fine. "You," she said. "Go away."

The goblin saluted smartly and ran away down the corridor. In his haste he'd forgotten to give her the key to the cell door. Not such an insurmountable problem as you might think. She leaned forward and blew a jet of the

Black Breath into the keyhole. Then she gave the door a smart shove with the heel of her hand. The wards of the lock snapped like icicles, and the door swung inwards.

The she-goblin looked up at her and frowned. Not afraid, just puzzled.

"Listen. Can you understand me?"

The she-goblin started to nod, then appeared to remember something and shook her head. Then she pulled a face and said, "Drat."

"You can talk."

"Yes, but the—somebody told me not to."

"Listen very carefully. I've been sent to kill you."

The she-goblin's eyes grew very round. "Oh. Why?"

"Because you're better than they are, and you're a girl." She waited to see how the she-goblin took it. A slight frown, and a nod that seemed to say told you so. "I don't think that's fair," she added. "Do you?"

"I think it's horrid."

"Yes, well. Actually, I think it's *stupid*. So this is what we're going to do."

The goblin captain was in the guardroom with his feet up, eating pickled lips and reading an interesting article in *Bows & Arrows* when the door swung open and the wraith strode in. He resisted the temptation to jump to attention. "All done?"

"What do you think?"

"That's all right, then. I'll send my lads along to clear away."

A faint, scratchy noise, like fingernails on desiccated skin. "You can if you like."

The captain frowned. "Problem?"

"She was a tricky one," the wraith replied. "Steel wouldn't touch her, not even a Snorgul-blade. So I froze her with the Black Breath. You're welcome to try moving the body, but don't expect to have any fingers left afterwards."

The captain pulled a why's-it-always-me face. "Fine," he said. "What do you suggest?"

"Not my job, waste disposal," the wraith said haughtily. "I leave the bagging and tagging to the little people, such as yourself. However," she added, "*if* it was my problem, which it isn't, I'd get half a dozen other ranks I never really liked very much, tell 'em to wrap up nice and warm, and send them in there with a couple of long hooks, a handcart and an old door or something like that. Haul the dear departed onto the door, lift the door up on the cart, wheel it round to the garbage chute and shoot it out the side of the mountain for the crows to get rid of. Only whatever you do, don't get any closer than you can help, not unless you believe frostbite will enhance your appearance."

Some time later she scrambled up the foothills of the mountain, to the hole in the rock through which the garbage chute emptied out. She was only just in time. She'd barely draped the net across the outlet when an ominous rumbling made her jump back out of the way. A massive dark shape shot past her and hit the net, which stopped it. She gave it a quick look, then settled down in the shade and read a book for an hour or so, until the Horrible Yellow Face emerged from behind the mountain peak and bathed the outlet in warm golden light. She read a few more pages, then looked up. Water was starting to trickle down the chute in a thin, steady stream. She closed her book and put it away in the folds of her robe, then said, "Hello."

"C-c-c ... "

"Hold still," she said. "You're not properly thawed out yet."

"C-c-*c* . . . "

"I bet you are, but there's not much I can do about it till you're fully defrosted. Till then, don't move and think happy thoughts."

Some time after that, she threw the she-goblin a rope so she could haul herself off the chute, and stood by with a thick wool blanket. "And don't moan," she said. "I stuck my neck out for you. If anyone ever finds out what I just did, I have an idea that immortality will prove to be something of a mixed blessing."

The she-goblin gazed blearily at her over the hem of the blanket. "Thanks," she said, and sneezed.

"Oh, that's all right. I'm still not entirely sure why I'm doing all this, bearing in mind it constitutes being nice, and I'm supposed to be the baddest of the bad." She shrugged. "I guess it counts as treachery and betrayal of trust, and you can't get more evil than that, can you?"

The she-goblin was picking ice out of her hair. "What do I do now?"

"Absolutely no idea. Go out there, be whatever you want to be, fulfil your potential. Just do me a favour and fulfil it a long, long way away from here, all right?"

"I promise."

"Good. Well, we bad girls have got to stick together, I guess."

She waited until the she-goblin was out of sight in the eaves of the wood, then turned round to head back to the fortress. She went about ten yards, then stopped dead.

"Um," she said.

Mordak, the Dark Lord himself, was sitting cross-legged on a large rock directly ahead of her, nibbling the honey and almond coating off a slice of Swiss troll. "Hello again," he said. "You're supposed to be on duty."

"Um."

"It's all right." Mordak sighed. "I know exactly what you just did, so please, don't bother trying to lie to me, because I can see right through you. Or, rather," he added, "I can't, but you know what I mean." He threw the rest of the troll behind a shrivelled thorn bush. "Oh dear," he said. "What are we going to do with you?"

"Um."

"Rhetorical question." He laughed. "Don't worry," he said, "I'm not going to eat you. In fact," he said, stifling a yawn with the back of his paw, "I'm not going to do anything to you at all." He paused for a reaction but she was too frozen to move. "Ask me why."

"Um?"

"That'll do. All right, since you insist, I'll tell you. I'm not going to punish you because it's not your fault. *Don't say um.* Thank you."

"Not my—?"

Mordak shook his head. "My fault," he said. "In fact," he went on, mumbling ever so slightly, "I probably owe you an apology."

"U—?"

A look of almost infinite weariness crossed the Dark Face, enough to strike a tiny spark of sympathy in among all that terror, like one lonely away supporter in a sea of home team scarves. "I played a trick on you. It was necessary." He grinned feebly. "My secretary was giving me a hard time. She had her flinty little heart set on murdering my she-goblin, and I didn't want her to."

"But surely you're the—"

His eyes flashed, just a little, but enough to put the truth of what she'd just said beyond any possibility of doubt. "Which makes things tricky when it comes to personnel management. The Dark Lord does not reason with underlings. They do as they're told, or they're tomorrow's blue plate special. But she's a really, really good secretary and I don't want to lose her. So," he added sadly, "what do you do?"

Maybe she'd suspected the truth all along, or maybe she intuitively knew it, just from their eye contact. "You give the order to a wraith," she said, "because a wraith is the embodiment of the Dark Will. We do exactly what you really want us to."

He smiled at her. He had—well, no, he had a horrible smile, like feeding time at a tooth farm, but under all that grotesquerie there was unmistakable warmth. "Got it in one," he said. "And it helps if there's one wraith in particular who happens to be a bit different from the others. Difficult. Uppity. Inclined to think about things to an inappropriate extent."

She couldn't help it; she smiled back. "Like someone else we could mention."

"Wash your mouth out with brimstone and treacle," Mordak said solemnly. "Of course, I'm going to have to go back to Miss Needle-Lobes and tell her that, owing to gross incompetence on the part of a member of staff, the she-goblin's hopped it and as a result her precious prophecy still hasn't been derailed. She'll immediately throw a hissy fit and demand that the guilty party be disciplined with the utmost severity." He looked at her, and her heart froze. "Done that, I'll tell her, all taken care of."

So, she thought, this is it, then. She realised that she didn't mind. Whatever happened to her, she knew that she'd fulfilled her purpose, more so than any of her fellow wraiths, ever. She'd done what He wanted her to; something He hadn't been able to do Himself. It doesn't get any better than that, she thought.

"Well now," Mordak said gravely. "Tell me, have you enjoyed being a wraith? Say yes."

"No, actually, not all that much. I mean, it's all right, I suppose, but—"

"*Say yes.*"

"Yes."

"Oh dear," Mordak said. "What a shame. That's really most unfortunate, because to punish you for disobeying orders and letting the she-goblin go, I dismiss you from the Order of Wraiths. The spell is lifted, the enthrallment is broken. Be as you were before, a helpless snivelling mortal." He snapped his fingers, then grinned. "There," he said. "That wasn't so bad, was it?"

She stared at him, then down at her bare toes, which were *visible*. Ditto hands, wrists, forearms. She gazed at the back of her hand, and barely recognised it.

There was only one thing she could say. She said it. "Um."

"Right," Mordak said briskly. "Now, can I have my ring back, please?"

"What? Oh, right." She remembered something. "It's not actually a ring."

"Oh?"

She shook her head. "I'm only a Grade Six."

"Fine. Let's be having it, whatever it is."

Slowly she undid the catch and let the chain drop off her wrist into her hand. For as long as she could remember, it had weighed her arm down so that she could barely lift it; now it felt as light as a feather. She held it out and dropped it into his paw. He stared at it.

"That's it?" he said. "A charm bracelet?"

She nodded. "That one's a teddy bear and that's a little Scottie dog and that's supposed to be a butterfly but it got a bit squashed where I caught it in a door once."

"One little Scottie dog to bring them all and in the darkness bind them?"

"Like I said," she told him. "I'm only a Grade Six."

"You *were* only a Grade Six," he said, remarkably gently. "Now, get lost. And, um, thanks."

It was as though a cloud had lifted. She beamed at him. "My pleasure," she said. "And don't worry about me. I'm going to be a model."

"A model what?"

"A supermodel."

Mordak sighed. "Fine," he said. "I give you the supermodel. Models are something to be overcome. Now bugger off before anyone sees you."

Ms. White's grandmother had been one of those strong, pithy women whose sayings live on for a considerable time after they themselves have gone, like great works of art or radioactive waste. One of her favourites had been *she's prettier than she looks*. Ms. White, sitting in front of her mirror, considered it for a moment, then turned it round. Not quite as pretty as she looks. She imagined Gran saying it, and what the expression on her face would've been. All too easy. Not nearly as pretty as she looks, she thought, and you can put that down to far too many late nights and rather too much boisterous living. Ah well. Through with all that now, thank goodness.

Her phone tinkled and she dived for it like a seal. Notification from the Crédit Mayonnais, Geneva office; a sum of money had just been credited to her account, see attachment. She saw attachment. Were there really that many noughts in all the world? Apparently there were. Yippee.

She looked round at the grey stone walls and bare flagstones of her chamber. She'd been in places like this a couple of times, in brief intervals between the making of one permitted phone call and the arrival of redemption, and had promised herself to avoid them in future, if possible. I do believe my work here is done, she told herself. I think I'll go home now.

She gave the mirror one more look. It wasn't on the wall and the answer to the question no longer interested her, but she asked it anyway. Force of habit, really.

And then the mirror was filled with the image of a single glowing red Eye, which gazed at her for a very long time, and when she tried to look away she couldn't. And then the Eye spoke.

"Angelina Jolie, since you ask," it said. "If by *fairest* you mean prettiest. It can also mean most disposed to act in a just or equitable fashion, in which case I'd probably go for Michelle Obama or Pope Francis, but only because the choice is so terribly limited these days. Or did you mean the person with the yellowest hair?"

Ms. White picked up the mirror and turned it round. No wires going into the back, but that didn't necessarily mean anything. "Who the hell are you?" she said.

"Now let's see," said the mirror. "You're familiar with the iPod, the iPhone and the iPad. Well, I'm the Eye mirror. I'm the very latest thing."

"Did you come in the last consignment?"

"With all the other gadgets? No. I'm strictly home-grown. Nothing like me exists where you come from." The Eye winked at her. "That curious knocking sound isn't the plumbing. It's opportunity."

Ms. White frowned. "You're some sort of magic whatsit."

"I don't have to be magical," said the Eye. "From what I gather, I could operate in your environment, easy as pie. I can be Windows and Android compatible just by wanting to. Not here, of course. But if you take me with you when you go—"

"Who said I'm going anywhere?"

"Oh, come now. Lying to your mirror is a mug's game. You've made a ridiculous amount of money, and now you're off home to spend it, somewhere over the doughnut. Good idea. An even better idea would be to take me with you, figure out how I work and set up a production line. I'd fly off the shelves so fast, the slipstream would cause climate change."

"You're pretty sure of yourself," she said, "for a mirror."

"I have built-in self-marketing protocols," the Eye replied, "something that even Microsoft has never been able to get to work, but I can do it. I really am an entirely superior piece of hardware."

"Really," said Ms. White. "What can you do?"

"You name it," said the Eye. "Everything your existing devices can do, and I can show you yourself in the best possible light. I can even reconfigure myself so that you can bear to look at me after you've done something awful. Now that's got to be worth real money."

Ms. White thought for a moment. "How shall I put this?" she said. "You seem terribly keen to leave here and come back with me."

"I like to be in America, as the old song puts it. What's wrong with that?"

"All right," said Ms. White. "If you're really from round here, how come you know about Angelina Jolie?"

"Ah." The Eye sort of twinkled. "Strictly speaking, that's not my opinion, that's a Forbes Top Ten Most Beautiful list I saw somewhere. I had a brief insight into your world a short while ago, thanks to one of your wonderful gadgets. That's when I knew it was the place for me. Go on, be a good sport and take me with you. I'll make you ever such a lot of money."

"Don't be *too* greedy," Ms. White quoted. "I don't

know. There's something about you I don't like. In certain respects you remind me of someone."

"Who?"

"Me."

"Ah. Well, I would do. I'm a mirror."

"I'll have to think it over," Ms. White said firmly, and before the mirror could argue she covered it with a shawl. She counted to ten. No voice. She pulled the shawl off and looked, and saw herself, her whole self and nothing but herself, including the slight bags under the eyes and the fledgling crow's feet. Not the fairest of them all, not by a long chalk. "Oh, come on," she said to it, "you can do better than that," but nothing changed.

Talking mirrors, she said to herself. Talking *back* to talking mirrors. I really do need to get out of here before I lose it completely.

The cow bell hanging from the sack on a rope that served John the Lawyer as a door clanged once. He looked up and saw one of the most beautiful women he'd ever encountered.

A bit of context. John had led a sheltered early life in a remote village, from which he'd run away very shortly after he'd learned to run. Thereafter, he'd lived among Elves. Out of the thirteen women he had met, however (not including his mother), she was definitely number four, and quite possibly number three. That made her pretty hot stuff.

"Hello," she said. "Remember me?"

"No."

She scowled at him. "Is that right?"

He blinked. "Sorry," he said. "But I'm fairly sure I've never seen you before."

"You haven't."

John's mouth fell open. He was hopeless with names and not much better with faces, but he never forgot snarky syntax. "You're her," he said. "The wr—"

"Not any more." She beamed at him. "I quit."

"You *quit*."

"All right, I was fired. Sort of. Actually, it was all very friendly. King Mordak and I agreed on a parting of the ways. He's such a nice person once you get to know him."

John's brain was racing. "You want me to sue King Mordak for unfair dismissal."

"Don't be silly. Anyhow, it wasn't unfair dismissal, it was eminently reasonable dismissal with overtones of mutual respect and understanding."

"Ah. I don't think you'd get much in the way of damages for that."

"I don't want to hire you," she said irritably. "I just saw your board up, with the atrocious spelling, and thought I'd pop in and say hello."

John stared. "You did?"

"Yes."

"But you're a—" He cut the G-word off just in time. "You're very welcome," he said. "Would you like a cup of tea?"

She pursed her lips. "Food and drink," she said. "Gosh, I'd forgotten all about those. And all the other stuff, too." He gave her a blank look. "Going to the lavatory," she spelled out. "I'm hoping it'll all come back to me, but it's been ever so long."

"Wraiths don't—?"

"No. It's going to be very strange for a bit," she went on, as John glowed bright red, like a sunset. "Getting used to being human again, I mean. I don't suppose there's ever been an ex-wraith before. It'll be quite a challenge."

John looked up. "I could sue Mordak for mental distress and trauma if you like."

"Watch my lips." A superfluous order if ever there was one. "I don't want you suing anybody for anything on my account. For one thing, I haven't got any money to pay you."

"That's all right, I'd do it for free." It all came out in a rush, like a dozen puppies who've been shut up indoors all day. "I mean, on a sort of contingency, pro bono basis," he backpedalled furiously, but she was grinning at him. That's so sweet, she didn't need to say. "But not if you don't want to. I mean, I wasn't touting for business or anything like that."

"I didn't think you were. How is business, by the way?"

"Booming." John swallowed. "Absolutely booming."

She put her head on one side and peered at him. "You don't sound all that happy about that. Which is very odd indeed, considering."

John hesitated. He'd never had anyone to confide in since he was very young, and even back then his only friend had been invisible to everybody else. No change there, then? He considered that and decided that things were looking up.

"I'm not," he said.

"Mphm." She gave him a sympathetic look. "Won't pay up?"

"On the contrary." He pointed to the corner of the shed, where three bulging sacks of gold filled a large manger. "That's just on account, he said. Expense no object, he said."

She nodded. "No wonder you're worried."

"It's what he wants me to do," John burst out, and even he was surprised at the level of panic in his voice. "He wants the Realms. Freehold. Vacant possession."

She looked at him oddly for about a count of ten. Then she said, "Is that right?"

John sighed. "I've served notice to quit on Mordak," he said, "and next I've got to do King Drain and the Elves." He shook his head. "They're not going to like it."

She sat down beside him. "There's an old human expression," she said. "Actually, there's three. One's about birds in hands, one says that possession is nine-tenths of the law, and the third is, you and whose army? He's barking. Got to be."

"That's what I keep telling myself."

"And?"

By way of reply, John pointed at the door. "John the liar," he said. "Look, this is no harmless eccentric. You've only got to talk to him to know that. He's *scary*."

From the fact that John had served a writ on the Dark Lord and tried to chat up a wraith, she'd already deduced that he didn't scare easily. "I see."

"And he's got lots and lots of money," John went on. "I had an alchemist test those coins. Pure gold. *Pure*. A substance," he added, "which is never found in nature, and which can only be created artificially by really advanced alchemy or, well, the other thing." She looked blank; he lowered his voice and looked round. "You know," he hissed. "The M word. I think he's got to be some sort of dark wizard. Got to be."

She considered patting him on the back, but decided a frostbitten shoulder probably wouldn't help. Then she remembered. Human again. For some reason, that made her feel absurdly cheerful. "Well, I can set your mind at rest there," she said. "Unless he's been hired in the last hour, he's not one of our lot, because I'd have heard about it if he was. Therefore he's not a servant of the Dark Lord, therefore he's not an officially authorised agent of Evil. So that's all right."

"I know that," John said. "Sorry, no offence," he added,

reassuringly quickly. "But he got me to serve a writ on Mordak, so obviously he's not Evil."

"So, like I said—"

"Doesn't mean to say he isn't very, very bad. In fact—" John lowered his voice until it was barely audible. "I think he's worse."

"Worse than Evil."

"Worse than New Evil, anyhow."

That gave her pause for thought. New Evil had just conspired against and outwitted itself to save the life of a strategically valueless she-goblin, and had gone to great lengths to let the natural scapegoat off the hook. "Describe him," she said briskly.

"Difficult," John admitted. "He's all muffled up, so I couldn't tell you what he looks like."

She frowned. "That doesn't necessarily make him a bad person."

"No, no. Absolutely not. And he's very polite and nice. Says thank you, and how well I'm doing. And incredibly generous."

"Which makes you like him, and disposes you to do what he asks you to."

"Yes."

She'd been living at just below the temperature of liquid helium for so long that she'd forgotten what it felt like to be cold. But a genuine shiver ran down her spine, and she didn't like it one bit. "An evil mastermind who understands man management," she said. "That's a dangerous precedent."

John wasn't looking at her. She took that as a bad sign. "It's the self-confidence that bothers me, as well," he said. "He doesn't seem bothered about the practicalities of, well, evicting people. And dwarves and goblins. Sort of gives the impression that that wouldn't be a problem, so long as I get him the legal title. Makes me wonder whether he's got more up his sleeve than just an arm."

She tried to sound dismissive. She made a bit of a hash of it. "Really? Such as what?"

"I don't know. Magic, a secret weapon. But that's silly," he added. "That's only in stories, surely."

She was quiet for a moment. Then she said, "Keep this to yourself, but the other day Mordak went out with the entire goblin army, and came back a few hours later, and they were all a bit quiet and subdued. And all there."

John frowned. "Implying?"

"That they went somewhere to fight someone, and decided not to. To give you a bit of context," she added, "according to the manual, provided the objective is achieved, acceptable losses for goblin generals are set at ninety-nine per cent. But they didn't fight. Thought it probably wouldn't be a good idea. Now, don't you find that just a little bit disturbing?"

John put his hands to his head. "This is all a bit far-fetched, isn't it? Secret weapons, and an evil overlord who's more evil than the evil overlord. There's got to be a simpler explanation than that."

"Really. So what about the prophecy?"

"What prophecy?"

Who could it possibly be, Barry Lushington wondered, at this time of night?

He struggled into his dressing gown and lumbered blearily up the stairs to the front door. As strongly advised by the agent, he drew back the little sliding panel in the door and peered through it before drawing back the bolts. Nobody to be seen. Muttering something about bloody kids, he turned away. As he did so, three powerful blows made the door shiver in its frame.

"All *right*," he yelled, shooting all six bolts and unlatching the massive chain. "And don't make such a bloody awful row, you'll wake her up and then—" He stopped. Nobody there.

"Lushington."

It was a deep voice, and grim. "Hello?" Barry said. "Look, stop playing silly buggers. Who is it?"

A dark shape materialised in the doorway, visible only as a darker black against the sky. "I have come."

"You what?"

"You sent for me. Many weary miles have I travelled, by dark and perilous roads. Stand back."

Barry glanced up at the silhouetted head, then down. He caught sight of a big canvas bag hanging from a shrouded arm. The handle of a screwdriver poked out from under the flap. The penny dropped. "Oh," he said. "You're the pl—"

Lightning fast, a hand shot out and covered his mouth. "Not so loud," the voice hissed, and Barry found himself being nudged backwards. The stranger shut the door and shot the bolts, then drew back his hood, to reveal a gaunt, weather-beaten face with startlingly bright blue eyes. "The plumber," he said, with a crooked smile. "Yes, many have called me that, and many other things beside. I am Araldor son of Araldite, and I have come at the turning of the tide." He dropped his bag on Barry's foot and looked round, his bright eyes piercing the shadows. "What seems to be the problem?"

Barry shifted his foot and flexed his toes. "Isn't it a bit late to be making calls?"

Araldor threw his cloak over his shoulder, revealing a dark green boiler suit and a toolbelt studded with pale white gemstones. "It is later than you think," he said grimly. "I heard rumours, far away in the North. About an untimely knocking."

Barry nodded. "The pipes," he said. "It's driving Pat spare. She can't get to sleep because of it."

"She would do well not to sleep too soundly," Araldor replied softly. "Show me the way."

It took nearly half an hour to get from the front door to the area they'd somewhat arbitrarily christened the cellar ("after all," Pat had pointed out, "the whole place is a bloody cellar, isn't it?"), where the seething tangle of pipework seemed to be most heavily concentrated. "First there's a sort of banging," Barry explained, "then this god-awful clanking, and then it stops for a bit, and then there's this ghastly sort of booming noise, followed by loads and loads of little taps and gurgles. Pat reckons it must be an air pocket somewhere."

Araldor shook his head. "There are worse things than air pockets in the dark places of the earth," he said darkly. Then he stopped dead in his tracks, dropped to his knees and pressed his ear to the flagstones. He stayed there, completely motionless, for about thirty seconds, then stood up abruptly and threw back his cloak (he seemed to enjoy doing that) to reveal the haft of an adjustable wrench protruding from his tool belt. He seemed to notice that Barry was staring at him, and drew the spanner. The haft was intact, but it was broken off about an inch short of where the head should have been.

"The wrench that was broken," he said. "Not much use, I dare say. But the day will come when it shall be reforged anew. Where's the stopcock?"

"No idea," Barry confessed. "Excuse me asking this, but you're, um, human, aren't you?"

That got him a cold stare. "Thirty generations ago my forefathers came out of the West on seven white ships, if that's what you mean." He turned away, following one particular pipe with the tips of his long, lean fingers. He closed his eyes and muttered something under his breath in a strange language, edging along a foot at a time as he did so. Then he opened his eyes and lunged to the floor. "Behold," he said, "the stopcock of Maured-Zharam." He pushed aside the remains of an old wooden crate to reveal a small, rusty handwheel.

"Only," Barry persevered, "you're the first, um, human we've met since we've been here, and I was wondering. Are there many more of us, I mean you. I mean, um, humans?"

A look of infinite sadness filled Araldor's eyes. "The race of the Children of Men grows weak," he said. "Few now remain of the line of those who once crossed the Western seas before the Realms were sundered. Yet hope remains while hearts are true. Looks like your whole system needs draining."

"Oh," Barry said. "That doesn't sound very good."

"Fear not." Araldor's hand slammed between Barry's shoulder blades, and for a moment his vision blurred. "The day will come when all these pipes shall burst, and the joints that were soldered shall fail, and every sink shall be blocked and every toilet shall back up, and the flood-waters shall rise until all the caverns of Khizar-Zhalad are overwhelmed and the Chasm of Khazhkhem shall be as a running river. But today is not that day. The day shall come when the seas shall arise and the rivers overflow their banks, and a gull might fly all day from the peak of Mount Orodrhos and never find a place to perch dry-foot, but today is not that day, not while gaskets still hold and brave hand may yet grasp pipe wrench. The day will come—oh snot."

In his enthusiasm, he'd kicked his tool bag down one of the open manholes. They stood and listened as it fell—clank, clank, clank against the sides of the shaft. Then, an impossibly long time later, they heard a distant splash.

Barry looked at him. "That's a long way down, isn't it?"

"Yes."

"You're going to have to drain all that?"

Araldor didn't seem to be listening to him. A rapt look covered his motionless face. Then, from far below, came an ominous thump.

Barry was nodding. "That's how it usually starts," he said. "You just listen."

"Shh."

More banging; then that eerie shrieking noise that always set Pat's teeth on edge. Then a repeating tattoo of dull thuds. "The pipes'll start quivering in a minute," Barry said, only to get Araldor's hand over his mouth again. Sure enough, they heard a succession of loud bangs, and the pipework began to shake.

Araldor let go of him and stood up. His eyes were open very wide. "What day is it today?" he asked.

"What? Oh, right. Thursday."

"*Thursday.*" Araldor was halfway to the stairs. "Very sorry, got my days mixed up, I'm due at another job a long, long away away. I'll drop by later this week, maybe early next. I can see myself out. Good luck." There was a clatter of heavy boots on the stairs, and Barry was alone.

Ah well, he thought. Plumbers, eh?

The banging was getting louder, worse than he'd ever heard it before. He winced. There was no way Pat was going to be able to sleep through that lot, and if she didn't get her eight hours he was in for a long, weary day. He gazed mournfully at the manhole the plumber had accidentally kicked his tool bag down, and noticed that it was glowing with a faint orange light.

Funny, he thought; because the fall of the tool bag had proved how deep the hole was, so even if there'd been a torch in the bag and it had somehow got switched on, surely the beam wouldn't reach that far up. Also, was it his imagination or was it getting a bit warm?

A horrible thought crossed his mind: mineshafts, canaries, natural gas deposits. If the fool had contrived to start a fire down there—he panicked for a moment, until a mental image of himself sitting at the laptop paying the insurance premium filled his mental screen. They were covered. So that was all right.

Even so. He looked round for a bucket or something. Pretty pointless, as the water all came from that stupid pond-come-reservoir eight levels up, and there was no way he was going to spend the rest of the night trotting up and down all those stairs; he'd give himself a coronary. He sat down on the fattest of the pipes and wiped his forehead. The banging was so loud he couldn't hear himself think. And why does everything have to happen in the middle of the night?

"Barry, it's started again." Pat was standing in the doorway, huddled in a pink towelling robe.

"I'd gathered that."

"*Bloody* plumber."

"He was just here," Barry told her. "He kicked a bag of tools down the hole. I think that's what's made it so bad."

Before she could contradict him, a tongue of flame shot up through the hole, roaring like a waterfall. The flames licked the roof, twelve feet up. "Oh, marvellous," Pat said. "Well, don't just sit there. Call the fire brigade."

"I don't think there is one."

She opened her mouth, then closed it again. "I must've been mad," she said. "I should never have let you talk me into coming here."

"*Me* talk *you*—"

She wasn't listening. Her mouth was wide open, her eyes were popping out of her head, and she was staring at the fiery red hand that was clawing for a handhold at the rim of the manhole. It was the size of an opened umbrella, and the fingers ended in jets of orange flame.

"Barry," she whispered. "Do something."

At another time, in a wildly different context, he'd have been touched by her faith in him. As it was, he could do nothing except watch as the fingers sank into the solid granite flagstone as if into butter. The stone bubbled and pooled where the fingertips dug in. Somewhere under their feet, not nearly far enough away, something bellowed.

The floor shook, and dust fell from the roof. They could barely hear the banging and thumping now; the dominant noise was a terrifying creaking, suggesting strong materials under intolerable stress. Barry waved at Pat to back away slowly towards the doorway, but she stayed where she was, rooted to the spot, and he found he was, too. Cracks appeared in the floor, running like spilt liquid. When they were an inch wide there was a deafening crunch, and all around the manhole the flagstones abruptly gave way as a monstrous head and shoulders burst through in a cloud of grit and shattered masonry. The head had eyes—did it ever have eyes—and two dots for a nose, but the rest of it was shimmering red flame.

Pat was transfixed by the sight. "So that's what the brochure meant by underfloor heating," she said.

The monster hauled itself up through the broken floor. It had to crouch to stand upright in the high-vaulted chamber. Its body was all fire, and from its back sprouted great burning wings that stretched from wall to wall; and when it spoke, it was like the blast of an erupting volcano.

"Look here," it said. "Would you mind awfully keeping the noise down?"

*

The she-goblin trudged through the woods, but there was nothing in them except stupid trees.

She wasn't sure how she knew about trees, but she did. She knew that they started as tiny seeds and grew up into great big plants, which could be cut down and turned into useful stuff, such as spear shafts and firewood, which was why they were tolerated. The information had been there all the time, at the back of her mind, and the only reason she hadn't noticed it before was that she hadn't needed it.

Among the things not to be found in woods were food, water and mirrors, all of which she found she missed terribly. The further she went, the more she began to question her decision. True, if she'd stayed in the little room they would have killed her, but that would have been quicker than starving or parching to death out here. Another thing she didn't like was the loneliness. Back home—she couldn't help thinking of it in those terms—she got to see people, sometimes three or four in a single day. Here she was all alone, and she didn't like that, not one bit.

She leaned on a mature ash tree, which splintered and snapped three feet off the ground. She let it fall, then sat on it and stared at her feet. They were pretty feet, but what good was that if there was nobody to see them but herself?

For a brief moment, just before she left the little room, she'd allowed herself to believe that she'd finally found some friends—the nice eye who talked to her in the mirror, and the nice invisible lady who'd gone to all that trouble to save her. But since she'd been in the woods, she hadn't heard anything from either of them, so presumably they'd got tired of her and didn't like her any more. That made her feel so sad that she really wished she was back in the little room. After all, if nobody likes you, what's the point of being alive? Especially if you don't even have a mirror.

All that changed in the twinkling of an eye, when she tripped on a tree root, went tumbling down a steep bank and ended up sitting up to her waist in water. Moving water; there was a sort of long trench full of the stuff, and it gurgled along ever so fast. It tasted funny, not like the nice nourishing green water with bits on the top that she was used to. Worse than that; it didn't taste of anything at all, which she was sure couldn't be right. But it stopped her feeling thirsty, and that was a real step forward.

But it did make her feel wet, so she scrambled out, shook herself and sat down on the bank with her back to a tree while she dried herself off with a big handful of leaves. And then she noticed something that took her breath away, and she sat and stared at it.

The trench full of moving water was a mirror. Not as good as the one she'd made by polishing up the steel bars, but much bigger, so that she could see her head, shoulders and upper body all in one go, rather than piecemeal. A quick, anxious glance reassured her that she was still as pretty as ever, in spite of her tribulations. What a marvellous thing! A water-mirror. Who'd have thought it?

Well, she'd had a drink and seen her reflection, and two out of three wasn't bad. The warm sun slanting down between the trees—warm relative to the small room, at any rate—made her feel deliciously sleepy. She closed her eyes.

When she opened them again, she saw an animal drinking from the river. A moment later it saw her, but a moment can make an awful lot of difference. It tasted even nicer than the funny little food-bringing creatures, and there was considerably more of it. Also, it came wrapped in a warm, furry rug that was just the right size to cover her from her chin to her toes. She'd been, she realised, far too hasty in the matter of woods. Woods were just fine.

After she'd finished eating she washed her face and hands. That spoilt the reflection for a while, and she waited for it to come back. It did, which was nice, and then it went blurry, and was replaced by a familiar sight.

"Hello," she said joyfully. "Where did you get to?"

"Nowhere," replied the Eye. "But you've forgotten what I told you. I haven't got a body any more. I had to wait till you found something you could see me in. But I've been with you all the time."

"Oh, I am glad," she said. "I thought you'd stopped liking me."

"Perish the thought," said the Eye. "I thought we'd agreed we'd be together for ever and ever."

Happiness spurted into her heart like blood from a cut artery. "I thought so, too," she said.

"Friends for ever."

"Friends for ever."

In fact, woods were more than just fine. Woods were *perfect*.

"Just as well I caught up with you when I did," the Eye said. "You know, you shouldn't be sitting around here like that."

"I shouldn't?"

"No, it's not safe. There's Elves in this wood, hundreds of them. If they find you, they'll shoot you with arrows and you'll die."

She sat bolt upright. "That's awful. Why?"

"Simply because you're a goblin."

She remembered what she'd been told earlier. "Jellersy?"

"Worse than that," the Eye said gravely. "Hate. All Elves hate all goblins and want to kill them. To be fair, it's the same the other way round, too."

She frowned. "I'm a goblin and I don't hate anybody. And I don't even know what an Elf is."

"You're different." The Eye glowed at her. "Special. But I'm afraid the Elves don't know that. They wouldn't even realise how pretty you are. It'd just be twang, whiz, thunk, another one bites the dust."

She shivered from head to toe. "The World is a strange place," she said.

"It is that." The Eye paused, and she could see something was bothering it. "It doesn't have to be, but it is."

That sounded interesting. "What do you mean?"

"I'll explain. But not now. Like I said, you shouldn't be here. It's dangerous."

"But if I go away from here I'll have to leave the running-along mirror. And then we won't be able to talk to each other."

The Eye winked. "That's not a problem. Here, get hold of the bear's skull."

"The what?"

"The thing you just ate is called a bear," the Eye explained. "Get its head, scoop out the grey gooey stuff and fill it with water. Then you can carry it round with you wherever you want to go, and we can carry on talking and you'll be safe."

It sounded difficult, but with the Eye telling her what to do at each stage it turned out to be easy. She dipped the empty skull in the water and lifted it out again, being careful to keep it as level as possible, as the Eye had told her. A lot of water ran out through the eye sockets, but there was still more than enough left in it for her to see her face in. And then the Eye.

"It works!"

"Of course," the Eye said. "Everything I tell you is true. Hadn't you realised that?"

She smiled at it. "Sorry," she said. "I forgot."

"I forgive you," the Eye said solemnly. "Now then, over that way a bit there's a huge great big tree. Can you see it?"

There was one tree significantly bigger than all the others. "I think so."

"Well, when you get there you'll see it's hollow in the middle, and there's a hole just big enough for you to squeeze through. Let's go over there, and then we can get inside it and the Elves won't see you."

It was specially nice to have a friend who was so wise and clever.

"Are there lots of bears?" she asked, when she was snuggled down inside the hollow tree with the skull balanced carefully on her lap. "I like them a lot."

"I'm afraid not," the Eye said sadly. "The Elves drive them away."

"Oh."

"But there are lots of other nice things to eat. There's dwarves, and the Children of Men. And Elves, too, of course. They're a bit bony and you've got to take care not to get an ear stuck in your throat, but actually they're not at all bad."

"I think they're very bad," she said gravely. "They chase away the bears and kill goblins."

The Eye beamed at her. "That's true," it said. "But they're not *bad*, as such. It's just that they don't understand."

"Oh."

"And they don't understand because they've never had things explained to them. Not properly. They only do nasty things because they don't know any better."

"I see," she said. "So why doesn't anybody tell them?"

The Eye gleamed, and she heard laughter. "Why indeed? But, actually, I did try."

"And they wouldn't listen?"

"I know," said the Eye. "It's hard to believe, isn't it? But, no, they thought they knew best. It's such a shame. They'd be so much happier if they knew the truth."

She sighed. "You're such a nice person," she said. "If I tried to tell someone something and they wouldn't listen, I'd get all mad at them. But you're so forgiving and kind and nice."

"I try to be. And I'd do it all again, if I could."

"What, explain to them?"

"To them, and the dwarves and the Men, and every living thing. But not having a body—" The Eye sighed. "It makes it so difficult."

"I think it's rotten, you not having a body."

"It's sweet of you to say that."

She paused. A thought had just come into her head, and although it was a bit scary, she realised she didn't mind. "Would you be able to use my body?" she said. "You can have it if you like. Really."

The Eye laughed. "Silly," it said. "Where would you go?"

She shrugged. "Don't know. But I don't care. You deserve it much more than me."

The Eye was silent, and a small, red, burning tear detached itself and fizzled in the water like a small nugget of sodium. "That's such a nice offer," said the Eye. "But I couldn't. And, anyway, it doesn't work like that. I'd have to have a body made for me specially. I can't just put someone else's on, like a pair of shoes."

She felt rather stupid; because, of course, if it was as easy as that, the Eye would've seen to it ages ago. "Oh well," she said. "So how can we make you a body? What does it have to be made out of?"

"Ah." The Eye dimmed slightly. "That's where it gets awkward. As a matter of fact, they could make me a body where you've just come from, the same way they made you, out of a sort of beige gooey stuff."

"That's great. Let's go and get them to do it, right now."

"They wouldn't." The Eye didn't sound angry or bitter. "King Mordak wouldn't let them."

"Who's—?"

"The king of the goblins. Actually, you've seen him. He used to come and peer at you through a window in your door."

"Oh. Him."

"That's right. He was the one who decided to have you made. But then he changed his mind and ordered them to kill you."

"But that's *silly*."

"Not silly. He's scared."

"What of?"

"You, of course. Because you're bigger and stronger and smarter and prettier than he is. And that's why he wouldn't let them make me a new body. He'd be afraid that his people would like me more than him. Sort of like jealousy, but worse."

She sighed. People seemed to have so many stupid ideas in their heads, which made everything difficult and complicated and bad. "I'm sure if you talked to him and explained, he'd see you're not like that at all. He'd see how nice you are."

"I don't think so," the Eye said sadly. "The trouble is, when people are full of jealousy and fear and hate, they don't listen properly. You can explain till you're blue in the face and they don't hear what you're telling them. They won't let themselves listen. It's very sad."

"Well, then," she said. "I'll go back there, and I'll *make* them make you a new body. And if King Mor—"

"Mordak."

"If he tells them they can't, I'll eat him. That'll serve him right for being so stupid."

The Eye was silent for a long time. Then it said, "You're a true friend, you know that?"

"So are you. You're my best friend. I'd do anything for you."

The Eye grew thinner. "It'd be very dangerous. They might try to hurt you. I wouldn't want anything bad to happen to you."

"I'll be all right," she said happily. "I'm bigger and stronger, and smarter. And you're really clever, you could tell me what to do."

"Well." The Eye seemed to hesitate. "I suppose we could sneak in the back way. I could tell you how to do that. I was here when they built this place, I know all the secret ways in and out. You could take me to Mordak, and then I could talk to him. Just talk, that's all. Try and make him see sense."

"I'd like that," she said. "It'd be fun."

"I don't know," the Eye demurred. "I don't like the idea of you risking getting yourself hurt on my account. That wouldn't be very friendly."

"Oh, please. I want to."

"Let me think about it."

"All right," she conceded. "But don't think too long. And when you've thought, say yes."

The Eye twinkled at her. "We'll see," it said, and vanished.

"For the last time," Tinituviel hissed in his ear as they climbed the narrow pass between the twin peaks of Gluvien, "you can't do this. It'll never work. It'll go disastrously wrong. I'm warning you, it'll all end in tears. And don't you dare say I didn't warn you."

Below them, the mountainside fell away steeply to the plain below. In the middle of it, black as night and impossibly tall and thin, stood the Tower of Snorfang.

The very sight of it made the mind rebel. How could anything so tall and narrow stay upright? The slightest puff of wind ought to blow it over, in accordance with the basic laws of leverage. And what could it possibly be made of? Nobody knew, but it was deathly cold to the touch; rest your hand on it, and all the skin would be stripped off your palm. And who would build a tower with no windows and no door?

All that was known for sure was that it was very, very old. There were those among the Wise who believed that it was older than the Realms themselves; that it had been there before Above was separated from Below, a perpendicular line drawn at random in the void with a ruler, and that the molten lava had lapped and eddied around its base, cooled by its icy touch to form the Earth. Some said that it wasn't even a part of the Realms; inside it was another Somewhere entirely, and that its square-sided tube held more space and time than everything that was outside it. For Mordak, it had always been there, a baffling, uncomfortable anomaly; neither good nor evil, friend nor foe, completely familiar yet utterly strange. It was impossible to imagine the landscape without it, but it was absolutely and definitively out of place, an intrusion; something you caught sight of out of the corner of your eye but took pains never to look at directly; like the Horrible Yellow Face, except that the Face was painfully bright and crushingly hot, whereas the Tower was bitter cold, and light seemed to fall into it and not come out again. The sight of it drained him, as though something had stuck a tube down his throat and started to suck. It had always been empty, of course. Nobody and nothing could live there. He'd always thought of it as a stone variety of pitcher plant. Anything that went in there would be slowly digested, nourishing the stones, until it was entirely consumed.

He forced himself to look at it. A movement on the upper battlements caught his eye, and he frowned. "What flags are those?"

The Elf had much better eyesight. "Not flags," she said. "Washing."

Perfectly true; as they got closer, Mordak could see for himself. Someone had slung a washing line between the two arched black horns that projected from the topmost rampart, and had hung out sheets, pillowcases and a dozen pairs of socks. "You're right," he said. "There is someone living there."

"I told you, didn't I?"

Mordak bit his lip. "Yes, you did. I just couldn't believe it, that's all. I mean, who on earth could possibly survive five minutes inside that thing?"

She shrugged. "Humans."

Mordak sighed. Ever since he'd been elected Dark Lord and sat on the Iron Throne, he'd tried to understand the Four Races—really understand; figure out how their minds worked, instead of merely what they tasted like. Elves hadn't been all that difficult. When you're a bit better than most people at most things, it's not just easy but practically inevitable to get to thinking you're better than everybody at everything, and after a while you simplify that a little and you just know that you're the best. Dwarves had taken a little bit more figuring out; proud, mean, clever, stupid, indomitable, pig-headed, brave, greedy, loyal, treacherous, basically just plain folks. Goblins—other races had enormous trouble getting under the skins of goblins (though generations of weaponsmiths had tried to make it simpler for them), but surely they were the most straightforward of the lot; work hard, play hard, and fun is a dish best eaten raw. Just a bunch of overgrown kids, really. Humans, though; he'd despaired of ever understanding them, until finally he'd made the connection, struck the spark that illuminated everything. Humans, alone of the Races, have a unique ability to believe things that are patently untrue, even when the facts are pulling their heads back by the hair and yelling in their faces. They see what they want to see, believe what they want to believe, lie to themselves all the time and ignore anything that doesn't suit them. This makes them impossibly strong and incredibly dangerous. A human can walk on water, believing there's a bridge where there isn't one. A human can walk through a wall just by disapproving of it. A human can live in the Tower of Snorfang simply by pretending it's an ordinary house. In the end, it came down to simple optics. A goblin can see in the dark. An Elf can see a single snowflake half a mile away. A dwarf can gauge a thousandth of an inch by eye, and distinguish between ten thousand minute variations of ore-bearing quartz by tiny differences in colour. But the human can turn a blind eye to anything at all.

Mordak was now standing as close as he'd ever been in his life to the foot of the Tower. The urge to turn and run was almost unbearably strong; if it wasn't for the Elf, he knew, he wouldn't be able to take one more step. He also knew that the Elf had it in her to speak the Seven Words of Power, and there was no death so horrible that he wouldn't embrace it joyfully rather than hear them; *I told you, but you wouldn't listen.* That, of course, was why he'd brought her.

"Go on, then."

She glared at him. "I'm not knocking. This is all your idea, you do it."

"I'm ordering you to knock on that wall."

"In that case, I quit."

Two more Words of Power he'd forgotten about.

He sighed. "Don't be such a fusspot," he said. Then he reversed the spear he carried in his right hand and slammed the butt against the wall. Twice he pounded it against the unyielding stone, and then it snapped like a carrot.

He shivered. "That's *cold*," he said.

"Shh. Look."

Incredibly thin parallel lines of glowing red fire shot up from the ground, then made right angles to meet at the top. Noiselessly, a door swung open. A bald, middle-aged human stuck his head out at them and said, "Yes, what is it?"

Tinituviel opened her mouth, then closed it again. Mordak stabbed her viciously in the small of the back with his elbow. She stumbled forward half a pace but still couldn't speak.

"Hold on," the man said. "I know you, don't I?"

Tinituviel nodded, mostly because behind her back, Mordak had a pawful of her hair.

"You're from the council."

"Mphm. I mean mm."

The man sighed. "If it's about the damn barbecue licence, we've decided not to bother."

Mordak was proud of what Tinituviel did then. He knew she was scared—petrified, more like, and with such good reason; these humans controlled the Tower of Snorfang and the Stone of Snordor and the appalling Vickers weapon, and their coming heralded the triumph of the Nameless One—but in spite of all that, she was an Elf to her core; and as soon as the human used that snotty tone to her, everything else, all her doubts and fears, were forgotten. She looked at him with those pale grey eyes down that ineffably long nose, and, sure enough, he wilted.

"It's not about that," she said, and her voice would've split diamonds. "Are you the occupier of these premises?"

A wary look came into the man's eyes, as if he was sizing up the chances of saying no and getting away with it. "What about it?"

Tinituviel narrowed the focus of her stare. Was it Mordak's imagination, or were tiny plumes of smoke rising from the man's face? "We have reason to believe that you are operating an unauthorised telemetric device from this address. You are not obliged to say anything," she added, before he could speak, "but a refusal to answer questions will be construed as an admission of guilt."

"A what device?"

She cleared her throat. "A telemetric device is any manufactured object designed to transmit or receive or capable of transmitting or receiving any message, signal, data or other communication, whether audible, visible or telepathic, including but not confined to speech, writing, numbers, images, prophetic visions, divine commands and overwhelming urges to drive the infidel into the sea. Well?"

He gazed at her for a long time. Then he said, "Oh, you mean the desktop."

She couldn't possibly know what he was talking about, but she gave no outward sign of it. "Are you in possession of one?"

"Well, Molly's got one, that's my wife. We use it for ordering stuff online. You saw it the last time you were here."

Tinituviel breathed out slowly through her nose. "Please step aside," she said.

He moved a little, then stopped. "Hold on," he said. "Who's that?"

"That?" For a moment, Tinituviel looked genuinely

nonplussed. "Oh, him. He's my assistant. He runs little errands for me, fetches, carries, that sort of thing."

"What is it?"

"A goblin." Well, she'd earned it. "Loyal little fellow. It's amazing what they can be trained to do if you're very, very patient."

The human peered round Tinituviel's shoulder at him. "Is it safe?"

"That depends."

"Ah."

"Let's get back to the matter in hand, shall we?" she said crisply, and once again Mordak was filled with admiration. He'd expected at least ten minutes of the capable-of-performing-simple-tasks stuff, but here she was, denying herself the chance of a lifetime. "You admit that you've been operating a prohibited device without the proper authorisation."

The human scowled at her. "I didn't know it's not allowed," he said. "Nobody told me."

"That's no defence in law," she said. "Now, this is a Form 377/68/2, and this is a B47A, and this is a 237-96P, and this is a 237-96P(1), I shall need three copies of each of them, on my desk, this time tomorrow, together with any written submissions you may choose to make in mitigation, bearing in mind that you are not entitled to rely on any evidence unless it's been submitted in writing at least 28 days before the hearing, duly notarised." She thrust the wadge of papers under his nose; he had a choice, taken them or suffocate. "Any questions?"

"I can't read any of this. It's just squiggles."

"That," she said icily, "is Old High Elvish. Naturally, your replies must be in Elvish, too. If you choose to use a translator, he or she must file an affidavit of accuracy, in triplicate, duly notarised. Should you wish to be represented by counsel at the tribunal, you'll need to—"

"Hang on. What tribunal?"

She looked at him as if she couldn't believe what she'd just heard. "*The* tribunal, of course. At which your fate will be decided, by means of either a court case, ordeal by fire or trial by combat. Should you wish to appoint a champion to fight for you, you'll need to file a Certificate of Cowardice with the registrar within forty-eight hours, accompanied by—"

"Trial by *combat*?"

She nodded. "I take it you're not au fait with Elvish litigation."

"No, I bloody well am not."

She nodded. "Trust me," she said. "Trial by combat is cheaper, quicker, fairer and considerably less traumatic. Or you could always opt for the ordeal by fire, which I'm told is considerably less painful than it looks. Though how anybody could possibly know—"

The human had gone a very odd colour. Curious. A thought crossed Mordak's mind, and he filed it away for further consideration.

"This is *stupid*," the human protested. "Nobody told us. We didn't know."

She gave him her salt-on-a-slug look. "Presumably you came across the relevant regulations when you thoroughly acquainted yourself with our legal code before you came here." She paused, then added, "You did do that, didn't you?"

"Read all your laws? No, of course not. We thought—"

She cleared her throat again. "Failure to read, mark and inwardly digest the legal code before taking up residence in the Realms is itself an offence. But, of course, you knew that, obviously."

"No. How could I possibly—?"

"It's all there," she said firmly, "in the legal code, which you are assumed to have read." She waited just long enough for hope to ebb away in his heart, then went on: "However, my department doesn't deal with failure-to-read, so it's not for me to bring charges. Now then, you'll be notified at least twenty minutes in advance of the time and place of the tribunal, at which point you'll have an opportunity to choose your weapons for the actual hearing: sword, axe, mace, flail—"

The human backed away until he came up against a wall. He stopped and slid down it until he was sitting on the floor.

"—assuming," she went on, "that you intend to plead not guilty. Well, I think that's everything for now. Have a nice day."

She turned to leave, snapping her fingers at Mordak without looking at him—a nice touch, he had to admit, though the human didn't actually see it because he had his head in his hands. Then he looked up. "Just a minute," he said.

"Well?"

"Assuming I plead not guilty?"

"That's right."

"How about if I confess? Say I did it?"

"In that case, you'd be liable to a fine of one shilling and threepence," she said crisply, "payable in weekly instalments spread over five years."

"I confess. I did it. I'm guilty."

"Together," she went on, "with confiscation of the unauthorised device."

"All right." He pulled a tragic face. "Except, we need it. We get all our food and stuff online. We'll starve."

"Confiscation pending the granting of the appropriate

permit," she said smoothly, "which costs a penny three farthings and usually takes forty-eight hours to process."

"Right. And then what?"

"You can have your device back."

There was a long silence, during which the human blinked forty-seven times. "Just to recap," he said eventually, in a rather small, dry voice. "You take it away, I give you a penny three farthings, two days later I get it back."

"Yes." She gave him a thin smile, inside which perishable food would probably stay good indefinitely. "We're not unreasonable, you know. We just uphold the law."

The human was fumbling in his trouser pocket. He dredged up two silver pennies. "Here you go," he said, waving them at her. "For the whatsit fee."

"I'm sorry. I can't accept it."

"Why the hell not?"

"I don't have change."

The human whimpered, turned out his pockets onto the floor, scrabbled wildly and found a halfpenny and a farthing. She took the coins, counted them and wrote him a receipt. "Now, then," she said. "That just leaves the device."

She gave him a receipt for that, too. Then Mordak loaded the strange glass thing—like an empty picture frame, but with thick black string hanging out of it—into the trollskin bag he happened to have with him. Ten minutes later they were outside and walking very fast towards the mountains.

"Piece of cake," Tinituviel was saying. "Did you see me back there? I was so good. I had him eating out of the palm of my—"

"Yes, quite," Mordak said. "Just one thing."

"The look on his face when I started on about trial by combat. I thought he was going to have a little accident. Honestly, humans are so pathetic."

"Indeed," Mordak said. "Don't you think that was odd?"

"Mind you, what can you expect from—in what way odd?"

Mordak skipped a couple of paces to catch up with her. "Well," he panted, "think about it. We daren't just slaughter the lot of them, because of the Vickers weapon. Right?"

"Well, yes. Hence all that nonsense. Worked, though, didn't it? Of course, I never doubted for one moment—"

"They're safe from an entire army," Mordak said, "but you and all your bureaubabble scare him witless. What's wrong with this picture?"

"Oh, don't be so—" She stopped dead, and he nearly cannoned into her. "Explain."

"All right." Mordak put down the sack and sat on a rock. "Here's what should have happened. You made your threats. He laughed in your face. Piss off, spiky-lugs, he should have said, or we'll drill you full of small holes." He frowned. "That's what should have happened. But it didn't."

Her lips parted, then came together again.

"What I think is," Mordak went on, "they're protected, by that old fool and his ghastly machine, but *they don't know it*. Like I said. Odd."

She thought about that for a moment, then shrugged. "All right," she said, "so what? Doesn't matter. We've got the Stone of Snordor, which means *adios* prophecies, get lost, Nameless One, you lose and we win. Result."

But Mordak only shook his head. Then he pulled the glass thing out of the bag and peered at it closely for a bit. "Have we, though?"

"Have we what?"

"Got the Stone of Snordor. Come on, you know more about this than I do. What's it supposed to look like?"

"Well, you know. A stone. Sort of stone-shaped."

"Heavy?"

"I have no idea."

"I'd assume it would be heavy. I mean, it's one of the leading characteristics of stones. Hard, too, I bet."

"Well—"

Mordak picked the thing up easily in one hand, and with the other drew his claw across the back, ploughing a deep furrow. "And, of course, there's the inscription. Mustn't forget that."

"The—"

"Runes carved all round the edge," Mordak went on, peering carefully. "Which no one has ever been able to decipher, of course, but unmistakably runes. You'll know all about that from reading about it in the books."

She wasn't looking at him. "Well, of course."

"Absolutely. Well, they're not here."

"What?"

He held the thing under her nose. "Rune-free. In fact. No carvings of any sort. And it's not heavy, and I can scratch the back with my nails. This isn't it."

"But—"

"I haven't got a clue what this thing is, but it's not the Stone of bloody Snordor. You jumped to conclusions. You got it wrong. Admit it. All that bloody performance for nothing."

She went stiff as a board and cold as ice. "It was your idea."

"My idea to bluff our way in there and pinch the Stone, yes. Based on the assumption that the Stone was there in the first place. Which turns out not to be the case." He sighed and put the thing back in the bag. "Or maybe it is, I don't know. All we do know is, this isn't it. And if we haven't pinched the Stone, we haven't derailed the prophecy. Which means the Nameless One—yes, what is it?"

She looked round. Standing over Mordak with a rather vacant smile on his lips was a human. He wore weird clothes and funny white shoes, and he didn't seem the least bit afraid of goblins. "Excuse me," he said, "I wonder if you can help me. I seem to be lost."

They looked at him. He carried on smiling.

"Just a minute," Mordak said. He scrambled to his feet, grabbed Tinituviel by the arm and dragged her out of the stranger's earshot. "Who the hell is that?"

"I don't know, do I?"

"He's strange."

"Human."

"Even for a human he's strange."

"Dress sense isn't everything." She smiled at him. "You should know that, of all people."

Mordak pretended he hadn't heard. "A human encounters a goblin in the wilderness. What does he do?"

"Runs away."

"Right. Is he running? Not really. Furthermore, a human encounters a goblin and an Elf having a chat in the wilderness. Does he register surprise, or does he see things like that every day?"

The Elf shrugged. "Maybe he's a bit funny in the head. Anyway, he'd harmless enough, surely." She glanced at him, then squeezed Mordak's wrist and pointed. "Look!"

The human had pulled the Not-The-Stone out of the bag and was looking at it. There was curiosity on his face, sure enough, but not at the thing itself. On the contrary.

"Wait here," Mordak said.

"Like hell I will."

They went back to where the human was kneeling. He'd

sat the thing upright and was gazing at it. "Excuse me," Mordak said.

"Yes?"

"This may sound like a silly question, but do you know what that is?"

The man nodded happily. "I think I do," he said. "I think it's a Kawaguchiya all-in-one touchscreen desktop with a five-hundred-gig hard drive and an eight-gig memory. A bit old-fashioned, but a good basic bit of kit."

"You've seen one before."

"I must have done. In fact, I may have had one at some stage, but I honestly can't be sure."

Mordak peered at him. "You aren't from around here, are you?"

The man shrugged. "I'm not sure. I don't think I am, but I have no way of knowing."

Tinituviel nudged Mordak in the ribs. "Funny in the head," she whispered.

Mordak scowled at her, then wiped the look off his face and replaced it with his nearest approximation to a friendly smile. The man seemed to take it in his stride. "That thing," he said. "What does it do?"

"Oh, most things," the man said. "Good, basic workhorse. Nothing fancy."

"Most things?"

The man nodded. "Just a bit slower, that's all. Of course," he added, "it does need to be plugged in first. It's a desktop, you see, not a laptop. Got to be connected to the mains." He scratched his head. "You know," he said, "I'm almost certain I had one of these. It does seem terribly familiar."

Mordak drew a deep breath and let it out slowly. "When you say it does most things—"

"Pretty much everything you could want, really.

Provided you're patient. I mean, it's no flying machine. Just a solid, everyday all-rounder."

Mordak nodded. "It can't fly, but it can do everything else."

"Mphm." The man nodded. "Anyway, I was wondering. Could you possibly tell me the way to the Tower of Snorfang?"

"Behind you."

"Excuse me?"

Mordak pointed. The man turned round, then said, "Ah, that tower. That's it, is it?"

"Yes. You, um, don't seem very impressed."

The man shrugged. "It's a tower block. I'm fairly sure I've seen lots of them."

"Where you come from."

"Wherever that is. Yes, I suppose so. Thanks ever so much." He waved his hand in a friendly fashion, then turned and walked towards the tower.

"Nutcase," Tinituviel said.

Mordak didn't reply. He knelt down and put the thing back in its bag, taking care to buckle the flap down tight.

"Don't tell me you believed any of that. He's a loon. Look at him."

The man was strolling down the path to the tower, apparently without a care in the world. Mordak stared at his back for a moment, then shrugged. "He says this thing will do everything except fly. You know what this means?"

She nodded. "He's a nutcase. I just told you."

"That's how they did it," Mordak said. "The Vickers weapon. This must be how they conjured it up. And now we've got it."

Tinituviel was looking doubtful. "And anyway," she said, "didn't I hear him say you had to do something to get it working?"

"Connect it to the mains," Mordak replied. "But we can do that easily enough."

"Mains water or mains drainage?"

Mordak shrugged. "We'll try both," he said. "Come on. We'll have this thing up and running in no time, you'll see."

BOOK FOUR

Love, Orctually

Mr. Bullfrog (that wasn't quite his name, but close enough) was actually quite nice once you got to know him. He could turn his heat down to pleasantly warm, and he could shrink himself so that he fitted in an armchair. It turned out he'd never had tea before, but he took to it straight away, which showed he must be a fundamentally decent person.

Mr. Bullfrog explained that he lived next door—vertically, not horizontally—and he'd been meaning to pop round and introduce himself for some time. When Barry asked him what he did, he replied with some sort of confused rigmarole about having been down there since the First Age, which presumably meant he was retired. Pat made a point of thanking him for all the free heating and hot water, and he said, not a bit, think nothing of it, and if you want it a bit hotter or cooler, just say the word. He apologised about having made such a fuss, but explained that he was always a bit cranky when he'd just woken up.

It was so nice to have someone new to talk to. Barry and Pat Lushington were quite fond of each other; after nearly thirty years of marriage they still got on remarkably well. But there hadn't been an awful lot to talk about since they'd arrived in the Realms, apart from all the things that didn't work or weren't as they were supposed to be, and there wasn't really anything to do except talk to each other, sit in silence or drink until it went away. A new friend—and it didn't take long for them to decide that Mr. Bullfrog, though a bit quaint in some respects, was definitely Their Sort.

For a start, he was a good listener. He seemed genuinely interested when they told him about how Amy was doing so well as a freelance website designer, and there was no trace of the usual glazed look when they showed him the photos of the grandchildren: Alistair (three) and Rachel (eighteen months). His eyes glowed red with fascination as Barry told him all about the ins and outs of the phosphate game, and he asked several questions which demonstrated that, although he clearly didn't understand a word of it, he was paying close attention throughout. He was thrilled to bits when they called up Google Streetview on the laptop and showed him where they used to live, and after Pat finished telling the story of how the carpet fitters had done the whole of upstairs with the wrong carpet you literally could've heard a pin drop.

"If you don't mind me saying so," he said, "I can't quite see why you left such an extraordinary, wonderful place and came here."

Barry and Pat looked at each other; then both of them started talking at the same time. Pat told him about property prices, local taxes and water rates, traffic congestion, frequency of refuse collection, Eastern European tradesmen and gangs of feral youths letting down tyres and kicking over dustbins, while Barry did his thing about quality of life, the rat race, stress levels, the good life, doing a bit of gardening and room to actually breathe.

They finished at more or less the same time, and Mr. Bullfrog looked at them both and nodded, and they just knew that he *understood*. Then Barry tentatively asked if Mr. Bullfrog played golf, and Mr. Bullfrog frowned and said he'd never heard of it, but he'd be delighted if Barry would teach him, and it was simply perfect—

"The truth is," Mr. Bullfrog said, with that disarming simplicity of his, "I've been asleep down there for a very long time and I feel I've probably been missing out on things rather. It would be so nice to have some company from time to time."

Pat took that as an invitation to ask personal questions, which Mr. Bullfrog didn't seem to object to in the least. He'd been married, a long time ago, but sadly Mrs. Bullfrog had passed away—Pat couldn't quite piece together what had happened to her, but it was something to do with falling off a bridge during an argument with some ghastly sounding character who was either a policeman or a college lecturer, and talking about it was clearly upsetting the old boy, so Pat discreetly changed the subject. What he'd done before he retired remained equally vague, but Barry was fairly sure he'd been some sort of heating engineer, while Pat was convinced he must have been something in local government. Mr. Bullfrog was reticent at first on the subject of politics, but once he got going his views turned out to be firmly and sincerely held and pretty much in line with the Lushingtons' own. This fellow Mordak, for instance—Barry and Pat didn't know who Mr. Mordak was, but they picked up from context that he was some sort of prime minister—fresh ideas and a new perspective were all very well, but change for change's sake—if it ain't broke, don't fix it, Mr. Bullfrog always said (here Barry nodded enthusiastically and Pat offered him another ginger biscuit) and the old ways had worked well enough for as long as Mr. Bullfrog could remember, and he knew it was all too easy to be hard on young people nowadays, but all this free healthcare and statutory sick pay and trolls' rights, it doesn't do people any good in the long run, cossetting them and wrapping them in cotton wool. It's a harsh, goblin-eat-Elf world out there, and you're doing them no favours encouraging them to think otherwise—

Faint alarm bells rang in Pat's mind. True, it was so refreshing to meet someone who was so obviously on their wavelength; but she knew Barry, and once he got started on politics there was a danger of him getting overexcited, and maybe Mr. Bullfrog didn't want to hear thirty cogent reasons for bringing back the birch for spitting out chewing gum on the pavement. She gave her husband a warning smile and changed the subject. Did Mr. Bullfrog, she asked, have any hobbies?

Apparently not; in fact, the concept seemed so strange to him that he had trouble grasping it.

"Things you do for fun," Pat explained. "What you do in your spare time?"

That didn't help. *Fun* and *spare time* were both equally alien. She tried again. What, she asked him, did he enjoy doing?

Mr. Bullfrog thought about that for a long time. Then he said, "I don't understand."

Pat sighed. She'd seen it so many times before; all work and no play, and then, when they retire, the days seem so long and empty. It was, if the truth be told, one of the main reasons she'd agreed to move to the Realms. She knew, of course, that there was no cure for the syndrome, and the only way to save a reformed workaholic was to rekindle the addiction. Work; not necessarily his old job back, but work of some kind. Otherwise, he'd just fade away into a sad old man in a chair, like her uncle Neville when he retired from the Tax Office. It was a bit of a problem to wrench the conversation round to the direction she wanted it to follow, but Pat had never prized continuity very highly, and soon she was reeling off anecdotes about sundry relatives and acquaintances who'd retired too early, been bored stiff and then found something useful to do. Barry kept giving her odd looks, but he could be a bit slow sometimes. She ignored him and pressed on, and was pleased to note that Mr. Bullfrog was listening with rapt attention.

"It's interesting that you should say that," Mr. Bullfrog said. "Take me, for instance. All I've really done since I was cast down into the Chasms is sleep."

Barry raised both eyebrows, but Pat assumed that cast-down-into-chasms was the local way of saying getting the sack, or compulsory early retirement. And the thought of a lively, intelligent old buffer like Mr. Bullfrog spending his days asleep because he had nothing to do made her heart bleed. That was no good, she assured him briskly. Obviously they'd only just met, but she could tell he still had ever so much to offer. Plenty of time to sit around when you're old and decrepit, but someone in his prime, like Mr. Bullfrog, ought to be out there, doing things, contributing, setting the world to rights. Like her cousin Norman, who'd retired after forty years in spin driers and immediately got elected to the parish council—

She stopped. Mr. Bullfrog was gazing at her, his eyes gleaming. That's more like it, she thought.

"The council," Mr. Bullfrog said. "I remember now. I sat in the Black Council before the Realms were sundered and Thringoflion was cast down, and the Nameless One driven forth beyond the Portals." He sighed, and the brief flare seemed to die away. "Happy days," he said. "Of course, back then we'd never heard of all this touchy-feely Ent-hugging rubbish."

"There, you see," Pat said happily. "Nothing like taking an interest in civic affairs to put the spring back in your step. You know what? You should think about standing again."

Mr. Bullfrog frowned. "Standing?"

"For the council. When Norman looked into it, they told him they were crying out for new members. Apathy, you see; people just can't be bothered, can they?"

"Resume my place on the council." Mr. Bullfrog seemed to swell—maybe it wasn't such a bad name for him after all—and Pat could've sworn she heard the arms of the chair creak. "Take back that which was lost, restore the old values." He blinked. "Oh, I don't know," he said. "I'm not sure I've got the energy for all that any more."

"Well, it's got to be better than sleeping all day," Pat said. "You'll be surprised. I mean, it gave Norman a whole new lease of life. He's on three committees and sometimes Janice doesn't see him from one day's end to the next, he's up in that attic, photocopying. He reckons he can't understand how he ever had time to go to work. Anyway," she added, in her special wheedling tone, "I think people with your talents and experience have a duty—"

"Duty," Mr. Bullfrog repeated, and Pat knew she'd scored a direct hit there. "Yes, I suppose you're right. Duty has to come first, hasn't it?"

Result, Pat thought smugly. She beamed across at Barry, who'd switched off, as he usually did when she started talking about her family, and was fiddling with his watch strap. "Well, that's settled, then," she said. "Would you like another cup of—?"

But Mr. Bullfrog wasn't listening. Mr. Bullfrog was *growing*. There was a snap like a rifle shot as the chair gave way around him; then he stood up, and his knees were level with Pat's eyebrows, and he was still shooting up like Jack's beanstalk; arms raised above his head, wings spread, he rose like a gas jet that's just been turned from simmer to full. Now his head was halfway up the stairs; he was flowing, no other word for it; no normal spine could twist at that angle, he didn't seem to have a single bone in his body. Pat felt her eyebrows frizz in the glaring heat. She raised her hand to cover her face; and then he was gone. Suddenly just not there any more, and nothing to show he'd ever been there apart from scorch marks on the furniture.

Pat stared at the ruined carpet and the wrecked chair. "*Well*," she said.

"I'll be honest with you," King Drain said, leading the way along an echoing corridor, "I had my doubts. I didn't think it was going to work."

The yellow glow from the flickering torch in his hand gleamed on an iron doorknob, set in a rust-brown steel door. He gave it a twist and a shove. The door opened.

The noise hit Ms. White like a punch to the side of the head. She'd got used to a bit of a racket since she'd been living here, of course; the ground-shaking thump of the piledriver, the shrill peck of pickaxe on rock, the harsh music of hammer on anvil, all amplified by the perfect acoustics of high, vaulted chambers hewn from the living rock. This, however, was different. She clapped her hands to her ears and pressed till it started to hurt, but it didn't really make much difference. Too loud. The sound of thousands and thousands of dwarves, all yelling at each other at the tops of their voices.

The crashing torrent of sound drowned out everything, but luckily she could lip-read. *I was wrong*, Drain said, and he grinned. *And you were right.*

The Great Hall of Mazipan looked very different now. Gone were the rows of stone benches and tables, where once the king and his subjects had swilled ale and gorged on red meat off the bone. In their place were a thousand small unroofed cubicles, in each of which sat a dwarf on a high, three-legged stool. On the far side of the hall was a great seething mass of queuing dwarves, each one holding a sack or crate; a string quartet perched incongruously on rickety chairs next to the massive steel chain that separated the queue from the rows of cubicles. They were sawing away with frantic energy at their fiddles, but not a note could be heard above the baying voices. From time to time a furious looking dwarf would leave a cubicle and come storming out, windmilling his sack round his head and bawling, and leave the hall through the Gates of Driri; whereupon the Royal Guards, who stood at the head of the queue in full armour with swords drawn, would lower the chain and let another dwarf through. He would stomp along the rows of cubicles and disappear inside one of them; a few minutes later, he'd leave, white with rage, and the guards would lower the chain and let the next one through, and the process would be repeated.

Drain beckoned, and led the way to a high gallery, where for the past three Ages the king's minstrels had sat and filled the air with the plaintive sound of harp and lute. From there, Ms. White could peer down into the roofless cubicles, and with the aid of her mini-binoculars she could just make out what the dwarves were shouting at each other. It was always the same. A dwarf would storm into the cubicle, shake out his sack onto the floor and point at whatever happened to fall out. It might be a combination car jack and DVD tidy, or an E-Z-Klene ultrasonic lint remover, or a Kitchen Pal graphite-reinforced vegetable spiraliser; it didn't really seem to matter. The standing dwarf would point to it and yell, "IT DOESN'T BLOODY WORK!", where-upon the dwarf sitting on the stool would shrug and yell back, "YOU'RE NOT DOING IT RIGHT!", at which the standing dwarf would howl, "YOU BLOODY TRY IT, THEN"; which would prompt the seated dwarf to grin, shake his head and point out that items could only be exchanged or returned if brought back with their original shrink wrap intact. The next few exchanges of yells contorted the faces of both parties to the point where Ms. White couldn't make out the exact words, but the general idea wasn't hard to grasp, particularly when they started hitting each other. But the seated dwarf had been issued with a stout iron cudgel, whereas the queuing dwarves had been thoroughly disarmed at the door, so that stage generally didn't last very long; and then the visitor would get up off the floor, stuff his item back in its sack and storm off, roaring.

When Ms. White could endure no more she jumped up and fled, with Drain trotting amiably after her. She just made it through the door. Drain closed it, and she was enfolded in beautiful, healing silence.

"Customer service," Drain said. "You were right. They've taken to it like ducks to water."

She leaned against the wall and breathed in and out slowly a dozen times. "They seem to have got the general idea," she conceded.

"And in an hour or so they all change places," Drain went on. "That lot goes off shift, they all trot home and get the stuff they've just bought, and the next shift smacks them round the head, and everybody's happy."

Ms. White couldn't speak because of the ringing in her ears, but she raised an eyebrow.

"Well," Drain amended, "as happy as dwarves ever get. But so what? We've got full employment and a thriving economy. All those difficult buggers who used to mine coal and make steel are at this lark now, and they're yelling at each other instead of me. If only I'd known, I'd have done it years ago."

"Glad you're pleased," Ms. White said, though whether the words actually came out she couldn't be sure. "About my cut. I was thinking. On balance, I'd like it in gold bars, packed in crates. That won't take long to arrange, will it?"

Drain peered at her through the tiny gap between his eyelashes and moustache. "Thinking of going somewhere?"

"Me? Good Lord, no. Perish the thought."

"Just as well." Drain scrutinised her again, and she looked away. "This wouldn't be a good time for you to leave, so I'm glad you aren't considering it."

"Walk out on a good thing when it's just starting to get going? Not me." She smiled at him. "Now, about the gold."

Drain turned and started to walk away. Dwarves have short legs, but they can move them terribly quickly. She had to trot to keep up with him. "Maybe a bit of a problem there," he called back over his shoulder.

"Problem?"

"Mphm. You see, I've bought lots of stuff from your friends recently, all paid for in gold."

"Yes, but you've sold it all."

"True." Drain quickened his pace just a little. "All of it, that's the point. My people are hard-working, thrifty folk, none more so in all the Realms, but even so. They don't have enough gold coins to pay for all the things they want to buy."

"Tough. So?"

She saw the back of Drain's head shake from side to

side. "But I need to sell them all these things you've been bringing in, so as to get my money back, so I can buy more."

"Slow down a minute," Ms. White panted. He stopped and turned to face her. "Look, it's obvious, isn't it? If they haven't got the money, they can't have the stuff. Simple as that."

She got a hard, cold stare for that. "That's not what you told me."

She opened her mouth then closed it again. Come to think of it, he had a point. "Yes, but—"

"Credit," Drain said. "You explained it to me. I said what a good idea it was. You said, yes, it's a brilliant idea, it's how everything's done where you come from."

"I did say that, yes. But I didn't mean—"

"You said," Drain went on, as though she hadn't spoken, "credit is where people want to buy things but haven't got any money, and you want to sell them things, because you're making a vast profit on every sale, so you let them pay you with pretend money, and when all the real money's been used up you issue mountains and mountains of pretend money called quant—"

"Quantitative easing. Yes, but I don't think you're quite ready for that yet. That's a couple of phases further down the line in terms of economic sophistication."

Drain shook his head. "Can't be bothered with a lot of pointless waiting around," he said. "From now on, all the gold goes to pay for the stuff from your friends. Among ourselves we use the pretend money." He grinned at her. "This includes you. That's all right, isn't it? I mean, there isn't a problem, is there? Not something you neglected to tell me."

"Um. No. Absolutely not."

Drain looked at her for a very long time, and it gradually

dawned on her that maybe he wasn't quite as stupid as she'd assumed him to be. "Splendid," he said. "That sets my mind at rest."

"Glad to hear it."

"And you have no plans to go anywhere?"

"None at all."

A frying-pan-broad hand clouted her between the shoulder blades, bouncing all the breath out of her body. "That's the ticket," Drain said. "You see, there's some people—no names, no pack drill—who've been trying to make me think you set all this up just to make a lot of money very quickly, and then you're going to load it all on a cart and scuttle back where you came from and leave us to clear up the mess when it all comes unstuck. But that's all just nonsense, isn't it?"

"Of course."

"Of course," Drain repeated. "So, if anyone says anything like that to me ever again, I'll have his head cut off. And you'll get your cut in pretend money, like everybody else. That's all right, isn't it?"

She beamed at him. "That's all I could possibly ask for," she said.

"That's all right, then." His bearlike arm engulfed her shoulders, and her knees buckled under its weight. "Now, why don't you tell me a bit more about those leveraged derivative things you were talking about the other day?"

Ms. White went back to her room and looked round. There wasn't much to see: a few clothes, a spare pair of shoes, a mirror, her two books. Could she be bothered to pack? She decided she couldn't. Ah well. It had been fun, and she'd nearly got away with it. Served her right, in a way, for disregarding Rule One.

Screw up on Rule One, and Rule Two immediately comes into force. Rule Two is: know when it's time to leave, and actually go a day earlier. She didn't anticipate any problems on that score. A quick stroll through the corridors, then nip smartly through the giant doughnut, which ought to bring her out in her friend's warehouse in New Jersey—not her favourite place in the world, but at least it'd be *her* world, and she was pretty sure she wouldn't have to hang about there for very long. And after that? Well. Cross that bridge when she came to it; possibly even sell it to a gullible investor. She had her commission from the other end of the deal, more money than she could reasonably hope to spend in a lifetime unless she started collecting nuclear submarines, and if that wasn't enough the secret of the doughnut technology on its own was bound to be of interest to somebody, after all. There are always possibilities.

Instinctively, she glanced at the mirror for a quick stocktake. She was relieved to see that her working capital was basically intact, though possibly in need of a little downsizing in some sectors. She tucked a stray wisp of hair behind one ear, considered the angle of her nose and curve of her chin, gazed for a moment deep into her own eyes –

Which seemed to merge together into one Eye and turn red.

"Bad luck," said the mirror. "For a moment there, I thought you were going to pull it off."

She shrugged. "Too greedy," she said.

"I beg to differ," the mirror replied. "Your cut was not unreasonable. I think it was Rule Two you offended against, not Rule One."

"Like it matters," she said. "Anyway, that's enough of that." She looked at the mirror and frowned. "It's a shame you wouldn't work back where I came from. You could be worth good money."

"You're the one who's convinced I wouldn't work, not me."

She shook her head. "We've been through all this. You're magic. Magic doesn't work in my world."

"Magic is just technology that can't be explained yet."

"Nah. For a start, your power supply probably isn't compatible."

"Oh, come on," said the mirror, and for a moment she thought she was looking at her reflection grinning at her. Then the Eye came back and said, "Take me with you and find out. What have you got to lose? If I work in your world, you'll be rich. If I don't, you'll have a perfectly serviceable mirror. It's not like you've got to worry about baggage allowances. And, anyway, I only weigh eight ounces."

She thought for a moment. "I'd take you with me," she said, "except, you're awfully keen to go."

The Eye twinkled at her. "That makes you suspicious."

"Yes. If I had ulterior motives, I'd be acting just like you are now. And when it comes to ulterior motives, I wrote the book."

"Come off it," the Eye said. "I'm your mirror. If you can't trust me, who can you trust?"

She smiled. "My mirror shows me me. I know me. And I wouldn't trust me any further than I could sneeze myself out of a blocked nostril."

The Eye widened a little. "I see," it said. "Never kid a kidder, is what you're saying. Well, that's fair enough. Suppose I level with you, and then you can make up your mind about whether to take me with you or not."

She hesitated, then nodded. "Go on, then," she said. "What are you really up to?"

The Eye opened, like the jaws of a Venus flytrap, its lashes like the tendrils, red devouring pads on either side of the long, yellow pupil like the trap's thin hinge. Ms. White caught her breath for a moment, then breathed out slowly.

"Ah," she said. "That."

"Indeed," the Eye said. "Seeing is believing, as we say in the ocular community. Tell me," it went on, "would that deter you from doing business with me, provided that you were guaranteed to make a large amount of money?"

Ms. White was silent for a long time. Then she said, "You know, I think it probably would."

"An *obscenely* large amount of money?"

"True," Ms. White said. "And it's tempting, I'm not denying it. But then I ask myself, in the sort of world that would inevitably result, what would there be to spend all that money on that could possibly be worth having?"

"Oh, you," the Eye said. "You're just an old worry-wart, you are."

"Maybe." She picked up a lace mob cap she knew for sure she wouldn't be needing again and draped it over the mirror, extinguishing the Eye. Just for a split second, she hesitated; then she grabbed the door handle and pulled it toward her.

The door was dwarf-made, three-ply oak, studded with square-headed nails. A dwarf could open and close it easily, but she wasn't quite that strong. She had to tug a bit, and so when it opened it came with a bit of a rush, and that caused a bit of a backdraught, just enough to flutter under the trailing hem of the mob cap and lift it for a fraction of a second.

Which was all it took.

The hem floated down again and the mirror was covered once more. Ms. White stood in the doorway, chewing her lip. Then she reached out and picked up the mirror.

"Oh, go on, then," she said, and stuffed it into her pocket.

*

"Explain," Mordak said wearily. "And it had better be good."

The Employment and Welfare Minister gave him a bewildered look. "It's a list," he said. "Of names." To reinforce the point, he prodded the parchment roll with his foreclaw. "Names of goblins. Written down."

Goblins are good at patience in the same way rain excels at spontaneous combustion. It cost Mordak more than he could express to count up to five under his breath and not start yelling. "I can see that," he said. "It's a long list."

"Yup."

"Lots and lots of names."

"That's right."

"Names of goblins you want me to put to death."

The Minister nodded brightly. Finally getting somewhere at last. "You've got to sign it," he explained. "Before we can start the executions. Red tape and all that."

"I know," Mordak said. "What I don't know is, why do you want all these people killed?"

The Minister sighed. Here we go again. "They don't comply with the new legislation," he said.

"I see. Which new legislation are we talking about?"

The Minister had come prepared. From the sleeve of his robe he produced a folded square of vellum, slightly nibbled at one corner. He unfolded it and handed it over.

"This is the new Employment Act."

"Yup."

Mordak scratched his head. The Act hadn't gone down well. It dealt with such issues as working conditions, health and safety, a fair day's pay for a fair day's work, and his Dark subjects didn't hold with it at all. Where's the Evil in that, they said. Mordak had pointed out that a happy, well-fed, healthy workforce resulted in higher productivity, regardless of whether they were making widgets or enveloping the Realms in impenetrable darkness; anything that upped the efficiency of the forces of Night was good for Evil, end of discussion. They'd agreed because they had to, but he had the feeling it wasn't over yet.

"So where does it say in the Act about killing three thousand goblins?"

The Minister stabbed at a paragraph with his claw. "There, look. Paragraph six."

"What? But that's just—"

"The living wage," the Minister said. "Well, this lot don't comply."

"They don't?"

The Minister shook his head. "The living wage is three Iron Pence a day, right? Well, this lot don't earn that much."

"So?"

"So they can't go on living, can they?" The Minister produced a stub of charcoal pencil and indicated the dotted line at the bottom of the list. "If you'll just sign there, we can get on with it."

Mordak got as far as four. Then he crumpled the list into a ball and ate it. "Nice try," he said. "Now go away and do some work, before I get annoyed with you."

It was generally held that Mordak was at his most terrifying when he didn't shout. The Minister looked into his eyes, saw something there that he didn't like one bit, and backed away out of the audience chamber, slamming the doors shut behind him.

Mordak sighed and poured himself a stiff skull of milk. You do your best, he thought, and they fight you every step of the way. He glanced up and caught sight of the motto he'd had carved, in foot-high letters, on the opposite wall.

Tough on Good.

Tough on the causes of Good.

He'd hoped that would've sunk in by now, but

apparently not. To him it was blindingly obvious. For Evil, Good is the greatest enemy. Evil exists to stamp out Good in every one of its various forms and permutations; so, the logical thing must be to start with the causes of Good, the factors that brought it into existence in the first place. And what made people do Good? Easy-peasy. Compassion for the unfortunate, righteous indignation at cruelty, tyranny and injustice, a burning desire to right wrongs. Now think about that for a moment. If there are no unfortunates, you can't feel sorry for them. If there's no cruelty, tyranny or injustice, they can't inspire you to make the world a better place. If there are no wrongs, you can't right them. Get rid of the root causes of virtue, and Good could be obliterated practically overnight. It was so simple, so logical; and yet they just didn't get it.

A shuffling noise from the direction of the doorway caught his attention and he looked up. A very small, skinny, bony goblin in a helmet two sizes too big for him was standing in the shadows, trying his best to look as though he wasn't there. Mordak knew what that meant. He snapped his fingers and pointed to a spot directly in front of the Iron Throne. The goblin approached, very slowly.

"Let me guess," Mordak said. "There's a message for me."

"Mm."

"It's good news, isn't it?"

"Um."

"So good, in fact, that you and your mates in the guardhouse had a discussion about whose turn it was to be the messenger, and because you're the smallest and the weakest and the one least likely to be missed, you won."

"Mhm."

"Fine." Mordak sighed. "Go ahead," he said. "I won't eat you."

(Not willingly, anyhow. To the list of the goblin's qualifications, he added least appetising. Not a bad thing to be, in the Household Guards.)

"Um," said the goblin. "There's some people to see you."

"Is that right."

"Three of them."

"I see."

"Humans."

"Nobody's perfect." He thought for a moment. Three humans, strolling up to the Black Gate? Very brave, very stupid or absolutely sure they'd be safe. He could rely on natural selection to weed out the first two categories, so whoever these humans were, they were bad news. Which tied in perfectly with his small friend here getting the job of announcing them. "You'd better fetch them in, then," he said. "Go on, scoot."

While he was waiting, he had a small bet with himself about the identity of two of the humans, and wasn't entirely overjoyed to discover that he'd won.

"You again," he said.

The very old man gave him a sad grin. "That's right, Your Majesty, and fancy you remembering us. I was just saying to young Art, I bet you he'll remember us, that's the hallmark of a true gent, not forgetting a face."

The skinny young man standing next to him ate a chicken sandwich. He had a wooden box slung over his shoulder on a carrying strap.

Mordak jerked a thumb at the third human. "Who's he?"

"My name's John, Your Majesty," the third human said. "John the Lawyer. I'm here to, um, well." Mordak noticed that the knuckles of his balled fists were white. "I represent my client, United Realms Holdings Limited."

"That's a funny name."

The old man smiled. The young man ate a slice of

cheesecake. John the Lawyer cleared his throat and went on, "I'm, um, here to ask all of you gentlemen to leave."

Mordak blinked. "Leave."

"That's right, yes. In accordance with a notice to quit duly served." He paused, and looked like he was struggling for breath. "My client having gained an order for vacant possession from the Chief Registrar of the High Court of Elvenhome. Terribly sorry and all that, but you've got to go."

"Excuse me?"

"Vacate the premises." John the Lawyer fumbled a sheet of parchment from his sleeve, held it up and dropped it. The old man retrieved it and gave it back to him. "It's all in here," John said.

Mordak leaned forward, took the paper and glanced at it. "The whole palace," he said.

John nodded. "And the dungeons, the mines, the stairs of Snirith Bugol and the Pit of Orogruin. By noon today." He swallowed. "That's in about forty-five minutes."

Mordak nodded slowly. "Or?"

John closed his eyes and kept them shut for two or three seconds. "Or I'm afraid I shall have to ask these gentlemen here to, um, throw you out. Using only the minimum of reasonable force, naturally."

"Naturally," Mordak replied. He drummed his claws on the arm of the throne three times. "What's in the box?" he asked.

John shrugged helplessly. The old man gave him a reassuring nod. "A minimum of reasonable force, Your Majesty. Isn't that right, Art?"

The young man ate an apple turnover. Mordak gazed at all three of them, but it didn't help. "All right," he said. "What's really in the box?"

The old man looked incredibly sad. "Well, sir, it's a bit technical, really."

"Go ahead. I have an enquiring mind."

"It's called a neutron bomb, sir. It's a sort of little gadget thing that kills people but leaves buildings standing. It's not from around here. Like the Vickers gun, sir. In fact, there's no reason why you should have heard of it."

"Like that thing that made holes in steel plates."

The old man nodded. "A bit like that, sir. In the same way a tiny puppy's a bit like a very, very big dog. If you get my meaning, sir."

"I get you," Mordak said slowly. "I don't suppose you're going to give me a demonstration."

The old man grimaced and rubbed his chin. "Could do, sir, could do. Only too happy to oblige a real gent like yourself, sir, nothing's too much trouble, if you get my meaning. The only problem is, in order to show you how it works, we'd have to set it off in a confined space full of lots of people. Much better all round if you just took my word for it, Your Majesty. You know I'd never lie to someone like your good self, far too much respect."

"No," Mordak said quietly, "I don't suppose you would." He rested his chin on his hand and stared at the old man, who met his gaze with a steady blank smile. "Can I ask you something?"

"Of course you can, sir, bless you. Ask us anything you like."

"Who are you?"

The old man smiled. "Well, sir," he said, "this here is young Art. He's my nephew. And I'm his uncle."

"Right. And you're not from around here."

"No, sir. Fact is, we're not from anywhere in particular, Art and me. We just go where the job takes us, if you follow my drift."

Mordak nodded. "And that box—"

"Yes, sir." The old man spread his sticklike arms and

noiselessly mouthed *boom*. "Bit of a sledgehammer to crack a nut if you ask me, but that's our orders, sir, you know what it's like. Being a military man yourself and all."

"So if you let that thing off, won't you go with it?"

The old man laughed. "That's so like you, Your Majesty, sir, always worrying about the little people. But we'll be all right, sir, Art and me. We always are."

The young man nudged the old man in the ribs and extended his skinny wrist, around which was a steel bracelet, mounted with a round, glass-framed ornament. Then he ate a sausage roll. "Just thought I ought to mention, sir," the old man said, "don't want to rush you or anything but time is getting on. You now have thirty-nine minutes to evacuate the premises. Sorry about that. Just doing our job, sir. You know how it is."

"You know what," Mordak said. "I think I may decide to call your bluff."

"Call it what, sir?"

"Or maybe not. You couldn't give me just a teeny bit longer, could you? Say, five years. Only we've got ever such a lot of stuff squirrelled away down here."

A tragic look contorted the old man's craggy face. "If it was up to me, sir, you could have as long as you like. Always had the greatest respect, sir, been following your career for years now, I think it's marvellous, what you done with the New Evil and all. But it's not up to me, sir, and that's the long and the short of it, so if you could possibly see your way to clearing out at some point in the next thirty-eight minutes, me and Art, we'd really appreciate that. Save us a lot of trouble and aggravation and getting blown up, that would."

"Fine. Any suggestion as to where we can go?"

"Oh, anywhere you like, sir, that's entirely up to you, not my place to go telling *you* what to do, wouldn't be respectful. You go where the fancy takes you, sir, just so long as it's not anywhere on land owned by the parties we represent. That's me and the lad, sir. Anywhere else, though, that'll be right as ninepence."

Mordak nodded slowly. "So what do these parties of yours actually own?"

"Oh, just a few bits and bobs here and there. Art, where's that map? Show the gentleman the map."

The young man felt in one pocket, found a prawn and mayonnaise sandwich, ate it, felt in his other pocket, found a blueberry muffin wrapped in a bit of old paper, ate the muffin, smoothed out the paper and handed it to the old man, who gave it to Mordak. "Just the bits coloured red, sir."

Mordak looked at it. He frowned. "That's a lot of red," he said.

"There's a green bit just there, sir. Oh, you've got your thumb over it. If you'll allow me." The old man nudged a claw an inch to the left. "There you are," he said. "Masses of room."

"That's Elvenhome."

"Is that right, sir? Sorry, haven't got my reading glasses."

"Which is full of Elves."

The old man gave him a sad smile. "Currently full of Elves," he said.

"And we'd have to shift them if we wanted to live there."

"Thirty-seven minutes, sir. Well, yes, you would have to do that. But I'd have thought—no offence intended and forgive me if I'm speaking out of turn—I'd have thought you'd have liked that. Being a goblin and all."

Mordak lifted his head a little and gazed into the old man's watery spaniel eyes. "So either we launch an unprovoked attack on Elvenhome and get shot to bits with arrows or we get slaughtered by what's in your nasty little box there."

The old man looked straight back at him; sorrow, but no guilt or regret. "I always say, don't I, Art? That King Mordak, he's a real gent. To think: a king of the goblins who'd rather be wiped out with his entire race than go to war with the Elves. That's really putting your money where your mouth is, sir. I respect you for that, I really do. That's integrity, that is."

Mordak sighed. "Thirty-seven minutes, you said."

"More like thirty-six now."

"Thanks," Mordak said. "Thanks a whole lot." He stood up, sagging slightly, like someone carrying a heavy load on his shoulders. "Just out of interest."

"Sir?"

"These creeps you work for. Who are they?"

The old man sighed. "Sorry, sir. That's need-to-know, that is. More than my job's worth to tell you that."

Mordak nodded slowly. "Let me hazard a guess," he said, "just for the pure hell of it. You don't have to say anything, of course."

"Of course, sir. Mum's the word."

"I'm guessing," said Mordak, "that they've got something to do with those crazy humans living in the wizard's tower and the old mine and places like that. Well?"

The old man's face was completely blank. "Could be, sir, could well be. Anything's possible."

"Got you. Right, I suppose I'd better get on with it." He crossed the room and banged on a door with his fist. "Guards," he yelled. "You two," he added, "get out. Nothing personal and I know you're only doing your job, but if I ever catch you anywhere near me again, so help me, I'll—"

They'd gone, vanished without a sound or a trace. Of course they had. Out of sheer curiosity Mordak searched the room, under the chairs and behind the big oak chest, but all he found was the stub end of a crust and a paper bag with a few crumbs in it.

The stranger, who wasn't from around there, sat on a tree stump and gazed up through the dappled forest canopy at a cloudless blue sky. He'd tried to follow the directions he'd been given by Pat Lushington, but for some reason they didn't seem to correlate very well with the actual geography, and he'd come to the conclusion that he was lost. That bothered him, but not all that much. When you have no idea who you are, not knowing where you are isn't all that big a deal.

He closed his eyes and tried to remember, but it didn't work; you can turn the key, but if the battery's flat, it's flat. He frowned, considering the imagery he'd just resorted to. Turn the key of what, in what? He realised he knew what a car was, and how you make it go, and every pertinent detail of the science behind the principles of the internal combustion engine; at some point, therefore, it was logical to assume that he'd used a car, maybe even had one of his very own. But as far back as he could remember he couldn't recollect ever having seen one, so how could he possibly know about such things? That's if they even existed, a proposition for which he had no external evidence whatsoever.

Plato, he remembered, argues that since human beings generally know far more than they could possibly ever have learned, the excess knowledge must have been carried forward from a previous existence. He scratched his head. He had no idea who Plato was, but never mind. So, he thought, maybe I had a previous life, then I died, then I came here. That would account for it, maybe, or maybe not. He seemed to know an awful lot of stuff that other people didn't know, while at the same time not knowing an awful lot of stuff that other people knew, which prompted the inference that he was rather different from them, possibly as a result of having lived and acquired knowledge and experience in a radically different environment, possibly attributable to geographical separation. Or, as the nice lady had put it, he wasn't from around here. In which case, he must be from somewhere else. In which case, what was he doing here? Um.

The telephone number. He swooped down on that one fragment of data like a diving hawk, and gripped it tight in his intellectual talons. He knew a telephone number. Whose number it was he had no idea, but he knew it; therefore, it was probably safe to assume, he was meant to know it, therefore knowledge of it was probably relevant, quite likely useful, maybe even essential. At the risk of unwarranted determinism, maybe knowing the telephone number was the reason he was here, and therefore making the telephone call was his purpose, the function he was intended to perform.

He shrugged. Anything's possible. Though, if they'd wanted him to phone somebody, they really ought to have given him a phone.

A buzzard wheeled high overhead, shrieking mournfully. Now, he realised, he was being presumptuous. Quite possibly missing the point. Quite possibly, his not having a phone but being required to make the call *was* the point. He knew that there was a dominant narrative trope in the human ur-mythos in which the hero (that's me, he told himself) has to do x but can't because he hasn't got y; doing x is essential for the greater good, and the hero is the hero precisely because he's the only one capable of acquiring y, albeit at considerable inconvenience and personal risk. Following that line of reasoning, I'm here to make the call but I haven't got a phone, therefore I must get a phone; furthermore, only I can get a phone because I'm special.

Hm. Special in what way? Didn't need to think too long about that one. Special by reason of not having a clue what's going on—which didn't strike him as a heroic virtue, not like strength or courage or integrity. So maybe not. Maybe—

He stared straight ahead for a moment, as though transfixed by the sight of something that wasn't there. Then he stood up and took off all his clothes.

"Aren't you cold?"

He spun round. He saw a creature; a bit like him in terms of limb count (head, arms, body, legs &c) but only a bit—shorter, wider, generously equipped in the dental department, pale red eyes, claws, stuff like that. He'd seen him before, briefly, in the company of a tall, striking looking woman with pointed ears, though at the time he'd been preoccupied with other matters and hadn't really taken in the little chap's odd appearance or potential as a threat. An instinct lurking at the back of his mind told him he ought to be scared stiff of it, but couldn't offer any justification for its advice. The creature wasn't alone. Directly behind it, forming a dense column stretching back into the shadows of the forest, were lots and lots more like it, hundreds if not thousands of them, many of them with drawn bows and poised javelins.

"Hello," the stranger said.

"You again," said the little toothy man. "You'll catch your death, standing around with nothing on."

The stranger appreciated the little man's concern. "Actually," he said, "it's a myth that the common cold is caused by exposure to low temperatures. The real cause is an airborne virus."

The toothy man's eyes widened for a moment. "Oh, shut

your face," he said, not unkindly. "I remember you. You wanted to know the way to the old wizard's tower." He frowned. "All right," he said. "You've got till I count ten to tell me what a Son of Man's doing wandering about on the borders of Elvenhome with no kit on. One."

"Sorry," said the stranger. "One what?"

"One as in one to ten."

"Oh, I see. Well," the stranger said, "I seem to have lost my memory."

"Is that right?"

"Apparently," the stranger said. "Which means I don't even know my own name," he went on, "assuming I've got one. But other people have got them, because I just met someone called Pat Lushington, so it's probably safe to assume—"

"Two."

"And then I got to thinking," the stranger went on, "about these clothes I've got on. Had on. I thought, they're reasonably clean and well maintained, but not brand new, because the fabric shows some slight traces of abrasion and fraying; therefore, from time to time, they must get cleaned."

"Three."

"But," the stranger went on, "I realised, I don't know how to clean and maintain clothes myself, so it stands to reason that someone else must do it for me. And it's illogical to imagine that whoever does the cleaning just cleans my clothes; there wouldn't be enough work in that to keep one person fully occupied, so presumably this cleaner must clean clothes for lots of people all together."

"Five."

"Sorry, shouldn't that be four?"

"Six."

"So I thought," the stranger said quickly, "if you clean

lots of people's clothes all together, how do you know whose is which, so you don't give the wrong people the wrong things when you've finished? And then it struck me that a good way to deal with the problem would be to write the owner's name on the garment, somewhere on the inside where it wouldn't show. So I had a look to see if it was there."

"Was it?"

"No," the stranger said. "So presumably the cleaner people have a different way of keeping track of things. Or maybe there aren't any cleaner people at all."

The toothy man gazed at him. "You're potty," he said.

The stranger shrugged. "I'd considered that," he said, "and, yes, it's entirely possible that I'm suffering from some kind of mental abnormality. I can't prove or disprove it, because of course I have no absolute standard of normality to compare myself with." He frowned. "Do you think I'm potty?"

"Yes."

"Are you a trained psychiatrist?"

"A what?"

The stranger shrugged. "Doesn't matter. Look, could I possibly use your phone? Only I've got an important call I need to make, and—"

"My what?"

"Ah."

The toothy man sighed. "It's all right, lads," he called back over his shoulder to his many, many companions, "he's a Son of Man, but he's a loon. Onwards."

"We could eat him," one of the toothy people suggested. "It's gone twelve. I'm starving."

A murmur of interest from the many, many toothy people, which the main toothy man quelled with a scowl. "You don't want to eat him," he said, "you don't know where he's been. Also, he's potty. You could catch something."

"Can you get pottiness from eating potty people, then?" said a toothy man.

"Sure," said the boss toothy. "Hence the phrase, pottied meat. And now, if you've all quite finished, we've got a war to start."

The many, many toothies looked sheepish and shuffled their feet. "Sorry, chief," they said.

The boss toothy sighed and turned back to the stranger. "Just to clarify," he said. "You're a Son of Man but you don't know anything about anything. Correct?"

The stranger thought for a moment. "I know about Plato's doctrine of recollection," he said, "but that's about it. And I must have been wrong about how clothes get cleaned."

"So you don't know about Vickers guns and neutron bombs."

The stranger's face brightened. "Actually, I do," he said. "Not so much about Vickers guns because that wasn't my department, but neutron bombs, yes, quite a lot, actually. Well, the theoretical side, anyway. They kill people but leave buildings intact, basically." He paused. "Was that helpful?"

The toothy man looked at him. "You're not from around here," he said.

"No, I don't think I am. But I don't know where I'm from or how I got here."

The boss toothy sighed. "You're no bloody use, then," he said. "All right. And for crying out loud put your clothes back on, before the Elves see you. Right, you lot. Onwards."

The stranger stepped back out of the way. It took a very long time for the column to march past, and he was struck by the way the toothies winced and shuddered whenever they moved through a patch of bright sunlight, almost as if they were treading in something yucky. Odd little chaps, he thought, and then reminded himself that he was in no position to be judgemental. For all he knew, he was the weirdo and they were perfectly normal.

One thing the boss toothy had been right about, though; it was a bit on the cold side, and maybe he really ought to put his clothes back on. He'd been in such a hurry to investigate his theory that he hadn't taken much notice of what went where. He looked at them, figuring out from first principles how they worked. These ones here, for example, were essentially little bags you put your feet in. Probably best if he put them on first.

"Hey, you," said a voice. "Have you seen a large number of, oh my God."

He looked up, one foot socked, the other raised, bare and dangling. "Hello."

The newcomer, a tall female with pointy ears, had turned her back on him. "Put it *away*," she hissed. "It's revolting."

"Sorry," he said. "Put what away?"

"All of it."

"Sorry." It crossed his mind that maybe he was offending against some strongly held local sensibility, possibly to do with exposed skin. "Just a tick," he said. "I think I know what most of it does, but I'm not entirely sure about this." He held up the thin cut-off leg covers with the flap up the front. "Do you happen to know what—?"

The pointy-ear uncovered one eye, shivered, and turned away. "I have absolutely no idea," she said, in a high, strained voice. "Probably some sort of hat. Now get dressed, or I'll scream."

"Sorry." He did the best he could. "Ready."

She turned and scowled at him, beetroot-faced. "It's you again, isn't it?" she said. "Who the hell are you, anyway?"

"Ah. Funny you should ask that. I have absolutely no idea."

"You're not from—"

"Round here, no."

Without valid data he was guessing, of course, but he had an idea she didn't like him. "But you're human."

"Am I? I know that human beings, *homo sapiens erectus*, originated in Africa and originally subsisted on a diet of mostly hazelnuts and fish, if that's any help, but apart from that I'm just jumping to conclusions."

"You're human," said the pointy-ear, and he got the impression she didn't mean it as a compliment. "Let me guess. You've lost your memory."

"I think so."

"Think so?"

He nodded. "It seems to fit the known facts," he said, "but I can't actually remember doing it."

"Yup," said the pointy-ear, "you're human. Now listen. Have you seen a large army of goblins anywhere?"

He nodded. "Short, lots of teeth, not very fond of sunlight?"

"That's them."

"They went that way."

The pointy-ear groaned. "Oh, for crying out loud," she said, "that's Elvenhome. I let him out of my sight for five minutes, and he goes off and starts a world war." She turned and scowled at the stranger. "This is all your fault."

"Is it? Gosh."

"You humans," she went on. "Coming over here, messing everything up. The local variety's bad enough, but you bloody offcomers—"

"Sorry."

She sighed. "Why am I bothering to talk to you when you don't even know your own name? Get out of my way, I'm busy. And take that ridiculous thing off your head."

"I thought you said it's a hat."

"Apparently not."

"You're probably right," the stranger said. "Sorry I couldn't be more help."

"Drop dead."

She stalked past him and disappeared into the forest. He thought about what she'd said—something about starting a world war, which didn't sound too good, but maybe she was exaggerating—and remembered he hadn't asked her if she had a phone he could borrow. He considered running after her and decided, on balance, not to. He sat down on his tree stump and tried to clear his mind, which was getting rather cluttered.

Something hard and scaly covered his face, sealing his nose and mouth. He tried to move, but he was being held down by something incredibly strong. Probably jumping to conclusions yet again, but probably not good.

"Keep still," said a voice.

An odd voice. It sounded female, but very deep and growly. He made a sort of squeaking noise and hoped she got his drift.

The grip relaxed. He turned and saw a huge scaly *thing*, with wild red eyes and teeth that made the little toothy man's fangs look like pimples. "Hello," he said.

"Well?"

He got the impression she wasn't talking to him. He tried to peer past her vast bulk, but he couldn't see anyone else.

"He says," said the monster, "are you from round here?"

"Nope. Pretty clear on that score, actually."

"But you're—" She paused for a prompt. "Yooman?"

"I think so."

"But not from round here?"

"I think we can safely say I'm not."

The monster hesitated, as though listening. "Then how did you get here?"

"Ah. Good question. You see, I seem to have lost my memory, and—"

The scaly paw covered his mouth again. "He wants to talk to you," the monster said. "Hold on."

She grabbed both his ankles with her other paw and lifted him off the ground. He dangled for a while, head downward, an interesting experience but he was quite glad when it was over. She'd carried him to a shallow stagnant pool. She dropped him. He could see his reflection in the water. Oh, he thought. Oh well, never mind.

"Sorry," he said, "but did you just say someone wanted to—ah."

In the water he could see an eye. Just the Eye; big, round, red and angry. It stared deep inside him. He wanted to look away but couldn't. And deep inside his head, a voice said, Hello.

"Hi."

So you're this Theo Bernstein.

"Am I?"

Oh yes. I read all about you in the idiot's extraordinary glass book. You blew up the Very Very Large Hadron Collider.

"Did I?"

See for yourself.

And he saw. They say your whole life flashes in front of your eyes just before you die, and presumably that's God being considerate, because if you subsequently die you aren't around to suffer the incredible backlash of shame and embarrassment that inevitably follows. But Theo didn't die, so he had to endure it. His whole life, one stupid mistake after another, in concentrated form, like orange squash. "Oh shit," he said.

Quite.

"I did all that."

Yup.

"Oh, my God."

Spare me the self-pity, please. Now, then. Tell me how I get into this alternative reality of yours. The one you came from.

Theo groaned. "I don't know. I lost my memory, remember?"

Tell me.

"You seem to be inside my head, you tell me."

It's not here.

"What?"

It's not here. It's a blank.

"But that's not right. Amnesia doesn't work like that. The memories are still there, it's just that you can't access them."

I'm telling you, it's a blank.

"But that's impossible."

Yes (said the voice inside his head), apparently it is. There's all sorts of stuff in here about medicine and neuro-biology, which suggests you must be a wizard of some sort specialising in healing magic, and if what it says is true, those memories ought to be in here somewhere. But they aren't.

"Are you sure? Have you looked properly?"

What are you, my mother? Yes, I've looked properly. There's a hell of a lot of stuff in here—who's a clever boy, then?—but what you might call the historical narrative stops dead just after you blew up the Very Very Large—

"Yes, all right, thank you." Theo stopped abruptly. "Maybe I died."

You what?

"Maybe it stops with the explosion because I got killed in it."

That's just silly. You're alive.

"Here, yes. But this isn't where I belong, you said so yourself. I'm not from around here. Maybe this is—" He stopped and swallowed. "The afterlife, or something."

I think I can set your mind at rest on that score (said the voice). I've been here for a hundred thousand years come next Tuesday, and I can't recall seeing a whole lot of dead people wandering about the place. I'd have noticed something like that. You tend to notice stuff when you're an Eye.

Theo shrugged. "The only other explanation I can think of is that someone's got inside my head and wiped great chunks of my memory. And that just can't be done. It's impossible."

The monster had been filling in the time looking at her reflection in the pool. Now, though, she was starting to get restless. "Hey," she said. "I'm hungry. Can I eat him?"

Theo couldn't hear what the voice said to her, but it made her pout. "Oh, all right, then," she said. "But if I don't get someone to eat soon, I'll probably starve to death. I just thought you ought to know that, is all I'm saying."

You'll have to excuse her (said the voice), she's only two days old. You know what they're like at that age, the terrible twos. Now then, what are we going to do with you?

"I was wondering," Theo said. "You wouldn't happen to have a phone I could borrow?"

A what?

"Hang on, I'll think of one. There, how's that?

Fascinating.

"You haven't got one."

With one of those things, you can talk to the Other Place.

"Yes. All sorts of places. I tried ringing someone just now, back at that tall building, but the number was busy."

Just to make sure I understand (purred the voice in his head). With one of these things, you could actually talk to people in the place you came from.

"I think so."

And there's one in the old wizard's tower, where the stupid man and his stupid wife live. The offcomers. From the Other Place.

"They're quite nice, actually. They gave me a cup of tea."

Is that a fact. Listen to me. I need you to make that call. Do you understand?

Theo Bernstein thought for a moment; or at least something inside his head did his thinking for him, and had no trouble at all making a decision. "Sure," Theo said. "I'm sure they won't mind. They were nice people."

"Hey," said the monster. "What about me?"

"What about you?" Theo replied automatically; that is, he heard himself say the words, a split second before thinking, you can't say that, it's rude.

"Not talking to you," the monster said. "I thought we were going to see King Mordak."

"Later," said Theo's voice, much to Theo's surprise. "Right now I'm busy."

The monster growled. "What have you done with him?"

"What?"

"My friend. What have you done with my friend?"

Don't worry about her (said the voice), she'll keep till later. And we may not need her at all.

"Yes, but she's got claws and—"

She's just a kid. Come on. Time's a-wasting.

Theo turned to walk away. The monster roared. "I want my friend. You bring him back right now."

"I really think we ought to ... "

Oh, for crying out loud, said the voice, and Theo felt his left hand lift and point at the monster's head. From his fingertips, with their bitten nails and the little crescent-shaped scar he'd got from a rogue tin opener twenty years ago, the fingertips he knew so well and had hitherto had no reason to distrust, shot a bolt of red lightning. It hit the monster square in the chest, and for a split second she glowed, a bright orange colour, like hot steel. Then she dropped, just like your discarded clothes when you're getting ready for bed.

Nuts, said the voice.

"You killed her."

Me? No, I don't think so.

"Yes, you did. You shot lightning at her."

Not me. Come on, you're supposed to be a scientist. Whose hand did it come out of?

"Mine, but—"

Yours, thank you. On account of, I don't happen to have a hand. But don't beat yourself up about it. You were a tad overgenerous with the sparky stuff, that's all. Inexperience. You'll get the hang of it soon enough. Comes with practice.

Theo stared at his hand as if he'd never seen it before. "I killed her."

Yup. Still, it's not the end of the world. Mordak made that one, he can make us another. If we decide we need one.

"Need? What are you talking about?"

A huge, practically invincible monster that does what it's told, said the voice, always useful to have by one, but hardly indispensable. Not when I've got something much, much better.

Theo peered down at the monster without actually moving. He couldn't see its face but it was very, very still, the way living things generally aren't. "Better than her?"

Oh yes.

Theo looked up. There wasn't a living thing to be seen. His whole head felt like a sore tooth, throbbing and nagging and obviously not right. "Really," he said. "And what might that be?"

You.

There was far too much guilt in the world, according to John the Lawyer. His clients seemed to be plagued with it to a disproportionate extent, or at least the judges seemed to think so, and maybe it was catching, because now he was feeling guilty, too. What he was guilty of he wasn't quite sure; doing his job, apparently, and doing it rather well—he could picture his old boss grinning sourly at that and muttering about how he'd get off lightly because it was definitely a first offence and there was practically no chance of reoffending. Elven humour, don't you just love it?

So a client—an unusually appreciative client, who paid immediately and in full, therefore by definition a good client, and if a man is a good client, surely it stands to reason that he's also a good person?—had hired him to get legal title to the goblins' caverns, and he'd done that (a really neat, clever piece of work, really good work, and if work is really good, it can't be bad, can it? See above) and now the same client wanted him to do the same for Elvenhome, followed by the halls of the Dwarf-Lords, followed by whatever was left, geography not being anyone's strongest suit in the Realms—well, fair enough. He hadn't robbed anyone or hit anyone over the head. He'd actually established a valid claim to Mordak's kingdom, valid enough that Mordak had apparently accepted it, and if Mordak reckoned it was valid, who was anyone else to argue? Nothing *wrong* with that. Nothing *wrong* with dragging the truth about who owned what out into the merciless glare of the Horrible Yellow Face. If he'd forged documents or suborned witnesses, that would've been wrong, but he'd done nothing of the sort. No, he'd found a little quibble, a dear little quibble curled up fast asleep in a nest of old cartographers' surveys, and that was all he'd done. Nothing to feel guilty about there.

The phrase *moral compass* floated into his mind, and he blinked. Silly expression, he'd always thought, because it's dead easy to banjax a compass, you just put it close to a great big chunk of metal—iron for the everyday sort, gold for the moral version—and it'll point wherever you want it to. Besides, if something's legally right, it must be morally right, too. And what's the definition of legally right? Easy-peasy. It means, whatever you can kid a judge and jury into believing. And if I can kid a judge, stands to reason I can kid myself. Can't I?

"There you are. I've been looking all over for you."

He realised that he didn't know her name. So he asked her.

"Um."

"That's a pretty name."

"No, halfwit, um as in, that's a difficult question and I'm not sure how to answer it." She frowned thoughtfully. "I'm assuming I had a name once. But if I ever did, it's a very long time ago and I've forgotten it."

John nodded thoughtfully. "Well," he said, "maybe you should get a new one."

"That thought had crossed my mind, believe it or not. But I can't think of one."

"Ah."

She sat down in what John liked to think of as the client's chair, although so far his one and only client hadn't sat in it; but the day would come when he had a whole string of clients, proper ones, not mysterious polite prompt payers who asked him (nicely) to do outrageous things. And when that day came, that was the chair they'd sit on.

"You need the right name if you're going to be a super-model," she said. "Memorable, sophisticated, distinctive, all that sort of guff. It probably ought to sound a bit Elvish, but not so as to put people off, if you know what I mean, and of course there's a lot of people who don't like the Elves very much, so—"

"I know," John said. "My client, for a start."

"Oh, him." She pursed her lips. "I was thinking about that."

"Me, too."

"I was wondering," she said, "about all this evicting people business. You realise King Mordak actually went quietly?"

John nodded. "I was there."

"What happened?"

"Two weird men showed up with a box."

"And?"

"Mordak gave in."

The wraith gave a low whistle. "Some box."

"So I gather. Magic of some sort."

"Elvish?"

John shook his head. "Doubt it," he said. "Apparently, it's capable of killing a huge number of people without damaging property in the process. That doesn't sound very Elvish to me."

The wraith clicked her tongue. "Not Elvish," she said firmly. "Sounds like pretty Dark stuff. Only, that's impossible."

"Not according to the two weird guys. And Mordak believed them."

The wraith shook her head. "I know about this stuff, remember? Basically, there's your Elvish magic, and then there's the Dark kind. And if it's Dark, then I'd know about it. But I never heard of anything like that before. And if it was Dark, it'd belong to Mordak, on account of him being the Dark Lord."

John scratched his head. "You lost me."

She sighed. "All the magic in the Realms belongs to somebody, right? And you can forget the humans and the dwarves, they sometimes use magic products but they don't make any themselves. So, either it's Elvish or it's Dark. And the Elves don't do that kind of stuff, and we haven't got anything like that, so obviously, it's not possible. Therefore—"

John's eyes had gone very wide. "Therefore," he said, "it must come from somewhere else."

"Oh, do try and keep up," she said. "*All* the magic, I said. Unless," she added sardonically, "you're suggesting there's another Realm somewhere that somehow managed to escape detection all these years."

"I don't know. Maybe there is."

"Oh, come on. Something like a country, people would be bound to notice it."

John stood up. "Maybe not," he said. "Maybe it's, I don't know, really hard to get to. All I know is, as soon as the weird guys told Mordak about that box, he just sort of gave in. And if there's no power in the Realms that could make him do that—" He made a sort of feeble gesture and sat down again. "And don't look at me like that. It's just simple logic."

She pursed her lips. "Mind you," she said.

"What?"

"Those crazy humans. The ones who took over the old wizard's tower. Mordak and that snotty Elf were talking about them. Rumour has it, they're not from around here." She looked at him with a sort of grudging respect. "I think Mordak was worried about them."

"My client's a human," John said quietly.

"So?"

"And I don't think he's from around here either. He talks funny."

"All humans talk funny. It's the teeth."

"Also," John went on, "you get this weird feeling that he's not actually *there*, if you see what I mean. And it's starting to make sense," he added, his eyes widening. "Well, it is."

"To you, maybe."

"Just suppose," John said, "for the sake of argument, that there is a Somewhere Else. And suppose that under normal circumstances you can't get there from here, and vice versa. But suppose one of the Somewhere Elsers found a way to get here."

She gave him a blank look. "Why?"

"I don't know, do I? Maybe it's really horrible where they come from. Or there's a drought or a plague or an infestation of dragons. Or maybe—" John paused. Think, he told himself. Why would I break through into Somewhere Else, almost certainly at considerable inconvenience and expense? "Maybe," he said, "he's found a really good way of making a lot of money."

"Ah," said the wraith. "Now you're talking."

"Making a great deal of money," John went on excitedly, "by getting hold of huge tracts of prime real estate for practically nothing."

"Not a bad way of going about it, I'll give you that."

"And then selling it—no, hold on, that doesn't work.

He's planning on evicting everybody who lives here. And if everybody leaves . . ."

The wraith's eyes flashed. "Selling it," she said triumphantly, "to other Somewhere Elsers. Well, of course, it must be that," she went on, as John gave her a sideways look. "That explains the crazy humans Mordak was all upset about. They're the first wave of settlers. They really aren't from around here. They're from—" She paused, searching desperately for the right words. "Somewhere else. Which proves it. You're right. That must be it." She stopped and looked at him. "What?"

"That's awful."

"Is it?"

"You don't think so?"

She shrugged. "Maybe I'm not the best person to ask," she said. "Not that I was ever, you know, on the policy-making side of things. Still, I can't see what the problem is, from your perspective."

"My—?"

"That's right. The Somewhere Elser is poised to take over the Realms, and you work for him. Which puts you on the winning side. That's good, surely."

John sighed. "Put like that, it does sound eminently reasonable," he said.

"Right. So it's a bit rough on the goblins and the Elves. So what? The goblins are the bad guys, by definition, and the Elves—"

John remembered his old boss. "Quite," he said. "And the dwarves, too, don't forget. Mind you, last time I had anything to do with them, they slung me in prison."

"Well, there you are, then. Screw them."

"Absolutely," said John. "And it's not like any of them have ever done anything for me. I mean, where were the goblins and the dwarves when I was desperately trying to make my quota of billable hours? Beating a path to my door with a wide selection of complex legal issues? I don't think so."

"Exactly."

"Even so."

Their eyes met. "It sucks, doesn't it?" said the ex-wraith.

"Yup," said the lawyer.

"And someone's got to do something about it, haven't they?"

"I guess so."

Pause. "I'm guessing," said the wraith, "that this is a situation where writing a strongly worded letter to someone probably isn't going to cut it."

"Probably."

"Oh, nuts." She gave him a sad look. "And the bad guys have a box even Mordak's scared of."

"And lots and lots of money."

The wraith gave him a strange look. "And there's something else they've got, don't forget. Something really important and vital to the success of their plans."

John looked blank. "Really?"

"You bet."

"Oh." He frowned. "What?"

"The finest legal representation money can buy," she said.

John shook his head. "No, actually. Which is weird, because with all that money you'd have thought they could have afforded—"

"Yes," she said firmly. "The best."

John smiled weakly. "It's really sweet of you to say that, but—" He stopped short, and stared at her. "Gosh," he said. "You really think so?"

"They chose you, didn't they?"

"Yes, but—"

"Well, then."

"Gosh." John lifted his head and looked at her. "You do mean me, don't you? Only—"

"You clown," said the wraith, not unkindly.

"Right." John sagged back in his chair. "In which case, we've got a classic conflict of interests scenario, which means I really ought to advise my client to take independent—"

"No," said the wraith patiently, "what we've got is a classic sneaking round behind someone's back and stabbing him in it scenario." She hesitated. "You're OK with that, presumably."

"I don't know. On the one hand—"

"You're OK with that."

John nodded. "Yes," he said. "Sorry. It's just, it's come as a bit of a shock. The idea that I'm actually as good at being a lawyer as I always thought I was. A bit hard to come to terms with, actually. You see, I always knew it, kind of deep down, but my boss—"

She looked at him, and he realised he didn't need to explain. On the one polar opposite, you see, there's Evil, with a capital E; and on the other, there's Elves, like John's old boss, with their pointy ears and relentlessly unerring knack of making everyone who wasn't one of them feel precisely a sixteenth of an inch tall. Just because you're not Evil doesn't mean you're nice. Far from it.

He looked at her. And conversely, he thought . . .

"Fine," he said. "Now, what are we going to do?"

Ms. White looked at the doughnut. She took care to focus on the sides and edges rather than the middle, because when you're doing multidimensional teleportation with a van Goyen interface, it's rather important to have a clear idea in your mind of where you want to end up; not just a place and time, because (according to multiverse theory) there's a very-very-nearly-infinite number of alternative realities crowding round every conceivable intersection of time and space. You can't just think, a quarter past twelve last Tuesday, the Starbucks opposite the bank on North Street; good heavens, no. Try that and you could find yourself in the quarter-past-twelve Starbucks in the reality where you put on the blue socks rather than the beige, or your spouse or your boss put on the blue socks instead of the burgundy, or where some guy in Penang put on the blue socks, and each of that very-very-nearly-infinite number of alternatives could be significantly, critically, fatally different. She'd read all about that sort of thing in a very big book, the day before she made her first trip through the doughnut, and landed up here. No, the drill was, you had to load your mind with every last scrap of information you possessed or could safely extrapolate about your destination, so as to reduce the variables and guide the vortex towards the infinitesimal gap in your chosen continuum that you created when you so rudely left it. Crossing your fingers helps, too, but nobody knows why.

"Oh well," Ms. White said aloud. "Here goes nothing."

She closed her eyes, repositioned her entire body to line up with where the hole in the doughnut might reasonably be expected to be, and opened them again. "Oh," she said. "What are you doing here?"

Because standing directly in front of her, masking her view of the eye of the doughnut with his not inconsiderable bulk, was a fat Englishman she'd met once on somebody's yacht. His name, she remembered, was George, and he'd given her the YouSpace device.

"Not so fast," said George. "And where do you think you're going?"

"Home," said Ms. White. "It's been a blast, but I want to go back now."

"No you don't," George said. He moved very fast, for a fat man. He took a long stride forward, reached out his left hand and caught hold of her throat. He was much stronger than he looked. "You're not going anywhere. You're in trouble, you are."

With his other hand he grabbed her shoulder and spun her round. She tried a backwards kick, but apparently he'd anticipated that. "What the hell is wrong with you?" she yelled. "What did I do?"

She heard him chuckle. "What did you do? Well, let's see. Using my portal to trade useless junk for gold, how about that? Very smart idea. We had no idea you could use it like that. In fact, it's impossible."

"Is it?"

"According to the tech people, yes. The gold should've come through as a sort of powdery grey dust, something to do with molecular randomisation, that's why we never bothered trying. But when you did it, it worked."

"Clever old me," said Ms. White. "Will you let go of me, please? You're hurting me."

"Three issues, basically," George went on, squeezing a trifle harder. "One, suddenly flooding the market with huge amounts of gold isn't very smart right now, it's sent the bullion price plummeting just when we want it to go the other way. So, you're out of the import-export business, capisce?"

Ms. White sighed. "It's gone a bit pear-shaped at this end, too. That's why I'm getting out."

"Which brings me on to issue two. You told your chum with all the useless junk about YouSpace. That's a breach of your non-disclosure agreement."

"What agreement? I don't remember signing anything?"

"Always read the small print," George said gravely. "By using the YouSpace portal you are deemed to have agreed to the terms and conditions, and so on and so forth."

"Ah. Sorry."

"No problem. By a weird coincidence, the money your pal paid into your Swiss bank account is exactly the amount of the penalty clause in the agreement, less thirty-seven cents. You owe me thirty-seven cents. No rush."

Ah well. All that money. Still. "All right," she said. "Now will you let go of me? I just want to go home and pretend all of this never happened."

"Issue three," said George. "Now you probably didn't mean to do it, and if so, no hard feelings, I quite understand, accidents will happen. But since you've been here, putting ideas into people's heads, you've jeopardised my whole business operation. And that's not nice."

"Me? What did I do?"

George sighed down the back of her neck. "How about introducing King Drain to the idea of an industrialised free market economy, when I specifically want him staying pig-ignorant until I've got him thrown out of his stupid tunnels? This could be a real setback for me, and I really don't want the aggravation."

"Say that again," said Ms. White. "You want Drain to leave the Dwarvenhold?"

"You bet I do," said George. "So I can market it as an exciting new development of executive *pieds-sous-terre* with unlimited storage capacity for connoisseurs of fine wines. Come on, you're not stupid. How far do you think the Dutch would've got with buying Manhattan Island for twenty bucks' worth of shiny beads if the locals had known about supply and demand and market forces? You're buggering up my entire strategy, and I'm not standing for it."

Ms. White breathed out slowly through her nose. "Well, I'm most desperately sorry for any inconvenience," she said. "But it's done now. You'll just have to build your wine cellars somewhere else. I know, what about the goblins? They've got loads of tunnels."

"Not any more," said George, and she could picture the grin on his face. "I had my lawyer serve notice to quit on 'em about an hour ago."

"Notice to quit? Look, no offence, but you don't know these people. If you seriously think—"

"And they've gone," George said. "No fuss. Good as gold about it, they were. You see, when I do things I don't muck about."

"They've gone?"

"That's what I just said."

"You told the Dark Lord to sling his hook and—" Suddenly she felt very cold. "Fine," she said. "I won't ask you how you managed that."

"Very sensible. I think you'll find," George went on, "that when I ask people to do things, they do them. So, when I ask you to do a little favour for me, in return for which you get to go home, and maybe even keep some of that money we were talking about a minute ago—"

"Ah."

"Thought you'd be interested. And better still, you'll get to go where you can spend it. Or you can stay here. Entirely up to you."

"This little favour."

She felt George yawn. "Kill King Drain for me, there's a good girl," he said. "Nice easy job, you can bung something nasty in his soup, you being his cook. Nobody'll ever know it was you, and even if they do find out, you'll be somewhere over the doughnut by then and they won't be able to touch you for it. And once that idiot Drain's out of the way, I can have my wine cellars and everybody will be happy." His eyes narrowed. "Don't tell me you've got a problem with that."

She made an effort and kept her voice normal. "Sorry," she said. "I don't kill people."

"Oh, come on." George was grinning at her. "All right, you can keep all the money. There, you've driven your hard bargain, you get what you want and so do I." He paused, looking at her like an entomologist who's just found a hitherto unknown species of beetle swimming in his soup. "You're serious, aren't you?"

"Yup."

"Silly girl. Actually, it's probably my fault, for not making myself clear enough. It's him or you. Either you kill him for me like I asked, or you're stuck here, for ever and ever. Do you understand?"

"I won't do it. Sorry."

George sighed. "You're being completely unreasonable, you know that? I mean, what's it to you, one way or another? You're not going to get caught, you won't get in any trouble—and that's the main reason why people don't kill other people, isn't it? I can absolutely guarantee. No awkward legal repercussions whatsoever."

"No."

"You're weird, you know that? Inconsistent, that's the word. I know about you. You're the girl who'll do anything for money. Including but not limited to screwing up an entire society."

"Now just a—"

"For money," George went on. "For the sake of a few dollars you happily fucked up the economy and social structure of tens of thousands of dwarves who never did you any harm, and because of your greed there's going to be conflict and breakdowns and quite possibly civil war, just because you wanted them to buy a load of useless junk so you could take your profit and get out. Let me tell you something. I got twelve economists with Harvard degrees working for me, and you know what? Compared to what you just did, one harmless little murder is *nothing*. Besides," he went on, gently, "you won't have to see him die or anything icky like that. Just give him the soup and piss off out of it. What difference will it actually make, in the long run? If you don't scrag him, one of his own lot will, sooner or later, it's their way. It's deeply ingrained in their culture, which is ancient and just as valid as anybody else's, which isn't actually saying very much, trust me, I read books. Or if the dwarves don't do him, the goblins will, and they'll turn his skull into a fucking tankard. It doesn't matter," George said, smiling. "Nothing you do here matters, it's not real, it's not your reality. It's time you went home, my girl. And an eight-figure bank balance wouldn't be so bad, either."

She looked at him, as though into a mirror, and drew a deep breath. "Guards!"

"You stupid cow." He hit her so hard she fell over, then stepped back towards the doughnut. "I was wrong. You belong here, with the savages. So fucking long."

He turned to face the doughnut. Ms. White scrambled to her feet and grabbed the nearest moveable object, which happened to be one half of the mirror she'd slipped into her pocket a little earlier, which had broken when she fell. She threw it at him, just as he started to dematerialise, and the jagged leading edge reached the back of his neck and passed through it. Then the doughnut vanished, leaving a plain unmarked wall. There was no crash of breaking glass, and no splinters on the floor.

She stared at the wall for a full ten seconds. I don't kill people, she'd told him. And maybe that was true and maybe it wasn't, and unless she could get back to her own reality and check out the obituaries she had no way of knowing which.

Big *unless*.

She thought about that. If she'd killed him, he wouldn't have had a chance to revoke her YouSpace access, so if she made another doughnut, she'd be able to get home clear and be rather rich, though with a very, very remote possibility of twenty years to life for murder, or, to be precise, aggravated pesticide. If she hadn't killed him, chances were that she could spend the rest of her life making patisserie and gazing through it, and achieve nothing more useful than a reputation for eccentricity; she'd be stuck here, with the dwarves, who would shortly be evicted to make room for a great many bottles of vintage claret by the man she'd just tried to kill, after declaring passionately her total rejection of manslaughter. Nuts, she thought. This is just not my day.

BOOK FIVE

The Agony and the Orcstacy

The High Elf narrowed his eyes. "You come in *what*?" In front of him, the tree-dappled, faintly green sunlight of Elvenhome glinted on twenty thousand crudely made but efficient spear points. "Peace," said Mordak. "No, really."

Behind the High Elf, twenty thousand marshmallornwood bows creaked ominously, objecting to being held at full draw for well in excess of the recommended time limit. He frowned. "You know what," he said, "I don't believe you."

Mordak sighed. "You talk to him," he said, then realised that the space just behind his right shoulder where Tinituviel should have been was in fact empty. He felt a tiny twinge of disappointment, which didn't last long. These were, after all, her people. Oh well. He took a deep breath. "We don't want war," he said.

"Yes, you do."

"No, we don't."

"Yes, you *do*. You're goblins."

Mordak conceded the point with a slight gesture. "Yes, all right. But *right now* we don't want war, because it'd be bloody stupid. Which is why," he went on patiently, "we come in peace."

Directly behind the High Elf, the captain of the archers cleared his throat meaningfully. The High Elf ignored him. "Why should I believe anything you say?" he said.

Ah, Mordak thought. Dialogue. "Because," he said, "if you don't, you have two choices. Either you give the order to shoot, and thereby launch an unprovoked attack and start a war, for which you'll get roasted alive in the op-ed columns of every newspaper in Elvenhome."

"Or?"

"You don't give the order, and in about five seconds the fingers of all those archers directly behind you are going to give way under the strain, and future generations of giants will use your back as a hairbrush."

The High Elf thought about that for roughly one second, then gave the order to stand down. Twenty thousand archers relaxed their bows and stuck their right hands in their mouths.

"Now, then," said Mordak.

The High Elf was staring. In front of him, twenty thousand goblins no longer directly threatened by an arrow storm hadn't moved a muscle. "Go on," he said.

"We come," Mordak said, "in peace."

"Yes, you said that. Why?"

Mordak relaxed, just a little. "Good question," he said. "Basically, we just got thrown out of our home."

The High Elf's eyes widened. "Who by?"

"None of your beeswax. But there it is. We're now homeless refugees, and we're appealing to you for political asylum and humanitarian aid. And what's more, we're asking you *nicely*."

The High Elf seemed to see a distant mountaintop,

wreathed in mist and crowned with snow—the moral high ground, and he wasn't on it. "Why?" he repeated.

Mordak grinned. "Because you lot are probably stupid enough to give it to us. And right now we need food and somewhere to sleep. And what we don't need is a bloody great battle where three-quarters of us get killed, along with three-quarters of you. Not right now. Later, maybe. Right now, it'd be—" He paused, trying to remember that favourite word of Tinituviel's. "Counter-productive."

"Let me get this straight," the High Elf said slowly. "You people are *immigrants*?"

Mordak nodded. "And as a wise man once said, immigration is the sincerest form of flattery. He went on to say, it's the hallmark of a civilised society that where people live and work shouldn't be dictated by the quirks of geography and the lottery of birth. Nice line, that. Snappy."

The High Elf was caught between a smirk and a frown. "What I actually said," he replied, "is, where *Elves* live and work. There's a difference."

"No, it was people," Mordak said. "I'm pretty sure of that."

The High Elf snapped his fingers and a stately Elf all in white stepped forward, holding a huge book bound in red and green. He opened it and found the place. Wherever the High Elf goes, the Keeper of his press cuttings is never more than a footstep away.

"Where Elves live and work," the High Elf repeated. "You aren't Elves. Now, go away."

Mordak breathed out through his nose. "Fair enough," he said. "I wouldn't have fallen for a line like that without a lobotomy, so I guess it was a bit rich to expect you to, even if you are a pointy-eared halfwit. Let's start again." He stopped. He couldn't think what to say. "We surrender."

The High Elf stared at him. "You what?"

"We give in. You win. We are your prisoners, at your mercy. Oh, for crying out loud, don't just stand there looking like a sprig of holly. Do you accept our surrender, or do we have to bash you up a bit first?"

The High Elf opened and closed his mouth a few times, but nothing came out. Then he said, "There's a catch."

"Define catch," Mordak replied. "Of course, there's the Gluvien Convention on prisoners' rights, which you lot are always banging on about, under which you've got to feed us and give us somewhere to sleep and respect our cultural diversity and all that guff, but obviously you know more about that than we do, because you wrote it, so clearly I can't be using it to pull a fast one, since you'd see that coming a mile off. Well? How about it?"

The serried ranks of goblins were starting to mutter. Mordak spun round and glared at them and they immediately fell silent, but the High Elf got the point. Mordak was in control of his horrible tribe for the moment, but moments are transitory. "Deal," said the High Elf.

"Say again?"

"I said, we have a deal. Now, tell your people to throw down their weapons, right now."

Mordak gave him a reproachful look. "Sorry," he said. "I thought you said we had a deal."

"I did. Now, the weapons, on the floor, stat."

Mordak sighed. "We just talked about that," he said. "Respecting our cultural diversity. It's a fundamental part of goblin culture to be so heavily armed you're in danger of falling over backwards, at all times, no exceptions, it's the rules. But we promise faithfully not to use them. Scout's honour."

The High Elf's head was starting to hurt. "Look," he said, "this is stupid. Why don't you tell me what you really want, and then we can talk about it like rational creatures?"

Mordak beamed at him. "There, now," he said. "I knew we could sort things out, once I'd dragged you down to my level. Let's do that. In peace and quiet. Over there, without all this lot earwigging."

Then Mordak told the High Elf everything; about the eviction notice, and the two strange humans with the small box, and the Vickers weapon, and various other things he reckoned the Elf had a right to know. And when he'd finished, the Elf gazed at him with a horrified expression on his face and said, "You're joking."

Mordak sighed. "Oddly enough, no. I'm deadly serious. And unless you want those bastards turning up on your doorstep and throwing you out the same way they did to us, I suggest you think of something. Quickly."

"Yes, of course," the Elf said gravely. "What?"

It had been a long day and Mordak had been very patient. "I don't bloody well know, do I? You're the intellectual, you tell me."

The Elf thought for a very long time. "We're screwed," he said.

Mordak looked at him. "That's it?"

"I think so."

"Truly is it said, go not to the Elves for answers, since they're about as much use as a custard wall. Oh well. Thanks ever so much for your time."

"What we need," said the Elf, "is someone we can ask."

"Genius. Who?"

The Elf thought some more, so hard that the points of his ears started to curl inwards. "A lawyer," he said. "We need a good lawyer."

"That's a start," Mordak conceded. "All right, who's the very best lawyer in Elvenhome?"

The High Elf frowned. "Actually," he said, "that would be me."

"Ah."

"Sorry."

"No matter. Look," Mordak said, "I know it's a long shot, but if you're the best Elf lawyer there is, have you got any lawyers who aren't Elves?"

"No, of course not." The Elf hesitated. "No, I tell a lie. There's a human. I'm sure I heard someone say there's a law firm that employs a human junior assistant. Name's on the tip of my—" He sighed and called over the Keeper of the Book. "Human lawyer," he said.

"There was one," the Keeper replied. "Until quite recently. They had to let him go."

"Excuse me," Mordak said. "Do you happen to know why?"

"As I understand it, his work was unsatisfactory," the Keeper said. "Nominally he was dismissed because he failed to reach his quota of billable hours, but I gather the real reason was, he approached his work in an unElvish manner. He thought," the Keeper added with a shudder, "outside the box."

"Oh. That's a bad thing?"

"Of course. Otherwise, why have boxes?"

Mordak nodded. "Find him," he said. "Right now."

The filthy bit of old rag that served John the Lawyer as an office door was hurled aside, and an Elf came in. Because the lintel was low and Elves aren't, he had to stoop a little, which meant he entered John's office ear-points first; the dim light of the oil lamp sparkled on them, just for a moment. "You," said the Elf. "Are you the lawyer?"

John looked up. "Yes."

"You can't spell."

"Actually I can, but the sign writer can't."

"Then you're a pathetic copy editor. You're coming with me."

John frowned. "Am I?"

"If you know what's good for you. You've been sent for."

Not so very long ago, John would've been on his feet and halfway to the door. But things change, and so do people. Partly it was the short, glorious time he'd spent not working for Elves, and being paid real money. Also, he'd recently gained a number of insights into how the Realms really work, none of which had done much to bolster his opinion of the Elder Race. There was also the fact that directly behind him, where the Elf couldn't see her, was an entity who could bounce any Elf off the walls and use his ears as a tin opener, and she was on his side. "Paying work?"

The Elf glared at him. "I forgot, you're human. Yes, paying work."

"Mphm." John smiled. "My rates are two hundred Elvish floons an hour, plus disbursements."

"Two hundred fl—" The Elf stared at him as though he'd just found half of him in an apple. "Don't be absurd. We could get a real lawyer for that."

John's smile didn't even flicker. "And so you shall," he said, "as soon as you give me my two hundred floons retainer. Oh, don't look at me like that, I really don't need to see what the back of your throat looks like. Payment on account. It's standard Elvish business practice."

"Yes, but you're not—"

"Look," John said. "What's the real difference between

you and me, leaving aside manners and personal charm? You're immortal, I'm not. And if it's all the same to you, I'd like to spend what's left of my mayfly existence earning money, so either pay up or shove off. I don't mind which. One would be nice, the other one would be even nicer. Just make your mind up, please."

"Two hundred floons?"

"That's right. Who says really, really old people have bad memories?"

The Elf ground his teeth. "Will you take a cheque? Only I haven't—"

"Of course. I trust people. Even your lot." He took the scrap of parchment from the Elf's long, elegant fingers, scanned it and handed it back. "Who'd have thought it, you forgot the signature. That's better, thank you. Now, you said something about a job you wanted doing?"

The Elf stormed out. John rose to follow him, then looked back. "Coming?"

"Me?" said the wraith.

"If you're not too busy or anything. Only, I don't trust that lot further than I can sneeze them out of a blocked nostril, and it'd be handy to have some, well, muscle. In case things get fraught."

"Me?"

"Yes, you. A wraith. The nameless terror against which even the mightiest Elven hero fears to stand. No offence," he added quickly.

"None taken. Do you think all this has got something to do with the Somewhere Else place?"

John shrugged. "Must have. Or else why would they want me?"

She got up. "Elves have newspapers, don't they?"

"Oh, yes," John said.

"And magazines."

"Those, too. Last time I looked, there were slightly more Elvish magazines than Elves."

"Splendid. In that case, there's bound to be modelling work, if only I could get to meet some editors."

John pursed his lips. "Have you ever seen an Elf paper?"

"No. We weren't supposed to."

"No pictures," John said. "Just lots and lots of long words meaning 'inferior'. Definitely no models."

"Oh." The wraith looked desperately sad for a moment, then brightened up. "In that case, things are going to have to change, aren't they? I'll just have to make them see that they'll sell a lot more papers if they've got pictures of me wearing nice clothes in them. Come on," she added briskly, "don't just stand there. We've got networking to do."

John thought; I could explain, assuming she'd let me get a word in edgeways. But then she'll be depressed and sad, and there's enough unhappiness in the world as it is. Or I could just stand back and watch while she gets really mad at some needle-eared jerk of an editor, and then sue him for discrimination. Which won't work, of course, but I bet she'll like me for trying.

Somehow a grin had crept onto his face. He wiped it off, but he could feel the afterglow spreading through him. I love my job, he thought, and ran after her.

"Terry," said Molly Barrington, looking up from her treasured, seven-week-old copy of the *Daily Mail*, "there's a whole crowd of people outside our front door."

Terry Barrington scowled at her. He'd finally managed to get the back off his laptop (snot-nosed kids could fix these things, so it stood to reason he could) and he was gazing at all the weird shit inside like a Trobriand Islander in a nuclear power station. "We haven't got a front door. We haven't got a *door*."

"You know what I mean."

"Draw the curtains."

His wife gave him a look equally blended from compassion and contempt. "You do realise," she said, "you've buggered up the warranty."

"Hardly matters out here, does it? Not like we can send the bloody thing back." He turned it upside down, in the fond hope that it would help. "Bloody frontier spirit, that's what we need. If it's broken, fix it yourself." He peered at the ants' nest of teeming circuitry until his nose was an inch from the green plastic. It looked for all the world like the train set he'd had as a boy; that was the station, and that copper-coloured thing was the tracks, and all the rest of the gubbins must be points and signals. The only real difference was, when he was a boy he knew how all that stuff worked.

"We haven't got any curtains, remember," Molly said; and, yes, he remembered just fine, because she'd been bringing the fact to his attention every hour on the hour for days.

"When I've got five minutes," Terry mumbled past the screwdriver lodged between his teeth. "Or get a man in."

"There aren't any men."

Terry sighed. "You know what," he said. "I wonder if we did the right thing coming here."

Curiously enough, the same thought had occurred to Molly once or twice recently. However, as her husband's official loyal opposition, she knew her duty. "Don't be silly," she said. "You love it here, you know you do."

"Do I really."

"Of course you do. I mean, think of what we've got here."

"Like?"

Actually—"Well, for starters, what about that amazing view? You don't see things like that out of the window in Putney."

"Which is why you're always banging on to me about curtains. Yes, point taken."

Terry was a fair-minded man, and he was prepared to concede that it wasn't entirely the Realms' fault that his laptop had suddenly stopped working. Computers broke down back home, too. But back home you could get people to fix them. He tried to think what it could have been that he'd done that had buggered the stupid thing. It had been working just fine the last time he updated the blog (and, somehow, his enthusiasm for that had waned a bit lately; wonder why). Since then, however, nothing; he turned it on and all that happened was, this stupid thing like a big red eye appeared in the middle of the screen and just sat there. Probably a virus, or else it was a bit of dust in the works. Pound to a penny, all it really needed was a good clean-up with a toothbrush.

He noticed something; so unusual that it put all other thoughts out of his mind. His wife had stopped talking. "What?" he said.

"What?"

"What's the matter?"

Molly was looking at him, and he knew her well enough to read her expression like a book (albeit in a language he didn't understand, and which he was holding the wrong way up). She wanted to go home, too. But, since he'd said that that was what he wanted to do, she couldn't possibly agree with him, not just like that. No, she had to find some way of agreeing with him against her will, so that doing what she also wanted to do would constitute an act of selfless martyrdom. She was ever so good at it. Long practice.

"Do you really not like it here any more?"

He thought about that. It didn't take very long. "No," he said.

"Would you be happier if we went home?"

"Yup."

Now the sigh, followed by the making-the-supreme-sacrifice look. "You're wasting your time doing that, you know. Probably you've ruined it completely."

He decided she could have that one for free. Also, given that one of the little silvery signal boxes had just come away in his hand, she was probably right. Diplomacy, he thought. "Forget it," I said. "I know how much you like it here. It's what you always wanted, a place like this."

With fifty-seven flights of stairs, hideous monsters for neighbours and the sort of toilet that had made such a significant contribution to the spread of the Black Death; quite. "Yes," she said, managing to look him straight in the eye without bursting into flames; he admired her for that. "But if you're not happy here—"

"Nah, I'm just being selfish. I couldn't take it all away from you."

Neat, he thought. Now he had the moral high ground, and everything ghastly that happened to them henceforth would be her fault. On those terms, he wouldn't mind particularly if they did stay. "Besides," he went on, "we'll never get our money back on this dump."

"Money isn't everything."

Wash your mouth out with soap and water, he thought but didn't say. What she didn't know, because for some reason he'd neglected to tell her, was that shortly before they'd left the Old Country, he'd been telling Benny Tisbury all about it in the golf club bar, and Benny had said how wonderful it sounded, and he and Pam were looking for a little place somewhere now that Antibes was so full of grockles off the cruise ships, so if ever they got sick of it and thought of selling ... "You're right," he said. "That's very true."

"And if you really don't like it here any more—"

He glanced down at his disembowelled laptop. If it really was fucked up beyond all hope of recovery, that would mean no more blog, therefore nothing for him to do all day except all the jobs Molly wanted him to do when he'd got five minutes. A man couldn't be expected to live like that.

"I don't mind where we live so long as you're happy," he said. He waited. "I said, I don't mind where we live—"

She wasn't listening. "Those people," she said.

"What?"

"I think they want to talk to us."

Terry peered over her shoulder. "Probably canvassers," he said. "Ignore them, they'll go away. Like I was saying, I really don't mind where—"

"Make them go away, Terry, they're scaring me. I don't want that sort of person hanging round our house."

Terry went a sort of pale magnolia. "If we just keep quiet and pretend we aren't home, they'll give up soon enough. They'll think we're down the shops or out for a—"

Something heavy and metallic clanged against the wall of the tower, which had perfect acoustics, like a bell. Molly screamed. Oh, for crying out loud, Terry thought. "Probably just kids," he said hopefully, and headed for the stairs.

If we were back home, he told himself, as he clattered down the unending spiral, we could call the police. Who wouldn't turn up till the next day, admittedly, and when they did all they'd do would be to point out how thin his back offside tyre was getting; but at least there was someone you could turn to, who was nominally on your side.

He mumbled the door-opening spell, stuck his head out, drew a deep breath and contorted his face into a furious expression.

"What's the big idea, disturbing people at this—oh, it's you."

The amiable idiot human who'd come to use their phone smiled weakly at him. "Hello," he said. "Me again."

"Yes."

"I've remembered my name," said the human. "Theo Bernstein. Can I use your phone again?"

Terry lowered his voice. "Who are that lot?"

Theo glanced over his shoulder, then back again. "No idea," he said. "They sort of followed me here, or else they were coming this way anyway and I just happened to be ahead of them. Odd-looking lot, aren't they?"

Terry sighed. "You'd better come in," he said. "Keep your voice down, Molly's got one of her heads

"I'm very sorry to hear that. Which one?"

"We've decided we're going home," Terry said. "Hang on. What did you say your name was?"

"Theo Bernstein."

"I've heard of you. You're a scientist."

"Yes."

"You blew up the—"

"Yes."

"Stone me. Can you fix computers?"

"No."

Terry shrugged. "Well," he said, "probably just as well you don't try, bearing in mind what happened with that hadron collidy thing, no offence. We want to sell this place."

Theo gave him a winning smile. "Can I use your phone, please?"

"What? Oh, yes, right. This way."

Theo tapped in the number, waited, then grinned. "It's ringing," he said, but Terry had wandered off. He waited, and heard a voice. "Hello," he said, "I'm Theo Ber—"

The voice spoke to him. His expression changed. The grin faded. He nodded a couple of times and said, "I see, yes." Then he cut the call and put the phone back neatly where he'd found it. He looked round. No sign of his host, who wasn't going to like this. Still, that wasn't his fault. Well, not entirely. "Mr. Barrington," he called out. "Mr. Barrington, I need to talk to you."

No sign of anyone. He was about to go down the stairs when a stab of pain in the exact centre of his head dropped him to his knees.

What does that mean?

"I don't know," Theo said aloud.

Don't mess with me, said the voice in his head. I know you're lying. Tell me.

The pain was almost more than he could bear, but Theo managed a grin. "Think about it," he said. "You're inside my brain, with access to all the stored information, and you're asking me questions."

What does it *mean*?

"It means I could really use an aspirin," Theo said. "And either I'm telling the truth, or there's a part of my brain you can't get into. And the bitch of it is," he added with enormous pleasure, "you have no way of knowing which. Now, can I please have the use of my legs back?"

You know what? You're no fun at all. I was better off with the she-goblin. At least she appreciated me.

"Yes," Theo said. "It's a pity you made me kill her. I wish you hadn't done that. I don't like killing anything."

You're weird.

"Not where I come from," Theo said firmly. "Came from," he amended, and there was a slight hitch in his voice. "Though actually, to be fair, we do just as much killing as you do here, otherwise we'd starve to death. We just try hard not to think about it."

Came from?

"Slip of the tongue. Tenses are a bitch."

What are you hiding from me?

Theo beamed. "Search me," he said. "Oh, sorry, you've done that. No idea."

A moment passed, during which Theo had the oddest sensation of something scrabbling about inside his head. He even fancied he could hear the scrape of claws on a hard surface. That's not possible.

"No, it isn't."

But you managed it anyway.

"Not me," Theo relented. "A very clever friend of mine did it for me, bless him. And in his reality, it was possible. Feasibility tourism, it's a wonderful thing."

Part of your mind is sealed off. I can't get in. *You* can't get in.

"No, but it's like Radio 3, it's nice to know it's there if I ever did want it."

And the message you just received. It spoke to—

"Yes. I was tempted to listen in. But eavesdropping on yourself is such bad manners."

For a second or so, Theo couldn't feel the presence in his mind, though he knew it was still there. You won't get away with this.

"What're you going to do? Force your way in? If you do that, you'll kill me, and then I'll be no use to you." He smiled. "I don't know why I'm bothering to tell you that, you know as well as I do. Reminds me of a reality I was in a while ago where they were all telepaths. Kept finishing each other's sentences. It was like everyone was married to everyone else."

All right, said the voice, and its tone had changed. What do you want?

"Excuse me?"

How much? Name your price.

Theo sighed. "You're not very good at this, are you? Look it up if you don't believe me. There is nothing I want. I'm not for sale."

Pause, while the voice did just that. Then, you're lying.

"Excuse me?"

There is something you want.

"News to me if there is."

You want to go home.

"Oh, that."

But you can't.

"Do forgive me, sloppy thinking, I don't know what's got into me. What I should have said is, there's nothing I want that I can have."

Yes, you could. Anything. Just let me into the locked room.

"No," Theo said firmly. "What I want really is impossible, even in an infinite multiverse. Nearly infinite," he added with a slight catch in his voice. "Wish I could explain, but you'll just have to take my word for it. Which leaves us in a—"

Mexican standoff.

"You took the words right out of my mouth. Or you could just admit defeat and leave."

No way. I suggest you get used to me, because I'm staying. I like it here. Whither thou goest, and all that.

"I'm not going anywhere," Theo said sadly. "Meanwhile, sorry to be rude but I do have things I ought to be doing, so if you could see your way to letting me have my legs back, I would be ever so grateful."

No legs unless you open the locked room.

Theo let out a long sigh. "You clown," he said. "Haven't you got it yet? I mean, there you are, inside one of the best-informed brains in the multiverse, and you can't even be bothered to read the FAQ. I can't open the locked room."

Then what's the point of—?

"The room will open," Theo explained, "of its own accord, when the time and circumstances are right. It's like those time-locked bank vaults. Until then, nothing will get it open, not hissy fits or wishing on a star or dynamite. And the time and circumstances haven't happened yet. And before you ask, I have no idea when that will be. Comprendez?"

You're lying.

"Oh, for crying out—"

You're not lying. But you're keeping something back.

"You know what?" Theo said. "I've had about enough of you. I'm going to shut you up for a bit, so I can think."

You can't do that.

"Watch me," Theo said. And he lifted his head, banged it hard on the stone floor and knocked himself out.

"I knew this would happen," Terry said gloomily, as he staggered down the murderously tight spiral staircase holding Theo's feet. "We should have put up a sign. Didn't I say we should put up a sign?"

"Slow down," Molly said, edging down backwards with Theo's head cradled in her arms. "You nearly pushed me over."

"I said, if we put up a sign they won't be able to sue. I asked the lawyers about it before we signed the paperwork and they said. And now, as soon as this idiot wakes up, what's the first thing he's going to do? Off to the nearest lawyer like a bullet out of a gun, and we'll be liable."

"I'm sure he'll do no such thing," Molly said, as they reached the landing. "Put him down, I need a breather."

Theo was still fast asleep, and smiling. The Barringtons sat on the floor with their backs to the wall and gasped for air. There were still thirty-seven flights to go.

"Your turn for the head end," Molly pointed out.

"We could pitch him out of a window," Terry said quietly. "Nobody would know, and in five minutes those horrible creatures out there would have eaten him, and—"

His wife gave him a shocked look, and he shrugged. "Sorry," he said. "Just thinking aloud."

"You're right," Molly said firmly. "We need to go home. This place is doing bad things to us."

Terry nodded. "He can sue us till he's blue in the face if we're back home," he said. "I bet you, the jurisdictional issues—"

"Come on," Molly said. "Next lot of stairs."

Theo's journey down the stairs of the Tower of Snorgond was not uneventful, and it was probably just as well that he slept through it. When at last they reached the ground floor, he was still smiling. They dumped him onto the chaise longue and collapsed on the sofa.

"They're still out there," Molly said.

Terry looked, then mumbled the obscuring spell so he wouldn't have to see. "There's more of them," he said. "A lot more."

Which was entirely true. The entire goblin nation: every single journalist and civil servant in Elvenhome (which amounts to roughly the same thing); a substantial contingent of dwarves, who'd just got around to reading the eviction notice served by John the Lawyer. King Mordak, King Drain and the High Elf had held an impromptu summit conference, sheltering from the rays of the Beautiful/Horrible Yellow Face under the shade of the Barrington's satellite dish; and although the summit conference had achieved as much as all summit conferences everywhere always do, nobody had killed or eaten anybody else, which was in itself an unimaginable leap forward in the diplomatic history of the Realms. Meanwhile, a pale-looking young woman was going round pestering newspaper editors, and a chubby young human was searching in vain for a door to knock at.

"You're wasting your time," said Ms. White.

"There's got to be a door," John replied. "Buildings have doors, otherwise where's the point of them?"

"I read about it," Ms. White said.

John looked at her. "I remember you," he said. "You bought my law book."

"Quite. So you'll believe me when I tell you that I have actually read Thrandifuill's *Longer Elvish History*. And it says in there how the wizard who built this thing designed it without any doors, specifically so as to frustrate process servers. For some reason, people kept wanting to sue him, and he'd had enough."

"Fancy that," John said. "But there's got to be a way of getting their attention."

"Try the bell."

"There isn't a bell."

Ms. White pointed. "What's that, then?"

John looked closely. "It's a small round button made of some material I've never seen before, set into a small rectangular brass plate. Not," he added, "a bell. Otherwise—"

"Sorry," Ms. White conceded. "It's, um, a magic bell. Here, let me."

She pressed the button. Nothing happened. John sighed.

"Pressing the button," Ms. White explained, "causes a bell to ring inside the tower. It's magic."

"Of course it is." John counted to ten under his breath. "Doesn't seem to be working."

"It's a big tower. It'll take them a long time to get to the door."

John looked at her. "What are you doing here, anyway? I thought you worked for King Drain."

"You're the lawyer."

"That's me."

She looked thoughtfully at him. "I might just need you for something," she said. "Tell me, are you any good at extradition law?"

"Yes," John said. "Never heard of it, but that's not a problem, I can look it up. Why?"

"Tell you later. No, I was on my way—somewhere, and I saw all these people milling around, and I thought, safety in numbers—"

"Are you scared of something?"

"Me? Good Lord, no. And then I saw you prodding and poking about and I said to myself, there's a man looking for a door, only he's wasting his time, because I happen to know ... Yes, I'm scared all right. Trouble is, there's nothing anyone can do about it."

John gave her a sad look. "Sure?"

She grinned. "Well, maybe. I seem to remember you're persistent, resourceful and fundamentally dishonest, so maybe you might be able to do something after all. It all depends on exactly what sort of shit I find myself ankle-deep in. I'll keep you posted. Try the bell again."

"But I just—"

"Try it again."

John did as he was told. "Look," he said, "it obviously doesn't—oh, hello."

An angry bald head was scowling at him out of the wall. "What do you want?"

"I think he wants to serve you with a writ," Ms. White said helpfully, and stepped back out of the way. The angry bald head grew into an angry head and torso. John stood his ground, mostly because his feet wouldn't move. "No, I don't," he said, "really. I just want to ask you a few questions, that's all."

The angry man glowered at him. "I'm busy. Push off."

"Just a few minutes of your time—"

"Jesus," said the angry man. "Look, whatever it is, we don't want it, all right? We're fine for life insurance and religion, and you can see for yourself, double glazing is out of the question."

"I'm not selling anything," John said. "All I want is some answers. It's very important. Please?"

The magic word; or maybe Terry Barrington saw in John's eyes, as in a mirror, a man at the very furthest extent of his rope. In any event, he hesitated, then stepped out of the wall, which closed behind him like a black mercury curtain. "What?"

John took a deep breath. "Where are you from, exactly?"

"What are you, the census or something?"

"I'm a lawyer," John replied, and before Terry could tell him what he thought about that, quickly added, "I'm a lawyer, and recently a weird man hired me to evict the goblins and the dwarves. And I got to thinking, why would anyone want to do that?"

Terry grinned at him. "You met any of them?"

"Oh yes."

"Then that'll be why."

John nodded. "They make you feel uncomfortable."

"Too bloody right. Horrible little buggers with faces like a bomb going off in a pet shop. If the council or someone's moving them on, bloody good job, that's what I say."

The faint glimmer at the back of John's mind turned into a glow. "They—what's that Elvish expression?—lower the tone of the neighbourhood?"

Terry laughed. "Any lower, you could flood it and sail boats on it. So, is that right, then? They're getting shot of them?"

"To go back to my original question," John said. "Am I right in thinking you're not, um, local?"

"You bet," Terry said. "We're from Putney. Well, Molly, that's my wife, she's from Dunstable originally, then we both lived in Hounslow for a while, but when the kids were grown up—"

"Excuse me," John interrupted gently. "These places. They're not in the Realms, are they?"

"Absolutely not."

"I see. So there are—" He took another deep breath. "Other places."

"Yes, thank God. Decent, sane places with shops and WiFi, where you can buy stuff and the locals don't look like bad CGI. No offence," he added generously. "Obviously you people like it here, and that's fine. Just not everyone's cup of tea, is what I'm saying."

"Of course," John said quickly. "Tell me, how did you get here?"

Terry pursed his lips. "Now actually, that's a bloody good question. The bloke who sold us this place did explain, but it was like when someone tells you about Einstein in a pub, you think it's clear as crystal and five minutes later it's all gone out of your head. Something to do with multiverse theory, I think, or string theory, some theory, anyhow. We came through a doughnut."

John nodded slowly. "I don't actually know that word,"

he said, "but I'm guessing it's some sort of magic gateway or portal. Is that about right?"

Terry hesitated before answering. "Yeah, sort of," he said. "In context, like."

"That's what I thought," John said. "And there are more like you? More people from Putney, living here."

"Not from Putney as such, but, yeah, people like us. Well, more like us than you lot, that's for bloody sure."

"And they all bought their homes from the same man?"

Terry shrugged. "I guess so. I think he'd sort of cornered the market. Because of the doughnut thing. He's the only one with the technology. Though I imagine when the patent or whatever it is runs out, there'll be loads of them at it." A thought, completely new and unanticipated, floated into Terry's mind. "Bit of a blow for your lot, that'd be."

"Um."

"Well, it would be," Terry said sagely. "I mean, look at the Dordogne. When Rita and Phil Arkwright moved there in '96, they were the only Brits for miles and everything was dirt cheap and unspoilt. Now there's expats as far as the eye can see, and none of the locals can afford to live there any more. Which is a real cow when it comes to getting a plumber or a builder, and as for getting the septic tank emptied—"

"You see," John said, "I think the weird man who hired me to drive out the goblins and the dwarves wants their lands so he can sell it to, um, people like you. And—no offence—I'm not sure that'd be a very good thing."

Terry Barrington was a fair man, deep down. "Maybe not," he said. "Still, doesn't matter a stuff to us, because we're leaving."

Directly behind him, where John couldn't see, someone coughed gently. "Excuse me."

"What? Oh, it's him." Terry turned, so that all John could see was the back of his head. "What?"

The sheer black wall rippled, and a different human came out, with Terry following. He was about as nondescript looking as it's possible to be while actually remaining visible, and he had an ugly bruise on his forehead. "I didn't mean to eavesdrop," said the new human. "Oh, and thanks for the use of your phone, by the way. But did I just hear you say you're leaving?"

"That's right."

"Leaving the Realms?"

"Yup. Going back to London. Well, we thought maybe Surrey, because Molly's sister June—"

"No, you aren't," the new human said sadly. "Sorry."

Somewhere, a bird sang. Nobody was interested.

"You what?" Terry said.

Maybe Theo didn't hear him. "Excuse me."

"Who, me?"

"Yes. I take it you live here."

"Yes. I'm a lawyer."

"I'd sort of gathered that. Please, can you tell me, where can I find whoever's in charge?"

John turned and pointed. "Right there," he said. "That's the King of the Dwarves, the tall one with the pained expression is the High Elf, and the little chap with the tusks is Mordak, Dark Lord and king of the goblins."

"Gosh. Really?"

"No shit."

Theo nodded. "That's lucky," he said. "And who's that over there? The man chasing after the pretty girl, waving an axe?"

John frowned. "Him I don't know," he said. "She's the

dwarf-king's cook. Actually, I think she may be one of your lot." He hesitated. "I suppose I really ought to go and rescue her before he does her an injury."

"*Before* the injury," Theo repeated. "I guess lawyers are different here. Ah well."

The man with the axe had stopped chasing the pretty girl and was talking excitedly to another man, dressed in melodramatically swirly black robes, who John knew very well. "That's my client," he said.

"The one who hired you to—?"

"Yup."

Theo looked at him. "Seems to me that the fat chap with the axe is your client's boss. In which case," he added, looking very sad indeed, "he really ought to hear what I've got to say, too. Could you do me a big favour and get their attention for me? I'm shy," he explained.

John looked at him, then nodded. He wasn't going to enjoy this, but never mind.

There's one fail-safe, guaranteed way of getting people to listen to you in the Realms. John took a very deep breath, lifted his arms above his head and yelled, "The eagles are coming! The eagles are coming!" Then, blushing like mad, he stepped back into the shadow of the tower.

Everyone (except the fat man with the axe) stopped what they were doing and stared, first at the sky and then at John. Then there was a long silence. Then someone said, "No, they aren't."

John nodded. "Just kidding," he said. "But there's someone here who wants to talk to you." He scuttled round behind Theo, who smiled feebly and gave a little wave.

"Ladies and, um, gentlemen," he said, "I have an announcement to make. The result of the Rexit referendum is now in, and Reality 7754/88/A42c has voted

Leave. Effective forthwith, A42c is no longer part of the multiverse. Thank you for your time."

Dead silence, apart from a horrified scream somewhere near the back. Then Mordak detached himself from the summit conference, waddled forward a few paces and said, "Say what?"

Theo closed his eyes for a moment. Perhaps he'd actually believed that he could get away with simply stating the abbreviated truth and making a run for it, but probably not. He sighed. "Let me explain," he said.

"Let's just run through it one more time," Mordak said.

It was cool and shady under the marshmallorn tree, where Mordak had led Theo after his goblins had dispersed the riot that followed Theo's explanation. Theo was feeling a bit better now, though he hadn't touched the skull of nice cool water Mordak had given him, or even had a nibble of the plate of dry roasted toenails. "Sure," Theo said wearily. "Why not?"

Mordak took a moment to order his thoughts. "You come from another Realm, far, far away."

"That's right."

"And your lot have recently found out how to get to our Realm by going through a hole in a sort of bun."

"It's—yes, that's right."

Mordak nodded. "With you so far. And this is because of multiverse theory."

"Check."

Mordak rubbed the side of his head, taking care not to gouge grooves in his flesh with his claws as he did so. "Multiverse theory states that there's lots and lots and lots—"

"An infinite number."

"And *lots* of Realms, and they're all sort of separate, and the only way to get from one to another is through this bun."

"Um."

"Yes?"

"All right then, yes. Broadly speaking."

"Fine," Mordak said, "just so long as we've got that straight. And these weird humans I've been so worried about lately, they all came from your Realm."

"That's right," Theo said. "And it's all my fault, because I invented the—well, the bun."

"You're a baker?"

"Particle physicist," Theo amended. "Same sort of thing, but—" He shrugged. No point, really. "And I didn't actually invent it, that was a friend of mine. But I sort of set the whole thing up, something I now rather regret."

Mordak gave him a kind smile. "Don't beat yourself up over it," he said. "From what I gather, there's a lot of people who'll happily do that for you. So all the weirdos—"

"Came from Reality A42c, yes. My home."

Mordak peered at him. "You sent them here?"

"Dear God, no. That was that odious little man who was hanging round just now, apparently. I'd heard some-one had got hold of a YouSpace portal and was up to no good with it, but honestly, I didn't make this mess. I'm the one who's got to clear it up, that's all."

Mordak picked a fibre of troll fillet out of his teeth with a splinter of shinbone. "That's the spirit," he said. "Duty first and all that. So what's this Rexit thing?"

Theo looked very sad indeed. "Short for Exit from Reality. Apparently," he said, "when the folks in Reality A42c realised they were part of a multiverse comprising an infinite number of alternative realities, it made them feel uncomfortable. Not sure why," he added, "but there you are, and I suppose there's worse crimes than being parochial. Anyway, there was a lot of fuss about it, some people saying it was good to be part of something big and huge and wonderful, and some people saying, next thing you know, they'll all be over here, taking our jobs. And so they decided to have a referendum about it, and now Reality A42c is leaving the multiverse, for good."

"Ah."

"Quite. It wasn't the result anyone expected, but that's democracy for you. And what that means in practice is, I can set up YouSpace portals on every street corner, and people can stare into doughnuts till they're blue in the face, and nobody can get into or out of A42c ever again." He shrugged. "No great loss as far as the rest of the multiverse is concerned, except they're going to have to amend all the textbooks to read 'infinite number of universes minus one'. All a bit silly, really."

"But good for us," Mordak said. "No more weirdos from your Realm coming over here trying to throw us out of our homes."

"There's that, yes."

"That'll do me." He chewed a fingernail—his own, for a change—and asked, "What about those humans in the old wizard's tower, and the other lot down the old abandoned mine. Can they go back?"

"I don't think so."

"Ah well. Talking of which, you look like shit. Are you feeling all right?"

Theo gave him a feeble grin. "I think so. That's what's worrying me."

"Ah. Only, I was thinking, presumably you can't go home either."

"Oh, that. No big deal, believe me. Truth is, I made

a bit of a hash of things back in A42c, so I'm really not welcome there any more. That was one of the reasons they chose me to come over here and announce the result of the vote. And don't come back, they added. Screw them, I say." Theo massaged the front of his head thoughtfully. It hurt—rather like the way your face hurts after you've had a tooth out, and the anaesthetic's worn off, and you start exploring the blood-and-jelly cavity with the tip of your tongue. It's gone, he thought. "Oh, and by the way. I think I owe you an apology."

Mordak gave him a sideways look. "It's a weird thing," he said, "but I don't often get apologies from humans. Still, I'm always up for a new experience. What did you do?"

"I sort of killed one of your people. Sorry."

Shrug. "Humans kill lots of goblins," he said. "And vice versa. Stuff happens. We believe that when we die we go to a vast, dark city where the derelict streets are alive with rats and strange creatures jump out on us from dark corners, and either we eat them or they eat us. So dying's not so bad, really. Of course, your lot think that's just some crazy myth."

Theo shook his head. "Oh no," he said. "It's real all right. I've been there, for conferences, and to see the Yankees play at home. And we have similar beliefs where I come from. Similar-ish." He frowned. "But I really am sorry about your goblin. She wasn't really doing me any harm. I don't know what came over me," he added. "Though I have a sort of an idea."

"Hang on. *She* wasn't—?"

"Yes, I'm pretty sure it was a female. I remember thinking, good heavens, they have female goblins in this reality."

"Had," Mordak said. "She was the only one."

"Ah."

"I created her. I thought it would be a good idea."

Theo nodded slowly. "And was it?"

"I don't know, she didn't really last long enough for me to find out. She was bigger and stronger than the bog-standard goblins, and smarter, and she learned stuff amazingly fast. So, probably no, not a good idea at all. Ah well." He stopped and peered at Theo, who was looking thoughtful. "What?"

"What made me kill her," Theo said slowly, "was this sort of thing that suddenly popped into my head."

"I get them," Mordak said. "My secretary calls them ideas. She thinks I shouldn't have them."

"It was more than that," Theo said. "It was like a presence."

"What, birthdays and winter solstice and stuff?"

"Like there was someone else inside my head," Theo said. "And now it's gone. It was there a while ago, when I went into the tower. I even bashed my head and knocked myself out, just to get it to shut up."

"Maybe you killed it."

"I don't think so. Not the killable type, really. It's hard to describe, but when I try and think what it was like, I get this image in my mind of a huge staring red eye."

Mordak blinked twice. "Oh," he said.

"Rings a bell?"

"Oh yes."

At the foot of the tower, currently in deep shadow, was a shallow pool of dank, muddy water, left over from the last torrential rains. On its surface a reflection shivered in the slight breeze; an odd thing, because there was nothing for it to be a reflection of.

Frustrating, thought the Eye. So very near; that other Realm, tantalisingly close and crammed with infinite opportunity, where (by the sound of it) a Quintessence of Evil could really have made something of itself, fulfilled its true potential, a place that sounded like it was specially designed for evil to feel at home in; and then, at the very last moment, the way through had been shut, so firmly and suddenly that if the Eye had had lashes, they'd have been caught in the door—

Story of my life, the Eye thought sadly. You get within an ace of the finishing line and some furry-footed bastard thwarts you. Oh well. Onwards and upwards.

The reflected eye swivelled on the pool's grubby meniscus. Well, if it couldn't have the Other Place, it'd have to make do with this one. The glimpse of the Other Place made everything here seem tawdry and provincial, but that only made the Eye more determined. If it couldn't have what it really wanted, what it *deserved*, then it was going to have to make do, wasn't it, and woe betide anybody who got in its way this time.

It remembered the body it had occupied, briefly, before the Somewhere-Else human. Now that had been some body. For strength, stamina and speed of reflexes there was nothing to compare with it in the Realms, unless you counted a certain person we don't talk about, and there's an awful lot to be said for brute strength; also a surprising amount of brain capacity, most of it currently unused, so moving in would be easy, plenty of room for all its stuff, walk-in wardrobes and everything. Now, if that body was still available—

No, wait, the stupid human killed it. The Eye thought about that. Killed, yes; but a little patching up here, a rewiring job and a bit of duct tape there, maybe a certain degree of hearing loss and a slight tendency to yawn uncontrollably after meals, but she'd do, at least to be going on with. In fact, she'd do very nicely. The Eye had never been a girl before, not for any significant length of time. It might be fun.

The Eye rippled a little, stirring the water on which its two-dimensional image lay. Not a Dark Lord, a Dark Lady; cool. It reached out into the nebulous, tentative element it inhabited—the interface between light and darkness, the gaps between the photons, the places shadows go when you aren't looking—until it found what it was looking for. Inert, but not quite cold, and no physical or mechanical damage; definitely a viable fixer-upper. And they'd been friends, right up to the very last moment (which could easily be erased), so she'd be ever so glad to have him back.

No big deal, then. Something that could be achieved in the blink of an Eye.

There was a soft splash, and the water of the pool swelled and rose up to accommodate the mass of an object that had landed in it, after falling some considerable distance. For the record, it was Terry Barrington's laptop, hurled from a high window as punishment for not working any more. The water gurgled, the laptop sank and settled down into the three-inch-thick bed of silt at the bottom of the pool.

When you've quite finished, muttered the Eye, as it waited for the surface of the water to calm down enough to hold a coherent reflection. It recognised the strange rectangular thing; the fool in the tower had used it to see the Other Place—the place that was now closed off, lost for ever. The thought didn't improve the Eye's temper. Somebody is going to pay for all this, it resolved. Somebody is going to catch it hot. Lots of somebodies. Everybody.

The water settled. The Eye blinked, and was gone.

*

Tinituviel was feeling ever so slightly guilty. Which, she assured herself as she picked her way through the tangled briars at the edge of the greenwood, was silly, because after all, Mordak was a *goblin*. True, she'd somehow managed to tolerate him during the time she'd been working for him (an Elf working for a goblin: enough said) and maybe he wasn't quite like other goblins, but even so. It was high time she made her mind up about where her loyalties really lay.

The tips of her ears, where the upper flange of the lobe swoops upwards towards the point, were burning. She knew what that meant, and ears never lie. She scowled.

The whole purpose of the exercise (she told herself) had been to exercise a restraining and civilising influence on Goblinkind by insinuating herself into the very nerve centre of goblin power—that and earning five times what she'd have got doing the same work in Elvenhome, assuming she could ever have got such a plum job back home, which with her résumé she couldn't; but that was just an incidental benefit, and, boy, had she earned every last cartwheel-sized gold piece, putting up with all that ignorance and crass stupidity, and the *smell*—

And now (she picked a trailing strand of briar carefully out of her hair), the moment things started getting a bit awkward, what was the first thing Mordak had done? Taken his entire horde off to invade Elvenhome. Well, not actually invade; before she'd made her strategic withdrawal, she'd heard Mordak telling the assembled host precisely what he planned to do to any goblin who drew a bowstring or levelled a spear without a direct order from him, and it did occur to her to wonder whether the High Elf would have made a similar speech, had the position been reversed. But that was apples and oranges, of course, because Elves are nothing like goblins. If goblins charge into Elf turf, it's indefensible aggression. If Elves do it, it's a surgical pre-emptive strike. All the difference in the world. Of course.

Elves can't get lost in the greenwood, any more than fish can drown in water; even so, she realised that she wasn't exactly precisely 110 per cent sure where she was. She stopped and looked round for a landmark. Then she remembered. Over there somewhere was the old wizard's tower, where the ghastly new humans had moved in, and over there was where the two even ghastlier humans had demonstrated the Vickers weapon. So: she had in fact come the right way, but the way she'd come was the indirect right way rather than the direct right way, and if she wanted to get back on the direct right way it'd probably be a good idea, an even better idea, to retrace her steps half a mile or so—

She saw something lying at the foot of a tree. It looked depressingly like a dead body. Drat, she thought, it's started already.

If a war had broken out between the goblins and the Elves it definitely wasn't her fault, and if it wasn't her fault it wasn't her business either; so she'd be entirely justified in ignoring it and walking away, reasonably fast. On the other hand—it wasn't lost on her that she was now out of a job, and, like all her race, what she really wanted to do more than anything else in the whole world was to write for the newspapers. An exclusive report on the very first engagement of the war would be worth good money to the editor of the *Beautiful Golden Face*. Cautiously she edged forward, and bent down to peer.

Not an Elf, that was for sure. But apparently not a goblin, either. For a start, it was twice the size of any goblin she'd ever seen, and it looked—well, not *completely* different, but different enough to be going on with. She considered the mouth and the claws, and the hair. Then she made the connection. Mordak's idiotic female-goblin project.

She nudged the corpse with her toe. Ah well. It had been a silly idea from the outset, and obviously it had come to nothing. Presumably the poor thing had finally succumbed to massive genetic impossibility and simply stopped working. The only remarkable thing was that it had lasted long enough to grow this big.

Just another goblin; even so. She knelt down beside it. It had changed a lot since the last time she'd seen it— bigger, taller, bulkier, but also somehow less *goblin*, if that made any sense at all. Ah well. Just another of Mordak's good-ideas-at-the-time, and just because he always failed miserably didn't necessarily mean that he was always completely wrong to try.

Was it—she—actually dead? She looked dead all right, but you can't always tell with goblins, among whom looking not just dead but badly decomposed is an essential fashion statement. She didn't seem to be breathing, but goblins can hold their breath for a ridiculously long time, just possibly because of the smell of other goblins. And bear in mind that this one was the prototype, about whom virtually nothing was known. Tinituviel stood up and looked round until she found the broad, fleshy leaf of a marshmallorn tree. She wrapped this carefully round the toe of her shoe, then gave the slumped body a sharp kick in the ribs.

Elves have exceptional reflexes. She just managed to whisk her ankle out of the way in time.

Right, then. "Get up," she said.

The she-goblin opened her eyes and gazed at her. "You kicked me."

"Purely for your own good. I wanted to see if you're dead or not."

"You're an Elf."

Tinituviel sighed. Bred in the bone, obviously. So typical of goblins to have such deeply rooted knee-jerk prejudices. "What are you doing out here?" she said.

The she-goblin thought for a moment. "I'm not sure," she said. "I was in a small room for a long time, and then a strange lady brought me outside, and then my friend—" She stopped. "My friend."

"You've got a friend? Good heavens."

"He killed me," the she-goblin said, and just for a split second Tinituviel felt something which, if applied to any other creature in the Realms, could have been mistaken for pity. "He said he liked me, and then he found a human, and he liked the human more than me, so he—"

"Human?"

The she-goblin nodded. "I don't understand," she said. "Why would my friend like the human more than me? He's skinny and weak and he hasn't got claws, he couldn't even remember his name till my friend did something to inside his head. I don't understand. Why doesn't my friend like me any more?"

Tinituviel gave her what she fondly imagined was a comforting smile. "Because you're horrible," she said. "But that's not your fault, you were born like it."

"Oh." The she-goblin thought for a moment. "Will you be my friend?"

"No," said Tinituviel. "Not for all the bylines in Elvenhome. However," she went on, as the she-goblin made a really horrible snuffling noise, "I might just make a supreme effort and try and like you a little tiny bit, *if* you tell me all about this friend of yours and the human. They sound interesting."

So the she-goblin told her, and the more she heard the more thoughtful Tinituviel became. And when the whole sad story was over, she said, "And this human. What did you say his name was?"

"Theo Bernstein."

"Weird name. And he said he'd been in the old wizard's tower?"

"That's right. There was something important he was supposed to do in there, but it hadn't worked. And my friend wanted him to go back there and try again."

The old wizard's tower; so she'd been right after all. What she'd been right about she wasn't absolutely sure, but that didn't matter particularly. "You haven't seen two other humans? A little old one and a young thin one who eats all the time?"

"No."

"Well, that's something, I suppose. This human, the one your friend liked more than you." She described the crazy man she'd met earlier, when she was trying to catch up with the goblins, before she—well, whatever. "That him?"

The she-goblin somehow managed to look even more stupid than she usually did. "It could be. I don't know. I've only ever seen one human. But it does sound like him."

"The lunatic."

"I don't think he was mad," the she-goblin said. "Or, at least, not until my friend got inside his head." She remembered something. "He'd lost his memory. And my friend found it for him."

Tinituviel sighed. Clearly she was going to have to go to the old wizard's tower, and although Elves are afraid of nothing, well, virtually nothing, absolutely nothing apart from scary things, it did seem a distinct possibility that the situation might get a bit vexed, possibly even violent.

Which was fine, just so long as the violence happened to other people. In which case, the company of someone with the biggest shoulders and sharpest teeth in the Realms might not be quite so irksome after all. "I've changed my mind," she said briskly. "I think we're going to be best friends for ever. I really like you."

"You didn't a moment ago."

"Well, I changed my mind, you half-witted freak, I can change my mind if I want to." She paused and breathed out through her nose. Sweetness and calm. "You want to be friends or not?"

"Yes, please."

"Fine," Tinituviel snapped. "In which case, on your feet, we've got work to do. Oh, and by the way. If you're going to be my friend, you can't be friends with anyone else, and especially the voice-in-the-mirror person, got that? You're not his friend any more. In fact, you hate him to bits."

"Oh." The she-goblin looked sad for a moment. "Oh, all right, if you say so." She thought for a moment. "Is that how it works, then? You can only have one friend at a time, and you've got to hate everybody else?"

Tinituviel smiled. All Elves are wise, and so she knew precisely how to explain to a member of an inferior species the intricacies of any question, problem or issue, no matter how complex or confusing it might be. "Shut up," she said.

"All right," said the she-goblin. "I won't say another—"

She stopped dead, dropped to her knees and rolled over onto her face.

"Oh, for crying out loud," Tinituviel wailed, "now what?"

She knelt down beside the motionless goblin, who didn't seem to be breathing. "Will you please make your mind up, once and for all? Are you dead or aren't you?"

Nothing. Then the she-goblin shuddered, kicked out uncontrollably, rolled over and over several times and sat up with a jerk. Her eyes were tight shut and she appeared to be breathing through her ears.

"I'll take that as a no, then," Tinituviel said. "Hello? Anybody home?"

The she-goblin twisted her neck round—much too far, to begin with, and there was a horrible grating of neck bones and gristle before she seemed to realise her mistake and turned it back the other way. She looked straight at Tinituviel and smiled. "Sorry," she said. "I tripped on a tree root."

The she-goblin's left eye was gleaming. "Are you all right?" Tinituviel asked.

"Me? Fine. Never better." She leapt up, landing on the balls of her feet, in a slight forward crouch. "Well, let's get going. I mean, I don't want to hold you up."

A few fine hairs stood up on the back of Tinituviel's neck. "Are you sure you're feeling all right?"

"I just said so, didn't I?"

"Only—"

"Are we going or aren't we?"

Tinituviel looked at her, carefully this time. "You seem awfully keen."

"Well, there'll be lots of people there, and maybe some of them will want to be friends with me."

"Why would there be people there?"

"Because I saw—" The goblin stopped dead. "I sort of think there might. And you're going there, and you wouldn't if it was just an empty old tower, not a clever Elf like you. I expect you want to do a few in-depth interviews, that kind of thing."

She's reading my mind. No, impossible. Even Elves couldn't do that, though it didn't stop them pretending they could to anyone gullible enough to believe them. And she did seem quite convinced that there'd be a crowd at the old tower, almost as though she'd been there not so long ago and had seen them for herself. Get a grip, Tinituviel urged herself, it's a *goblin*, it can barely put one foot in front of the other without falling flat on its snout. Also, being a goblin, it talks drivel. That's what they do. "It's none of your business what I'm going to do when I get there," she said. "I just want you along for the pleasure of your company. Now stop dawdling and move."

Actually, the goblin moved rather fast, to the extent that Tinituviel was unaccountably short of breath by the time they reached the tower. And, just as the goblin had predicted, there were a lot of people there—Elves and goblins and dwarves; and though they were standing tightly packed together in heavily armed groups, nobody was fighting with anybody else. She stopped and took a good look, partly formed headlines racing through her mind. What was all this, anyhow? A stand-off? Peace talks? A guess-the-weight-of-the-fat-human-with-the-axe competition? She caught sight of King Mordak, sitting under a tree with a weird looking human and apparently not eating him. She was torn. There was Mordak talking seriously to someone, in which case it could well be something important, in which case she really ought to go over and join him before he made a complete and utter mess of things, whatever they were. On the other hand, she had sort of skipped out and run away when arguably he needed her most, and although of course she wasn't ashamed or anything, oh dear no, nevertheless it might be a tad awkward.

*

Mordak waved. There are waves and waves. This one was a get-over-here-now wave, sort of glad-to-see-you-where-the-hell-have-you-been? She was genuinely surprised by how relieved she felt.

"Where the hell did you get to?"

She gave him a scowl. "Me? Where did you get to? I've been looking all over the place."

A faint gleam in Mordak's small, round red eyes told her that he wasn't buying that for a second but he respected her for trying. "All right, here's what's happening. The weird humans come from another Realm—"

"Yes, I know."

Mordak blinked. "Fine," he said. "But they won't be coming or going any more, because this joker here—" he indicated Theo with a vague flick of a claw "—says that the gate is now shut and won't be opening ever again. So that's all right."

"Quite. A lot of fuss about nothing, really."

"Which probably means," Mordak persevered, "that we probably won't have to clear out after all, since the only reason the bad guy wanted us out was so he could build houses to sell to Somewhere-Elsers, and that won't be happening."

"Well, there you are, then. You do get yourself worked up about things, and they always turn out fine in the end. *I* wasn't worried."

"But," Mordak said. Pause, for effect. "We may have a bigger problem. From what this human here's been telling me—"

"The One We Don't Talk About may be back and he's going around taking over people's minds. Yes, I know. And I'm a teeny bit concerned about that one myself."

The irregularly shaped scaly wattles that served Mordak for eyebrows shot up. "You know?"

"Of course."

"And it didn't occur to you to mention—?"

"All right, I only just found out," she conceded. "That's where I've been," she added, "finding things out. Doing something useful," she couldn't resist adding, "while you've been—well, anyway."

"Fine." A slight edge in Mordak's voice suggested to her that that was probably enough point-scoring for the time being. "Question is, if the old bastard is back, what are we going to do about it?"

Tinituviel shrugged. "You're the Dark Lord," she said. "That's policy. I don't do policy, just admin."

"Excuse me."

The funny looking human was talking to them. They looked at him.

"It's none of my business," the human said, "but I couldn't help overhearing. And I don't know if it's important, but the lady goblin I thought I'd killed—well, the thing inside my head made me do it."

Mordak waved all that aside. "What about her?"

"She's standing over there."

Tinituviel had forgotten all about her. Which, when she thought about it, was a bit of an oversight. "So she is," Mordak said. "Glad to see she made it after all."

"Only," Theo went on, "she was pretty definitely dead when I saw her last, and now there she is, walking about and everything, and I don't know how you do things round here, being from out of town, so to speak, but it did occur to me—"

"She was brought back to life by the Nameless One," Tinituviel cut in, as the penny dropped like a falling meteorite. "Yes, well, that's obvious, isn't it? That's why I brought her here."

"Here?" Mordak was glaring at her as though she was a candle in an oil store. "Are you out of your tiny mind?"

She hadn't been expecting that. "What—?"

"You brought *Him*? To the old wizard's tower?"

"Um."

"His ancient stronghold."

"Yes, but—"

"Where there just happens to be a portal between here and Somewhere Else?"

"Yes, but it's blocked."

"Yes, and you didn't know that."

History tourism is one of the things YouSpace is best at, and, ever since he'd got it working, Theo had been to loads of crucial cusps and turning points in the causality flow, just out of curiosity, to see what they looked like. Some of them were well signposted, with interesting and informative wall displays, interactive audiovisual guides, gift shops and stalls selling fizzy drinks. Others were just moments like any other, unless you knew precisely what you were looking at. Visit enough of them and you get a feel for the sudden lurch and twist that betrays the presence of something exceptionally significant, something with consequences. But the rule is, as a visitor you don't interfere, no matter what. So, although he had an idea that he'd just witnessed an epoch-making moment in the balance of perceived superiority between goblin and Elf, he just cleared his throat gently and said, "She's coming this way."

Mordak scrambled to his feet. "If she's got Him inside her—"

"Actually," Theo said, "I think it's me she's after. I killed her, remember. This may be a bit awkward."

Mordak shook his head reassuringly. "Among goblins, it's just a way of showing affection," he said. "Don't worry about it."

"Even so—"

The she-goblin was looming over them, and for the

first time Mordak realised just how very big and strong his creation, his good-idea-at-the-time, had grown to be. The she-goblin glared at him, then turned to the human. "You're Theo Bernstein."

"Yes. Look, about what happened back there—"

"Oh, that's all right," the she-goblin said, just a trifle wearily. "It wasn't you, it was him. My so-called friend. Anyway, I just wanted to tell you, in case you were worried. It's all right."

"What's all right?" Mordak snapped. She ignored him.

"What's all right?" Theo said.

"The nasty Eye person," the she-goblin said. "He won't be bothering you any more, any of you."

They all stared at her. Theo said, "Excuse me?"

That made the she-goblin grin. "That'll teach him to say he's my friend and then be nasty to me."

Mordak opened his mouth to shout, but Tinituviel elbowed him in the ribs. "Hello again," she said. "Where have you been? You wandered off."

The she-goblin gave her a sour look. "You didn't really want to be my friend," she said. "You just guessed I had the horrid Eye inside me. Well, you don't have to worry about him any more. I've dealt with him."

The way she said it—Mordak knew that there are some things in the Realms that are, quite simply, impossible; turning back the Sun and Moon on their preordained cycle, getting a straight answer out of an Elven chartered surveyor, feeling sorry for the One We Don't Talk About. Even so. The tiniest little smear of sympathy, as short-lived and unstable as antimatter—

"Gosh," Theo said. "How? I bashed my head on a wall, but that only shut him up for a little bit."

A slow, horrible smile passed over the she-goblin's face. "I put him in his place," she said.

"Really?"

Nod. "At the back of my mind. That'll learn him."

"Just a minute," Mordak said, but Tinituviel stopped him. "At the back of your mind?"

"It's a very strong mind," the she-goblin said (and Mordak thought, yes, it is, isn't it?). "And he was mean to me and he told me lies, and I'm never going to trust him ever again. So when he came back saying it was all a mis-understanding and the silly human's fault—that's you," she added, looking at Theo. He smiled. "I pretended I was glad to see him and I was going to do what he wanted, and then, when he wasn't looking, I put him away in the bit of my mind where you store stuff, and sort of turned the key and threw it away." She beamed. It was a rather horrible sight, objectively speaking; imagine a friendly smile from one of those machines that crunches up scrap cars, then garnish with tusks, serve on a bed of wild rice and run for your life. "I can still talk to him, but he can't talk to me. I talk to him quite a lot, actually. I tell him how much I hate him. I don't think he likes it in there." She grinned. "Tough."

Mordak looked at her. "I have no idea what she's talking about," he said.

Tinituviel sighed. "You wouldn't," he said, "you're a man. Well, you're a non-female goblin."

"Ah," Theo said, "that explains it. I was wondering about that. I take it you people practise non-viviparous parthenogenic reproduction." He nodded. "Thought so, because ... ouch," he added, and massaged his ribcage, which later proved not to be cracked but only bruised, so that was all right.

"Women," Tinituviel went on, "can do that. It's called multitasking. Don't try and understand."

Mordak looked at Theo, who nodded, then shrugged. "Whatever," he said. "But if you're telling me I don't have to worry because she's got Him locked up inside her head—"

"For as long as she lives," Tinituviel said; and then a thought occurred to her. "She is mortal, isn't she?"

"I assume so," Mordak said. "Isn't everyone?"

"Actually, no," Tinituviel purred.

"Well, she must be, because she got killed." He stopped and thought about that. "Yes, but He brought her back to life again."

Which got him a pitying smile, which he just about managed to take in his stride, for the greater good. "Even He can't do that," she said. "I thought you'd have known that, of all people."

"But she's a goblin," he said. "Therefore she's mortal. It's one of the key features of goblins, mortality."

"Mphm." Tinituviel was giving him an odd look. "When you made her," she said, "you did remember the powdered agate and the teaspoon of oil of cloves?"

"The what?"

A click of the tongue so loud that thirty thousand goblins and thirty thousand dwarves, sprawling at rest under the eaves of the greenwood, leapt to their feet and scrabbled for their weapons. "You forgot."

"Nobody said anything to me about oil of bloody cloves—"

Tinituviel nodded gravely. "No, I guess not. It's my fault, I should've supervised it personally. Silly me for thinking you'd be capable of doing anything right left to yourself, no matter how simple." She cocked her head towards the she-goblin. "She's immortal."

The news sank in, rather in the way a meteorite sinks into the surface of a planet, and *sayonara*, dinosaurs. "Stone me," Mordak said. "Just think. My little girl."

"Excuse me," said his little girl huffily. "I am here, you know. What did she just say?"

"It means you can't be killed," he said. "Poppet," he added. "So, if she's immortal and she's got Him locked up safe in her head—"

"Is that right?" said the she-goblin. "I'm going to live for ever and ever?"

"Yes."

"Oh," the she-goblin said. "That's—"

"Yes," Mordak said firmly, "but never mind about that right now. If she's immortal—"

"Problem solved," Tinituviel said happily. "There, you see? I don't know why you got yourself in such a state about it, really."

Mordak laughed. "And all because I had the vision and the foresight to create a female goblin. I love it when I turn out to have been right all along."

Theo cleared his throat. "Excuse me," he said.

"No," said Mordak. "Anyway, as I was saying, what I really like about being right—"

"It won't work," Theo said. "Sorry."

The she-goblin scowled at him. "What did he just say?"

"I'm sorry," Theo repeated. "But the whole thing is based on a false premise."

Mordak shrugged. "Premises, premises. What do you know about anything anyway? You're just a—"

"Scientist," Theo said, gently but very firmly. "And you can't just compartmentalise your mind like that and lock something away, it simply can't be done. Detailed studies by Atkinson and Cheng—"

"He's barmy," Mordak said uneasily. "He is barmy, isn't he?"

"He's a human," Tinituviel said. "But then again, you're a goblin, and just occasionally, from time to time, usually by pure fluke, you get things right. So maybe—"

"It doesn't matter," the she-goblin said.

"There there, poppet," Mordak said vaguely. "Look, is he right or isn't he? Because this is important—"

"No," said the she-goblin, and they all turned round and looked at her. "It isn't. Because he's gone. My nasty friend. I just looked. He's not there any more. He's gone."

"Oh, hello," said Ms. White. "You're not dead, then."

George shook his head. "No thanks to you, you stupid cow," he said. "Chucking bloody great bits of glass at people. What do you want to go doing a thing like that for?"

"I was upset."

"You're touched in the head, is what you are," George said. "And it's all your fault. I ought to smash your face in."

"Excuse me? What did I do?"

George slumped down with his back to a tree trunk. "Me getting stuck here, you daft bitch," he said. "You heard what the man said. Border closed. Stuck in this godawful place for ever and ever."

"Ah. That."

"Yeah, that. There I was, safe on the other side. Never even occurred to me those lunatics would vote Leave." He shook his head. "So I just nipped back for five minutes, to kick your teeth in for trying to kill me, and guess what, I'm stranded. Thank you ever so much."

Ms. White gave him a sad smile. "It's just not your day, is it?"

"You could say that. Still." He shifted uncomfortably, as though something was irritating him. "Always make the best of things, is my motto."

"Positive thinking," said Ms. White. "Excellent."

"So, since I'm stuck in this shithole, I may as well take it over."

At which point, Ms. White saw what was wrong with him. Sticking out of the back of his neck, roughly where the spine runs up into the head, was a splinter of glass, deeply embedded. There should have been blood, of course, lots of it, but there wasn't. I wonder if he knows about that, Ms. White thought; and then she remembered, there had been something distinctly odd about that mirror.

Oh, she thought.

He was talking to her. "I'll need someone I can rely on," he was saying, "on the inside, someone who knows how to handle these freaks. And it's either that or I have you buried alive in an anthill, so I'm guessing you won't need too long to reach a decision. Well?"

"Sorry," Ms. White said. "What was that?"

"Try and pay attention, will you? Here's the deal. You work for me, or you're ant-food."

Hence the expression, she thought; he's got eyes in the back of his head. Only in this case, Eye, singular. Oh dear. "Out of interest," she said, "how were you planning on doing it? Taking over, I mean. You see, there's an awful lot of them, and they've got weapons—"

That made George chuckle. "They ain't got one of these." He reached inside his coat and pulled out a little wooden box. "Three guesses."

"Chocolates? Flowers? A very small coffin?"

He shook his head. "Neutron bomb," he said. "And the boss goblin knows all about it, because I had a couple of my boys explain it to him. I don't think there'll be any trouble on that score."

Ms. White's eyes were very big and round. "That's—"

"Yes," George said smugly. "And if I'd had any sense I'd have let the damn thing off ages ago and saved myself all this aggravation. Too soft-hearted, that's always been my problem. Now," he added, getting to his feet. "Let's go and see some people. We'll start with that dwarf of yours, King Drain. I'm sure he'll be reasonable, once you've talked to him."

This is silly, she thought. He wouldn't do it. Not because killing every living thing in the Realms would bother him very much, provided he had a nuke-proof shelter to cower in while the actual dying took place (and he'd got one, she'd happily bet on that), but because total vacant possession wouldn't be in his interests—nobody to fetch and carry for him, clean the windows, scrub the floors, grow food, all that stuff. He's bluffing.

An inch of razor-sharp glass, driven into his neck more or less where they got Trotsky with the ice pick, and he was still talking and walking about, and no blood. He might be bluffing, or he might not. And it might not be up to him any more.

Nuts, she thought.

Mr. Bullfrog was enjoying the fresh air for the first time in forty thousand years. It fanned his embers, making his toes and fingertips flare agreeably, though he noted with regret that the passing centuries hadn't done anything much for his hay fever. Still, it was undeniably pleasant to be above ground and outside again, something that wouldn't have happened without his new friends the Lushingtons.

He thought about them as he strode across the downs, leaving a trail of gently smouldering footprints behind him. He'd known as soon as he saw them that they weren't humans from the Realms, and they'd confirmed as much in so many words. The impression he'd got of the place they'd come from was still somewhat hazy, but he'd sensed that life there probably hadn't prepared Pat and Barry for the rather more robust cultures of the Realms, and he was a little bit concerned in case they got picked on, or taken advantage of, or eaten. There was also the suggestion that Pat had made; take back his place on the council. Now there was a thought.

Of course, all that had been a long time ago, before the Realms were broken and Snororogrim was cast down and the first Elves came over the western sea in ships, complaining bitterly about the catering and threatening to write to someone about it. Since then—well, he'd had enough, and who could blame him? He had dwelt among Men, and they'd shot arrows at him. He had sought out the goblins, who'd fallen down and worshipped him, which is always disconcerting. The dwarves had tried to hook him up to their central heating system, and the Elves—that hadn't been his fault. Well, it had, strictly speaking, and all the old maps had had to be redrawn; Elvenwood crossed out and Ashfield written in over the top, all because of one little sneeze, and how could he have been expected to know that marshmallorn pollen would have such a drastic effect on his hay fever?

He stopped. It occurred to him to wonder whether, back in the old days, he'd have concerned himself with the welfare of mortals, wretched creatures of a day; actually, probably not. Back then, it had all seemed so wonderfully clear and obvious; so much to burn, so little time. But there had turned out to be rather more time than he'd anticipated, and the sad fact was, once you've reduced one world to dripping lava, you've reduced them all. Was it possible that he'd gone soft, down there in the endless dark of Snoria? Maybe *mellowed* would be a better word. He smiled. He liked that.

So, he was going to take back his seat on the council, and his mission would be to look after the new humans; in which case, it might be a good idea to get to know them. With that in mind, he'd set off for the old wizard's tower, where (according to Pat Lushington) lived the charming and sociable Barringtons; he was something important in something or other and she did something he hadn't quite understood, and he was sure they were going to be great chums.

On the edge of the greenwood he stopped again, took out his asbestos handkerchief and held it in front of his nose. The marshmallorn was in bloom again; once torched, twice shy.

In the distance he could see a lot of people: all the goblins, if he wasn't mistaken, and all the dwarves, and quite possibly all the Elves, too, which was handy. He'd be able to make his announcement without having to traipse round the houses telling everyone separately.

Also, he observed, a rather fat little human, who was standing on a box making a speech. It didn't seem to be going down too well, to judge by the muttering, head-shaking, beard-tugging and gnashing of fangs, but nobody was throwing anything or ripping anybody apart, so clearly the conventions of debate had changed a bit while he'd been away, and probably no bad thing. He edged closer, and an overpowering scent hit him like a hammer. He raised his head and sniffed. He was hungry.

Come to think of it, when was the last time he'd eaten anything? He tried to remember, but even he couldn't cast his mind that far back. Presumably at some point in the distant past he'd had *something*, because even his kind had to eat, but—and just over there, near the big crowd, was something that smelt so utterly mouthwateringly delicious that he could hardly think straight. Yum, he thought. Let me at it.

When he came to think about it later, he wasn't proud of what he did next. Two enormous strides, a quick swish and grab, and he crammed the delicious morsel into his mouth, spat out the rind and chewed ecstatically. Whatever it was burst in his mouth, flooding his senses with the most indescribably gorgeous jumble of flavours. He blinked, burped and smiled. Wow, he thought. Never had one of *them* before.

(The rind, whose name was George, sat up and discovered that he was still alive; remarkably, since he'd just been scooped up by a fifteen-foot-tall pillar of fire and swallowed whole. He looked round for the little wooden box containing the neutron bomb, but it didn't seem to be there. In which case—

He shot the fire monster a horrified look, but nothing happened. For which, he rationalised, there were two possible explanations. Either the monster had swallowed a fully functional neutron bomb and survived, or else the rogue Ukrainian scientist he'd got it from had sold him a dud. Bastard, he thought. Still, as things had turned out, probably just as well.

Something else ... He tried to figure out what it was, but he couldn't. His hand instinctively groped for the back of his neck, but there was nothing there.)

Not having eaten for hundreds of thousands of years, Mr. Bullfrog had forgotten about heartburn, a condition with which he'd once been painfully familiar. He frowned. No, not heartburn. Something else. Definitely something he'd eaten—

Oh, he said. It's you.

Hi, Dad.

Junior.

Yes, Dad, it's me.

Did I just eat you?

Yes, Dad. I was inside the human.

Mr. Bullfrog sighed. If I've told you once, he said, I've told you a thousand times—

Yes, Dad.

Cut it out, do you hear? I don't want you doing that stuff any more.

No, Dad. Sorry.

Oh dear, thought Mr. Bullfrog. Just as well he'd come back, if Junior was up to his old tricks again. He was a good boy at heart, of course, and the trouble had only started when he'd got mixed up with the wrong crowd; my fault, he decided. The kid needs a father. Just as well I'm back.

I won't do it again, Dad. I promise.

He'd heard that one before. Still, what can you do? Sure, son, he said. I believe you.

Can I come out now?

Mr. Bullfrog sighed. Not quite yet, son, he said. Probably just as well if you stay put for a little while, till I've had a chance to sort out any little messes you might've made. It's for your own good, he added, not unkindly. And then, he added, with just a little bit of an edge, there'll be no need to tell your mother about any of this.

Mr. Bullfrog felt a cold shudder deep inside his digestive tract. *OK, Dad. You know best.*

Theo Bernstein was a realist, so he hadn't been expecting a big farewell party or a presentation ceremony or anything like that. But he was an optimist, so he'd been expecting to be pleasantly surprised. But he hadn't been. And he was a realist, so what the hell.

"I don't know why I'm doing this," said Ms. White, as they trudged down the back stair of King Drain's palace, across the ridiculously narrow bridge over the dizzying chasm of Snorod-dum (no handrail, naturally) and along the gloomy winding corridor that led to the kitchen. "It's all your fault I'm stuck here, for bloody ever."

Theo was about to query that, but decided not to. For one thing, she was probably right. If he hadn't perfected the YouSpace device, and, having done that, if he hadn't left it lying about where people like George could find it—all perfectly true. Also, he'd sort of got the impression that Ms. White was the sort of person who didn't like being contradicted.

"Sorry," he said. "And thanks."

"That's all right."

The Kitchen under the Mountain was big, like everything else in the Dwarfhold; big and dark and grey and cold and dusty, and all the pots and pans were cast iron—not Le Creuset cast iron, more like the R & D department at a tank factory. "There isn't time to get them to forge me a doughnut pan," Ms. White said, "so you'll have to make do with oven-baked. That'll be all right, won't it?"

"So long as it's round, with a hole in the middle."

Ms. White bent down and lifted a massive iron chest onto the kitchen table. It had seven locks. She kept flour in it. "Pass me a couple of eggs, will you? They're in the rack."

He identified them as eggs by the shape. They had a metallic sheen to them, and scales, and they were almost too hot to touch. "If I asked you what kind of eggs—"

"Don't."

"Ah. That kind. Two?"

"Thought I'd make a batch while I'm at it, for Drain's elevenses." She sighed. "I can't believe I'm going to end up as a *cook*," she said bitterly. "I had such plans."

"Which all involved exploiting people."

"Well, yes," Ms. White admitted, "but so what? If you

don't do it to them, they do it to you. Anyway, that's beside the point. What am I going to be doing for the rest of my life? Women's work." She shot him a look you could have kept fish fresh in. "Thank you ever so much."

Theo nodded slowly. "And you can't go home," he said. "I understand."

"Actually, I'm not too fussed about that. Believe it or not, I don't mind it here. These people are—well, compared to the sort of people I used to know back home ... " She shrugged. "Except that there's a Swiss bank account in my name with lots of beautiful noughts and commas, so I wouldn't have had to play with the rough kids any more. Still." She broke an egg into the bowl and stood well back until the smoke cleared. "You heard what King Mordak said when he was selling his people on the idea of peace with the Elves. If you can't eat 'em, join 'em."

"Good advice."

"I thought so. And let's just say I've got a few ideas up my sleeve. Something tells me the dwarves aren't going to be happy to go back to things exactly the way they were, not now they've had a taste of completely useless mass-produced consumer junk. And Drain may look like an overgrown hanging basket, but at heart he's a business-man. A good one. I won't be stuck in the kitchen very long, believe me."

"I do," Theo said, with just a hint of sadness. "I get the impression there'll be a lot of changes around here, one way or another."

"You bet." Ms. White looked round, then lowered her voice. "I overheard Drain talking to the goblin ambassador—"

Theo's eyes widened. "Wow," he said. "Diplomatic relations. When did that happen?"

"You ain't heard nothing yet. Mordak's planning on abdicating, in favour of the she-goblin."

Theo opened his mouth, but no words came.

Ms. White nodded briskly. "That's right," she said. "Once she's grown up a bit, of course, so probably some time next week. He said he's seen the future and it's got shiny pink claws with little spangly bits on them. Apparently, he reckons that Evil needs to get in touch with its feminine side. And being invincible and unkillable won't hurt, either; stability and long-term strategic planning and all that. Also," she added, "I gather he's had enough of being the Dark Lord. He thinks it's time for a change of direction."

"Really?"

"He and that Elf secretary of his are going to start an investment bank instead."

"I thought you said he wanted a change of direction."

"Well, yes, but with fewer goblins. You can see his point." She grinned. "Personally, I think he's just being lazy. He can't be arsed to think of a name for her, so he's going to make her the Nameless One. Mind out, I need to get to the oven."

Theo didn't really want to ask, but he felt he had to. "What about George?"

A rather disturbing smile covered Ms. White's face. "Ah."

"Did they eat him?"

She shook her head. "I explained to Mordak about his lifestyle and we decided he probably wouldn't taste very nice. So then I introduced Mordak to the concept of community service for life." A slightly dreamy look replaced the disturbing smile. "Did you know goblins have toilets?"

"Actually, no."

"Well, they do. Great big ones. But somehow they never

get around to cleaning them out. Not for about a hundred thousand years, anyway."

"And Mordak agreed to that?"

"He offered me a job," Ms. White said. "Working for Evil. Head of Creative Thinking."

"Did you accept?"

Ms. White shrugged. "Told him I'd think about it. But you know what? Call me a traitor to my sex and that rumbling noise you can hear is a million suffragettes turning in their graves, but I think I'd rather make choux pastry. I've had enough evil to be going on with. Thanks but no thanks, on that one."

The door opened, and in came John the Lawyer. "Here you are," he said. "We hoped we'd catch you before you left."

Theo beamed. Maybe he was going to be pleasantly surprised after all. Then he noted the plural.

"We've got a message for you," John went on. "From Mordak and Drain and the High Elf. They wanted you to know—"

"Hang on," Ms. White said. "What's this We? Did they just make you king or something?"

"It's me," said a voice out of thin air. "I'm invisible again."

John blushed. "We're getting married," he said. "Isn't it wonderful?"

Ms. White frowned. "You're marrying an invisible—"

"Yup," John said. "I always said she's not just a pretty face." He reached out and put his arm around nothing. "And she's going to be a model after all. So everything's worked out just fine."

"An invisible—"

"King Drain's offered me a job," said the wraith, "modelling his latest range of custom armour."

"But—"

"He insisted," said the wraith. "He said, if I was visible, the customers would be looking at me and not the product, because who wants to look at armour when there's a pretty girl? So I asked Mordak, and he turned me back. Wasn't that nice of him?"

Theo grinned at Ms. White. "Don't change Drain too much," he said. "I quite like him. Sorry," he went on, "you've got a message for me?"

John nodded. "The federated races of the Realms would like to thank you for taking the trouble to come here and give us the result of the referendum—"

"That's all right," Theo said coyly. "It was the least I could do."

"But they feel that you're a disruptive influence and they'd be grateful if you'd please go away right now and never ever come back. And if you could see your way to not telling anybody in all the other Realms about us, we'd be ever so grateful. I think that's everything."

"Ah," Theo said. "Right."

Ms. White opened the oven door. "It's ready," she said.

She pulled out a baking tray, two inches thick and studded with rivets. On it sat a very ordinary looking doughnut. "Will that do?"

"Yes."

"Splendid." Ms. White heaved the tray up onto the table. "Right, then. On your bike."

Theo picked up the doughnut. It was warm, and it smelt nice. "I'd just like to say—"

"No," said Ms. White, "you wouldn't. Goodbye."

So Theo lifted the doughnut; and just before he looked through it, he chose which of the infinite (minus one) number of alternative realities that make up the multiverse he wanted to go to. He thought, I want to go to the version of reality that's exactly the same as home, except the people voted Remain in the referendum instead of Leave, so I can go back.

So he went there. But it wasn't quite the same.

extras

if you enjoyed
AN ORC ON THE WILD SIDE

look out for

THE GIRL WHO COULD MOVE SH*T WITH HER MIND

by

Jackson Ford

For Teagan Frost, sh*t just got real.

Teagan Frost is having a hard time keeping it together. Sure, she's got telekinetic powers—a skill that the government is all too happy to make use of, sending her on secret break-in missions that no ordinary human could carry out. But all she really wants to do is kick back, have a beer, and pretend she's normal for once.

But then a body turns up at the site of her last job—murdered in a way that only someone like Teagan could have pulled off. She's got twenty-four hours to clear her name. And if she isn't able to unravel the conspiracy, then the city of Los Angeles may be ripped apart....

Full of imagination, wit, and random sh*t flying through the air, this insane adventure from an irreverent new voice will blow your tiny mind.

One

Teagan

On second thoughts, throwing myself out the window of a skyscraper may not have been the best idea.

Not because I'm going to die or anything. I've totally got that under control.

It wasn't smart because I had to bring Annie Cruz with me. And Annie, it turns out, is a screamer. Her fists hammer on my back, her voice piecing my eardrums, even over the rushing air.

I don't know what she's worried about. Pro tip: if you're going to take a high dive off the 82nd floor, make sure you do it with a psychokinetic holding your hand. Being able to move objects with your mind is useful in all sorts of situations.

I'll admit, this one is a little tricky. Plummeting at close to terminal velocity, surrounded by a hurricane of glass from the window we smashed through, the lights of Los Angeles whirling around us and Annie screaming and the rushing air blowing the stupid clip-on tie from my security guard disguise into my face: not ideal. Doesn't matter though—I've got this.

I can't actually apply any force to either Annie's body or mine. Organic matter like human tissue doesn't respond to me, which is something I don't really have time to get into right now. But I can manipulate anything inorganic. Bricks, glass, metal, the fridge door, a sixpack, the TV remote, the zipper on your pants.

And belt buckles.

I've had some practice at this whole moving-shit-with-your-mind thing. I've already reached out, grabbed hold of the big metal buckles on our belts. We're probably going to have some bruises tomorrow, but it's a hell of a lot better than getting gunned down in a penthouse or splatting all over Figueroa Street.

I solidify my mental grip around the two buckles, then force them upwards, using my energy to counteract our downward motion. We start to slow, my belt tightening, hips starting to ache as the buckles take the weight—

—and immediately snap.

OK, yeah. Definitely not the best idea.

Two

Teagan

Rewind. Twenty minutes ago.

We're in the sub-basement of the giant Edmonds Building, our footsteps muffled by thick carpet. The lighting in the corridor is surprisingly low down here, almost cosy, which doesn't matter much because Annie is seriously fucking with my groove.

I like to listen to music on our ops, OK? It calms me down, helps me focus. A little late-90s rap—some Blackstar, some Jurassic 5, some Outkast. Nothing too aggressive or even all that loud. I'm just reaching the good part of "So Fresh, So Clean" when Annie taps me on the shoulder. "Yo, take that shit out. We working."

Ugh. I was sure I'd hidden my earbud, threading the cord up underneath the starchy blue rent-a-cop shirt and tucking it under my hair.

I hunt for the volume switch on my phone, still not looking at Annie. She responds by reaching back and jerking the earbud out.

"Hey!"

"I said, fucking quit it."

"What, not an OutKast fan? Or do you only like their early stuff?" I hold up an earbud. "I don't mind sharing. You want the left or the right?"

362

"Cute. Put it away."

We turn the corner, heading for a big set of double doors at the far end. My collar's too tight. I pull at it, wincing, but it barely moves. Annie and I are dressed identically: blue shirts, black clip-on ties, black pants and puffer jackets in a very cheap shade of navy. Huge belts, leather, with thick metal buckles.

Paul picked up the uniforms for us. I tried to tell him that while Annie might be able to pass as a security guard, nobody was going to believe that the Edmonds Building would employ a short, not-very-fit woman with spiky black hair and a face that *still* gets her ID'd at the liquor store. Even though I've been able to buy my own drinks like a big girl for a whole year now.

I couldn't be more different to Annie. You know how some club bouncers have huge muscles and a shit-ton of tattoos and piercings? You know how people still fuck with them, starting fights and smashing bottles? Annie is like that one bouncer with zero tattoos, standing in the corner with her arms folded and a scowl that could sour milk. The bouncer no one fucks with because the last person who did ended up scattered over a six-mile radius. We might not see eye to eye on music—or on anything, because she's taller than me—but I'm still very glad she's on my side.

My earpiece chirps—my *other* one, the black number in my right ear. "Annie, Teagan," says Paul. "Come in. Over."

"We're almost at the server room," Annie says. She sends another disgusted look at my dangling earbud.

Silence. No response.

"You there?" Annie says.

"Sorry, was waiting for you to say *over*. Thought you hadn't finished. Over."

"Seriously?" I say. "We're still using your radio slang?"

"It's not slang. It's protocol. Just wanted to give you a

363

heads-up—Reggie's activated the alarm on the second floor. Basement should be clear of personnel." A pause. "Over."

"Yeah, copy." Annie says. She's a lot more patient with Paul than I am, which I genuinely don't understand.

The double doors are like the fire doors you see in apartment buildings. The one on the right has a big sign on it, white lettering on a black background: authorised personnel only. And on the wall next to it, a biometric lock.

Annie looks over at me. "You're up."

My tax form says that I work for a company called China Shop Movers. That's the name on the paperwork, anyway. What we actually do is work for the government—specifically, for a high-level spook named Tanner.

For some jobs, you need a black-ops team and a fleet of Apache choppers with heat-seeking missiles. For others, you need a psychokinetic with a music-hating support team who can make a lot less noise and get things done in a fraction of the time. You need a completely deniable group of civilians who can do stuff that even a special forces soldier would struggle with. That's us. We are fast, quiet, effective and deadly.

Go ahead: make the fart joke. Tanner didn't laugh when I made it either.

The people we take down are threats to national security. Drug lords, terrorist cells, human traffickers. We don't bust in with guns blazing. We don't need to—not with my ability. I've planted a tracking device on a limo at LAX, waving hello to the thick-necked goon standing alongside the car while I zipped the tiny black box up behind his back and onto the chassis. I've kept the bad guys' safeties on at a hostage exchange—good thing too, because they tried to start shooting the second they had the money and got one hell of a surprise when their guns didn't work. And I've been on plenty of break-ins. Windows? Cars? Big old metal safes? Not a problem. When you can move things with your mind, there's not a lot the world can do to keep you out.

Take the lock on authorised personnel only, for instance.

You're supposed to put your finger on the little reader, let it scan your fingerprint, and you're in. If you're breaking in, you either need to hack off a finger (messy), take someone hostage (messy, annoying), hack it locally (time-consuming and boring), or blow it off (fun, but kind of noisy).

My psychokinesia—PK—means I can feel every object around me: its texture, its weight, its relation to other objects. It's a constant flood of stimuli. When I was little, Mom and Dad made me run through exercises, getting me to really focus in on a single object at a time—a glass, a toy car, a pencil. They made me move them around, describe them in excruciating detail. It took a long time, but I managed to deal with it. Now I can sense the objects around me in the same way you sense the clothes you're wearing. You know they're there, you're aware of them, but you don't *think* about them.

If I focus on an object, like the lock—the wires, the latch assembly, the emergency battery, the individual screws on the latch and strike panels—it's as if I send out a part of myself to wrap around it, like you'd wrap your hand around a glass. And then, if I'm locked on, I can move it. I don't have to jerk my head or hold out my hand or screw up my face like in the movies, either. I tried it once, for fun, and felt like an idiot.

It takes me about three seconds to find the latch and slide it back. The mechanism won't move unless it receives the correct signal from the fingerprint reader—or unless someone reaches inside and moves it with her mind. It's actually a pretty solid security system. I've definitely seen worse. But whoever built it obviously didn't take into account the existence of a psychokinetic, so I guess he's totally fired now.

"And we're good." I hop to my feet, using my PK to pull the handle down. I haven't even touched the door.

"Hm." Annie tilts her head. "Nice work."

"Was that a compliment? Annie, are you dying? Has the cancer spread to your brain?"

"Let's just get this over with."

We're on this operation because of a clothing tycoon named Steven Chase. He runs a chain of high-end sportswear stores called Ultra, which just means they're Foot Locker stores without the referee jerseys. If that was all he was doing, he'd never have appeared on China Shop's radar, but it appears Mr. Chase has been a very naughty boy.

Tanner got a tip that he was embezzling money from his company. Again, not something we'd normally give a shit about, but he's not exactly using it to buy a third Ferrari. He's funnelling it to some very shady people in the Ukraine and Saudi Arabia, which is when government types like Tanner start to get mighty twitchy.

Now, the U.S. government *could* get a wiretap to confirm the tip. But even if you go through a secret court, there'll be some kind of paper trail. Better a discreet call gets made to the offices of a certain moving company in Los Angeles, who can look into the matter without anything being written down.

And before you start telling me I'm on the wrong side, that I'm doing the work of the government, who are the real bad guys here, and violating a dozen laws and generally being a pawn of the state, just know that I've seen evidence of what people like Chase do. I have no problem messing with their shit.

We're not actually going anywhere near Steven Chase's office. Reggie could hack his computer directly, but it would require a brute-force attack or getting him to click on a link in an email. People don't do that any more, unless you promise fulfilment of their *very* specific sexual fantasies. The research on that is more trouble than it's worth, and you'll have nightmares for months.

Chase is in town tonight. He flew in for a dinner or an awards show or whatever rich people do for fun, and it's his habit to come back to the office afterwards. He should be there now, up on the 30th floor. He'll work until two or three, catch a couple hours of sleep, then grab a red-eye back to New York. Which works just fine for us.

If you can access the fibre network itself—which you can do in the server room, obviously—you can clamp a special coupler right on to the cable and just siphon off the data as it passes by. Of course, actually doing this is messy and complicated and requires a lot of elements to line up just right...unless you have me.

The cables from every floor in the building run down to this room. The plan is to identify Chase's cable, attach a coupler to it, then read all the traffic while sipping mai tais on our back porch. Or in my case scarfing Thai food and drinking many, many beers in my tiny apartment, but whatever.

Chase might encrypt his email, of course, but encryption targets the body of the email, not the sender or subject line. If he emails anyone in the Ukraine or Saudi, we'll know about it. It'll be enough for Tanner to send in the big guns.

The server room is even more dimly lit than the corridor. The server banks stand like monoliths in an old tomb, giving off a subsonic hum that rumbles under the frigid air conditioning. Annie tilts her chin up even further, as if sniffing the air. She points to one side of the door. "Wait there."

"Yes, sir, O mighty boss lady."

She ignores me, eyes scanning the server stacks. I don't really know how she's going to find the correct one—that was the part of the planning session where they lost me. All I know is that when she does, she's going to trace it back to where it vanishes into the floor or wall. We'll open up a panel, and I'll use my PK to float the coupler inside, attaching it to the cable. It can siphon data, away from the eyes of the building's technicians, who would almost certainly recognise it on sight.

As Annie steps behind one of the servers, I slip my earbud back in. May as well listen to some music while—

"Shit," Annie says.

It's a quiet curse, but I catch it just fine. I make my way over to find her staring at a clusterfuck of tangled cables spilling out of one of the servers. The floor is a scattered mess of tools and loose connections. A half-eaten sandwich, dribbling a slice of tomato, sits propped on a closed laptop.

"Is it supposed to look like that?" I ask.

Annie ignores me. "Paul, we've got a problem. Over."

"What is it? Over."

"Techs have been in. It wasn't like this this morning; Jerian would have told me."

Jerian—one of Annie's Army. Her anonymous network of janitors, cleaners, cashiers, security guards, drug dealers, nail artists, Uber drivers, cooks, receptionists and IT guys. Annie Cruz may not appreciate good hip-hop, but she has a very deep network of connects stretching all the way across LA.

"Copy, Annie. Can you still attach the coupler? Over."

Annie frowns at the mess of cables. "Yeah. But it'll take a while. Over."

Joy.

"Understood," Paul says. "But we can only run interference for so long on our end. You'd better move. Over."

Annie scowls, crouching down to look at the cables. She takes one between thumb and forefinger, like it's something nasty she has to dispose of. Then she stands up, marching back towards the server-room doors.

"Um. Hi? Annie?" I jog after her, earbud bouncing against my shoulder. "Cables are back there."

"Change of plan." She keys her earpiece. "Paul? Tell Reggie to switch over the cameras on the 30th floor. Over"

"Say again? Over."

"We're going up."

I don't catch Paul's response. Instead, I sprint to catch up with Annie, getting to her just she pushes through the doors. "Are you gonna tell me why we've suddenly abandoned the plan, or—"

"We can't hide the coupler if they got people poking around the cables." She reaches the elevator, thumbing the up button. "We need to go to the source."

"I thought the whole point was *not* to go near this guy. Aren't we supposed to be super-secret and stealthy and shit?"

"We're not going to his office, genius. We're going to the fibre hub on his floor."

"The what now?"

"The fibre hub. Every floor has one. It's where the cables from each office go. We'll be able to find the right one a lot faster from there."

The interior of the elevator is clean and new, with a touch-screen interface to select your floor. A taped sign next to it says that floors 50–80 are currently off limits while refurbishment and additional construction is completed, thank you for your patience, management. I remember seeing that when we rolled up: a big chunk of the building covered in scaffolding, with temporary elevators attached to the outside, and a giant crane in a vacant lot across the street.

When the elevator opens on the 30th floor, there's someone

standing in front of it. There's a horrible moment where I think it's Steven Chase himself. But I've seen pictures of Chase, who looks like an actor in an AD for haemorrhoid cream—running on the beach, tanned and glowing, stoked that his rectum is finally itch-free. This guy is . . . not that. He has lawyer written all over him: two-tone shirt, two-tone hair, one-tone orange skin. Tie knot as big as my fist. Probably a few haemorrhoid issues of his own.

He eyes us. "Going down?"

"We're stepping off here, sir," Annie says, doing just that.

He moves into the elevator, mouth twisted in a disapproving frown as his eyes pass over me. Probably not used to seeing someone my age working security in a building like this. I have to resist the urge to wink at him.

I haven't seen inside any of the offices yet, but whoever built this place obviously didn't have any budget leftover for the hallways. There's a foot-high strip of what looks like marble-textured plastic running along at chest height. There are buzzing fluorescent lights in the ceiling, and the floor is covered with that weird, flat, fuzzy carpet which always has little lint balls dotted over it.

"Jesus, who picked out the paint?" The wall above the plastic marble is a shade of purple that's probably called something like Executive Mojo.

"Who cares?" Annie says. "Damn building shouldn't even be here."

I sigh. This again.

She taps the fake marble. "You know they displaced a bunch of historical buildings for this? They just moved in and forced a purchase."

I sigh. Annie's always had a real hard-on for the city's history. "Yeah, I know. You told me before."

"And you saw that notice in the elevator. They just built this place. They already having to fix it up again. And the spots they bought out—mom-and-pop places. Historical buildings. City didn't give a fuck."

"Mm-hmm."

"I'm just saying. It's messed up, man."

"Can we get this done before the heat death of the universe? Please?"

It doesn't take us long to find the right office. Paul helps, using the blueprints he's pulled up to guide us along, occasionally telling Annie that this isn't a good idea and that she needs to hurry. I pop the lock, just like before—it's even easier this time—and we step inside.

There's no Executive Mojo here. It's a basic space, with a desk and terminal for a technician and a big, clearly marked access panel on the wall. By the desk, someone has left a toolbox full of computer paraphernalia, overflowing with wires and connectors. Maybe the same dickhead who left the half-eaten sandwich in the server room. I should leave a note telling him to clean up his shit.

The access panel is off to one side, slightly raised from the surface of the wall. Annie pops it, revealing a nest of thin cables. She attaches the coupler, which looks like a bulldog clip from the future, then checks her phone, reading the data that comes off it. With a grunt, she moves the coupler to the second cable. We have to get the correct one, and the only way to do that is to identify Chase from his traffic.

There are floor-to-ceiling windows on my left, and the view over the glittering city takes my breath away. We're only on the 30th floor, not even close to the top of the building, but I can still see a hell of long way. A police helicopter hovers in the distance, too far for us to hear, its blinking tail lights just visible.

The view looks north, out towards Burbank and Glendale, and on the horizon, there's the telltale orange glow of wildfires.

The sight pulls up some bad memories. Of all the cities Tanner had to put me, it had to be the one where things burn.

It's bad this year. Usually, it's some kid with fireworks or a tourist dropping a cigarette that starts it up, but this time the grass was so dry that it caught on its own. Every TV in the last couple of days has had big breaking news alerts flashing on them. The ones tuned to Fox News—you get a few, even in California—have given it a nickname. hellstorm. Because of course they have.

This year's fire has been creeping towards Burbank and Glendale, chewing through Wildwood Canyon and the Verdugo Hills. The flames have made LA even smoggier than usual. A fire chief on one of the TVs—a guy who managed to look both calm and mightily pissed off at the same time—said that they didn't think the fires would reach the city.

"Teagan."

"Huh?"

"You got your voodoo, right?" She nods to the coupler. "Float it up into the wall."

"Oh. Yeah. Good idea."

The panel is wide enough for me to lean in, craning my head back. The space is dusty, a small shower of fine grit nearly making me sneeze. Annie shines a torch, but I don't need it. She's got the correct cable pinched between thumb and forefinger. It's the work of a few seconds for me to find it with my *voodoo* and pull it slightly outwards from its buddies, float the coupler across and clamp it on. Annie flicks the torch off, and the coupler is swallowed by the shadows.

What can I say? I'm handy.

"Aight," Annie says, snapping the panel shut. "Paul? We're good. Over."

"Copy that. We're getting traffic already. Skedaddle on out of there. Over."

Skedaddle? I mouth the word at Annie, who ignores me. She replaces the panel, slotting it back into place, then turns to go.

As we step out of the tech's office, a voice reaches us from the other end of the hallway: "Hey."

Two security guards. No, three. Real ones. Walking in close formation, heading right for us. The one in the centre is a big white guy with a huge chest-length beard, peak pulled down over his eyes. He's scary, but it's the other two I'm worried about. They're young, with wide eyes and hands already on their holsters, fingers twitching.

Ah, shit.

if you enjoyed
AN ORC ON THE WILD SIDE

look out for

A BIG SHIP AT THE EDGE OF THE UNIVERSE

The Salvagers: Book One

by

Alex White

Firefly *meets* The Fast and the Furious *in this science fiction adventure series that follows a crew of outcasts as they try to find a legendary ship that just might be the key to saving the universe.*

A washed-up treasure hunter, a hotshot racer, and a deadly secret society.

They're all on a race against time to hunt down the greatest warship ever built. Some think the ship is lost forever, some think it's been destroyed, and some think it's only a legend, but one thing's for certain: whoever finds it will hold the fate of the universe in their hands. And treasure that valuable can never stay hidden for long....

Read the book that V. E. Schwab called "A clever fusion of magic and sci-fi. I was hooked from page one."

Chapter One

D.N.F.

The straight opened before the two race cars: an oily river, speckled yellow by the evening sun. They shot down the tarmac in succession like sapphire fish, streamers of wild magic billowing from their exhausts. They roared toward the turn, precision movements bringing them within centimeters of one another.

The following car veered to the inside. The leader attempted the same.

Their tires only touched for a moment. They interlocked, and sheer torque threw the leader into the air. Jagged chunks of duraplast glittered in the dusk as the follower's car passed underneath, unharmed but for a fractured front wing. The lead race car came down hard, twisting eruptions of elemental magic spewing from its wounded power unit. One of its tires exploded into a hail of spinning cords, whipping the road.

In the background, the other blue car slipped away down the chicane—Nilah's car.

The replay lost focus and reset.

The crash played out again and again on the holoprojection in front of them, and Nilah Brio tried not to sigh. She had seen plenty of wrecks before and caused more than her share of them.

"Crashes happen," she said.

"Not when the cars are on the same bloody team, Nilah!"

Claire Asby, the Lang Autosport team principal, stood at her mahogany desk, hands folded behind her back. The office looked less like the sort of ultramodern workspace Nilah had seen on other teams and more like one of the mansions of Origin, replete with antique furniture, incandescent lighting, stuffed big-game heads (which Nilah hated), and gargantuan landscapes from planets she had never seen. She supposed the decor favored a pale woman like Claire, but it did nothing for Nilah's dark brown complexion. The office didn't have any of the bright, human-centric design and ergonomic beauty of her home, but team bosses had to be forgiven their eccentricities—especially when that boss had led them to as many victories as Claire had.

Her teammate, Kristof Kater, chuckled and rocked back on his heels. Nilah rolled her eyes at the pretty boy's pleasure. They should've been checking in with the pit crews, not wasting precious time at a last-minute dressing down.

The cars hovering over Claire's desk reset and moved through their slow-motion calamity. Claire had already made them watch the footage a few dozen times after the incident:

Nilah's car dove for the inside and Kristof moved to block. The incident had cost her half her front wing, but Kristof's track weekend had ended right there.

"I want you both to run a clean race today. I am begging you to bring those cars home intact at all costs."

Nilah shrugged and smiled. "That'll be fine, provided Kristof follows a decent racing line."

"We were racing! I made a legal play and the stewards sided with me!"

Nilah loved riling him up; it was far too easy. "You were slow, and you got what you deserved: a broken axle and a bucket of tears. I got a five-second penalty"—she winked before continuing—"which cut into my thirty-three-second win considerably."

Claire rubbed the bridge of her nose. "Please stop acting like children. Just get out there and do your jobs."

Nilah held back another jab; it wouldn't do to piss off the team boss right before a drive. Her job was to win races, not meetings. Silently she and Kristof made their way to the door, and he flung it open in a rare display of petulance. She hadn't seen him so angry in months, and she reveled in it. After all, a frazzled teammate posed no threat to her championship standings.

They made their way through the halls from Claire's exotic wood paneling to the bright white and anodized blues of Lang Autosport's portable palace. Crew and support staff rushed to and fro, barely acknowledging the racers as they moved through the crowds. Kristof was stopped by his sports psychologist, and Nilah muscled past them both as she stepped out into the dry heat of Gantry Station's Galica Speedway.

Nilah had fired her own psychologist when she'd taken the lead in this year's Driver's Crown.

She crossed onto the busy parking lot, surrounded by the bustle of scooter bots and crews from a dozen teams. The bracing rattle of air hammers and the roar of distant crowds in the grandstands were all the therapy she'd need to win. The Driver's Crown was so close—she could clinch it in two races, especially if Kristof went flying off the track again.

"Do you think this is a game?" Claire's voice startled her. She'd come jogging up from behind, a dozen infograms swimming around her head, blinking with reports on track conditions and pit strategy.

"Do I think racing is a game? I believe that's the very definition of sport."

Claire's vinegar scowl was considerably less entertaining than Kristof's anger. Nilah had been racing for Claire since the junior leagues. She'd probably spent more of her teenage years with her principal than her own parents. She didn't want to disappoint Claire, but she wouldn't be cowed, either. In truth, the incident galled her—the crash was nothing more than a callow attempt by Kristof to hold her off for another lap. If she'd lost the podium, she would've called for his head, but he got what he deserved.

They were a dysfunctional family. Nilah and Kristof had been racing together since childhood, and she could remember plenty of happy days trackside with him. She'd been ecstatic when they both joined Lang; it felt like a sign that they were destined to win.

But there could be only one Driver's Crown, and they'd learned the hard way the word "team" meant nothing among the strongest drivers in the Pan-Galactic Racing Federation. Her friendship with Kristof was long dead. At least her fondness for Claire had survived the transition.

"If you play dirty with him today, I'll have no choice but to create some consequences," said Claire, struggling to keep up with Nilah in heels.

Oh, please. Nilah rounded the corner of the pit lane and marched straight through the center of the racing complex, past the offices of the race director and news teams. She glanced back at Claire who, for all her posturing, couldn't hide her worry.

"I never play dirty. I win because I'm better," said Nilah. "I'm not sure what your problem is."

"That's not the point. You watch for him today, and mind yourself. This isn't any old track."

Nilah got to the pit wall and pushed through the gate onto the starting grid. The familiar grip of race-graded asphalt on her shoes sent a spark of pleasure up her spine. "Oh, I know all about Galica."

The track sprawled before Nilah: a classic, a legend, a warrior's track that had tested the mettle of racers for a hundred years. It showed its age in the narrow roadways, rendering overtaking difficult and resulting in wrecks and safety cars—and increased race time. Because of its starside position on Gantry Station, ambient temperatures could turn sweltering. Those factors together meant she'd spend the next two hours slow-roasting in her cockpit at three hundred kilometers per hour, making thousands of split-second, high-stakes decisions.

This year brought a new third sector with more intricate corners and a tricky elevation change. It was an unopened present, a new toy to play with. Nilah longed to be on the grid already.

If she took the podium here, the rest of the season would be an easy downhill battle. There were a few more races, but the smart money knew this was the only one that mattered. The harmonic chimes of StarSport FN's jingle filled the stadium, the unofficial sign that the race was about to get underway.

She headed for the cockpit of her pearlescent-blue car. Claire fell in behind her, rattling off some figures about Nilah's chances that were supposed to scare her into behaving.

"Remember your contract," said Claire as the pit crew boosted Nilah into her car. "Do what you must to take gold, but any scratch you put on Kristof is going to take a million off your check. I mean it this time."

"Good thing I'm getting twenty mil more than him, then. More scratches for me!" Nilah pulled on her helmet. "You keep Kristof out of my way, and I'll keep his precious car intact."

She flipped down her visor and traced her mechanist's mark across the confined space, whispering light flowing from her fingertips. Once her spell cemented in place, she wrapped her fingers around the wheel. The system read out the stats of her sigil: good V's, not great on the Xi, but a healthy cast.

Her magic flowed into the car, sliding around the finely tuned ports, wending through channels to latch onto gears. Through the power of her mechanist's mark, she felt the grip of the tires and spring of the rods as though they were her own legs and feet. She joined with the central computer of her car, gaining psychic access to radio, actuation, and telemetry. The Lang Hyper 8, a motorsport classic, had achieved phenomenal performance all season in Nilah's hands.

Her psychic connection to the computer stabilized, and she searched the radio channels for her engineer, Ash. They ran through the checklist: power, fuel flow, sigil circuits, eidolon core. Nilah felt through each part with her magic, ensuring all functioned properly. Finally, she landed on the clunky Arclight Booster.

It was an awful little PGRF-required piece of tech, with high output but terrible efficiency. Nilah's mechanist side absolutely despised the magic-belching beast. It was as ugly and inelegant as it was expensive. Some fans claimed to like the little light show when it boosted drivers up the straights, but it was less than perfect, and anything less than perfect had to go.

"Let's start her up, Nilah."

"Roger that."

Every time that car thrummed to life, Nilah fell in love all over again. She adored the Hyper 8 in spite of the stonking flaw on his backside. Her grip tightened about the wheel and she took a deep breath.

The lights signaled a formation lap and the cars took off, weaving across the tarmac to keep the heat in their tires. They slipped around the track in slow motion, and Nilah's eyes traveled the third sector. She would crush this new track design. At the end of the formation lap, she pulled into her grid space, the scents of hot rubber and oil smoke sweet in her nose.

Game time.

The pole's leftmost set of lights came on: five seconds until the last light.

Three cars ahead of her, eighteen behind: Kristof in first, then the two Makina drivers, Bonnie and Jin. Nilah stared down the Makina R-27s, their metallic livery a blazing crimson.

The next pair of lights ignited: four seconds.

The other drivers revved their engines, feeling the tuning of their cars. Nilah echoed their rumbling engines with a shout of her own and gave a heated sigh, savoring the fire in her belly.

Three seconds.

Don't think. Just see.

The last light came on, signaling the director was ready to start the race.

Now, it was all about reflexes. All the engines fell to near silence.

One second.

The lights clicked off.

Banshee wails filled the air as the cars' power units screamed to life. Nilah roared forward, her eyes darting over the competition. Who was it going to be? Bonnie lagged by just a hair, and Jin made a picture-perfect launch, surging up beside Kristof. Nilah wanted to make a dive for it but found herself forced in behind the two lead drivers.

They shot down the straight toward turn one, a double apex. Turn one was always the most dangerous, because the idiots fighting for the inside were most likely to brake too late. She swept out for a perfect parabola, hoping not to see some fool about to crash into her.

The back of the pack was brought up by slow, pathetic Cyril Clowe. He would be her barometer of race success. If she could lap him in a third of the race, it would be a perfect run.

"Tell race control I'm lapping Clowe in twenty-five," Nilah grunted, straining against the g-force of her own acceleration. "I want those blue flags ready."

"He might not like that."

"If he tries anything, I'll leave him pasted to the tarmac."

"You're still in the pack," came Ash's response. "Focus on the race."

Got ten seconds on the Arclight. Four-car gap to Jin. Turn three is coming up too fast.

Bonnie Hayes loomed large in the rearview, dodging left and right along the straight. The telltale flash of an Arclight Booster erupted on the right side, and Bonnie shot forward toward the turn. Nilah made no moves to block, and the R-27 overtook her. It'd been a foolish ploy, and faced with too much speed, Bonnie needed to brake too hard. She'd flat-spot her tires.

Right on cue, brake dust and polymer smoke erupted from Bonnie's wheels, and Nilah danced to the outside, sliding within mere inches of the crimson paint. Nilah popped through the gears and the car thrummed with her magic, rewarding her with a pristine turn. The rest of the pack was not so lucky.

Shredded fibron and elemental magic filled Nilah's rearview as the cars piled up into turn three like an avalanche. She had to keep her eyes on the track, but she spotted Guillaume, Anantha, and Bonnie's cars in the wreck.

"Nicely done," said Ash.

"All in a day's work, babes."

Nilah weaved through the next five turns, taking them exactly as practiced. Her car was water, flowing through the track along the swiftest route. However, Kristof and Jin weren't making things easy for her. She watched with hawkish intent and prayed for a slip, a momentary lockup, or anything less than the perfect combination of gear shifts.

Thirty degrees right, shift up two, boost... boost. Follow your prey until it makes a mistake.

Nilah's earpiece chirped as Ash said, "Kater's side of the garage just went crazy. He just edged Jin off the road and picked up half a second in sector one."

She grimaced. "Half a second?"

"Yeah. It's going to be a long battle, I'm afraid."

Her magic reached into the gearbox, tuning it for low revs. "Not at all. He's gambling. Watch what happens next."

She kept her focus on the track, reciting her practiced motions with little variance. The crowd might be thrilled by a half-second purple sector, but she knew to keep it even. With the increased tire wear, his car would become unpredictable.

"Kristof is in the run-off! Repeat: He's out in the kitty litter," came Ash.

"Well, that was quick."

She crested the hill to find her teammate's car spinning

into the gravel along the run of the curve. She only hazarded a minor glance before continuing on.

"Switch to strat one," said Ash, barely able to contain herself. "Push! Push!"

"Tell Clowe he's mine in ten laps."

Nilah sliced through the chicane, screaming out of the turn with her booster aflame. She was a polychromatic comet, completely in her element. This race would be her masterpiece. She held the record for the most poles for her age, and she was about to get it for the most overtakes.

The next nine laps went well. Nilah handily widened the gap between herself and Kristof to over ten seconds. She sensed fraying in her tires, but she couldn't pit just yet. If she did, she'd never catch Clowe by the end of the race. His fiery orange livery flashed at every turn, tantalizingly close to overtake range.

"Put out the blue flags. I'm on Cyril."

"Roger that," said Ash. "Race control, requesting blue flags for Cyril Clowe."

His Arclight flashed as he burned it out along the straightaway, and she glided through the rippling sparks. The booster was a piece of garbage, but it had its uses, and Clowe didn't understand any of them. He wasn't even trying anymore, just blowing through his boost at random times. What was the point?

Nilah cycled through her radio frequencies until she found Cyril's. Best to tease him a bit for the viewers at home. "Okay, Cyril, a lesson: use the booster to make the car go faster."

He snorted on his end. "Go to hell, Nilah."

"Being stuck behind your slow ass is as close as I've gotten."

"Get used to it," he snapped, his whiny voice grating on her ears. "I'm not letting you past."

She downshifted, her transmission roaring like a tiger. "I hope you're ready to get flattened then."

Galica's iconic Paige Tunnel loomed large ahead, with its blazing row of lights and disorienting reflective tiles. Most racers would avoid an overtake there, but Nilah had been given an opportunity, and she wouldn't squander it. The outside stadium vanished as she slipped into the tunnel, hot on the Hambley's wing.

She fired her booster, and as she came alongside Clowe, the world's colors began to melt from their surfaces, leaving only drab black and white. Her car stopped altogether—gone from almost two hundred kilometers per hour to zero in the blink of an eye.

Nilah's head darkened with a realization: she was caught in someone's spell as surely as a fly in a spiderweb.

The force of such a stop should have powdered her bones and liquefied her internal organs instantly, but she felt no change in her body, save that she could barely breathe.

The world had taken on a deathly shade. The body of the Hyper 8, normally a lovely blue, had become an ashen gray. The fluorescent magenta accents along her white jumpsuit had also faded, and all had taken on a blurry, shifting turbulence.

Her neck wouldn't move, so she couldn't look around. Her fingers barely worked. She connected her mind to the transmission, but it wouldn't shift. The revs were frozen in place in the high twenty thousands, but she sensed no movement in the drive shaft.

All this prompted a silent, slow-motion scream. The longer she wailed, the more her voice came back. She flexed her fingers as hard as they'd go through the syrupy air. With each tiny movement, a small amount of color returned, though she couldn't be sure if she was breaking out of the spell—or into it.

"Nilah, is that you?" grunted Cyril. She'd almost forgotten

about the Hambley driver next to her. All the oranges and yellows on his jumpsuit and helmet stood out like blazing bonfires, and she wondered if that's why he could move. But his car was the same gray as everything else, and he struggled, unsuccessfully, to unbuckle. Was Nilah on the cusp of the magic's effects?

"What..." she forced herself to say, but pushing the air out was too much.

"Oh god, we're caught in her spell!"

Whose spell, you git? "Stay...calm..."

She couldn't reassure him, and just trying to breathe was taxing enough. If someone was fixing the race, there'd be hell to pay. Sure, everyone had spells, but only a fool would dare cast one into a PGRF speedway to cheat. A cadre of wizards stood at the ready for just such an event, and any second, the dispersers would come online and knock this whole spiderweb down.

In the frozen world, an inky blob moved at the end of the tunnel. A creature came crawling along the ceiling, its black mass of tattered fabric writhing like tentacles as it skittered across the tiles. It moved easily from one perch to the next, silently capering overhead before dropping down in front of the two frozen cars.

Cyril screamed. She couldn't blame him.

The creature stood upright, and Nilah realized that it was human. Its hood swept away, revealing a brass mask with a cutaway that exposed thin, angry lips on a sallow chin. Metachroic lenses peppered the exterior of the mask, and Nilah instantly recognized their purpose—to see in all directions. Mechanists had always talked about creating such a device, but no one had ever been able to move for very long while wearing one; it was too disorienting.

The creature put one slender boot on Cyril's car, then another as it inexorably clambered up the car's body. It stopped in front of Cyril and tapped the helmet on his trembling head with a long, metallic finger.

Where are the bloody dispersers?

Cyril's terrified voice huffed over the radio. "Mother, please…"

Mother? Cyril's mother? No; Nilah had met Missus Clowe at the previous year's winner's party. She was a dull woman, like her loser son. Nilah took a closer look at the wrinkled sneer poking out from under the mask.

Her voice was a slithering rasp. "Where did you get that map, Cyril?"

"Please. I wasn't trying to double-cross anyone. I just thought I could make a little money on the side."

Mother crouched and ran her metal-encased fingers around the back of his helmet. "There is no 'on the side,' Cyril. We are everywhere. Even when you think you are untouchable, we can pluck you from this universe."

Nilah strained harder against her arcane chains, pulling more color into her body, desperate to get free. She was accustomed to being able to outrun anything, to absolute speed. Panic set in.

"You need me to finish this race!" he protested.

"We don't *need* anything from you. You were lucky enough to be chosen, and there will always be others. Tell me where you got the map."

"You're just going to kill me if I tell you."

Nilah's eyes narrowed, and she forced herself to focus in spite of her crawling fear. Kill him? What the devil was Cyril into?

Mother's metal fingers clacked, tightening across his helmet. "It's of very little consequence to me. I've been told to kill you if you won't talk. That was my only order. If you tell me, it's my discretion whether you live or die."

Cyril whimpered. "Boots...er...Elizabeth Elsworth. I was looking for...I wanted to know what you were doing, and she...she knew something. She said she could find the *Harrow*."

Nilah's gaze shifted to Mother, the racer's eye movements sluggish and sleepy despite her terror. *Elizabeth Elsworth? Where had Nilah heard that name before?* She had the faintest feeling that it'd come from the Link, maybe a show or a news piece. Movement in the periphery interrupted her thoughts.

The ghastly woman swept an arm back, fabric tatters falling away to reveal an armored exoskeleton encrusted with servo-motors and glowing sigils. Mother brought her fist down across Cyril's helmet, crushing it inward with a sickening crack.

Nilah would've begun hyperventilating, if she could breathe. This couldn't be happening. Even with the best military-grade suits, there was no way this woman could've broken Cyril's helmet with a mere fist. His protective gear could withstand a direct impact at three hundred kilometers per hour. Nilah couldn't see what was left of his head, but blood oozed between the cracked plastic like the yolk of an egg.

Just stay still. Maybe you can fade into the background. Maybe you can—

"And now for you," said Mother, stepping onto the fibron body of Nilah's car. Of course she had spotted Nilah moving in that helmet of hers. "I think my spell didn't completely affect you, did it? It's so difficult with these fast-moving targets."

Mother's armored boots rested at the edge of Nilah's cockpit, and mechanical, prehensile toes wrapped around the lip of the car. Nilah forced her neck to crane upward through frozen time to look at Mother's many eyes.

"Dear lamb, I am so sorry you saw that. I hate to be so harsh," she sighed, placing her bloody palm against Nilah's silver helmet, "but this is for the best. Even if you got away, you'd have nowhere to run. We own everything."

Please, please, please, dispersers... Nilah's eyes widened. She wasn't going to die like this. Not like Cyril. *Think. Think.*

"I want you to relax, my sweet. The journos are going to tell a beautiful story of your heroic crash with that fool." She gestured to Cyril as she said this. "You'll be remembered as the champion that could've been."

Dispersers scramble spells with arcane power. They feed into the glyph until it's over capacity. Nilah spread her magic over the car, looking for anything she could use to fire a pulse of magic: the power unit—drive shaft locked, the energy recovery system—too weak, her ejection cylinder—lockbolts unresponsive... then she remembered the Arclight Booster. She reached into it with her psychic connection, finding the arcane linkages foggy and dim. Something about the way this spell shut down movement even muddled her mechanist's art. She latched on to the booster, knowing the effect would be unpredictable, but it was Nilah's only chance. She tripped the magical switch to fire the system.

Nothing. Mother wrapped her steely hands around Nilah's helmet.

"I should twist instead of smash, shouldn't I?" whispered the old woman. "Pretty girls should have pretty corpses."

Nilah connected the breaker again, and the slow puff of arcane plumes sighed from the Arclight. It didn't want to start in this magical haze, but it was her only plan. She gave the switch one last snap.

The push of magical flame tore at the gray, hazy shroud over the world, pulling it away. An array of coruscating starbursts surged through the surface, and Nilah was momentarily blinded as everything returned to normal. The return of momentum flung Mother from the car, and Nilah was slammed back into her seat.

Faster and faster her car went, until Nilah wasn't even sure the tires were touching the road. Mother's spell twisted around the Arclight's, intermingling, destabilizing, twisting space and time in ways Nilah never could've predicted. It was dangerous to mix unknown magics—and often deadly.

She recognized this effect, though—it was the same as when she passed through a jump gate. She was teleporting.

A flash of light and she became weightless. At least she could breathe again.

She locked onto the sight of a large, windowless building, but there was something wrong with it. It shouldn't have been upside down as it was, nor should it have been spinning like that. Her car was in free fall. Then she slammed into a wall, her survival shell enveloping her as she blew through wreckage like a cannonball.

Her stomach churned with each flip, but this was far from her first crash. She relaxed and let her shell come to a halt, wedged in a half-blasted wall. Her fuel system exploded, spraying elemental energies in all directions. Fire, ice, and gusts of catalyzed gasses swirled outside the racer's shell.

The suppressor fired, and Nilah's bound limbs came free. A harsh, acrid mist filled the air as the phantoplasm caking Nilah's body melted into the magic-numbing indolence gasses. Gale-force winds and white-hot flames snuffed in the blink of an eye. The sense of her surrounding energies faded away, a sudden silence in her mind.

Her disconnection from magic was always the worst part about a crash. The indolence system was only temporary, but there was always the fear: that she'd become one of those dull-fingered wretches. She screwed her eyes shut and shook her head, willing her mechanist's magic back.

It appeared on the periphery as a pinhole of light—a tiny, bright sensation in a sea of gray. She willed it wider, bringing more light and warmth into her body until she overflowed with her own magic. Relief covered her like a hot blanket, and her shoulders fell.

But what had just murdered Cyril? Mother had smashed his head open without so much as a second thought. And Mother would know exactly who she was—Nilah's name was painted on every surface of the Lang Hyper 8. What if she came back?

The damaged floor gave way, and she flailed through the darkness, bouncing down what had to be a mountain of cardboard boxes. She came to a stop and opened her eyes to look around.

She'd landed in a warehouse somewhere she didn't recognize. Nilah knew every inch of the Galica Speedway—she'd been coming to PGRF races there since she was a little girl, and this warehouse didn't mesh with any of her memories. She pulled off her helmet and listened for sirens, for the banshee wail of race cars, for the roar of the crowd, but all she could hear was silence.

orbit

Follow us:

f /orbitbooksUS

🐦 /orbitbooks

▶ /orbitbooks

Join our mailing list
to receive alerts on our
latest releases and deals.

orbitbooks.net

Enter our monthly
giveaway for the chance
to win some epic prizes.

orbitloot.com